Barefoot in Lace

The Barefoot Bay Brides #2

roxanne st. claire

Barefoot in Lace

Copyright © 2014 South Street Publishing, LLC

For permission or information on foreign, audio, or other rights, contact the author, roxanne@roxannestclaire.com

Cover art by Robin Ludwig Design Inc.
Interior formatting by Author E.M.S.
Seashell graphic used with permission under Creative Commons CC0 public domain.

ISBN-13: 978-0-9883736-9-3

Published in the United States of America.

Critical Reviews of Roxanne St. Claire Novels

"St. Claire, as always, brings a scorching tear-up-the-sheets romance combined with a great story: dealing with real issues starring memorable characters in vivid scenes."

— Romantic Times Magazine

"Non-stop action, sweet and sexy romance, lively characters, and a celebration of family and forgiveness."

— Publishers Weekly

"Plenty of heat, humor, and heart!"

— USA Today's Happy Ever After blog

"It's safe to say I will try any novel with St. Claire's name on it."

— www.smartbitchestrashybooks.com

"The writing was perfectly on point as always and the pace of the story was flawless. But be forewarned that you will laugh, cry, and sigh with happiness. I sure did."

— www.harlequinjunkies.com

"The Barefoot Bay series is an all-around knockout, soul-satisfying read. Roxanne St. Claire writes with warmth and heart and the community she's built at Barefoot Bay is one I want to visit again and again."

— Mariah Stewart, New York Times bestselling author

"This book stayed with me long after I put it down."

— All About Romance

Dear Reader,

Welcome back to Barefoot Bay and another romantic interlude with the Barefoot Bay Brides. These wedding planners might be quite skilled at creating picture-postcard nuptials on the beach, but not all of the ladies have found their own true loves...yet.

But we know that's going to change, don't we? Read on to kick off your shoes and fall in love with Gussie McBain, a spunky stylist whose hiding plenty under her plumage, and Tom DeMille, the one man who knows how to get under Gussie's wig...and clothes...and skin.

As is the case with every one of the (nearly forty!) books I've written, I had a team of breathtakingly talented professionals to help bring this story to life, and they all deserve umbrella drinks and close attention from the pool boy. My deepest gratitude to editor Kristi Yanta who guides me through the white water of every revision and makes sure I don't drown. Also, much love and appreciation to copy editor and proofreader Joyce Lamb, a master at the art; cover artist Robin Ludwig, who captures my world in an image and layout; my assistants Marilyn Puett and Maria Connor who make sure my life is in relative working order; and, of course, my precious little family, who love and support and encourage me even when they are so sick of hearing about how hard it is to write a book.

Special props to some research assistance on this one, too. Reader and friend Naomi Lahn gave me hands-on help on the French excerpts—*merci*, Naomi! Also, big *efharisto* to Anastasios G. Milios, who guided me through Greece (virtually) and introduced me to the gorgeous island of Karpathos.

Like every book set in Barefoot Bay, this novel stands entirely alone, but why stop at just one? All of the books and series are listed in the back. There are plenty of opportunities to go barefoot and fall in love!

— *Roxanne St. Claire*

Barefoot in Lace

roxanne st. claire

Dedication

This book and the story of love it celebrates is dedicated to my dear friend Sonia Tsirambidis Fakatselis, who inspires me every single day when we meet on the street.

My neighbor, my sister, and the owner of
Portokali Sky Accessories…
Sonia is as beautiful as the products she creates!

Chapter One

"Thomas Jefferson DeMille? You expect me to believe that's your real name?"

Ten feet away, the cashier's question stopped Gussie McBain dead in her tracks, almost making her drop two liters of Diet Coke in the aisle of the convenience store. *Thomas Jefferson DeMille*? She stared at the back of a tall man, who swiped back a handful of dark hair while broad shoulders rose and fell with obvious frustration.

Hadn't she read somewhere that that was famed photographer TJ DeMille's real name?

"Clear the card," he ordered in a sandpaper whisper.

"No can do." Charity Grambling, owner of the convenience store and undisputed Most Obnoxious Human on the entire island of Mimosa Key, tapped a credit card on the counter while she peered through bifocals to read what was in her other hand. "Because the name on this shiny black American Express does not match the one on this *expired* New York state driver's license, so I won't accept either one."

"What the hell are you talking about? Expired?" He leaned over the counter, the move pulling a white T-shirt tight, straining corded muscles and drawing Gussie's eye to

1

a tattoo script wrapped around his forearm. "It's still me, whatever the date. See? TJ DeMille, right there."

Gussie bit her lip. It *was* him! One of the most talented and famous photographers in the world was standing in the middle of the Super Min.

Charity remained unimpressed, raising a thickly drawn brow. "Thomas Jefferson, *really*? I wasn't born yesterday."

"No shit," he mumbled.

"The hippie hair and devil's paint are a dead giveaway."

Giveaway of what? Gussie took a few steps closer. Hippie hair? Hardly. More like handfuls of dark chocolate silk that fell carelessly over his neck and grazed his shoulders. Some strategically placed ink only added to his allure.

"I use my initials for work, and that's a business credit card." He bit out each word, impatience rolling off him.

"Sorry." Charity handed the AmEx and license back to him. "We do accept cash, however."

He snapped the cards from her hands. "Where's your ATM?"

"You'll need to visit the Mimosa Community Credit Union, over at the corner of Harbor and—"

"Never mind!" He gave a push to a pile of magazines, nearly toppling a bottle of Snapple onto a jumbo bag of Fritos. He turned away and marched out the door.

"Charity!" Gussie exclaimed when the welcome bell dinged in his wake. "Do you have any idea who that was?"

"The list of possibilities is long, but I'm going with a prison escapee. Did you see those marks on his arms?"

"They're called tattoos. Pretty mainstream these days."

"And that little silver earring? I'm almost certain that's a sign of an ex-con."

Gussie glanced outside to spot him standing next to a

small white sedan, thumbing a cell phone. Not the car she'd expect a man like him to drive, she mused, her heart rate increasing with each second she lingered over his delicious physique and chiseled, if angry as hell, features.

"I mean, just look at him," Charity said.

"No problem."

"What else can you think about a man with all those...those..."

"Muscles?"

"Exactly." She huffed. "Steroids, I'd bet my life."

"You'd lose that bet," Gussie said, squinting to get a better view of a body that looked more like he played rugby than pumped iron.

Charity rolled her eyes, shoving his pile of merchandise to the side, obviously not as concerned with a lost sale as the possibility of stopping a hardened criminal. "I don't trust a man who buys raspberry tea, Fritos, girlie magazines and"— she grabbed three supersized Milky Way bars—"more chocolate than a woman with PMS."

Maybe he's feeding a starving model. Gussie's attention slid to the top magazine, instantly recognizing TJ DeMille's masterful ability to capture both an ethereal yet utterly honest expression on his subject's face.

"*Vogue* is a girlie magazine now?"

"What kind of man buys it?" Charity demanded.

"The man who shot the covers," Gussie informed her. At Charity's confused look, Gussie pointed at the picture. "The top-notch, well-respected, highly in-demand photographer responsible for that image."

For a second, interest flickered in Charity's gray eyes, her weakness for local news and notoriety showing. "That explains the raspberry tea, then."

"How?"

"He's gay."

Actually, rumored dalliances with models would say differently, but Gussie ignored the gross generalization. "You should have *given* him the magazine and asked for his autograph."

"The only autograph I accept is on the credit card machine, as long as the card isn't stolen and the license is valid. Despite my name, there's no *charity* at the Super Min." Charity pointed to the liters of Diet Coke. "Cash or charge?"

"Cash." While she reached for her wallet, Gussie took one more look at the man still standing in the parking lot. The unforgiving Florida summer sun poured light over him, making his hair glisten and emphasizing the shadows under defined cheekbones.

"Ahem." Charity knocked inch-long nails gleaming with a fresh coat of Charged-Up Cherry against her counter. "Would you like to stand there and drool all over the magazines so I can't sell them to anyone now that Tommy Jefferson himself had his tattooed palms all over them?"

Gussie reached for the issue of *Vogue*, hardly aware that she stroked the glossy cover as she took one more look at the man who'd brought the image to life.

"Oh, for heaven's sake, pay for your soda."

Gussie tore her gaze from the parking lot to the beast in front of her. "Add the magazines," Gussie blurted out. "And candy. And Snapple. And whatever else he was buying. I'll take it all."

Charity's eyes grew wide behind her bifocals. "And do what with them?"

Help out a great talent. Great-*looking* talent. "None of your business."

She *pffted* out a breath. "Everything on this island is my

4

business. Like, why do you wear different-color wigs every day? Someone asked me about it, and I assumed, you know, chemo or something."

Gussie almost laughed, because how else could you even respond to such rudeness? "So that's what you told them?"

"I told them I'd find out." She leaned way off her little stool to peer hard at Gussie's face. "And all that makeup. What's the deal?"

A slow heat slid up her chest and onto her cheeks, which Charity probably couldn't see because of *all that makeup*. She dug for the snappy retort about how Charity could benefit from a touch of mascara and a magnifying mirror so she could actually find her eyebrows, but doing her good deed for the day beat out the need to snark at the old lady.

Reaching into her wallet, Gussie grabbed two twenties—those magazines were pricey—and slapped them on the counter. "I'll take it all. His and mine." She scooped everything into her arms, using the magazines to cradle his Snapple and her Diet Cokes.

"What the—"

"Keep the change," Gussie called as she hustled away, not pausing to second-guess the impulsive decision. The bell dinged as she shouldered the door open, just as the sedan pulled out of its parking spot.

"Don't leave!" she called out to the back of the car. Seeing his right-turn signal flash, she ran that way, bolting into the intersection, almost right in front of the car. "Hey!" The move nearly cost her a forty-dollar armload.

He slammed the brakes and jerked his head back in surprise, glaring at her with thick brows drawn together in incredulity.

"I have your stuff." She lifted her arms, rolling the Diet Cokes to a precarious angle on top of the magazines.

He still stared at her like she was a complete and total lunatic. Which, right at that moment, would be a fairly accurate assessment.

"Your...magazines," she called through his closed window, angling her whole body so one of the soda bottles lodged between her elbow and boob. "And tea and candy. I bought them for you."

He stayed in the driver's seat, clearly uncertain of the possible danger of a pink-wigged woman who'd spent way too much money for a stranger. Finally, he lowered the window.

"Why would you do that?" he asked.

She had no freaking clue, except she admired his work. And his body. So she'd either sound like a fangirl or stalker. "Just to be nice." Oh, so lame. Her elbow braced the armload so tight that her muscles started to burn. "And I kind of hate that woman who owns this place."

That made him smile, just a little. Just enough to trip Gussie's heart.

"That makes two of us. Hang on." He put the car in park and opened the door. Climbing out, he reached for the magazines and sodas, a lock of hair falling over his eye as he looked down at her. "Let me help you."

He reached for the Coke bottle as she moved to protect it from slipping so his fingers accidentally grazed her chest.

He drew his hand back—not terribly fast—but she felt the tea slip right between the magazines and her stomach. "Oh!" She gasped, leaning into him to save the glass bottle from the fall, but it slipped and crashed to the concrete, making them both jump back as raspberry tea spurted all over her sandaled feet and his faded jeans.

"Oh, I'm sorry," she groaned.

"It's...okay." He stepped back, shaking some liquid off his jeans.

She lifted one foot out of the mess, and the heavy issue of *Marie Claire* toppled, followed by *Vogue*, both of them splatting right onto the puddle of Snapple. "Oh, God. So much for being a Good Samaritan."

"Just don't drop the Fritos." He gingerly plucked everything else from her hands. "'Cause then I *will* have to rob the convenience store."

She laughed. "She's probably already called the cops."

"We could go all Bonnie and Clyde on her ass," he joked, meeting her gaze with disarmingly blue eyes, about the color of the sky over Barefoot Bay on a balmy Florida afternoon. "Wanna go rogue with me?"

Right about then, she'd have gone anywhere with him. "Tempting, but it would put a damper on my daily Diet Coke stop." She couldn't help but smile up at him. "I'm Gussie McBain, by the way."

"Gussie? You've even got an outlaw name and a cute disguise. I'm—"

"Oh, I know who you are," she blurted.

"You do?"

Regretting the admission that made her sound like some kind of crazed fan, she pointed over her shoulder. "I mean, I heard you tell Charity. Thomas Jefferson—or TJ—DeMille."

"Tom to my friends." He threaded his fingers through his hair to push it off his face, studying her with enough amusement and interest to make her feel even warmer than usual in the summer sun. "And good-deed doers."

For a long, crazy, heart-stopping few seconds, they stared at each other. Gussie felt her chest tighten and her stomach flip at the instant, palpable, electrifying connection.

"You're blocking the entrance!" Charity's grating voice broke the magic. "And look at that mess! You'll give all my customers flat tires!"

Charity shook her fried and dyed hair, pointing at him. "I know who you are now, mister. I made a few phone calls. Get on your way and take care of that mess your sister left behind. And you." Her finger slid to Gussie. "Find a pink scarf and lose the stupid wigs. You'd be pretty."

Gussie felt her cheeks flush as Charity backed into the store.

"We could take her," he whispered, his voice so low and sexy it practically pulled Gussie closer.

"And all the Fritos we can eat."

He gave a wry laugh, studying her again. After Charity's rude comment, he was, of course, looking at her wig. She should have been used to it—and the misperception that she was sick—but he was so skilled at finding and photographing real beauty that the scrutiny nearly flattened her.

"Here." He handed her the only magazine that made it through the small disaster, *Vanity Fair*. "I owe you at least this much for your effort, Gussie McBain."

"For a broken bottle of iced tea and ruined magazines?"

He gave the chips a noisy rattle. "You saved my Fritos and thus my backside. That's good enough for a return favor in my book." He stepped back to get in the car, but took one more moment, scrutinizing her again. "She's wrong, you know."

"You're not a criminal?"

He shook his head. "You already are pretty. I have an eye for these things, you know."

I know.

He slipped back into the driver's seat and closed the door.

Giving a casual wave, he drove off, leaving Gussie standing in the sun, speechless.

Gussie was still thinking about the encounter after running the rest of her errands and grabbing subs for herself and her two business partners. But thoughts of TJ DeMille—or Tom *to his friends*—disappeared the minute she got back to Casa Blanca Resort & Spa to find glum faces when she entered the Barefoot Brides offices.

Ari Chandler sat at the small conference table, braiding and unbraiding her long black ponytail, the way she always did when she was upset. At her desk, Willow Ambrose had her chin propped on her palms, a phone to her ear, an expression of defeat as she listened to someone on the other end.

"What's up?" Gussie asked as she dropped the bag of sandwiches on the table, along with the issue of *Vanity Fair*. "Did we lose a bride or something?" she asked.

"Not yet, but we have trouble for the Bernard-Lyons wedding."

Gussie cringed, falling into one of the conference table chairs. "Really? Then you probably don't want to know that I just saw the bride's parents checking into the resort when I walked through the lobby."

"Ugh." Ari dropped back and blew out a breath. "It's only a matter of minutes until Rhonda Lyons is over here demanding a full status report."

No doubt about that. Rhonda was the quintessential control-freak MOB who'd been breathing down their necks for the last six months in preparation for her daughter's wedding.

"This universe has been frowning on this wedding from the beginning," Ari mused. "Remember the snafu with the hundred-year-old save-the-date cards?"

"Hey, we only mailed them. Not our fault she had them printed by a friend who typeset the year as 1914." Gussie glanced at Willow, who now had a finger over her other ear and closed her eyes to concentrate on the call.

"What's the problem?" Gussie asked in a whisper.

From her desk, Willow held up a finger as she took a breath to talk. "Well, I certainly understand that couldn't be changed," she said. "We will keep looking. Thanks so much." She hung up, shaking her head as she looked at Gussie. "Dianne Stoddard found her husband with another woman," she said.

"She actually found him in the *shower* with another woman," Ari added. "Not to put too fine a point on it."

Gussie's jaw dropped. "Big Bill Stoddard? The guy who owns the hardware store? Gross."

"Apparently, *screws* are Big Bill's specialty," Ari deadpanned.

"What does this have to do with the Bernard-Lyons wedding?" Gussie asked, spinning through all of the options. "Are we buying props from the store or something?"

Willow shook her head. "Dianne left him and insisted her sister come along."

"Her sister?" Gussie thought for a minute. Mimosa Key wasn't a large island, but she hadn't lived there long enough to know all the residents and their dirt.

"Her sister, Maggie Wallace," Willow supplied.

Gussie gasped. "She can't back out this late. Rhonda will be apoplectic."

"I do *not* like the sound of that." The woman's voice in the doorway jerked them all around. A fearsome Mother of

10

the Bride if there ever was one, Rhonda Lyons glared at the three of them. "*What* will make me apoplectic?"

Just about everything, Gussie thought, barely biting back the comment. Ari bristled, but Willow was up before Rhonda could ask another question.

"Mrs. Lyons, how lovely to see you." Willow set her pretty face into an easy smile and reached out her hand. "We heard you'd arrived. How's your villa?"

Rhonda swept into the room, zeroing in on Gussie. "I heard you say someone's backing out of my daughter's wedding. Who? Don't tell me I have to break Hailey's heart."

Gussie swallowed, having already been on the receiving end of Rhonda's wrath when the beaded lace for Hailey's veil hadn't been available with a scalloped edge. She'd acted like her darling daughter would walk down the aisle with a garbage bag draped over her head.

"It's the photographer," Willow said, breezing around her desk to put a friendly hand on Rhonda's shoulder. "Nothing to worry about, Mrs. Ly—"

"The photographer canceled?" Rhonda's voice rose at least three octaves into a bona fide shriek, something they'd probably be hearing a lot of in the next four days. "For a wedding this Saturday? What kind of planners are you?"

"Good ones," Willow assured her, adding a gentle pat. "We have connections all over the county, state, and country. We'll get another photographer in plenty of time."

"Absolutely," Ari agreed, gesturing toward a notebook in front of her. "We're already working on it." Except that notebook was awfully full of crossed-off names, Gussie noticed.

"Working on it?" Rhonda was aghast. "You'd better be

doing more than 'working on it.' This is my only daughter, and Wayne and I have sunk a small fortune into this event, and I will not, I repeat, I will *not* accept a second-rate photographer."

"And you won't have to," Willow said.

"I want a solution and I want it *now*," Rhonda demanded. "In fact, I want to meet with the replacement photographer before the end of the day today. And I know that Maggie Wallace was excellent because I loved her work, so I expect someone equally talented, if not more so."

Ari and Willow shared a secret look that confirmed all of Gussie's suspicions: They had *nuthin'*.

"Who are we talking to?" Rhonda asked, pulling out another chair to join them at the table.

"Well, we..." Ari subtly pushed her list away.

"Names." She tapped the table, her fingers hitting the magazine Gussie had set there. "And sample portfolios, right now."

Willow and Ari stayed dead silent for a few long and awkward beats.

"TJ DeMille." The name popped out of Gussie's mouth, and all three of the women stared at her.

"I've heard of him," Rhonda said.

Willow leaned out of Rhonda's line of view to stare at Gussie in complete horror, then she quietly said, "But we don't want to make promises we can't keep."

"He's a really big name...as you know," Ari added, trying to hide her shock at the suggestion.

"He's huge," Gussie agreed, snagging the issue of *Vanity Fair*. "He shot this cover."

Rhonda's eyes widened. "Get him."

Willow and Ari blinked at Gussie when the order dropped silence over the room.

"I want him for this wedding," Rhonda said, inching closer. "You claim to be so good, prove it. Get this TJ DeMille for my Hailey's wedding. That ought to impress my tennis club. I doubt Sherry Wells is getting him for Brianna's wedding." She thought about that, nodding. "Yes, by all means, this is wonderful news. Get him."

And all three of them looked at Gussie.

"No problem," Gussie assured them all. And herself. Because it *might* be a problem. A big, fat problem. "I was just chatting with him." She went for a casual air, despite Ari's wide eyes. "And, as a matter of fact, he owes me a favor."

"Excellent." Rhonda stood, impervious and challenging. "I'm available for dinner and would like to meet with him at eight o'clock in the resort restaurant. I'll bring Hailey, but the final decision is mine, since I'm footing the bill." She picked up the magazine and narrowed her eyes at the movie star on the front. "And I don't expect to be charged one penny more than I agreed to pay the original photographer."

She sailed out of the room, leaving Gussie under the disbelieving gazes of her two closest friends.

"Please tell me you really know this guy," Willow said.

"And that he owes you a big, gigantic favor," Ari added.

"Kind of and maybe." Gussie wrinkled her nose. "I ran into him at the Super Min and saved him from Charity's wrath. Does that count?"

"Does that count?" Ari's midnight-black eyes blinked in surprise. "You meet him on the very day we need a photographer? Now that's what I call the universe doing her thing."

"That's what I call an opportunity," Willow added. "But

how can you possibly get someone of his caliber to agree to shoot a wedding?"

"I don't have a clue," Gussie admitted, pushing up and giving them a grin that covered her wave of self-doubt. "But I'm not going to let that stop me."

Chapter Two

T he noise never stopped. Whine, whirr, buzz, beep, and the occasional explosion. Something screeched and shrieked, and the constant sound of motors revving screamed for so long, Tom could swear he heard it in his sleep.

And he did, often. Because his twelve-year-old niece played her incessant, annoying video game of stupid little characters driving around in circles at all hours of the day and night.

Carrying the chips and candy as an offering for the broken raspberry tea he'd promised, he headed into the dimly lit den. Of course, Alex hadn't opened the cheap vertical blinds on the window. Or cleaned up the kitchen or made plans with a friend or watered the plants or done anything but play that mindless, brain-numbing game that occupied almost all of her waking hours.

Obviously, it was her only escape from grief and shock. Lucky girl. Tom had no such outlet for the miserable situation they were both in.

He stood directly between the television and the controller in her hand, holding out the Milky Ways and Fritos. "Healthy lunch, anyone?"

She leaned around him, not looking up, her attention still on the game.

"Alex?"

Her dark eyes narrowed, concentration intense.

He shifted left to block her again. "*Alex*."

Finally, she gave up, falling back on the recliner, her gaze as vacant and empty as the day he'd arrived. "You're in my way," she said, stating the obvious in her reed-thin voice.

He stayed there but put the snacks on the table next to her, smashing a frustration that was growing far too familiar in every exchange they had. "You haven't done anything today but play this game."

She blinked at him, her eyes dark against skin that would someday be pale and creamy but was currently dotted with preteen acne that only seemed to get worse since he'd arrived.

"Don't you want to do something else?" he asked, already knowing the answer. "Call a friend? Ride your bike? Something?"

"No." She set the controller next to the candy bars. "I'll go to my room."

"No," he said sharply—too sharply. "Don't leave, Alex. Just...don't."

But it was too late. She stood, barely reaching his shoulder as she slid by him, her waif-like body disappearing around the corner, leaving him wondering why his famed ability to get ice-princess supermodels to open up to him when he was holding a camera couldn't crack the shell around a twelve-year-old orphan.

Tom closed his eyes and walked as far away from the den as he could, which wasn't very far in this tiny house that bore his sister's lively fingerprints on every crocheted pillow and lacy curtain. It all reminded him that Ruthie had made a secure, loving, stable home for her daughter, and then left it all in the hands of the one person who didn't do *security*, *love*, or *stability*—him.

"Shit." Shoving his hair back and sighing hard, Tom went into the kitchen and stared out the window at the miniature backyard, noticing Ruthie's drooping, brown-tipped plants that he supposed someone should water.

But he'd never had a plant. Or a tract home. Or full responsibility for a kid who erected walls made of blank stares and noisy video games.

What the *hell* had Ruthie been thinking? She'd been thinking what most people who live in a state of denial, never dreaming something like an aneurysm or a car accident or a...*hemorrhage* could end their life in an instant.

But Tom knew better. And Ruthie *should* have known better, considering their childhood history. But apparently she hadn't, because she'd never bothered to change a twelve-year-old document that left Thomas Jefferson DeMille, least qualified person on earth, responsible for his niece.

What the hell was he supposed to do now?

Since he'd received the news that his sister had died and he'd dropped his camera on a shoot in Bora-Bora to get on a plane to a much less glamorous island off the Gulf Coast of Florida, he'd asked himself that question a thousand times. He was Alex's closest living relative, if you didn't count her father, who had been MIA for more than a decade and had already legally rejected his own daughter.

There was no answer to what he should do, only questions. How could he take care of a child when his career was one endless road trip? How would Alex fit into his lifestyle? Was it possible to incorporate a twelve-year-old girl into his crazy, chaotic world? Did he have a choice?

The questions were silenced by his buzzing cell phone with a reminder alarm.

Flight 615 to Majorca. Leaves in three hours.

Maybe it would, but he wouldn't be on the plane. He'd canceled the flight, the shoot, and the whole European trip weeks ago, but he'd forgotten to take some of the dates off his calendar. Or maybe he'd secretly hoped that he'd find a solution to this insurmountable problem and be able to make the trip anyway. He squeezed the phone, staring at the notification, unable to resist tapping the month view to see all the things he'd canceled in those hazy days when he'd arrived, bearing his own grief for the loss of one more person he'd cared about.

The city names blurred, like his old travel days, one into another.

Barcelona after Majorca. And then Nice and Monaco. Son of a bitch, he wanted to do that campaign for LaVie on the French Riviera. But he'd had his agent cancel it along with everything else for July and August.

And *then what?*

He smacked the counter so hard it stung his palm. "What the hell am I going to do?"

"You could find my dad."

He closed his eyes at the soft whisper, biting back the truth. Some lawyer had already found Steve Whitman, who lived in Oregon, had another family, and had done nothing but wave the legal papers that released him of any responsibility for the one he'd had twelve years ago with Ruthie.

Tom certainly didn't have the heart to tell this broken girl that her father didn't want her even though her mother was dead.

"That's not what your mom would have wanted," he said, choosing his words carefully.

"She wanted me to be happy."

"Of course," he said vaguely. And Ruthie had always been a little ditzy, and too trusting, and forgetful. Amusing as hell, but had she forgotten that Tom had already sacrificed a few years of his life to raise a young girl without parents? Otherwise, why would she let history repeat itself?

The front doorbell rang with a singsong interruption. More neighbors with casseroles? More of the colorful troupe of amateur actors from Ruthie's community theater? The visitors had slowed to a trickle in the past two weeks. Nice enough characters with good intentions and tons of offers of sympathy and prayers, but no one had any idea what to do with Alex, and none seemed close enough to suggest they take care of her while Tom lived his life. Or at least while he went to the south of France for a few weeks.

"Can you get that?" he asked, not eager to make small talk with strangers right then. Or ever.

She barely nodded before walking out of the kitchen. Tom stayed exactly where he was, breathing slow and steady, his mind back to the original and only problem he had. Not that he wanted to think of Alex as a "problem" at all. She was a kid, broken and beaten by life's cruel circumstances. He knew *exactly* how she felt. But what was he going to do?

He couldn't leave her, even for a few weeks. And what about long term? Maybe he could put her in a boarding school, or find a live-in nanny willing to stay while he traveled, or take her with him when she wasn't in school. Maybe that was a possibility.

"Um, she wants to see you." Alex stood in the kitchen doorway again.

19

"Who?"

She lifted a bony shoulder. "I thought she was from the theater group with that pink hair, but I've never seen her before."

Pink hair? A little shot of adrenaline rushed through him at the memory of the charming young woman from the convenience store. How had she found him? Without a word, he brushed by Alex into the living room, and sure enough, there she was, as pink and pretty as he remembered.

She smiled, showing small, straight teeth that fit pixie-like features. Still, she was more striking than classically "cute" and surprisingly intriguing. Not at all his usual taste in women, but purely attractive anyway.

"Hi." She bit her lower lip, her eyes bright and as wildly green as he remembered from the parking lot. Instantly, he imagined those sparkly eyes aimed directly at his camera, slightly shuttered, with a yellow-tinged light to accent the green. "Charity told me how to find you," she said.

He pulled himself out of the imaginary shot. "Charity?"

"That nice lady who owns the Super Min."

Behind him, Alex snorted softly. "Nice as a python."

The comment surprised him so much he turned to her, startled by one of the first emotive things he'd heard his niece say. "Um, Alex, this is Gussie, who swooped in and saved me from that python. Gussie, this is my niece, Alex Whitman."

"Gussie?" Alex asked, eyeing their guest with more interest than she'd shown in anything except a video game in the month he'd been there.

"It's short for Augusta," Gussie explained, with the tone of a person who'd offered the information a thousand or more times in her life. "I was born one minute after midnight on August first, so my mom named me Augusta. I was supposed to be Julia, for July."

"Do you have sisters named April, May, and June?" Alex asked.

She laughed easily. "Just a brother, Luke." Gussie turned to Tom, leveling him with those grass-green eyes. "I bet you're curious why I'm here."

As hell. "And how that woman came up with this address, that wasn't on my *expired* driver's license."

"Don't underestimate the nosiness of Charity Grambling," Gussie said.

Alex laughed, a sound so out of place that Tom had to look at her again, spying the faintest glint in eyes that had been nothing but dull for a month. "That's what my mom used to say. She called her Chump Charity."

Gussie snapped her fingers and pointed to Alex. "A Mario Kart fan?"

"Yeah. Are you?" Alex asked, her voice rising a bit.

"A fan and champion." She gave up an endearing smile, flipping her colorful hair with playful smugness. "I'm kind of unbeatable at anything with Mario's name on it."

"Do you play Mario Kart?" Alex asked with a note of rising excitement.

Gussie held up her hands as if on a steering wheel. "Princess Peach rules the road."

Alex let out a soft shriek. "I'm Rosalina."

Tom looked from one to the other, the conversation volley throwing him on so many levels. Not only did he not know what the hell they were talking about, he couldn't even wrap his head around the change in Alex. It was like someone had turned a light on inside her.

"Would you, um, want to play?" Alex asked. "Just one game, right now?"

"Well, I...I..."

"Maybe later, Alex," he said, trying not to throw too much cold water on the ideas. As much as he knew the spark in Alex had been lit by their unexpected guest, he took pity on the woman who probably hadn't hunted him down to play video games.

The light in Alex's eyes dimmed, gone as fast as it had arrived. "My mom liked to play it with me," she said on a sad whisper.

He bit back a grunt of frustration, furious at himself for killing the first sign of life.

But Gussie stepped forward and reached out a hand to Alex, sincere sympathy oozing from her. "Charity told me about your mother. I'm so sorry."

Alex swallowed and nodded. "Yeah, thanks. And sorry I asked."

"No, don't be sorry. I'd love to play sometime."

But Alex backed away, slinking into the hallway.

Damn it. *Damn* it.

"Oh," Gussie breathed a sigh of sorrow that reflected exactly how he felt. "I shouldn't have—"

"It's not your fault," he assured her. "I should thank you. I have no clue who Princess Whatever and Rosalina are, but you made her smile for the first time in weeks."

"The poor kid. And...you. I'm sorry for your loss. Her mother was your sister?"

He nodded and murmured, "Thanks."

She reached toward him, then pulled her hand back as if she realized she shouldn't touch him. "That has to be horrible. Family is everything."

Or it's nothing, depending on the cards you've been dealt. "Is that why you're here? A sympathy call?"

"Actually, no." She gave a self-conscious smile and

shuffled a little on bright red heels. "I came to ask you for that favor you said you owed me."

A favor? He eyed the pink wig, the artfully applied makeup, the flirty skirt, and wanted to know more about her. Like, what was she hiding under that rainbow of color? "Sure," he said. "What do you need?"

"A wedding photographer."

He frowned, not following. "You want me to recommend someone?"

"I want you to shoot a wedding. This weekend."

He stared at her, then smiled, slowly. And that grew to a real laugh, because that was about the funniest thing he'd ever heard. Except by the look on her face, she was dead serious.

And something told him this unusual young woman was not about to take no for an answer.

"I know that's like asking Picasso to fill in a coloring book," she said. "But is there any chance you would consider it just this once?"

"A wedding?" Was she on crack?

"I know this is a really hard time for you and your niece, and I don't mean to intrude on your time together, but maybe a fun wedding on the beach would help take your mind off the grief?"

Not enough to get him to strap on a camera and shoot the receiving line. He'd rather shoot himself. He was vaguely aware of the whirring sounds of the video game from the den, the noise filling in an awkward beat of silence.

"I'm sorry," he said simply. "I'm sure you can find another photographer."

Raspberry-glossed lips tilted in disappointment, and he hated the splash of guilt in his gut. But TJ DeMille was *not* a wedding photographer. It was bad enough he'd been turned into a permanent babysitter, but he wouldn't make his currently crappy situation worse by shooting a wedding.

"Okay," she said, the sadness in her acceptance still not wiping out the sparkling light in her bottle-green eyes. "I knew it was an outrageous request, but if you don't ask, you don't know."

"I like fearlessness in a woman," he admitted. "I like someone who knows what they want and goes after it."

Her expression grew hopeful.

"But I draw the line at wedding photography."

She let out a slow exhale. "Of course you do. Well, it was great to meet you. I didn't tell you this, but I'm a fashion blogger and stylist and a huge fan of your work."

"Really?" Then she should have known he didn't do happy brides and grooms. "Thanks."

"Well, I..." She glanced toward the hall. "Can I say good-bye to Alex?"

"Of course." He gestured for her to go first, a little surprised by the request. Was she still trying to get into his good graces so he'd say yes, or did she really care about a girl she'd just met?

Behind her, his gaze was drawn to the skirt that flipped around her thighs, showing long legs and a shapely backside. It was the first time he'd really gotten a good look at her body, which was slender and strong, but quite feminine. Her face had been captivating enough. If only she didn't cover it all up with the wig and makeup, even though both were applied with the hand of an expert.

She paused at the den door, leaning in. "Sounds like somebody's at the mall," she said lightly.

Instantly, the sounds stopped as Alex paused the game. Even that was a rarity, Tom thought.

"It's an easy course," Alex said.

"If you know how to find the escalator," Gussie replied.

Alex laughed, the sound still so out of the norm in this house that Tom couldn't believe he heard it. "Can you play now?" she asked Gussie.

"I…" Gussie turned to him, a question in her eyes, then suddenly she shook her head. "No, I can't," she said to Alex. "I have to go."

To find a photographer, even though there was one standing in front of her. Guilt kicked him in the chest, but he ignored it.

"Aww." Real disappointment echoed from the den, adding power to that guilt kick.

"Another time," Gussie said brightly.

But they both knew there wouldn't be another time. Unless…

"I hope so." The thin strand of desperation in Alex's voice added a knife slice to his already bruised chest.

Gussie stepped back into the hall and tipped her head, a sad frown pulling. "She's so sweet," she mouthed, slipping past him to return to the living room.

This time as he followed her, his gaze wasn't on her shapely backside or legs. Instead, he stared at the tile floor and gave into the certainty of what he had to do.

How hard would it be to take a few pictures at a wedding?

She moved quickly, getting to the front door a few seconds before he did. She opened it and then paused. "Thanks, any—"

"I changed my mind."

She leaned forward as if she hadn't heard him correctly.

"I'll do the wedding."

Then she blinked at him. "Wha…why? I mean, that's awesome, but what happened?"

He had a million ways he could go with this, but settled on the truth because it was always easier and less complicated than anything else. "So you'll come back and play that game with Alex."

She opened her mouth to respond, then shut it again, shaking her head.

"You won't?"

"I will. But you don't have to...although I really want you to." She laughed lightly. "What I mean is, I love kids, and I'd be happy to play with her, but not to coerce you into doing my wedding."

Her wedding? Of course...that hadn't even occurred to him. For some reason, some *wrong* reason, he'd gotten the impression she was...available. Wishful thinking on his part.

"I mean, I'd play with her right now, but you looked like you really wanted me to go and I already overstayed my uninvited visit."

He couldn't help smiling. She was genuine and adorable and...damn it, he *wanted* to shoot her wedding. "No, but I'll make you a deal. You spend a little time with my niece when it's convenient, and I'll give you the most beautiful wedding album you and your"—he angled his head, since it had to be said—"very *lucky* fiancé could ever imagine."

Her jaw dropped in surprise. "*I'm* not getting married." She pressed her hands to her chest with another laugh. "I'm the stylist."

So his instinct *was* right. "And a damn good one, I'd say."

"You don't know that yet."

"Yes, I do." He reached to take a playful tug of her brightly colored hair. "Look how you rock a pink wig."

A soft flush of that very color rose over her cheeks, making her even prettier and making him damn glad he'd

26

made this deal, a feeling that only deepened as she gave him the details and dates, and finalized dinner plans.

He didn't know why, exactly, but for the first time in a month, he felt a glimmer of happiness. Probably because he would be getting a camera back in his hands. Or maybe because of the stylist he'd be working with.

As he watched her walk away, he was certain it was the latter.

Chapter Three

Junonia was crowded, even midweek, since the resort's restaurant had become a destination not only for guests, but for discerning diners from all over Mimosa Key and the mainland, too. Still, Gussie had managed to persuade the hostess to give her a waterfront table, where she waited for her guests with way too many butterflies.

She still couldn't believe her good fortune. Ari and Willow had high-fived and danced in the office, and even Rhonda Lyons had sounded downright thrilled when Gussie called to confirm dinner with TJ DeMille, famed photographer.

To get him for a wedding was such a coup. Her stomach fluttered at the thought of working with him, of styling the shots and watching him hold the camera with those strong, sexy hands.

Whoa, girl. Keep it professional now. Shaking off the thought, she turned to appreciate the beach view, the panorama awash with a midsummer sunset that turned the nearly still water of the gulf a mix of tangerine and cobalt.

"That's my favorite color."

She whipped around at the sound of a man's voice,

meeting a gaze that was as gorgeous as the water and so…
"Blue."

"No, the orange." He pulled out the chair closest to her, openly checking out her hair, face, and the lacy yellow sundress she'd chosen to match her mood. "Very pretty."

"The sunsets at Barefoot Bay are amazing."

He smiled and unbuttoned a cuff of a crisp white shirt, casually rolling up the sleeve to get comfortable. And torture her with the sight of his masculine forearms. "I didn't mean the sunset."

She felt a familiar blush, along with the denial that always popped out when someone complimented her. But before she could speak, he touched the edge of her wig.

"Pretty in pink."

"Sometimes I wear purple or black."

He lifted an interested brow, and she braced for the questions, the inevitable "why" she'd fielded for much of her adult life, but it didn't come. Instead, he unbuttoned the other cuff and folded it up, revealing that string of blue ink she'd seen in the Super Min.

"So, here's your wedding photographer, reporting for duty." He winked and helped himself to her water. "But be warned." He gave a faux toast. "The last time I shot a wedding, I was about seventeen, and I got in trouble for spending too much time in the bridesmaids' dressing rooms."

She laughed. "Why am I not surprised?"

"But the shots were stellar."

"Still not surprised. I spent a little time this afternoon researching your most recent work."

"The layout in the *Vanity Fair* you bought?" He squinted, looking off to the distance as if remembering the shoot. "The lighting in Madagascar was brutal."

29

Reminding her just how preposterous it was to have *this* photographer shooting a wedding. "You really are a master of the art, both fashion and commercial."

He tipped his head in gratitude. "I try."

"You succeed. That Fendi campaign? All saturated color and simple shots with complex backgrounds."

He inched back, amusement making his blue eyes sparkle. "Nice of you to notice."

"I told you I'm a stylist and I blog about things like that."

"What's the blog called? I'll have to visit it."

She got a ridiculous thrill at the thought. "Get Gussied Up. I mostly talk fashion and style and blabber on about the weddings we plan and hold right here at Casa Blanca Resort & Spa. Nothing, you know, *major* like what you do."

He accepted a water of his own when a waiter stopped by. Which was a shame. Gussie kind of liked the idea of sharing a glass with him.

"Don't denigrate what you do," he said. "It's bloggers like you who get my work out there."

"I have to say I enjoyed glomming your work today. You really are a storyteller. There's always so much emotion in your work."

The amusement left his gaze, darkening to something else as he eyed her long enough to feel a spark of electricity in the air.

"I guess I sound like some kind of fangirl now," she said.

"Not at all." He glanced down at the table, his hand casually rubbing his arm, right over the words tattooed there.

"What does that say?" she asked.

He didn't look up, but his whole body grew still as he lightly grazed the purple ink that wrapped around his muscular forearm. "*Panta monos*," he said, turning his arm so she could read the script. "It's Greek for 'always alone.'"

She stared at the strange words, barely recognizing the Greek alphabet.

Πάντα μόνος. *Always alone.*

"Wow. How…" Sad. Serious. Such a personal statement. "Permanent."

He laughed. "That's the general idea of a tattoo."

She stared at the letters. "Always?"

He acknowledged the question with a nod. "Which is why my sister's decision, or lack of it, is so ironic."

"Her decision?" What did he mean? She'd done a little snooping around the resort, talking to some of the staff about Ruthie Whitman's death, and learned that the young, single mother died of an aneurysm while at work as a receptionist in a local dentist's office.

"Her decision to let me be the one to take care of Alex."

Gussie gasped softly. "She's…yours?"

"At least until she's eighteen." His jaw set as he stared ahead. "Imagine handing over the care and nurturing of your twelve-year-old daughter to a man who spends three hundred and fifty days of the year on the road, rarely stays in one city for more than a week, works all day, and plays all night."

That was his life? "Had you and your sister talked about this?"

He closed his eyes and gave his head a slow, dramatic shake. "No, we did not. We really didn't talk that often at all, a few times a year at best. Her passing was…completely unexpected." Closing his eyes with obvious grief, he helped himself to a healthy gulp of water. "My schedule doesn't allow for long family reunions."

But he was certainly having one now. "So, what are you going to do? Move here?"

He almost choked on the water. "Not likely. But I have to work." He managed a wry smile. "And there isn't much

31

demand for high-end photography on Mimosa Key, except for the occasional wedding."

She returned the smile, still wrapping her head around his predicament. "And there's no one else?"

"Her father's out of the picture. We don't have any other relatives." He stared out the window, the last rays of sunset reflected in his eyes as he studied the scenery. "I guess I'm going to adjust my life to take care of one very hollowed-out young girl. Which is why I was so moved by your ability to make her laugh today."

"Hollowed-out?" She sank into the palms of her hands, resting her elbows on the table. "I couldn't tell that from her at all. I mean, obviously she's sad, but she didn't seem...gutted." But who wouldn't be in her situation?

"She's distant and depressed, and I can't seem to connect with her, no matter how hard I try. And, believe me, I'm usually very good at getting people to take down their defenses, since it's a big part of my job."

"Maybe she's just more comfortable around a woman, since it was only the two of them."

He shrugged. "I don't know, but I'll figure it out. I'm short on friends in this town, so..."

She reached her hand out and laid it on his arm, right over his Greek pronouncement. "I told you, I love kids. I'd be happy to entertain her when I can. And I won't make you shoot any more weddings after this."

He repositioned his hand so he could wrap his fingers around hers, his hand every bit as strong and secure as she'd imagined. "Thanks, Pink."

The smile pulled at her lips, their eyes locked, their fingers deliciously entwined.

"So this is how you got him?" Rhonda Lyons's question snapped them apart.

Gussie sniffed a sharp breath as Tom stood, towering over the other woman and her daughter.

Rhonda paled a little, looking up at him, all of her fight fizzling out as the impact that TJ DeMille no doubt had on most women smacked her in the face. She opened her mouth to speak, but her gaze moved from his eyes to his hair to his chest and lower and back up again. Then color returned full force to her cheeks as she finally managed to look at Gussie.

"Can't say I blame you."

"Rhonda." Tom reached out his hand for the most accommodating and warm handshake in the history of greetings. "I can't tell you how honored I am to photograph your daughter's wedding."

The sarcasm, so subtle and sneaky, was lost on Rhonda, who still stared openly. Then Tom turned his killer smile on Hailey, a quiet young woman who'd long ago handed the reins of her wedding to her mother. "And our beautiful bride."

Hailey was actually speechless as she took his hand.

Meanwhile, Gussie's heart was slip-sliding around her chest so hard, she could have sworn she heard it crack a little. Great. Just what every girl needs...a crush on the guy who wanted to be alone, always.

Rhonda was a cougar with a weakness for vodka. Hailey was a pushover who let her mother run her show. Tom knew exactly how to handle those two—give one more booze and the other some sincere compliments. But the woman on his right was a bit of an enigma, making him want to finish the boring client dinner and get Gussie alone to take off some...layers.

Leaning close to Gussie as they walked out of the restaurant, he whispered in her ear, "Let's take a walk."

He felt her shudder a little. "We're really all ready for the wedding." In other words, she knew a walk wasn't to talk about event logistics.

He guided her to the door. "Ready with the bride and mother, but I still have to win over the stylist."

She laughed as they crossed a pavilion and kicked off their shoes, placing them on a stair that seemed to be built for the express purpose of holding shoes while their owners went barefoot on Barefoot Bay. "I'm won, trust me. I just hope you like my styling technique."

"You obviously know your business."

She waved off the compliment. "Not like some of the people you've worked with."

It wasn't the first time she'd directed a subtle dig at herself. Why wouldn't a woman as attractive and capable as Gussie be more confident?

"Like Simone Friar," Gussie continued. "What a stylist. She's brilliant."

"And a bitch."

"Or Max Adelman, who is a genius."

"And always two hours late."

"What about Chloe Hartman? She's got an eye for that shocking pop of color."

"And a penchant for pot."

Laughing, she elbowed him. "You're bursting my bubble. These people are my professional idols."

"You could do their job and you would be sweet, on time, and not high."

She shrugged. "Well, I'm *not* doing their job. I'm a

small-town destination-wedding stylist and a part-time blogger. So, let's get real. Working with you on a shoot is kind of a professional dream come true."

Hearing the wistful tone, he glanced at her. "That's your professional dream?"

"Not now, obviously. I love this business we've started, but…" She rewarded him with a smile that was both inviting and a little uncertain. "Doesn't every stylist dream of working for a big fashion magazine or a top-notch photographer?"

"So do it."

She shook her head, her dreamy expression melting into determination. "Oh, no. I committed to my two closest friends to launch a business, and we're getting more successful and better known with each wedding."

"Why did you do that, if you have other professional dreams?"

"Because…" She took a slow breath, measuring her response. "Some things are more important than seeing your work on the pages of *Vogue*."

"Like?"

"Like family," she replied without a second's hesitation.

He frowned, realizing she'd mentioned she was from the Boston area and told Alex she had a brother, but hadn't talked about any other family. "Where's yours?" he asked.

"Well, it depends on which family you mean. Ari and Willow are like my sisters now, and they are family, which doesn't have to be blood."

The statement hit him harder than he'd expected, but he pushed the emotional response back to the dark corner where he kept thoughts like that. "Are they all from Boston, too? Were you childhood friends with these women?"

"Oh, no. We met when we were all on the board of the

American Association of Bridal Consultants, which had us traveling together every month to different destination-wedding locales. We cooked up the idea of combining our talents into one business and chose Barefoot Bay as our location. I threw in with them because I wanted the solid sense of a team and that security that comes with knowing someone has your back. Do you get that?"

Did he get that? Better than anyone. He also knew how...*fleeting*...it could be. He lifted his arm and pointed to his *panta monos* tattoo. "*I* have my back," he told her.

"Oh, that's right, you're the Lonesome Dove."

"I prefer eagle."

"And eagles fly alone? Well, have fun with that. Like I said, family is everything, and they are mine."

Family is everything. He swallowed a response that would only sound bitter and angry. "What about the family that you were born into?" he asked.

Her expression flickered slightly. "Cracked and broken up, I'm afraid."

He wasn't exactly sure what that meant, but he recognized the hitch of pain in her voice. "As in..." he prodded.

"As in my family is not a solid foundation to stand on, and since I really need and want that, I have chosen to build my life with these dear friends."

She regarded him for a moment, the moonlight making her eyes a soft, pale green, but then she closed them as something hit her. "How thoughtless I am," she said suddenly. "I shouldn't be talking about family to a man who recently lost his sister. I'm so sorry."

"No, that's fine." He paused as they reached the water's edge, the sand as cold and hard as his heart right then. "I usually avoid the subject of family, even before this latest tragedy."

"What about the rest of your family?" she asked. "You said there are no other close relatives."

"My parents were killed in a car accident when I was seventeen. Ruthie was thirteen."

He heard her suck in a soft, shocked breath.

"We lived with my grandmother, who Ruthie lovingly called Cruella DeMille."

Gussie gave a sad smile, listening.

"And when she died, I raised Ruthie until she was eighteen."

"Oh, God." She gave his arm a squeeze of sympathy. "No wonder you don't talk about your family. You've lost three people."

He nodded, absolutely unwilling to tell her the number didn't stop at three. It would have killed the whole night.

"Is that why you take such emotional pictures?"

The question surprised him. "I've never thought of it that way, but maybe."

"Your shots are always so poignant."

"Thanks, but that's not because of my past. I told you I can find a subject's vulnerability point. It's my secret power."

She gave a quiet laugh. "Good to know. Is that better than X-ray vision?"

"Very similar, actually. And that's how I get a great shot. Models especially will tell me anything."

She gave him a playful nudge. "'Cause you're cute."

He got a hold of her elbow and eased her a little closer so their feet were in the cool water. "So are you."

"Not exactly."

He turned her so they were facing each other, considering if he should tell her he was about to use that secret talent or let her figure it out. For a few heartbeats, they looked at each other, a nice, positive attraction as heavy as the humidity in the air.

Brushing back a few strands of her hair, he inched infinitesimally closer. "Why do you wear this?"

She answered with a casual shrug of one shoulder. "It's my signature look."

"Hmm."

"It is," she insisted.

"Is that why you don't think you're pretty?"

Her eyes grew wide, like he was a doctor tapping around and had found the very spot that caused pain. "I never said that. Charity did."

"And she's wrong," he assured her.

She gave a little eye roll, telling him she didn't think Charity was wrong at all.

"But you do always wear a wig?"

"Not always. Sometimes I wear hats."

Her expression shifted subtly, susceptibility working its way to the forefront as he found her tender place, the thing that made her teeter on the edge between fierce and fearful. He wanted to see that on her face, wanted to memorize it. God, he wanted to take a picture of it.

"Take the wig off."

She stared at him, motionless.

"You can do it," he said. "I don't care if you're hiding a bad hair day or you're bald as the proverbial cue ball. I want to see you, Augusta McBain."

"You're looking at me, Thomas Jefferson DeMille."

"But I'm not seeing all of you." He got a little bit closer, threading his fingers into the hair until he felt the netting underneath.

"Don't," she said.

He relaxed his hands instantly, obeying her order. "Then

tell me the real reason you wear it, and I'll never mention it again."

For a long, long time, she didn't move, didn't even breathe. He was certain she was making some kind of decision. To trust or not trust. To share or not share. To give or not give. It was like watching a woman decide whether she'd let herself be seduced. Only it was a hundred times sexier.

After a slow, deep inhale, she put her hands on the sides of her head and carefully lifted the wig out of his fingertips. As the bangs brushed upward, he saw more of her. A high, beautifully round forehead that finished the heart-shaped face. God had been in a very good mood the day He'd designed her.

Waves of honey-colored hair fell to her shoulders in soft, silky strands. It wasn't styled, but it had been twisted, so the strands curled a little, framing her face. Thick, sexy, naturally beautiful hair that would look stunning in any style.

"Why do you hide this?" he asked, incredulous because it wasn't what he had been expecting under that wig.

She swallowed, then turned. He managed not to hiss a breath at the sight of the back of her head, where there was no hair at all. Just a misshapen patch of cratered skin, disfigured and slashed with the marbled, mottled scars of a horrifying burn.

He saw her shoulders rise a bit, as if she shuddered under his scrutiny. He turned her around and wasn't the least bit surprised to see mist in her eyes.

"You know what I think is beautiful?" he asked.

"If you say my head, I'll know you're lying."

He let his thumbs run under her jawline. "Beautiful is a woman who survives and thrives no matter what life throws at her."

"Life didn't throw that bottle rocket. My brother, Luke, did."

"Oh." The sound was half grunt, half sigh, all pain for her. "That's awful."

"No, it's just something that happened." She reached up and pulled her hair off her face, making a ponytail. "My scar is ugly, so I cover it, that's all."

But somehow he didn't think that was all. Not for a minute. And that only made Tom want to peel off more layers of Gussie McBain.

Chapter Four

"It's no big deal," Gussie said, using that cavalier tone she always copped when someone saw the scar. She'd learned early that the attitude helped ease the other person's discomfort much more than her own.

"Your eyes would say differently," Tom replied.

And then there was the rare person who saw right though her devil-may-care act. Immediately, she fought the urge to stuff her head back into the safety net of her favorite wig. Instead, she concentrated on the look in Tom's dreamy blue eyes, a look that wasn't pity or shock or disgust or curiosity.

He looked...*intrigued*.

And that gave her enough courage to let the wig hang in her hand and feel the rare sensation of a tropical breeze on her hair and scalp.

"Well, the problem's in the back," she said, using another well-worn phrase. "It was a blessing I spun around the instant I did or that would have been my face."

He flinched with a millisecond of horror. "What happened?"

She rooted through all the different versions of the tale she'd accumulated over the years. The quick-and-dirty "childhood accident" or "wrong place, wrong time" was fine with the occasional stranger. The more detailed "my brother was drunk with his friends and accidentally shot a bottle rocket at my head" usually sufficed for the very curious. But then there were close friends who deserved a little bit more.

Where on the spectrum of trust did Tom land? She wasn't sure yet, so she went with the simple truth.

"Fourth of July accident when I was fifteen years old," she said. "I was at the Cape with my older brother, and he and his friends got...well, like crazy teenage boys get on summer nights at the beach. Next thing you know, I'm an Independence Day statistic."

"Holy shit," he murmured. "How awful. For both of you."

Somehow, the fact that he recognized how bad it was for Luke, and not just her, touched her heart. Truth was, it was worse for her brother than it had been for her, and he'd paid a higher price.

"Yeah, it"—broke up the most perfect family—"was hard."

"Hard has to be an understatement."

She turned to the water, oddly unembarrassed that he could see her scar. She knew how to partially cover it with a ponytail and some creative hairstyling, but it wasn't covered now. "Damn, you have a gift," she murmured.

"Don't change the subject."

"I'm not. I mean it. You weren't kidding when you said you have X-ray vision."

"I don't generally unleash that on innocent bystanders, but..." He got a little closer. "You fascinate me."

She did? He was the fascinating one with all his secret powers of perception. Silent for a moment, she listened to the water lap and the sound of distant laughter from the

42

resort.

"So, did you forgive your brother?"

The question stung, nearly taking her breath away. "If only I could."

"What do you mean?"

"After I got out of the hospital, he…" She swallowed hard, wishing so much this story had a different ending. "He left."

"Where did he go?"

She shrugged. "We don't know."

Tom looked as surprised as anyone when she told them the truth.

"Except for a few random calls after he disappeared, he dropped off the face of the earth."

"Damn."

"Yeah, damn." Old emotions, anger and hurt and frustration, bubbled up and threatened to spew. But she shouldn't tell him everything, not now, not here. This man barely knew her and had no connection to her. He wouldn't care about how her happy, stable, perfect family shattered from the impact of one wayward bottle rocket and one stupid girl on a hot July night fifteen years ago.

In her peripheral vision, she was aware that he lifted his hand and was going to—

"No." She jerked away from his touch before his hand made contact with the scar. "Please."

"Does it hurt?"

"Only my pride." She raised the wig. "My hair won't grow where the burn scar is, no matter how many transplant surgeries I had." She grabbed the hair that grew on either side of the scar. She kept it long, and with some creativity, she'd learned to get it under a hat or even make a ponytail to come out of the back of a baseball cap, but she never forgot that the scar was there.

"I battled it for years, then wigs came into style, and I made wearing one my own personal look, in a rainbow of crazy colors. That's it. Curiosity satisfied? Can I put it back on?"

"You don't have to wear it for my sake, only if it makes you more comfortable." He gestured toward the raised edge of sand formed by the last high tide. "Want to sit?"

"What I want to do is dive into that water." The admission tumbled out, and at his surprised look, she added, "I'm usually at the beach on crowded Sunday afternoons, so I never go underwater. I wear hats a lot."

"So let's go in."

She laughed at the suggestion. "I've shown you enough skin for one night."

"Then keep your clothes on." At her look, he laughed. "Underwear? I assume you've got some on. Colorful, if I had to venture a guess."

"Polka dot, actually."

He made a little grunt in his chest, kind of slow and dirty. "Did you know that they've done research and found that men are aroused by polka dots?"

"Men are aroused. Period."

"I can handle a swim. Can you?" He started unbuttoning his shirt, pulling the tails from his khaki pants. When he finished with the buttons, he shrugged out of the shirt, the moonlight catching cuts and cords of his muscles, and a soft tuft of chest hair nestled between impressive pecs. And more ink. His whole left pec was covered in swirls of purple and blue that looked like some kind of dragon. The tattoo ran over his shoulder and pec and down the side of his waist. She wasn't normally a lover of all that body art, but his was stunning, and she couldn't stop staring.

The pants hung low enough to show narrow hips and the tip of another tattoo...down there.

"We've all got some things hidden, don't we?" he teased, watching where her gaze had settled.

"Your hidden things are nicer-looking than mine." She scooped up his shirt and handed it to him. "But since I met— and *hired*—you today, I'm going to pass on the swim."

He took the shirt, letting their fingers brush, sending a hundred goose bumps down her spine. "I'm not ready to end the night." And there went a hundred more.

"Who said anything about ending it?"

His brows rose in interest.

"We've got a twelve-year-old opponent waiting to play Mario Kart."

His lips slid into a slow smile. "You do. I'll watch."

"Then let's go." She turned to walk away and head up the beach, but he snagged her elbow, stopping her.

"One more thing," he whispered in her ear, staying behind her. She waited, her breath catching. "I happen to think scars, any kind of scars, are beautiful."

And then he brushed the thin hair aside and pressed his lips to her exposed scalp, burning her skin, searing her heart, and making her want to spin around and take some of that kiss directly on her mouth. All of it.

But she fought the impulse, and broke the contact, walking a few steps away from him, knowing she was being very smart to turn down a night swim with a hot guy...but it still felt like the dumbest thing she'd ever done.

Momma's home! Alex slammed her finger on the controller to pause the game, but then reality bit. Momma couldn't be home. She was dead.

The pain in her gut, so familiar she barely thought about it most of the time, rose up to her chest and squeezed some more. Would she ever get used to it? Probably not. Definitely not.

Another soft female laugh, light and airy—like Momma's when she was excited about something—floated through the house from the living room.

Who was that? Alex stood slowly, dropping her controller to tiptoe down the hall, but before she reached the next room, she heard that laugh again and recognized it instantly. The pink-haired lady. *That's* who he'd gone to see?

A weird sensation seized her, something like anticipation and longing and familiarity all at once. That lady reminded her of Momma.

"Alex? Gussie's here to play that game with you."

Alex took a step farther, coming through the archway, sucking in a breath when she saw the lady wore a bright yellow sundress.

Momma would have *died* for that dress. She made a face, realizing how wrong that thought was. Momma *did* die.

"Not if you don't want to," Gussie said quickly, making Alex wonder what her face gave away.

"No, no, I do want to play."

"Great." Her tone was so friendly and natural, Alex relaxed a little, something she rarely did when Uncle Tommy was in the room. He was so dark and serious, and obviously hated her so much that Alex just wanted to hide from him.

"What should I call you?" The question sounded

awkward, and Alex could practically hear her mother correct her or cover for her daughter's lack of social skills. But Momma wasn't here, so Alex would have to stumble through conversations, and life, without her. "Miss…Something?"

"Gussie works for me," she said, coming closer. "Or Princess Peach."

Momma was Peach. Always, *always*. Ever since Alex taught her to play Mario Kart, Momma had been Princess Peach on the Sugar Scooter. She won only when Alex secretly let her, and then she would jump up and down and holler, "Peach rules!" and they'd both laugh, and Momma would point at the screen when Peach was on the podium like she was a boss.

"Or I can be someone else," Gussie said, probably because Alex had zoned out thinking about her mother. *When* would that stop?

"No, you can be Peach. It's fine." It was *right*, somehow.

She headed down the hall, fighting that weird sensation Momma used to call *déjà woo-woo*. She'd say, "We must have dreamed this was going to happen, Alex."

Alex *wished* all this was a dream. That she'd wake up and Momma would be sitting on her bed, making up her stupid poems and singing her silly good-morning songs.

"Would you like something to drink, Gussie?" Uncle Tommy's question broke through Alex's thoughts.

"Whatever you have," Gussie said. "I won't ask for Snapple, though," she added with a laugh.

Alex whipped around. "Why not?" Snapple had been Momma's number one favorite drink. "It's the best." Of course her uncle had forgotten to buy the raspberry Snapple Alex had asked for.

"Because I accidentally broke the bottle he was buying at Super Min today. Was it for you? God, I'm sorry I was such a klutz."

Alex burned a little, ashamed she'd assumed he'd forgotten. "S'okay," she said.

In the den, she turned on a light because she remembered Momma always wanted the light on when she played. Even when she got better at the game—which had taken months— she still needed the light to see the controller and remember which button was which.

"I don't need a wheel," Gussie said as she settled on the sofa. "I can play with the stick."

Obviously, this lady didn't need a lesson on the controllers. As Alex sat in the recliner, she couldn't help giving Gussie a curious look. "Why are you doing this?"

Oh, God, there she went again, blurting out stupid questions. But Gussie shrugged and smiled, glancing at the door and leaning closer as if they shared a secret. "I'm kind of addicted to the game," she admitted on a whisper. "It's hard to find a worthy opponent."

Alex smiled. "Me, too."

"I haven't played the latest version yet, have you?"

She shook her head. "Just this one. My mom was going to get me the new one for my birthday." And another crappy fact came tumbling out of her mouth.

"Well, let's see how we do with this one," Alex said quickly, probably because talking about her mother made people uncomfortable. She'd noticed that, even with the people who came to bring them food and make sure she was okay. No one really wanted to talk about Ruthie Whitman, but merely looked at Alex and made her feel even sadder.

Her uncle came in holding three bottles of water. "Unless you need something stronger to play," he said as he handed one to Gussie.

"Oh, no, I need my wits about me to win." Gussie winked

at Alex. "You might be better than I think."

Alex looked over her head at Uncle Tommy, who had a slight smile on his usually scowly face.

Gussie tapped her controller with one move, clicked through the Wii screens like a pro, then zipped through the characters.

"Hello, Peachy," she whispered when she picked her player and ride.

Alex's heart split wide open. Momma never said that, but Gussie was so much like her! Easy, happy, *fun*.

"Alex?" Uncle Tommy asked, making Alex realize she'd been staring at their guest.

"Oh, yeah, sorry." She returned to the screen and clicked on Rosalina. "You can pick the course."

"Let's start simple."

And just like that, Alex was back on the starting line at Mushroom Gorge, her thumb poised to hit the button exactly between seconds two and one to get a boost of speed that would leave her opponents in the dust.

Deep in her heart, she didn't know if she should be happy like a butterfly or curl up and feel guilty because...this wasn't Momma.

Except, before she blinked, Peach's Sugar Scooter was flying so fast, Alex didn't have time to do anything but *catch up*.

"Whoa," Alex muttered, leaning forward, a frown tugging. "Holy crap."

Gussie laughed heartily. "Weren't expecting that, were you, Rosalina?" She fell back into the sofa with the relaxed ease of an expert player.

Well, *that* wasn't like Momma.

"Which one are you?" her uncle asked.

Gussie and Alex shared a quick look, the kind two players

give each other when someone clueless watches the race.

"I'm on the top screen," Gussie said. "Watch and learn, my friend."

Alex heard him laugh and was vaguely aware of how close the two of them were on the sofa, but since she was currently in ninth place—*ninth!*—she paid attention to the game.

Alex stole a glance to her right. "How often do you play this game?" She was an adult, despite the funky hair and wild makeup. "Aren't you, like, forty or something?"

Gussie let out something between a shriek and a grunt, taking her eyes off the game to give Alex a *get real* look. "Are you kidding me? I'll be thirty on August first!"

"Oh, I'm sorry."

But not really, since the comment made Gussie slip out of the lead.

"Keep her distracted, Uncle Tommy!"

"Uncle Tommy?" Gussie almost choked she laughed so hard. "Oh my God, please tell me I can call you that."

"Not if you want to live."

But Gussie cracked up and looked at Alex, and they both laughed. Hard. Alex's shoulders shook, and her heart danced a little, and she almost couldn't catch her breath because it was like she'd forgotten how to laugh.

"Look at that." Gussie waved her controller. "I was so gutted by being called an old bag that I let that little worm Koopa Troopa get ahead of me."

Alex giggled. "I didn't say you were an old bag."

"*Forty?*"

"Now you know how to beat her, Alex," Uncle Tommy said, getting into it with them. "A well-placed insult obviously takes her off-track."

"Don't help the competition, *Tommy*," Gussie shot back,

effortlessly flying back into first and over the finish line.

Alex stared at the screen and her own pathetic finish. "How did that happen? I never lose this game." She fell back on the recliner, her whole body buzzing from the fight.

Or was it buzzing from something else? Fun. Laughter. That incredibly awesomely wonderful feeling of not being sad.

Next to her, Gussie was trying to explain to Uncle Tommy how the controller worked, but the conversation didn't interest Alex. All she could think about right now was how she felt, despite having lost the game.

She felt...*whole.*

It was the first time since Momma died that Alex felt like her arms and legs were connected to her body and her head wasn't about to thud on the ground and her chest didn't feel like a big empty pit of nothingness.

Could that happen from one game of Mario Kart? That she'd *lost?*

"Want to try something a little easier, Alex?" Gussie asked, a playful tease in her voice. "Moo Moo Meadows?"

Alex turned, absolutely unable to wipe the smile off her face. How weird was that? "How about Ghost Valley?" No one—not real or a computer opponent set to "difficult"—had ever beaten her at Ghost Valley.

"That's my favorite course." Gussie clicked through the game choices, barely looking at the screen. "Let me at it."

Uncle Tommy leaned his whole body closer to Gussie, his blue eyes—usually so scary to Alex—didn't look terrifying at all when they were directed at Gussie.

"You're a beast," he whispered, but Alex heard the tease in his voice.

Gussie grinned back at him, the two of them looking at each other as if...as if...

As if they *liked* each other.

Alex tried to wrap her head around that, but the game started and Gussie kicked her butt one more time. But for some reason, it didn't matter. This was too much fun.

They played six more games, and Alex lost every one. Still, she never wanted the night to end, but when it did, Alex did something she hadn't done since Momma died. She fell asleep without crying.

Chapter Five

An incessant, angry, relentless buzz hummed like a freight train under Tom's head.

"What the..." Managing to open one eye, he saw nothing but darkness. And heard nothing but the growl of—

His phone. He reached under the pillow and pulled out the cell, blinded by the light of the unidentified number on the screen. And the time. 6:15. Who the hell would call him at this hour?

Then his brain engaged, and he recognized the country code. France. He squinted at the words.

L'Eau LaVie S.A.

The French bottled-water company. Hadn't his agent canceled that job? Or had it somehow slipped through the cracks? Grunting, he tossed the phone on the floor and flipped over, letting his eyes adjust to the palest streams of sunlight through the metal blinds his sister thought qualified as window treatments.

The house was small and lowbrow, but, damn, there'd been some laughter in it last night. Alex's giggles had been music to his ears, and he knew who he had to thank for that.

The phone buzzed again, which was definitely *not* music

to anyone's ears. Well, shit, he was awake now. Reaching down, he patted the floor, found the phone, and thumbed the screen, mentally cursing his overpaid agent who probably handed the cancellation off to an assistant who'd screwed up.

His bad mood firmly established, he hit the screen hard. "DeMille."

"*Monsieur* DeMille!" The woman's voice was thickly accented, low-pitched, and unfamiliar. "Oh, *bien, bien*! *Madame Voudreaux, le directeur de*—"

"English or I hang up." You had to be rude to the French. It was the only attitude they really respected.

"*Bien*. Of course. I am sorry. I am Suzette Voudreaux, the vice president of advertising for LaVie."

The VP was calling? Shit. He sat up, his head clearing. "You were supposed to be contacted by my agent."

"Oh, we were, *monsieur*, and he explained your situation. May I offer my deepest condolences for the loss of your sister?"

"Thank you." He barely whispered the words, her genuine sympathy coming through enough for him to feel bad for hating on his agent and even worse for having to cancel the job. "And I'm sorry I had to bail. Your campaign sounded interesting."

He didn't take a lot of commercial product work, but they'd planned to shoot the iconic LaVie bottle as a fashion accessory, as he understood the concept, and they wanted TJ DeMille to give the photography that ultra-couture look. Which he totally could have done, except—

"*Monsieur*, I am calling personally to ask you to reconsider your decision."

It was hardly a *decision*. "I can't," he said simply. "I'm

not working...for a while." Except for a *wedding* this weekend. "The situation is complicated."

"I understand the situation, *monsieur*. And I have a proposal for you."

No, she didn't understand the situation. *He couldn't go.* He winced and rolled over, ready to dump the call.

"We are prepared to offer you a completely enhanced compensation package." She practically purred this news. "We will provide you a fully furnished three-bedroom apartment in the center of Nice."

Nice. That was exactly the problem—only it was spelled differently, even if it was pronounced the same. "I don't think you fully understand my—"

"You have a child in your care. We are completely aware of that, *monsieur*, and we will arrange for a full-time au pair unless you would prefer to bring your own, and we will cover her compensation as well. We will pay all transportation and costs, including the use of our president's private jet to get you to and from France, and of course, we will increase your base fee." She lowered her voice and whispered a number that made him mouth a dark and frustrated curse.

"In euro," she added at his silence, adding even more dollars to the pot.

"Really." He heard her murmur something in French to another person. Something that probably translated to "even DeMille has a price."

But he was wide awake now. He'd never considered taking Alex to France. Would it be possible? Legal? Did she have a passport? Would she go?

"I'll have to let you know," he said.

"Our meetings with the advertising agency begin on Wednesday in Nice, and you must be there," she replied.

"We are brainstorming sets and locations and making final decisions on the models. The theme is 'drink beautiful, be beautiful,' and your advice will be invaluable."

"I'll think about it." A lot.

"We want you there," she urged. "It will be good for you. What better place for a grieving young girl to spend your summer than the exquisite city of Nice, *non*?"

She made a lot of sense, but something told him Alex wasn't about to jump on a private jet and hit the Promenade des Anglais.

"While you decide, I will send you some of our concepts and storyboards for your consideration. And pictures of the apartment. It's owned by LaVie, and I assure you, it is lovely."

Oh, he bet it was.

"And only a short distance from the beach and Vieux Nice."

The Old Town of Nice. One of his favorite places in the world.

A moment after signing off on the call, he was at the desk in Ruthie's room where he'd stored all of her most important papers. Shuffling through the files, he found two passports, both valid.

He took a minute to look at Ruthie's picture, seeing how she'd changed…and yet remained the same girl he'd worried about and worked to raise all those years. Her smile had always been easy, her heart surprisingly light for a girl who'd lost her parents so young.

But then she'd met that asshole Whitman and lost her mind, and Tom's respect. Putting her passport away, he took Alex's and let his hopes soar. He needed to get away, needed to travel and work and leave this little island. And now he could. If only he could get her to say yes.

Maybe, after last night, she'd be willing to be a little adventurous and come out of her funk. Surely he could make her do that, right?

After a shower, he pulled on some clothes and headed to the kitchen in search of coffee, surprised to find Alex's bedroom door closed tight. She rarely slept late. He wondered if she slept at all some nights. He'd hear her moving about at one in the morning, then she'd be up and in front of that game before seven.

But last night had been different. She'd had an indescribable *connection* with Gussie.

And so had he.

Only he could describe it perfectly in one word: attraction. She'd driven herself home last night and denied him even the chance to steal a kiss good night, but that would change. It had to.

Coffee in hand, he lost himself in reading email after email from France.

By the time he'd finished, he was on fire for the idea of taking this job. They not only needed him, there wasn't another photographer in the world who could make this ad campaign celebrate beauty the way he could. Images sprang to life already, his juices flowing at the thought of the resources, the possibilities, and the—

"Hey."

It was the closest thing to a "good morning" he'd had in four weeks. "Hi, Alex. How'd you sleep?"

She shrugged a slender shoulder that slipped out of a ripped T-shirt and opened the pantry, reaching for her usual breakfast of chocolate-chip cookies and a side of Milky Way.

"Did your mom let you eat like that?" The minute the words were out, he regretted speaking.

Everything closed up—her eyes, her arms, her mouth. She started to leave without answering. Shit. He shouldn't even *try* to be a parent.

"Wait, wait, Alex. Stay here for a minute."

Slowing her step, she bit into a cookie but still didn't make eye contact.

"I want to ask you something."

"The answer is yes," she said, so quietly he almost didn't hear her.

"You don't know what I'm going to ask."

She finally turned, her dark eyes blank and cold. Ruthie had had those brown eyes, too, only they hadn't been cold. "I meant yes, she let me eat junk food whenever I wanted. She knew it was a mistake, but since I'm so skinny, she'd let me eat anything."

He nodded, not sure what to say to that. Like so many aspects of her life, he had no clue how to discuss what she ate, what she weighed, how she lived. Hadn't Ruthie given one second's consideration to how woefully ill-equipped he was to raise a young girl?

He turned on the barstool to face her and figure out how to introduce the idea of a long, long trip. Other than *carefully*.

"Did you have fun with Gussie last night?"

She gave a single nod. "She's nice."

"Yeah, she is."

"Do you like her?" Alex asked.

The question threw him, and not because it was possibly the first personal thing she'd ever asked. He couldn't believe she cared.

Again, he chose every word like a well-timed shot, getting his angle and aperture just right. "What's not to like? She's funny and"—adorable and sexy—"great."

"I meant do you *like* her. You know, how you like a girl."

Yes, he knew. But did she? How much did twelve-year-olds know, anyway? He had no clue.

"Well, I'd call her more of a woman than a girl, but yes, I do. Don't like the idea of wedding photography," he added, "but no getting out of it now."

She nodded, backing away, that state of semidiscomfort and semidistrust already enveloping her. Why couldn't he talk to her? What was it that created the weird barrier between them, and would it ever come down? It had come down last night. But Gussie wasn't here now to provide that buffer of some kind of female game-playing connection. Without it, he had no idea how to approach this.

But he had to. "I want to ask you a question, Alex," he said.

She stared back at him.

"How would you like to get away for a while?"

Another shrug. "I guess. I'm not doing anything today."

That was a bit of progress. "I actually meant for a long time."

Her eyes widened, and her translucent skin paled.

"I have an opportunity to spend a couple weeks in the south of France."

Her jaw slipped ever so slightly, encouraging him.

"In Nice," he said, adding a grin. "How about I take my niece to Nice?"

The rhyming joke fell flat between them as she blinked in surprise. "France? You can't make me go to France."

"I wouldn't make you, Alex, but—"

"No." She shook her head. Hard. "No way. No. I don't speak French."

"You don't speak much English, either." At her look, he

added, "I mean you don't talk a lot, and I thought it might help you forget—"

"Forget?" She whipped the word at him. "Forget my Momma? Is that what you mean?"

"No, I—"

"'Cause I don't plan to." Her voice rose with emotion. "Why don't you just go and leave me? I know you hate me."

"I don't hate you, Alex." Only the situation they were in. Maybe she couldn't see the difference. He tiptoed back into the white water. "And if we go, we could take a private plane, and we could talk to—"

"That would be kidnapping."

Kidnapping? Not if she's his ward. He'd just done the research and there were no restrictions on taking her anywhere, but he raised his hand, hoping to calm her. "I thought you might like to visit the Riviera and—"

"You thought wrong." She pivoted and headed down the hall, closing her bedroom door with enough force to qualify as a slight temper tantrum. Shaking his head, he pulled out his buzzing phone to read a text from Gussie McBain.

Can you come to the resort for some planning and prep today?

Anything would be better than staying here and staring at Alex's closed door, even fluffing tulle for the wedding. He texted back immediately, then put the phone down, rinsed his cup, and headed down the hall to let Alex know where he was going. Because God forbid he *leave* and *live* and not have any damn responsibilities.

He tapped, making an effort not to let his frustration come through in an angry knock.

"Come in."

He opened the door, unsure what he'd find. He'd spent about zero minutes in this room since he got here. It was her sanctuary, and a twelve-year-old girl's bedroom was about as foreign to him as the moon.

The first thing that struck him was how neat it was. For some reason, he'd assumed all teenage or near-teenage girls were slobs. But this room, with deep-purple walls and a snow-white bedspread, was practically pristine.

Alex sat on the floor, leaning against the bed, stuffing a notebook under a blanket on her lap. He'd probably walked in on private diary time. Something twisted in his gut when she looked up and her eyes appeared suspiciously damp.

"I'm going out for a while," he said.

She nodded, her blank expression firmly in place.

"I'm going to see Gussie at the resort." He didn't know why he felt compelled to tell her, but the slight spark of interest in her eyes made him glad he did. "Do you want to go with me?"

She didn't move for a beat or two, and he was certain she was about to say yes. Then she shook her head. "I'm busy," she said.

"Doing what?"

Her fingers slid to the notebook she'd barely hid. "Just...writing."

Should he ask what she was writing? Try for a connection? Or—

"You can leave now."

Or do as he was told. With a single nod, he stepped out of the room, eager to get back to the woman with whom they'd both connected. Maybe Gussie could give him some advice or help.

Because God knew he needed some.

Chapter Six

"We divide and conquer." Willow opened the giant binder that held the Bernard-Lyons Master Wedding Plan and turned it so Ari and Gussie could see. They were on the "final seventy-two," as they called the last three days before the main event, and details could be missed if they didn't track everything. "Since we all know the sane thing to do is separate this bride from her mother."

"So smart." Ari lifted a packet of files and photos in front of her. "You take the mother to the kitchen, Willow, and do a final tasting of the key menu items. I'll walk Hailey through the event and calm nerves with some outside air and soothing talk." She handed the files to Gussie. "I would normally do this since it's more about setting than styling, but since you roped him into helping us, why don't you take this prop checklist to the storage space in town with the photographer and start hauling some of the pieces? The most complicated one is the gazebo, but it fits in our van with some ingenuity and muscle power. I'm assuming this guy has a little of both."

Gussie imagined Tom hauling the gazebo in the Barefoot Brides's van. "He has both in spades, though I'm not sure he'll fall in love with the idea of hauling gazebo parts in ninety-two degrees."

"You'll make it fun," Ari said, and then caught herself. "You don't mind going over to the warehouse in Fort Myers with him, do you?"

A day alone in the warehouse? "Couldn't be more treacherous than walking the beach in the moonlight with him."

"You did?" The question came in unison from both Ari and Willow.

"Yup."

Ari and Willow shared a look that Gussie instantly analyzed. They didn't mind that there was more to the dinner than wedding planning, but they sure as heck minded not being told about it.

"And you were going to spill these beans, when?" Willow asked, leaning across the conference table as if ready to physically pull the details out of Gussie.

"It's not like anything major happened. We talked for a while, and I hung out with his niece and played a Wii game," she said. "After I told him I wouldn't go in the gulf in my underwear."

Ari gasped, but Willow started laughing. "That sounds familiar." She was referring to her fiancé, of course, a former Navy SEAL who loved nothing more than the water...with very few clothes on.

"This is different," Gussie assured them.

"Sounds like it," Willow said dryly. "Nick never stops at underwear."

"I talked him out of it and convinced him to get back to his twelve-year-old niece." She'd told them about the girl when she'd first closed the deal with Tom, and mentioned today that he had guardianship of her, but hadn't elaborated on what had happened last night.

"Did Rhonda and Hailey witness the stripping photographer?" Willow asked.

"They'd gone already," Gussie said.

"And nothing else happened but talking?" Willow prodded.

Gussie shrugged. "Not really. Well, I wigged out. Literally."

They both gasped. And Willow shot up from the table and walked to the office door, closing it with a solid thud. "Every word. Every detail. Now."

"There's nothing to tell," Gussie said.

"Coy is one accessory you don't wear well," Ari finally replied, crossing her arms and giving that look that reminded everyone that her sixth sense was as uncanny as her ability to read "the universe" and its vibes.

"I'm not being coy," Gussie insisted. "I mean, there's really nothing to share except we talked and made a, you know, nice connection, and he asked me why I wear wigs, and I showed him. No biggie."

"No biggie?" Willow asked, reaching her hand out to put a light touch on Gussie's arm. "You don't show that scar to many people, Gus. I think I knew you for five or six months before you explained the reason you love wigs and hats. Which is perfectly reasonable. You know this guy for, what, half a day, and you reveal your most personal truth?"

Ari slipped into a chair, nodding. "Willow's right, you know. This is significant."

Was it? For some reason, Gussie didn't want it to be significant. Probably because she knew what she wanted out of a man...and one who advertised "always alone" on his

64

arm didn't fit the bill. "He's mind-numbingly attractive, so I'm claiming a numb mind."

"Nick's mind-numbingly attractive," Willow countered. "And I didn't show my cards to him right away."

"Tom has a superpower," Gussie told them with a sly smile. "He gets women to reveal stuff, like secrets and scars and the things that make us vulnerable. That's how he gets such amazing photos, by taking down his subjects' barriers."

"Is he going to do that to our bride?" Willow asked, horrified.

Gussie laughed. "I don't think Hailey's hiding much."

"Except a deep-seated dislike for her mother," Willow said. "Which I totally understand."

Ari was still zeroed in on Gussie. "Can I make a point here?" she asked. "You were dating a guy before we moved here last year, and having to come clean about your scar is what made you break it off with him."

"You don't know that," Gussie shot back. Even though it was true and, dang it all, sometimes it seemed like Ari knew everything.

"I bet I do know that." She held out her hand to shake. "Bit-O-Honey or Necco Wafers? I bet both that you broke up with that guy because you didn't want to wig out."

Gussie lifted her hand to make the bet, then dropped it. "You know I'm not going to lie. Not even for Bit-O-Honey." She screwed up her face. "You have some?"

Willow stopped the conversation with a flat hand and determined look. "If you two start discussing the merits of that crap you call food right now, I'll scream. Ari's right. You didn't tell Ryan, and we *both* thought you would."

Gussie frowned, conjuring up an image of...bland. "Ryan, yeah. The tax attorney." The boring, staid, kissed-like-a-vacuum-cleaner tax attorney. "I remember him."

"You *remember* him?" Ari choked the question. "You dated him for two months."

"And he helped us incorporate when we started the Barefoot Brides," Willow added.

"He was forgettable, which is why I didn't want to get into the whole scar thing. It gets so complicated and draining. Why get into the whole history when I knew there was no future?"

"So there's a future with this photographer?" Willow asked.

"No, no. I mean…" What if he did stay on Mimosa Key to take care of his niece? A strange sensation of curiosity and longing wrapped around her. She wouldn't mind getting to know TJ DeMille better. "The chances of a guy like him settling down are zero to nil. He travels the world and doesn't really seem to care about much but moving on to his next assignment. Alone." She sighed. "Always alone is like his personal motto."

"And he's got guardianship of a twelve-year-old girl?" Ari asked, her voice rising with incredulity.

Gussie nodded. "She's a sweet kid, too, so it's really heartbreaking. I feel like taking the poor thing home myself."

"Gus." Ari narrowed her eyes. "She's not a stray cat."

Of course not, and Gussie had three of those at the moment.

"Get back to your hair," Willow said. "What made you tell him?"

She pushed back the straight, black locks she wore today. "I don't know. It gets to be a burden to cart around sometimes."

Willow leaned forward. "You don't have to cover it, you know." It wasn't the first time she'd made the suggestion.

"There are ways to wear your hair that it's barely noticeable."

"Easy for you to say, woman with a mane of healthy hair and no scars."

"None visible," Willow corrected with a wry smile.

Ari was still shaking her head, though. "The burden that it becomes is exactly why I'm so intrigued. This photographer must have something incredibly special."

"Many somethings. Head-to-toe somethings, as you will soon see. Trust me, hanging out with him—even hauling gazebos—is *not* a burden."

Ari and Willow shared a look so lightning fast that Gussie almost missed it, but like always, she suspected she could follow the silent exchange pretty well.

"Look, you two should be thrilled I'm doing this wedding with him," Gussie said. "It'll get my dreams of styling for the pros out of my system and confirm that the Brides was absolutely the right move for me. He's probably going to be a bear to work with, and I'll realize that the job is not for me and I'm exactly where I'm happiest."

Ari stood and walked to the window that looked out at one corner of the Casa Blanca parking lot, thinking before answering, as she often did. "You know what I'm going to say."

This time, it was Gussie and Willow who exchanged the knowing look. "You are where the universe wants you to be," they said in singsong harmony, imitating Ari.

"No, that's not what I was going to say at all."

"It's not?" Willow laughed.

"Then what?" Gussie asked.

"I was going to say…is that *him*?"

"Who? Where?" Willow was up in a flash. "That guy?"

Gussie didn't move from the table, listening to them coo.

"Look at that hair. It's sexy," Ari whispered. "I don't usually like long hair, but...wow. It's beautiful on him."

"Hair? Look at his face," Willow said.

"He has a face?" Ari asked, laughing. "I love a guy who rocks a plain white T-shirt and jeans."

"Especially with all that ink. Very nice arms, I might add."

Gussie fought the urge to join the ogling at the window. "Listen to you two. He's just a guy."

"Well, you might not have stripped down and gone swimming last night," Ari said, "but I would bet good candy you will tonight."

Gussie finally joined them at the window. "Bit-O-Honey?"

"Doesn't matter, I'm winning this one. Do you still have those Blue Raspberry Flipsticks? Put 'em on the table, woman."

Gussie let her jaw drop. "I'm not betting my Flipsticks!"

"Why should you worry if you're not going to lose? Keep your clothes on, and you'll keep your 'Sticks."

Gussie shifted her gaze to the man striding across the parking lot. He did rock a white T-shirt and old, snug jeans. But there it was, forever on his arm: always alone.

"Nah." She attempted a shrug. "Not 'Stick-worthy."

Ari choked again. "He's totally 'Stick-worthy. And who are you kidding? Wig's been off. Clothes are next. Come on, Gus. Make the bet."

"Enough, you compulsive candy gamblers." Willow held up her phone, indicating a message. "Rhonda and Hailey are on their way, too. It's show time."

Ari nudged Gussie. "Wager's on the table for the rest of the day. Bit-O-Honey for you if you say no, Blue Raspberry Flipsticks for me if you give in to what you obviously want."

Gussie narrowed her eyes in warning, then started to laugh. "Don't you realize that either way, I win?"

"Of course I do. Why do you think I made that bet?"

Gussie's hair was black today, a deep blue-black that made her eyes look like emeralds and her skin milky, with bright pink lips. The effect was...feminine. Sexy. Even in jeans and a loose top cropped high enough to show off a narrow midriff—or maybe because of that choice—she completely snagged his attention.

"You really don't mind doing this?" she asked as they left the resort together, bound for some kind of gazebo-gathering errand.

"Not at all." Frankly, he wanted to spend time with her.

Damn, boy. You better be careful.

"Excuse me?" she asked as she slipped out the door he held open for her.

Had he said that out loud?

"You said be careful?"

"Driving a van." He covered by trying to tug the keys out of her hand. "I watched you on the road last night."

She laughed. "That was a video game." She held tight to the keys, digging the edge of a persimmon-colored nail into his skin. "And your license is expired. Sit in the passenger seat and enjoy the scenery."

He snorted softly, giving up the fight.

She pointed to a white industrial-style van with a stylized Barefoot Brides logo on the side. "Don't judge," she ordered.

"Ah, the sweet life of a wedding photographer."

At the door, she stopped, crossing her arms. The move deepened the cleavage that peeked out of the V-neck and forced him to fight the urge to look down and enjoy.

"You're judging," she said.

"I'm appreciating the scenery, as I was told." He dragged his gaze from her body to her face, nice and slow. "No need to worry about my judgment or this job. I'm committed now." He tapped her chin for the sheer pleasure of seeing the response in her bright green eyes. "Anyway, it might be fun."

"Might? It *is* fun. I mean, if you even know how to have that."

"What?" he asked. "I can have fun. I had a lot last night," he admitted, placing his hand on the roof of the van, trapping her between his body and the vehicle. "You made a sad and sleepy house come alive."

She stayed still, smiling at the compliment. "That's good," she said. "And that is what I promised to do in exchange for"—she notched her head to the van—"your photography services. So, like it or not, get in."

Neither one of them moved, warmed by the sunshine and each other. "You know, if I'd been a smarter negotiator"— he inched closer to get a whiff of gardenia-sweet perfume— "Alex wouldn't be the only one playing games with you."

"I think you're playing one right now." She opened the door without breaking eye contact, lifting one brow. "Aren't you, Tommy?"

"Not really," he admitted. "But if I did, would you let me drive?"

"Nope." She slipped out from under his arm, disappearing around the back of the van. *Damn.*

He climbed in and watched her do the same, settling into the driver's seat with an air of authority that made him want to kiss her. Everything, in fact, made him want to kiss her. And he might, soon.

"So, did Alex come out of her shell a little after last night?" she asked. "Did we accomplish the mission?"

"For a while, yes." He blew out a frustrated exhale as she turned the ignition. "I thought we'd made a breakthrough, but this morning she still hates me."

Gussie considered that, shaking her head. "I actually think she's a little scared of you and maybe sensitive to how much of an inconvenience she is for you, but she doesn't hate you."

"Scared of me? I guess that's possible. When I arrived for the funeral, she looked at me like I was a tattoo-covered monster. But I've never said she was an inconvenience. Hell, I'm not *that* much of a monster." Was he? Had she picked up the vibe? "When she found out that her mother's will left her in my care..." He shook his head, remembering the look of horror on her face. "Call it terror or hate, but she doesn't want me there any more than I want to be there."

She gave him a sympathetic look before pulling out of the lot and heading down the beach road toward the mainland. "So, what are you going to do?"

"Long term, I have no idea. Short term? Well, I offered her a trip to the south of France and she said no."

"*What?*"

Exactly. "I'm getting pressured to accept a job in Nice," he said. "And by pressured, I mean they're laying on cash, an apartment in town, an au pair for Alex, and a private jet for transportation to and from the Riviera."

"And she doesn't want to go?" She sounded incredulous.

"She acted like I was going to drag her to a drug lord's house in the Colombian jungles and sell her into slavery."

"Oh." She shook her head. "The poor kid. She's probably

as confused as you are, and maybe France seems like a long, long way from home."

"It's only for a couple of weeks, before school starts." He turned from the water view to the one as lovely next to him. "I really wanted this job."

"What is it?"

"A commercial campaign for LaVie, the bottled-water company." As they drove off Mimosa Key and over the long causeway that connected the island to the mainland, he told her about the shoot, frequently interrupted by the kinds of questions someone who understood fashion photography would ask, and he enjoyed answering.

"You're going to kill that assignment," she said as she pulled into an office complex. "It's kind of like what you did with that whole 'flawless diamonds make flawless women' thing for DeBeers."

"Wow, you really do know my work."

"I did a huge blog on that campaign," she said. "It was styled perfectly. Bronwyn St. Marie, right? She's awesome."

The Aussie stylist was one of the best, but he was stuck on a different point she'd made. "You really do blog about my photographs."

She cringed a little. "I don't want you to think I'm some kind of stalker."

"Not at all. I'm flattered."

"Sounds like I'll want to blog again on this LaVie campaign."

LaVie. Damn, he wanted that job even more now. "But I can't take the assignment if Alex won't go."

"Maybe she'll change her mind," Gussie said. "In fact, if you think it would help, I'd be happy to tell her she'd be missing out on the trip of a lifetime."

"I bet she'd listen to you, but you don't have to."

"I want to," she told him. "And if that doesn't work, she can stay with me while you go."

He inched back, the offer genuinely surprising him. "Are you serious?"

"For a couple of weeks? I don't see why she couldn't play Mario Kart at my apartment as well as she can at her house."

For a second, he didn't respond, but stared at her while a dozen different thoughts popped through his mind. How could he turn down an offer like that? Would Alex want to stay with a virtual stranger? How easily could he arrange it? Would it be legal? Or fair to her? But one thought overrode all the others, the one he had to voice.

"You might be one of the sweetest people I've ever met."

Her eyes warmed at the compliment. "Nah, I'm just..."

He waited for her to finish. To say she was trying to pay him back for the wedding or she was lonely or she needed someone to watch her dogs. Something that wasn't purely altruistic and giving because...because that kind of person terrified him.

He could never return that level of selflessness. All it did was make him realize how selfish he'd become.

"I'm doing what anyone would do," she finished.

He had to laugh. "Well, considering no one else has stepped forward and made the offer, that's not true."

"Have you asked?"

"To be fair, no."

"There may be plenty of people willing to take her while you travel."

"But you were the one who said it first." The one who cared the most. "And you didn't know my sister and barely know Alex."

"But I know how she feels." Gussie looked out the

windshield, thoughtful for a moment. "I wasn't too much older than Alex when I was facing long, sad days in the hospital with my head bandaged and doctors talking about grafts and transplants and *dense masses of granulation tissue*." She gave a wry smile. "Med-speak for scar. There were days, and nights, and months, frankly, when I wondered if I could ever be normal again. And I think that's probably what Alex feels right now, desperate for normalcy."

He hadn't really thought of Alex's situation like that, but it made sense. "You think that's what she's going through? Not grief?"

"Yes, grief. Mourning, anger, fear." She turned her green gaze on him. "Didn't you, when your parents died?"

He thought back on the days, the mourning and grief so quickly replaced by a low-grade anger that never went away. "I had a sister to take care of," he said. "And maybe I didn't make Ruthie feel so great about that situation, either."

She tilted her head, a question in her eyes. "Then why would she consider you as a guardian? Maybe you were the best brother in the world, and she wanted nothing but that for her daughter."

Shaking his head, he couldn't agree. "She knew my lifestyle and schedule."

"She also knew *you*."

"Not that well since Alex was born. I'd been scarce and..." Miserable. Again, there was too much she didn't understand. "If I had been such a great caretaker, would my sister have fallen into the sack with the first guy who showed real attention to her and gotten knocked-up at eighteen?"

She laughed a little. "Does anyone even say 'knocked-up' anymore? She made a mistake, Tom, and that 'mistake,' which some would call a *choice*, ended up being a beautiful girl, and clearly, they had a great relationship, so she must have been a terrific mother."

He closed his eyes. "I feel like I'm to blame for that mistake."

"I doubt you could have put a chastity belt on her, so you should let it go. As far as Alex, we'll—*you'll*—figure it out."

But he'd caught the slip. *We'll* figure it out. We'll. *We.*

It had been a long time since Tom had been a "we." Once, years ago, he had known the pleasure of being a "we" and an "us" and a...couple. Without thinking, he looked at his arm and remembered his vow.

"Hey," she said, turning the tables by being the one to lift his chin and force his gaze to meet hers. "I bet I can convince her to go to France. Then your problems will be solved."

Hardly. Lost for a moment in her eyes, he stared, inching over the console to come closer, wanting to end this conversation with a soft kiss. But before he could, she suddenly turned to get the keys out of the ignition, and his lips landed on her cheek.

And still it felt good. Just not good enough.

Chapter Seven

Gussie's cheek burned from the touch of Tom's lips, even after she'd unlocked the warehouse door and led him into the dark space. Her body's reaction to the soft pressure of his lips was almost as surprising as her impulsive suggestion that she take care of his niece while he enjoyed the south of France.

No, her body's reaction was no surprise. Everything about the man attracted Gussie—his hands, his kiss, his laugh, his attitude, and even his talent. And her offer to help him out? Maybe not that surprising, either, but her open admission about those dark days in the hospital had been a little unexpected.

She had to remember this was the man with a secret talent to find vulnerabilities. Sure hadn't taken him long to find hers.

"This doesn't look like a warehouse," Tom said, checking out the dimly lit entryway.

"It's really inexpensive, unfinished office space that we got supercheap," she explained. "We needed somewhere to store all our stuff, which grows exponentially with each wedding. Come and see, but be warned, we don't pay for air conditioning except in the front area, so it can get hot in the back."

"Where's the gazebo?"

"Gazebo *pieces*," she reminded him. "In the way back, so follow me."

Unlocking the door to their suite, she switched on the lights and gestured him into the first room.

"There's central air here," she told him. "So this is where we keep all the things that are affected by humidity, like fine linens, table settings, canopy covers, and delicate sheer netting and tulle. Tables and chairs are in the next room. Lighting, chandeliers and torches after that. Then, miscellaneous weird things like columns and archways, a chocolate fountain, two fire pits, and the occasional pink cherub, which is from a wedding we'd rather not talk about."

Tom laughed softly. "That poor photographer."

"She was fine," Gussie told him. "Our usual photographer, Maggie, is great that way. She does whatever we want and goes with the flow and makes the brides feel like they have a say..." Her voice trailed off as she threw him a look that he completely understood.

"So, in other words, the opposite of me." He gave her a sly smile. "Hey, you wanted me."

When he smiled like that, she sure did. "And today, I want your muscles." Did she ever. "We have to drag the gazebo parts out to a loading dock. Once we have them out there, I'll bring the van around, but we have to come and go through this front door, which is only one of the inconveniences of this space." *Oh, God, stop chattering, Gussie.* It was just that he seemed to set her on fire with every intense look, making her neck and scalp tingle.

But that could be the heat.

"This way," she said, determined to stay all professional and not melt from the temperature *or* the man.

She gestured toward a narrow hallway, aware that he was

close behind her, probably checking out her ass. She threw a look over her shoulder, confirming the suspicion.

He looked up and gave in to a sheepish grin. "Hey, what can I say? First time I've seen you in jeans." He came a little closer, not touching but close enough that she could feel his body warmth and smell that sandalwood scent. "Looks good," he whispered.

She slowed her step enough that he continued right into her—although he certainly could have stopped. Instead, he purposely let their bodies touch. "Feels good, too," he added, just before backing away.

"Be careful, Tommy. You might start enjoying the wedding assignment."

He put both hands on her shoulders and held her, sending a wave of chills up her back despite the lack of air conditioning. "Too late. Enjoyment started last night. Now I'm having fun in the wilds of…where are we again?"

"Fort Myers."

"Yeah, that. Well, if I weren't here, I'd be in Majorca."

"So boring," she teased with a flip of her wrist. "And where is that, anyway?"

"It's an island in the Mediterranean off the coast of Spain." He was so close, his sigh ruffled over her cheek. "I was supposed to be on a shoot there until Tuesday, when I would have been headed, via a yacht with some friends, for Nice. I've already missed Barcelona, Paris, and London."

"I can't even imagine living that life."

"Yeah? I can't imagine *not* living it."

In the back room, she tapped on the light to reveal the deconstructed gazebo. "Sorry, but today you're living the manual-labor life. If you get the great big sections, I can handle the smaller boxes."

"Why don't I handle everything, and you get the van

pulled around? Show me where I have to take them."

"This way." She rounded the corner to the farthest wall of the warehouse and headed to the garage-style door that unlocked only from the inside. "So, do you travel constantly or do you get time to go home and veg?" she asked.

"I veg in penthouses and yachts or beautiful homes overlooking the sea."

At the door, she crouched to try to turn the manual garage-door latch. "But when do you get home?" As usual, the metal stuck, making her cringe as she used all her strength to turn it.

"Here, let me." He was next to her in an instant, his hand on the metal lever.

"It's the humidity." She backed away to give him a little space. "It always sticks."

He grunted as he tried to twist it, the sound echoing in the little room, making her aware of how close and warm the quarters were. As he leaned over, his hair fell across his face, hiding his eyes, giving her a chance to admire the streaks in the strands, like stained mahogany with highlights of amber. His hair was so thick and silky, her fingers itched for another touch. It would be soft and tickly, brushing through her fingers, over her body, down her—

"I don't have one."

Caught off-guard and in fantasy land, she had no idea what he meant.

"A home," he supplied when she didn't answer. "I don't technically *live* anywhere." The metal latch snapped open, the sound cracking like an exclamation point to his statement.

"What?"

He stayed crouched in front of her, face-to-face, inches apart. "I'm on the road at least three hundred and forty or fifty days a year. The rest, I simply find a place to sleep."

"And someone to sleep with?" The question escaped before she could bite her lip and stop it.

He looked up, humor sparking his blue eyes. "Why do you ask?"

"I wondered, is all," she admitted. "I mean, does 'always alone' mean you never have…real relationships?"

His expression grew slightly darker and more serious. "Every relationship is real. It just doesn't last."

She tapped his arm, the Greek letters hard to read in the dim light, but they both knew they were there. "So your warning label comes with an expiration date, too?"

He smiled, and then he stood, pulling the whole door open with him, letting a wave of hot tropical air into the space. He reached for her hand to ease her up, silent, but she couldn't help feeling like he wanted to say something. So she waited, feeling the heat bounce between them, despite the open door.

"Yes," he finally said. The single syllable, nearly a whisper, fell over her like one drop of warm rain. "But aren't you better off knowing that from the beginning?"

"The beginning…of what?"

He smiled, coming closer, close enough that he had to hear the thump of her heart and rush of blood in her veins.

He's going to kiss me. And she was going to kiss him right back.

He stroked her wig, pushing the hair over her shoulder. "You know, I wish you didn't wear these."

Damn it. Why bring that up now? "To be perfectly honest, once they know why I wear them, most people don't mention it again."

"I'm not most people."

No kidding. "Let's do the gazebo," she finally said,

pivoting and heading away to some safer place in the warehouse.

Back in the airless room where the gazebo was stored, they went to work hauling the crates from the shelves out into the hall. On the fourth trip back in, Tom started on the smaller boxes, easily hoisting them and carting them out, pausing to swipe at a sheen of sweat on his forehead.

He stared at the next stack of boxes, plucking at the white T-shirt that already stuck to his chest.

"Want me to get some cold water?" Gussie asked.

"In a sec." But before he lifted the next box, he grabbed the bottom of his T-shirt and yanked it over his head in one move. And there were those abs, that chest, and the swirly dragon tattoo again.

"Where'd you get that ink?" she asked, trying to cover up her pathetic staring.

He pointed to the head of the dragon, right over his heart. "This, in Malaysia." He trailed his fingers over his chest, lifting his arms to better show the body of the beast riding his ribs. "This, in Thailand." He turned so she could see his back, which was almost completely covered with the dragon's tail. "This is all mostly Australia and New Zealand." He turned again, showing a different swirled design on his right hip, mostly hidden. "Africa and Europe are covered here." He finished the turn and pointed toward the sleek muscle by his hipbone that led to something hidden by his jeans. "North and South America are for another time."

A slow trickle of sweat meandered down her neck. "Oh. I get it. One for every continent for the man with no home."

She stole another look at his bare chest, envious of the freedom he must feel, sweat dampening her midriff, under her bra, and down into her jeans, which hid no continental tattoos but were feeling...restricting.

His chest rose and fell with a slow breath, perspiration glistening on his beautifully cut pecs, the dampness highlighting each muscle and the dark circles of his nipples. He lifted one arm, making his chest tense as he swiped more hair off his face, revealing soaking-wet temples.

"Bet all that hair is hot," she mused.

"Not as hot as that lid you wear." He took a few steps closer to her. "I'd cut every inch of mine if you'd wear yours naturally."

Her next breath became almost impossible to take, and she practically swayed as she stared at him. Heat prickled her skin, her throat went dry, and suddenly every limb felt extremely heavy.

"Why would I do that?"

He got closer still, his gaze slicing through her, a predatory, demanding, irresistible set of blue eyes gutting her. "Why wouldn't you?"

She put her hand on her chest, where it stuck to the skin.

"I need water," she said. "I'll be right back." Forcing herself to leave, she headed a little too quickly to the room where they kept a small refrigerator stocked with water and soda.

She still had a few stars popping behind her eyes, but moving down the hall—and away from Tom—gave her a chance to breathe. The windowless table-and-chair room was nearly pitch black, and every bit as hot, so she didn't make it worse by turning on the overhead fluorescent light. Instead, she worked her way around six-feet-high stacks of chairs and rows of folded tables to the mini-fridge in the back.

There, she fell to her knees and yanked the door open, gulping the first wave of refrigerated air. She didn't remember being quite this hot in the warehouse, although she hadn't ever been faced with a man built like a god and looking at her like...*that*.

She lifted the hair of her wig to get some of the refrigerated air on her neck.

"C'mon, Gussie. Take it off."

His voice jolted her, and not just because she hadn't heard him come down the hall. But because it was low and sincere and slid over her, as cool as the refrigerated air, only it did nothing to chill her body. Quite the opposite.

She didn't answer, leaning closer to the cold air.

"It's only the two of us," he said. "And I've already seen what you're hiding. I don't want you to faint."

Then he probably should stopping searing her with every look and burning her with every touch.

"I took my shirt off."

Yes, that was a big part of the problem. "Not quite the same."

"Sure, it is." He was getting closer. She could tell without turning around. Maybe five feet behind her. "It's hot as hell, Gussie, and you'd feel better."

Before she took her next breath, he was next to her on the floor. She opened the door a little wider to share the cold air, but he reached in and grabbed a chilled bottle of water. He twisted the top and lifted it to her lips.

"Drink it. You're flushed."

"Of course I'm flushed. It's a hundred and ten in here, and you're"—hotter than that—"half naked."

He laughed, pressing the bottle to her mouth. "That's not why you practically passed out."

"Didn't help." She closed her eyes and tilted her head back, letting him pour some water into her mouth. It was so icy cold, chilling her mouth and dribbling down the side of her cheek. She didn't care, it felt so good.

"Ahh," she sighed after the drink. "Have some. You need it, too."

He leaned closer and flicked his tongue over the water on her cheek. "That's all I need."

She closed her eyes, heat that had nothing to do with the lack of air conditioning rising again. "More water," she murmured.

He complied, giving her another big sip, then he pulled the bottle back but kept it tilted so the stream poured over her chin and neck and chest. Instantly chilled, she shivered, but kept her head back because it felt so damn good.

"I need more," he whispered, coming right back to put his mouth over her jaw and capture a drop.

She stifled a laugh. "You could use the bottle."

"Too conventional." His lips followed the trail of water down her throat and over her collarbone.

"This is not making me cooler," she said, eyes closed and fingers curling into the rough industrial carpeting. If she didn't cling to something, she was going to grab hold of those ink-covered shoulders.

"My bad," he whispered, shocking her by pouring more water down her chest, soaking her shirt.

She shrieked and laughed, backing up, but it was too late. The crop top was soaked. "What are you doing?"

"Getting a drink." He looked down at the wet top, then lowered his head to lick right over her cleavage.

She couldn't help it. She put her hands on his shoulders, squeezing for the pure pleasure of feeling the muscles, then dragged her fingers over his skin, under his sweat-dampened hair and then over his scalp, moaning a little as she finally got to touch his glorious hair.

Threading the silk through her fingers, she practically cried at the glory of it. "You cut one inch of this, and I'll kill you."

Chuckling, he planted deadly little kisses up her chest and throat, finally reaching her mouth, his tongue surprisingly cool as he traced her lips to start the kiss.

There was no way to stop him, no way she could possibly convince herself that this wasn't the right thing to do. Instead, she tunneled her fingers deeper into his hair, angling his head to get him exactly where she wanted him, opening her mouth, and meeting every stroke of his tongue with hers.

Her body hummed with the clash of hot skin and cold water, his kiss divine on her lips while his hands were...on her wig. She clutched his head, and he did the same, easily slipping off the barrier that protected her from the world. He managed to get his hands in her real hair as he slowly pushed her onto her back and kissed every single drop of common sense right out of her.

So he had an expiration date? For one crazy second, Gussie couldn't have cared less...as long as it lasted through the next kiss.

Chapter Eight

He wanted her wig off. He wanted her top off. Hell, he wanted her to *get* off, but Tom settled for losing himself in her natural hair as he laid Gussie down on the floor.

Body to body, heartbeat to heartbeat, mouth to mouth. Every part of him was growing happier and harder with each kiss. So he increased the pressure where his hips rested over hers and was rewarded with a soft, quick whimper of pure pleasure.

And another that was not quite so pleasurable, but strong enough that he lifted his head to get a good look at her.

"I'm not going to lose that damn bet," she murmured, her expression taut, as if her body and brain were in the midst of a raging battle.

He frowned at the statement that made no sense. "What bet?"

"The one that will cost me Blue Raspberry Flipsticks. Look at this face," she said, staring right up at him. "What do you see?"

Soft, natural, golden-brown hair spread carelessly around, pouty lips wet from kissing, green irises lost in pupils wide with arousal. What did he see? Someone he wanted. He shifted so his hard-on didn't answer for him. "A beautiful woman."

"Nice try, but this face?"

"If you start talking about not being—"

"This is the face of a Flipstick hoarder," she said. "And I am not going to lose the bet. I mean, I want to lose that bet. You're making me really want to lose that bet, but I know that isn't smart at all."

He had no freaking idea what a Flipstick was, but he got the gist of what she was saying. "You bet on me? On sex with me?" he surmised.

"On *not* having sex with you. I bet against you."

He let out a soft choke of disdain. "What did I do to deserve that?"

"Nothing, but I'm not..." She let the words fade into silence.

"Interested?" he guessed.

She looked at him like he'd lost his mind. "I've got eyes and a working female hormone system. And hands"—she tugged at the hair she still held—"and a body."

"Quite a nice one, too."

Torturing him, she rocked her hips a millimeter, enough to get a rise. "Yep, the interest is there," she confirmed. "For both of us."

"So what aren't you? Willing? Free? Capable?"

She laughed. "I'm willing enough to make out on a warehouse floor. And I don't have a man in my life, so I'm free. And last time I checked, everything worked fine, so I'm completely capable."

"Then what's the problem?"

"Look, I met you yesterday. We're working together. And you..." She bit her lip, a sure sign she was trying to hold back what she really wanted to say. He was what? A drifter? A hedonist? A headache for a woman who wanted permanence and stability?

Instead of denying the truth, he relaxed against her, heading right back for that sweet spot under her ear he'd just discovered. "We can go really slow. We have all day."

She half-laughed. "It would still mean we met yesterday."

As much as it pained him, he rolled off her, and not only to give his erection a break. He wanted her to know he heard her, loud and clear. But he stayed on the floor next to her, casually picking up the water bottle and holding it over her.

"Still hot?"

"You wouldn't dare."

He tipped the bottle and dribbled more water right over her breasts, taking that as an excuse to stare at them, his mouth already watering and his hands itching. "How slow do we have to take it?" he asked.

She rolled onto her side, propping her head on one hand. "Do you always get the woman you go for twenty-four hours after you meet her?"

Most of the time. But he didn't want to blow this one with arrogance. "If it's meant to be," he said, purposefully vague.

"What the hell does that mean?"

"It means that..." His gaze dropped down to the water sluicing over her breastbone, forming a rivulet over her skin, and forcing him to reach one finger and slide through that sliver of transparent heaven.

Her eyes shuttered, but she didn't collapse into him like he'd hoped.

"It means that when it feels right and it's what we both want..." He trailed his finger up her throat so slowly he felt her swallow under his touch. "And there's no good reason to stop..." He glided over her chin, her lower lip, and slipped his fingertip into her mouth. "Then I do what feels right and good and..." He leaned forward, replacing his finger with his mouth to kiss her again.

She let him, not fully returning the kiss, but not stopping it, either.

"You really are a pleasure seeker," she said.

"Who isn't? You're a dipstick hoarder. Whatever that is, I bet you get pleasure from it."

She laughed, her eyes dancing and her smile wide and inviting. "Flipsticks. They're candy. Ari, the wedding set designer you met today? We both love vintage candy and have a weakness for a good bet. So we wager on things."

"Like who you'll have sex with."

"Or not, as the case may be."

He tipped the bottle again, letting only one drop fall on her cheek. It rolled toward her lips, and she licked it off with a quick flick of her tongue.

Which forced a little grunt of sexual frustration out of his throat. "How well do we have to know each other before the inevitable happens?" he asked.

She eyed him for a few seconds, letting the sparks ping between them. "Do you think it's inevitable?"

"Don't you?"

Her eyes fluttered closed when he said that, the way they would have if he had touched her somewhere sensitive and sweet. "I can't..." She bit her lip. "Never mind."

"No, not never mind. Why do you do that?" He leaned over her to look down into her eyes and freed her lower lip with one finger. "You start to say something and then don't finish."

"Because I remember why I shouldn't and stop myself before it's too late. Bad habit."

"Yes, it is. Say what you're thinking," he chided.

"I'm just trying to show caution and restraint."

"Caution is the death of a good shot, and restraint is a guarantee of boredom, and they both kill creativity. Why would you want to do that?"

"I can't…" She bit her damn lip again, but her eyes were smiling as she realized what she was doing.

"Say it, Gussie. You can't what?"

She put both hands on his chest and eased him back. "I can't hop into bed with a guy I know I have…no…" She swallowed hard. "No real connection with," she finished quickly. "It doesn't feel right. And I don't mean a forever kind of future, but a real connection."

Was she nuts? "This is a connection."

"A physical connection."

"So? You never have sex just for fun?"

"Not…no, I really don't." She shrugged, as if she didn't care how provincial she sounded. "I like to be in a relationship, which I'm going to guess is a word you like only slightly less than 'caution.'"

He couldn't argue with that truth. "Gussie, relationship and caution are up there with commitment, home, forever, family, and security on the Things That Tom Avoids List." At the flash of disappointment in her eyes, he sat up. "I don't mean to sound like an asshole, but I'm nothing if not honest."

"Not an asshole, just a bad bet. I don't like to make those." She pushed up. "You're honest, so I will be, too. I'm not the kind of woman who throws caution to the wind along with the rest of my clothes and screws your gorgeous brains out right here on the warehouse floor."

He nodded slowly. "I respect that. I hate it," he added, getting up slowly to end the almost tryst. "But I respect it." He studied her for a moment, not even sure what the feeling was that wrapped around his chest and squeezed. Attraction, affection, yeah. He'd been through all that. This was something different. This was…

A *connection*.

Exactly what he never wanted to have. And she needed.

So he should have been thanking her for putting a stop to the inevitable. Because with a woman like Gussie, it might not end as easily as he'd like.

For the second time in one day, Gussie was thinking about…expiration dates. Only this one was stamped on the egg carton and had passed three days ago. Would it kill her to eat them? Because she was starved, and the cupboard—at least the refrigerator—was bare if she didn't count old lettuce and some jelly. The pantry was full of nothing but candy and junk.

She lifted the edge of a plastic container that had once been a gorgeous chopped vegetable salad that Willow had made but was now a science experiment. She had to shop or—

Ari tapped on the kitchen door, opening it without waiting for an invitation. That wasn't unusual. Since the three of them had moved into the triplex Victorian and each taken a separate apartment on a different floor, they rarely knocked.

"Should I have brought my Bit-O-Honey?" Ari asked with a teasing smile as she came in. "Or do I get Blue Raspberry Flipsticks for dinner?"

"Either one would be an improvement over anything else in here." Gussie closed the refrigerator door and leveled a look at her friend. "Do you really think I did the deed at the warehouse? Have you met me?"

"You didn't come back for a long, long time."

"But I *did* come back, and you and Willow were gone."

"We had to take Hailey and Rhonda over to Bud's Buds for a last-minute check of the roses he got in, and then we zipped down to the Sweet Spot to talk cake issues."

"What kind of issues?"

Ari waved a hand. "Name it. I tell you, everything that could go wrong for this stupid wedding has."

"The mother of the bride is the only thing that's gone wrong with this wedding. How did it go with Bud?"

"The world's most miserable florist?" She pulled out a chair at the small eat-in table and slipped into it. "Somehow he managed to come through with blue roses that are not dyed."

"Awesome. He is grumpy, but good."

Ari tapped the table. "What's on the menu?"

"A marmalade omelet with a side of slightly tinged iceberg."

She made a disgusted face. "I want a burrito and beer."

Gussie dropped her head back and moaned with joy. "Yes! I'm so down for South of the Border. Let's grab Willow and beat the dinner crowd."

"Willow?" Ari gave her a *get real* look.

"What?" Gussie asked. "They have taco salads. I know she didn't lose a hundred pounds eating burritos, but after fighting Rhonda and Bud, I'm sure she'll want to vent."

"She probably is venting right now...to Nick." The slightly sad note in Ari's voice was unmistakable, along with the look in her expressive dark eyes. "But I think they're secretly wedding planning."

Gussie's eyes widened. "I thought she...we..." She

shook her head. "So much for the pact to be the wedding planners who never have weddings."

Ari shrugged. "She agreed to that before she reconciled with her parents, and now, well, I don't see any reason she shouldn't have a wedding if that's what she wants."

"I know. It was a lame pact made on two bottles of chardonnay."

"Three. And we're not exactly slammed next month, because it's too damn hot to have an outdoor wedding in August. If this were February, it would be different."

"So she's going to get married that soon, huh?" Gussie slipped into the chair next to her. "Well, from a scheduling standpoint, I might be a little busy."

Ari lifted a brow in interest. "With the photographer who's moved to town?"

"I don't know if he's actually 'moved' here as much as he's hanging out until he figures out what to do with his niece, who is the reason I may be busy." She explained Tom's situation with the job in France.

"And you offered to keep her?" Ari asked when Gussie finished.

"Only if she can't be convinced to go with him, which I still think any person in their right mind would do. You don't have to be so shocked. It's only for a few weeks, and it seemed like the right thing. Plus, I like her."

"What if he never comes back? What if he sticks you with her?" Ari shook her head. "I mean, can you really just take someone else's kid?"

"It's babysitting, Ari, not kidnapping."

"Oh, Gus, I don't know. That's a big commitment."

She shrugged. "I can handle it. I'd love it, in fact. You know I love strays."

As though on cue, Scooter, a fat black cat Gussie had

found shortly after they moved to Mimosa Key, wandered into the kitchen, whining for love and food. Instantly, Gussie was up, looking for a can, which meant Gensie and KayCee wouldn't be far behind. Sure enough, the tabby and the Persian came sauntering in, looking for Mom and food.

Ari watched Gussie open the cans, silent. But her knowing eyes said it all.

"What?" Gussie finally demanded. "I know that look. You're about to make some pronouncement about how the universe has directed Alex to me."

"No, but I could say something about how the universe is trying to tell you that you have a maternal instinct a mile wide and this part-time solution appeals."

"Not a maternal instinct as much as a familial one. Does that make sense?"

Ari shrugged. "Considering what happened to you and your family, of course it does."

Gussie sighed, relieved that Ari understood her so well. "I do miss what I had as a kid and would love to re-create that. But not with someone else's family." A slow pounding started at the base of her neck, as it did whenever she thought about her brother and her family. She rubbed the spot as if she could massage the memories away.

"You okay?" Ari asked.

"Fine. Just hungry. Why don't you grab your bag, and I'll go put a lid on? If we don't get over there soon, we'll have to wait an hour for a table."

But Ari didn't move, still looking at Gussie with her All-Knowing Face.

"What?" Gussie asked.

"You don't have to 'put a lid on,' Gus. Pull your hair back and most of the scar is covered. It's a thousand degrees in Florida in July, even at night."

So much for someone who understood her. How many times in one day did she have to have this conversation? "The wigs are *me*, Ari. They are my style, and I feel absolutely naked without them," she said.

"And you know if you met someone and fell in love, you'd have to get naked. Completely naked. No-wig naked. All the time, every night."

Gussie rolled her eyes. "Yes, I *know*. I was halfway there this afternoon."

"You were?" Ari shot up. "If you're holding out on me because of those Flipsticks..."

"The only person I'm holding out on is Thomas Jefferson DeMille."

"And how's he handling that?"

"Mmm." Gussie thought about that. "He's accepted it for now, but I don't think the 'we just met' excuse will last long. He is one determined man."

"So what's stopping you?"

"Besides the fact that I hardly know him?" Gussie asked. "I mean, I met him yesterday, and he'll be gone tomorrow."

"He better not be. He's doing our wedding this weekend."

"Well, not exactly gone tomorrow, but soon. But I don't want to get all worked up over a guy who doesn't even own a home, let alone plans to settle down and live a normal life." She could feel Ari's gaze on her and avoided it by picking up a dishtowel and refolding it.

"Maybe you'll be the one to change him."

"Said every woman who's ever met him. And then failed."

"Well, if he's that much of a player, you wouldn't be attracted to him. Maybe there's more than meets the eye, even if what meets the eye is pretty nice."

"That's what I keep thinking," Gussie admitted. "There's something very caring about him. He raised his sister and seems concerned about his niece. It's like he's a supernice guy wrapped in this cloak of 'I vant to be alone' that doesn't even ring true." She sighed and straightened the already straight dishtowel. "Did you get any of that when you met him today?"

"I didn't get past the hair and the biceps."

"I know, right?" From the other counter, her phone dinged with an incoming text. "But you would if you spent time with him because you have such a great sense of intuition with people." She picked up her phone and looked at the screen. "Oh, speak of the devil." Damn it, why did a text from him give her a thrill?

"Really?"

She clicked on the message and read. "He wants to know if I can meet him and Alex for dinner tonight." She looked at Ari. "He wants me to talk her into going to France with him, and if that fails, I guess I can suggest she stay with me."

"Oh, okay. You go, and I'll scrounge for leftovers upstairs."

"No, come with me."

Ari held up a hand to say no, but Gussie grabbed it and squeezed. "You have to come," she said as the rightness of the idea took hold. "You're such a good judge of character, Ari. And it's not a date since Alex will be there. It'll be fun. I'll text him back and tell him we'll meet them at South of the Border in half an hour."

She expected an instant yes, but Ari narrowed her eyes and held her hand out. "It'll cost you."

"Damn it." She yanked open the pantry door and dug into the open box of Flipsticks. "Here." She slapped about six into Ari's palm, getting a jaw-dropped look of shock in return.

"I would have settled for something less fabulous. A Twizzler or Good & Plenty. The 'Sticks are for sex." She put the Flipsticks back into Gussie's hand. "If Tom can wait, so can I."

Ari sounded pretty confident she wouldn't have to wait long. Well, she *was* a damn good judge of character.

Chapter Nine

It had been remarkably easy to persuade Alex to go out to dinner. Tom had to say only four words: *Gussie will be there*. He didn't mention that Gussie was bringing a friend. He didn't want anything to change her mind, since he was certain that once he got them together again, Gussie could convince Alex that she should go to France. And if she didn't, surely Alex wouldn't mind Gussie's generous backup plan.

He still wasn't sure of that idea, on many levels. It felt like shirking his responsibilities, yet he believed the offer was genuine. Would Ruthie have approved? He had to ask himself that question every time he made a choice for Alex now. Although sometimes he wondered how much Ruthie had really cared since she'd so cavalierly left her daughter's future in his hands.

But of course she'd cared. She'd merely thought she was invincible. Nobody was invincible. Nobody. Not strong, healthy women who seemed born to be mothers. Not...anyone.

Pushing the thought away out of habit, he repositioned himself on the bench where he and Alex sat outside under the bright red umbrellas of a Mexican restaurant the locals called the SOB.

The worst of the day's heat had faded with sunset, but it was still warm under a lavender evening sky, still sticky and heavy. Or maybe that was the silence between him and the young girl who sat in front of him, splitting her gaze between the table, the street beyond, and the menu.

Anywhere but him.

He dug around for something to say, even though it would only get a monosyllabic answer.

"So, did you remember to water those plants?" he asked.

"I forgot."

He bit back a sigh. "What did you do all day while I was gone?"

She shrugged, which he interpreted to mean "played video games." Then she closed her mouth over her straw and sucked down soda.

Everything in him wanted to ask if she'd given any more thought to France, but he resisted the urge, leaving that in Gussie's capable hands.

"Did you do more 'work' on...whatever it is you're working on?" he asked.

She looked up without taking her mouth off the straw, her eyes suddenly so much like Ruthie's it almost took his breath away. His sister hadn't been quiet. In fact, she'd usually had a smartass answer for everything. But funny smartass, not miserable smartass.

Alex hadn't inherited that trait, which would at least have been more tolerable than this silence.

"What is it you're working on, anyway?" he probed. "Writing something?"

"It's private."

In other words, shut the hell up. He shifted his gaze to the street, scanning the palm-tree-lined avenue for the woman he'd spent most of the day thinking about when he hadn't been trying to kiss her. "I wonder what color wig she'll wear," he mused.

That perked Alex up a bit. "How many does she have?"

"From what I can tell, a lot."

"Does she always wear them?"

"I think so."

"Why?"

He weighed the truth against the relief of actually engaging Alex in a conversation.

"She has a burn scar on the back of her head, and her hair doesn't grow there."

"Really?" She sat up and abandoned the soda. "How big is it? Have you seen it? How'd she get it?"

"Yes, I've seen it. It's not that big, and she'll tell you the story if she wants to." Maybe. Maybe it was private, and he'd just broken a confidence. He had no idea.

So maybe Gussie had been right when she'd said they needed to know each other better before sex. The idea made him a little uncomfortable, but then, everything about Gussie made him a little uncomfortable. And she also made him extremely comfortable, which was puzzling.

"Can I ask her tonight?" Alex asked.

"If it seems right." Over Alex's shoulder, he spotted two women walking and laughing, and it took him a few seconds to realize it was Gussie and her friend Ari. Was that her natural hair?

An unexpected zing shot through him at the sight of her long, golden-brown hair falling around her shoulders. He loved her hair like that, but then the two times he'd seen it, they'd been alone, close and, this afternoon, kissing. Maybe *that's* what he loved—Gussie with her guard down.

But then she turned to her friend, both of them laughing,

and he saw that the hair covered her whole head, so it must be another wig.

"There she is." He gestured in the direction of the two women crossing the street.

Alex whipped around, nearly knocking the bench over to get a look. "Who's that other lady?"

"Her friend and business partner."

Her shoulders fell as she turned back. "This is a *business* thing? I thought it was like, you know, dinner."

"It *is* dinner, Alex." He caught Gussie's eye as she approached their table, getting another unexpected zing when she smiled.

"But are we going to talk about taking pictures for that wedding?"

"I don't know what we're going to talk about." He stood, placing his napkin on the table, as the two women reached them.

"Hi, Gussie." Alex didn't stand, but looked up. Gussie instantly reached down and gave her a hug, something he suddenly realized he hadn't done since the day he'd arrived. Only because she never seemed like she *wanted* to hug.

"This is my friend Arielle Chandler," Gussie said, putting her other arm around her friend. "Ari, this is Alex and, of course, you met Tom today."

When they sat back down, Tom lightly took Gussie's hand to get her next to him and across from Alex, but she easily slid onto the bench next to his niece, leaving the space next to him for Ari.

He didn't like it, but let it go. After all, she was here to help him solve the France situation, no matter how much he wanted her close to him.

"So I heard we owe you dinner for all your hard labor," Ari said easily as she sat. "I'm usually the one stuck finding volunteers to help with the gazebo-gathering, so thank you."

"Not a problem," he said. "We had..." He glanced at Gussie.

"Fun," she supplied brightly, turning to Alex. "What did you do today?"

"I played some Mario and read a book and reorganized my closet."

Why couldn't she have told Tom that when he asked?

"Books, clothes, and video games!" Gussie exclaimed. "You might have had my dream day."

"What about you?" Ari turned to grab his attention.

"Uh, no books, video games, or closets for me today."

Ari laughed. "But did you have a good time at the warehouse?"

"Very good." He stole a glance at the woman responsible for that good time, but she'd turned on the bench to talk with Alex. And Alex was talking back.

"Gussie is a blast, that's one of the many things we love about her," Ari said, dragging him back into conversation. "Along with her incredible loyalty, her whimsical humor, and her unparalleled ability to make even the plainest bridesmaid look stunning, but not quite prettier than the bride. That's an art, you know."

He smiled at the flattering résumé recital. Did Ari think she had to showcase Gussie's qualities? Because he was getting familiar enough with every one.

"I know it is," he said vaguely, leaning a little to hear what Alex and Gussie were talking about, but Ari fired another question at him. Something about the setup for the wedding. Then another about his personal approach to the bridal party. And one more, forcing him to give up on the other conversation altogether.

Maybe that was better, since Alex seemed more alive than she had since they'd arrived.

"Are you, uh, interviewing me?" he asked Ari. "'Cause I'm pretty sure I got the job already."

She gave a low laugh. "You have the wedding job, yes. But"—she arched a dark brow and tipped her head toward Gussie—"what are your intentions toward my friend?"

Had he heard that right? Across the table, Alex let out a little shriek. "You would take me there?"

"Where?" Tom asked, letting the conversation with Ari drop.

"There's a Forever 21 open on the mainland," Alex said.

"What is that? Some kind of bar?"

Alex burst out laughing and looked at Gussie. "He's clueless."

"No, he's a man who would have no reason to shop for teen-girl clothes. But I did a whole blog about that store, and I think they have great stuff." She eyed Alex carefully, up and down. "You might be a tad young, but definitely too old for Justice."

"I know, right? Where does that leave me?"

Leave her for what? Some kind of justice?

"You are so in-between stores," Gussie said, true sympathy in her voice. "But I have some ideas we could check out at Forever 21, or even H&M."

Alex's face brightened. "Would you help me shop?"

Gussie glanced over at Tom, giving a sly wink. They ordered and made small talk, but when the food came, it was obvious Gussie and Alex were getting better and better acquainted without any help from him.

"She hasn't talked that much to me in all the time I've been here," he admitted quietly to Ari.

"Maybe you don't know what to talk to her about," the woman suggested.

Clothes? Video games? Trips to the mall? "That's an understatement."

"So can you answer my question now?" She lifted her margarita, looking innocently over the rim of the glass with large, dark eyes. "Intentions?"

He smiled. "So this *is* an interview."

"More or less." She sipped again. "No less about it, actually. Interview's on."

He took his own deep drink of cold beer. "She set you up to this, didn't she?"

"No more than you set her up to convince your niece of something."

Touché. "What do you want to know?"

"How bad she's going to be hurt when you disappear."

He frowned at her, trying to get his head around any possible way of answering that without actually answering it.

"If you're utterly amazing and truly a keeper, then she's going to be crushed," Ari said. "If you're an uncaring asshole, then she'll be fine, but we try to steer each other clear of the latter. Which are you?"

His frown deepened. "Doesn't matter. Either way, I'm the bad guy."

"Pretty much." Ari grinned. "But you'll be happy to know I'm encouraging her to broaden her horizons and have fun with you."

"Then I should—"

"No!" Alex's exclamation brought the conversation to a stop, which he should have appreciated, but all the joy was gone from his niece's eyes as she stared at him. "I'm not going to France," she said through ground teeth.

"Alex," Gussie said, putting her hand on Alex's arm.

"You just said you and your mom were going to go to Mexico for a vacation this summer. This would be a vacation, too."

"That was my mom, and he's…he's…"

"Your uncle," Gussie supplied. "Think of what an adventure it would be."

"I don't want an adventure," she murmured, pushing her barely eaten burrito away and skewering Tom with an accusing look.

"You don't know that if you haven't had one," Gussie said. "It would be like stepping into a video game for real. You would go on a private plane and stay in a beautiful apartment and taste French food, and think about the clothes in France. *Magnifique!*"

Slowly, Alex closed her eyes and let her shoulders fall. Tom knew better than to say a word. One wrongly spoken syllable, and Alex would shut down completely. Instead, they all waited in an awkward beat of silence.

"I think," Gussie said, leaning a little closer to Alex, "that your Momma would have wanted you to have the experience."

Moisture formed under Alex's lashes, and Tom lost the battle to stay still and quiet. He reached his hand across the table and put it on Alex's other arm so that he and Gussie were both connected to her.

"I'm pretty sure Gussie's right," he said, his voice sounding gruff as he worked not to push her too hard.

Finally, Alex opened her eyes and looked right at him. "You didn't know my Momma at all. You hardly talked to her for years."

There was a reason for that. He hardly talked to anyone who could ask probing, tough questions after his dark days in Greece. But this was no time to explain that. "Well, then,

105

maybe if we take a trip together, you can tell me all about her."

Something flickered in Alex's eyes. "But what if..." She looked down, unable to finish.

"What if what?" Gussie urged gently.

"What if I miss something here?"

"You won't miss anything here," Tom said. "I promise you'll be back before school starts."

"But what if..." She swallowed, something painful ravaging her expression.

"What if *what*, honey?" Gussie asked.

"What if my dad comes to get me, and I'm not here?"

Oh, man. His whole chest squeezed until his heart hurt. Is *that* what she thought was going to happen? He opened his mouth, but Gussie shot him a look and sidled closer to Alex.

"Oh, Alex," she said. "That's perfectly understandable that you'd feel that way, but if he did..." She dug for something, and Tom knew exactly what she'd come up with: nothing.

Alex's father was not coming for her.

"Do you think he's coming?" Alex asked Gussie, hope in her voice as if she thought this new person might be the one with different information.

Gussie stroked Alex's arm, not answering right away. Finally, she sighed. "I don't know anything about him, Alex, but I do know that a man who cares very much about you is sitting across from you, trying to do the right thing, offering you a gift, and trying to give you something happy to remember this summer. Why don't you give him a chance?"

For a second, he couldn't breathe. He didn't trust himself to even blink, because everything in him grew tight and heavy. Where did she come from, this unexpected gift of a good woman? He'd never known anyone like her.

Well, he had...once. And swore he'd never take that chance again.

"Okay, I'll go," Alex whispered.

"You will?" Tom asked, stunned.

"On one condition."

"Anything," he said. "Anything at all. Whatever you want."

She gave in to a slow smile, still staring at Gussie. "You come, too."

Chapter Ten

"That is the most brilliant idea I've ever heard!" Ari leaned forward like she was about to launch over the guacamole dip to shake sense into Gussie if she even thought about saying no.

Gussie blinked from Alex to Ari and back to Alex again. Both of them looked like the winning lottery ticket had just fallen out of the sky. Finally, she mustered up the courage to look straight ahead and meet Tom's eyes.

He looked more like a reflection of how Gussie felt—gobsmacked.

"I...can't," she murmured.

"Why not?" That came in unison from Alex and Ari. Alex, she understood. But her friend? Her good, trusting friend who'd come to scrutinize the man in question and help decide whether he was worthy of a fling? She'd send her off to France with the guy?

Gussie zeroed in on Ari. "Because we have weddings—"

"One," Ari said. "After this weekend, we have one wedding booked in August, because it's so hot and humid."

"But I have to be here for it."

"The Lucente-O'Dell wedding?" Ari flicked her fingers like the event was a pesky fly. "Piece of cake. Willow's the lead on that one, and everything is practically done. You really should go."

"Well, I...don't..."

"Have a passport?" Alex asked.

"She's a destination-wedding planner," Ari interjected. "Of course she has a passport."

"But I...shouldn't be away..."

"Everyone takes vacations in August," Alex insisted.

"I couldn't..."

"Yes, you could and you should," Ari said, as if it were finalized. "Right, Tom?"

"She has to go," Alex exclaimed, not giving him a chance to reply. "Because if she doesn't, I'm not going."

"Alex." Tom and Gussie spoke in perfectly timed unison.

"This is a big decision," Tom said, obviously choosing each word carefully. "Not something anyone could decide on the spur of the moment."

At least one person had some sanity at this table. Unfortunately, he was the one whose opinion mattered most.

"I don't know if I could—"

"It would be like stepping into a video game for real," Alex said, enough singsong in her voice that Gussie recognized it as an echo of her own words. "'You would go on a private plane and stay in a beautiful apartment and taste French food, and think about the clothes in France. *Magnifique*!'"

Alex looked so pleased with her memory, Gussie had to laugh. "Well, I *still* have to think about it."

"What's to—"

Ari cut off Alex's question by standing up and taking the girl's hand. "Alex, why don't you and I walk into town and stop by Miss Icey's for a cone and let these two talk about it?"

"Okay," Alex agreed, also pushing back.

Gussie opened her mouth to argue—and possibly drag Ari off to the bathroom for an explanation—but then she thought better of it. "That is a good idea," she said. "I have some questions for Tom about the...logistics." Like, did he like the idea *at all*?

In seconds, Alex and Ari were gone, leaving Tom and Gussie staring at each other.

"Um, I think I know what it feels like to go under a steamroller now," Gussie joked. "I really don't know what to say."

Leaning forward, he put his hand over hers, the touch warm and intimate. "Say yes."

Really? Her next breath was a little ragged, her stomach fluttering about while her heart rate tripled. How did he do that to her with two simple words?

"Yes?" She went for a joke, because his face was way too serious. "You've been telling me to say that all day, Tom. I think you're a bad influence."

"Yeah, 'cause a few weeks in France would be very bad for you." He added some pressure on her hand. "I'd like to have you there. You're amazing."

"I'm good with Alex." That had to be what he meant, right?

"And you're amazing." At her look of disbelief, he added, "I told you today I'm honest. So, yes, it's obvious you have an incredible effect on her and connect with her in a way I never could. You have the ability to magically put a spark in the eyes of a little girl who thinks life has beaten her."

Okay. That's why he wanted her there. Like a babysitter or companion—for his niece.

"But that's *not* why I want you to go." He held her gaze,

unwavering and direct. "I want to get to know you better."

She didn't answer, making him laugh. "You don't believe me, do you?"

"I admit to some skepticism."

He laughed, shaking his head. "Woman, you have got to up the confidence quotient."

"And I'm going to do that by going to Europe?"

"You're going to do that by"—he threaded his fingers through hers—"spending time with someone—two someones, actually—who think you're fantastic."

Good God, it was easy to believe him. Easy to forget his personal mantra and travelin'-man lifestyle. Easy to hope that this could be more than…

A trip of a lifetime.

"I don't know…" But she did. Deep inside, she did.

He smiled, slow and sweet and, dang it all, so sexy her whole body betrayed her with a hormonal tsunami.

"As you said to my niece"—he stroked her hand and inched closer—"there's a man sitting right here who is trying to do the right thing, offering you a gift, and trying give you something happy to remember this summer. Why don't you give him a chance?"

Because he was probably going to break her poor little heart into a bazillion pieces. "I don't know," she whispered. "Why don't I?"

"Looks like Nick's still here," Ari said as she pulled the car into the driveway, the headlights shining first on Nick's car, then on the wraparound porch that circled the first floor of their house. "Let's get Willow's opinion."

"Let's not bother her," Gussie said, gathering her bag. "We can talk to her tomorrow."

"Why? Are you afraid she'll say you should go?"

"Yes. She'll have me packed and out the door before you can say, *Bonjour, mes amis*."

"See, you do speak French."

Gussie shook her head, tired of the discussion. All she wanted to do was get up to her apartment and think about every single word Tom had said to her.

"Let's go at least tell her about it," Ari said.

"You know Willow will agree with you because love is blind, and she thinks we're going to find lightning in a bottle like she did."

Ari sighed wistfully as she turned off the engine and lights. "Could happen."

"A hot Navy SEAL with abs of steel and a heart of gold?" Gussie grunted. "There are so many of those running around."

"That's not what I want, at least not if the universe doesn't have that in the plans for me."

"It's not what I want, either." Gussie sighed. "But I have a question for you since you're all about 'there's one for everyone' and the universe is going to send him. What if you think he's the one and he doesn't think you are?"

"Are you asking that because of Tom or just as a general question of my beliefs?"

"Tom's not the one," she said, barely hearing her friend's question. "I mean, he's a ton of fun and great for my ego, but he doesn't know the meaning of forever. And the closer I get to thirty, the more I want forever." Or at least more than a few fun weeks.

Ari reached over and touched her arm. "I told you, I got a

really good vibe from him. And Alex is crazy about you. Why wouldn't you go?"

She was still trying to come up with a reason that made sense, other than she was scared to death to fall for a guy who'd break her heart.

"Come on," Ari said, opening the driver's door. "Let's see if they're dressed and interested in company."

"Okay," Gussie agreed. "Maybe Willow will be the voice of reason. Maybe she'll see that with less than a year under the belt of the Barefoot Brides, none of us is really in a position to take time off for romantic jaunts to the south of France."

"See?" Ari whipped around to make her point. "Even you are calling it a romantic jaunt."

"Well, I told you what happened at the warehouse. And I asked you to go tonight so you could give me your opinion on him." Gussie climbed out of the car and slammed the door harder than necessary. "I didn't expect you to betray me."

"Betray you? By helping you get an all-expenses-paid dream vacation? Maybe you can betray me sometime, too."

"Are you two betting again?" Willow's question surprised them both when it came from the darkened porch.

"Discussing," Ari said.

"Ending our friendship," Gussie corrected.

"Get up here." Willow appeared at the top of the three steps, gesturing for them to join her on the porch.

"Are you alone?" Gussie asked.

"Of course not." Nick Hershey's deep voice came from the corner, followed by the squeak of the swing. "Her soon-to-be better half is here."

"Are we interrupting anything?" Ari asked.

Gussie could have sworn Willow shot a warning look

over her shoulder at the man she loved, but it was too dark to be sure.

"We're just talking," Willow said. "What are you two ending your friendship about now? The last pink bubblegum cigar in the state?"

From the corner, Nick chuckled. "Is that the wager of the day?"

"We're not betting," Gussie said, folding into the corner of the rattan sofa. "We're discussing how thrilled Willow will be when she finds out one-third of the company is considering being gone for a couple of weeks in August."

"Who, you? When? Which couple of weeks?" There was definitely a note of panic in Willow's voice and another silent look exchanged with Nick.

Of course she wouldn't want Gussie to bail, no matter how few weddings they had in the peak of the hot summer months. They still had a business to run.

"Yes, me. And soon. Like, next week soon," Gussie said. "I took Ari to dinner with Tom and his niece because I needed a second opinion on the guy, and what do you know? She loves him."

Ari curled up on the other side of the sofa. "How can I not? He's awesome. I think he's a perfect fit for Gussie."

"Really?" Willow finally sat down on the swing, as close to Nick as she could be without actually burrowing inside him. "He is hot, Gus, no doubt about it."

Nick slid her a look, but let it go.

"Yes, he's hot," Gussie agreed. "And I'm attracted to him. And I made out with him on the warehouse floor today, but—"

"Whoa. You sure you want me to hear this?" Nick asked.

"You're practically family now," Gussie said. "But I

don't know if it's smart to get on a private plane, fly to the Riviera, stay in an apartment, and..."

Fall hard for someone I can never have.

Willow laughed. "So far, it doesn't sound like it would suck."

"Right?" Ari asked, happy for the support. "You'd have the time of your life with a guy who is not only attracted to you, but clearly cares about others." Ari crossed her arms, confident in her assessment. "You told me I can read people really well, Gus, and what I read was good. Did you see how he acted when his niece got emotional about her mother? He melted, for God's sake."

"And that's enough reason for you to encourage me to do something wild and spontaneous and potentially"— *heartbreaking*—"dangerous," she finished weakly.

"Is this guy a threat?" Nick leaned forward, making the swing screech. "What do you know about him?"

"Very little," Willow said.

"I know all I need to know," Gussie said. And she didn't mean from following his work. "He's a..." Man who has no home, lives the high life, and would never settle down and be a *family*. Not a family like the one she grew up in, not the family she wanted to re-create...perfect, whole, and happy. Did Ari and Willow even realize just how much she longed for that? Her dreams were more than having kids—Gussie wanted the wholeness of a real, solid family. She'd had it once and wanted it again.

"What's stopping you, really?" Ari asked. "Be honest, you're among friends."

"I guess I want to think about it for a while, and that's what I told him. A trip to Europe is a big commitment."

"And so is sleeping with him," Nick said.

Gussie gave him a light kick in the shin. "Way to remind us that Willow snagged the last greatest guy on earth."

"No, I didn't," Willow said. At Nick's look of dismay, she laughed. "I'm pretty sure there are two more for my best friends."

"There are," Ari said with certainty. "And maybe Tom's one of them."

Gussie snorted. "And maybe we'll see some pigs soaring next to the window of the private jet."

"So you're going?" Ari asked.

"You're missing the point," Gussie insisted. "I am deathly afraid of having my heart broken, Ari."

"I'm sorry." Ari reached across the sofa and put her hand on Gussie's arm. "I thought all you needed was a little prodding, and that guy seems like he'd be a lot of fun for you. Really, that was all I was thinking. He's really nice."

"And superhot," Willow added.

"So we've heard," Nick said dryly.

"Really, Gus, it was my mistake," Ari said, giving her hand a squeeze. "I thought the only thing stopping you was the commitment to work, and I wanted to reassure you we had it covered. I didn't think you were evaluating him for husband material."

Gussie felt her face burn, grateful for the dim light. "I'm not."

"And it is kind of the trip of a lifetime," Ari added.

After a beat, she realized Willow hadn't joined in, but instead was looking at Nick, both of them carrying on a wordless conversation the way only people in love could do.

"I guess I don't have a really good reason not to go," Gussie said, half to herself.

Willow took a deep breath and turned to the other two women, still holding Nick's hand. "Actually, we might have one for you, depending on how long you'll be gone."

"Might?" Nick asked, a tease in his voice. "There's no *might*, honey."

"He's right," Willow said. "Fact is, the Barefoot Brides actually *are* going to have a second wedding in August. My parents are able to come the last weekend and, well, we don't want to wait any longer, so…"

Gussie blinked, the rest of the statement not necessary, because they all knew what was coming.

"You're getting married!" Ari and Gussie exclaimed in unison, and they all popped up, the three of them hugging hard, with Nick wrapping his strong arms around the whole group.

"I know we always said we wouldn't have weddings ourselves," Willow told them.

"Big-deal weddings with crazy in-laws and plastic cherubs," Ari said.

"Of course you'll have a wedding," Gussie agreed. "And we will be there, no matter when and where it is."

Willow hugged them again. "Well, don't worry. It'll be right at the resort, and I promise small, intimate and, well, I'd say classy, but with a rock star for a father, I'm not guaranteeing anything."

"Well, I hope there are at least two bridesmaids," Gussie said.

"Co-maids of honor," Willow said. "If Gussie's not still in France with the superhot photographer."

"Ahem." Nick elbowed her.

"As if I'd go to France and miss your wedding. I should be back by the last weekend of the month." Then she caught herself. "If I go," she added quickly.

And her two best friends laughed, knowing her like the real sisters they were.

Chapter Eleven

At T-minus five hours before the Bernard-Lyons wedding, all three of the Barefoot Brides consultants went to work. This was when they forgot about their own lives, problems, candy bets, and future plans. Nothing mattered but making that day perfect for one starry-eyed, nervous-wreck woman—and maybe her mother—who'd spent her life dreaming about it.

At least, that's what Gussie told herself as she headed down the hall to the far end of the Eucalyptus spa to prepare the dresses, shoes, makeup, and jewelry for the bridal party, which would arrive in about an hour. Except, instead of Hailey's sculpted lace and imported satin slippers, Gussie's mind was lingering on a decision she'd yet to finalize.

Should she go with Tom to France? She'd already decided that she'd make her mind up by the end of the day, sensing that seeing him "in action" would seal the deal one way or the other.

Unlocking the dressing room door, she stopped to inhale the lingering scents of lavender and rose, makeup and hairspray and powder, instantly calm and happy.

She busied herself by taking out the gowns she'd hung

after last night's rehearsal dinner, starting with three sea-foam-green bridesmaids' dresses and then moving to Hailey's stunning Alfred Angelo A-line with an illusion boat neck. Not Gussie's favorite style, but it suited Hailey's understated personality.

She fitted the gown onto the dress form, spreading out the train for the most gasp-inducing effect when the bridal party arrived. Next, she headed back into the closet to find the shoes so she could line them up on one side, and on the way, she snapped on the sound system to play the soft classical music Willow loved and made sure the lights were set to perfection.

Carrying a load of five shoe boxes that blocked her vision—Rhonda had hers in here, too—Gussie navigated her way back outside when she heard a loud click.

"Perfection." Tom's voice was a little louder than the music. "Sheer perfection."

Gussie slowly leaned to the right to see around the shoe boxes. He was flat on his stomach, a camera up to his eye, his lens focused on the train she'd spread.

"What are you—"

"Shh. I'm getting you the money shot."

"Of a dress on a form?"

"The opening act, Pink." He snapped a few more, giving her a minute to lower the boxes and watch. And what a sight it was. Faded jeans hugging his ass and long legs spread wide to anchor him. His broad shoulders were propped up on his elbows, his hair fanning over the white T-shirt pulled snug over his muscular back.

White T-shirt? Wait a minute. "What are you wearing?"

"Work clothes. Shh." *Click. Click. Click.* And he rolled to his side to capture another angle.

"For a wedding?"

"I get dirty when I work." And he rolled again, all the way onto his back, looking right up at her. Well, the camera was. "Auburn today? I like it."

Click.

She backed away from the lens, lifting the boxes to cover her face. "Don't take pictures of me."

"Why not?"

Because there were few things she hated more in the world. "This isn't my wedding. I'm supposed to be totally in the background."

"I'm going to take pictures of everything, foreground and background. Then I'm going to make a masterpiece of a wedding album, and it's going to be so amazing that you..." *Click. Click.* And he popped to his feet with one smooth move, angling to the side to snap her surprised face. "Lower the boxes."

"Wha—"

"The boxes. Lower." He put his hand on the top box and pushed down, clearing his view of her face. "Look down at them."

She stared at him. "You don't take pictures of the stylist, Tom. You—"

He leaned right into her and kissed her on the lips. As she drew back, open-mouthed, he snapped the shot without even putting the camera to his eye. "Tom!"

"That one's for me. Let's start on the shoes."

She set the boxes on the makeup table, corralling her exasperation. This wasn't a good start to what would be a long day. "What exactly are you doing?"

"Uh, shooting a wedding? I believe that's what I was hired to do."

"You were, but—"

"We'll do it my way. And if you don't like it, then..." He

took one of the boxes and flipped it open, dropping the shoes to the floor. "Never mind. You'll love it."

He dumped the rest of the shoes, making a messy pile of sea-foam green and ivory satin, high heels, buckles, and bows. Then he started shooting, getting closer and closer and closer, until the last shot, which was nothing but the stitching on the toe of one of the bride's shoes.

When he finished, he grinned up at her.

"Do you spend a lot of time on the floor?"

"A helluva lot." He stood and lowered the camera. "Look, here's the only rule for today. You do what you do and I do what I do, and when those two things overlap, I get the final say if it affects a picture, and you get the final say if it affects the wedding style. Deal?"

"I—"

"Deal." He kissed her again, quick and playful. Too quick.

"What about when the bridal party gets here? You think Rhonda Lyons is going to let you take what photos you want to take?" Her eyes dropped to the skintight white T-shirt. "Dressed like that?"

He fought a smile. "I'll handle Rhonda and the bride and the party and photography. Trust me, this is what I do."

Actually, she was pretty sure this *wasn't* what he did. "You promised that whole elegant but lighthearted theme, remember?"

"It will be all that and"—he picked up the camera, his gaze moving over her shoulder—"more." Camera in hand, he walked to the ottoman, studying it, looked up at the chandelier and around the room. "Didn't expect to find this place in the back of the resort spa."

"When the Barefoot Brides moved in nearly a year ago, it

was clear that destination weddings would be a bread-and-butter staple of the resort's business, so Lacey, the owner, gave up two adjoining massage and facial rooms to make this dressing area."

His gaze fell on the makeup table, two silk settees, a wet bar, a dressing platform surrounded by mirrors and, under a glistening crystal chandelier, the oversize ivory silk and velvet tufted ottoman where brides loved to lounge, sip champagne, and pose for pictures.

"This place has your fingerprints all over it."

The comment really shouldn't have given her a little frisson of satisfaction, but it did. "That's because I designed it, inch by satiny inch." She gestured wide, as though introducing him to her pride and joy. "And it is my canvas to sprinkle stardust and transform nervous brides and giddy girlfriends from simple into stunning."

But he had a question in his eyes.

"You look as if you don't quite believe me."

"I *do* believe you. I can hear the passion and see the proof, but..." His voice trailed off.

"But what?"

After a second, he shook his head and let it go, turning to the tufted ottoman and the chandelier above it. "Is that on a dimmer?"

"Of course."

"Take it as low as it will go, will you?"

"Sure." She went to the switch and turned the dimmer knob to its lowest setting. With no windows and only wall sconces, the room quickly became shadowed.

"That's it?" he asked.

"That's as dim as it goes. Don't you need *some* light?"

He traveled around, on his knees, then put his hand on the satin tufted edges. "Not with this camera, but..." He moved the camera and looked at the ottoman, silent while he thought. After a beat, he gestured her over.

"Sit here."

"Tom, I..." *Hate to have my picture taken.*

"Sit. I need to do a light check." When she didn't move, he turned to her. "You do expect me to take pictures of the bride on this thing, don't you?"

"Well, that's what the photographer usually does."

"Usually being the operative word, so I'll have to do it somewhat differently. Sit here for me, Gussie."

She gave up the argument and perched on the edge.

"Lean back," he said, putting a hand on her shoulder to guide her where he wanted her. Then he held the camera up and aimed it right at her...

Breasts? She put a hand over her chest, suddenly aware of how thin her silk button-down shell was. "We generally focus on the bride's face."

"Generally," he said. "Usually. Always. Standard. Commonly." He moved the camera from his eye to look right at her. "Do any of those words sound like they describe what I do?"

She sighed and shook her head. "But this is a wedding, and you did agree to photograph it, so I do expect a little nod to convention."

"You will get your nod." His gaze traveled down again, lingering for a moment on her chest, then went all the way down to the light linen pants. "That's a different look for you."

"Work uniform." She plucked at the breathable fabric, every inch of it a subtle, understated sand tone. "I'm cool and comfortable for all the running around I do for a wedding, and I blend in. This day, these photos and, really, even this room are not about me."

"Mmm." He angled for a shot, so she put her hand in front of the lens, which looked quite a bit more expensive than what other wedding photographers used. "No more pictures of the stylist. The shoes and esoteric image shots to help tell the tale are fine, but not me."

"Why not?"

She was saved by the sound of female giggling and footsteps echoing from the hall outside. He reached down and gave her a hand, slowly pulling her up until her face was scant inches from his.

"Later, Pink. I'll get my shot. Right on that...tufty thing. But now let's work together."

He made the shot and the work and the tufty thing all sound way too sexy. Way.

Tom had expected the worst—an emotional bride, a pushy mother, a douche-bag groom, horny bridesmaids, a cheese-ball band, a drunken speech, and the sapfest of a father-daughter dance set to what would feel like a three-hour version of *Butterfly Kisses*. But the Barefoot Brides staged an elegant, sophisticated, and surprisingly low-key event that he dutifully recorded with a thirty-thousand-dollar Leica S2-P. Recorded *his* way, of course.

He also got the pure pleasure of working side by side with Gussie, observing her in her element, sprinkling her sugar dust, or whatever she called it, and a singular brand of infectious zest for life.

It just made him want her more.

Finally, Hailey and her weak-chinned groom—that poor schmuck didn't stand a chance against the tidal wave of a mother-in-law—headed to one of the villas, a little tipsy, veil, shoes, and tuxedo jacket long gone.

Using the moonlight and tiki torches for color, he stole a few candids of a teary conversation between the bride's parents and grabbed a great shot of some of the groomsmen heading into the resort bar to close it down.

"Hey, TJ."

He heard the woman's voice over the waning noise of the crowd, but knew it couldn't be Gussie because she'd never call him by his professional name. It had to be someone who wanted one more picture, no doubt. Slowly, he turned, only a little surprised to see one of the bridesmaids making her way toward him, her hair fallen, her shoes long gone. She was the prettiest and most flirtatious of the three, and he'd been trying to avoid her suggestive gazes since her third glass of champagne.

"Hey...Kaylie, is it?"

"Kayla," she corrected, zeroing in. "You almost done? We're hitting the bar."

"Nowhere near done," he told her.

She came closer, booze-brightened eyes dancing with hope. "I can wait. We can walk the beach. And I have a villa here if you want to, you know, talk."

"Too busy, I'm afraid."

She made a childish frown and fluttered a finger over the dragon on his bicep. "I'm sure you hear this all the time, but I think you're really cute."

"Cute? No, I don't get that often."

She giggled. "Hot? Cool? Come on." She slipped a finger up the sleeve of his T-shirt. "We have nice chemistry, don't you think?"

"The groomsmen are in the bar. You'd have better luck there."

125

She narrowed her eyes, predatory and determined, inching closer just as an arm scooped through his, and Gussie sidled next to him, the bride's veil and groom's jacket over her other arm, a pair of ivory satin shoes hooked off her fingertips.

"Need some closing shots over here, Tom. Kayla, honey, Courtney took your shoes, and they've all headed back to her villa for a post-party. They're waiting for you." She tugged Tom's arm. "This way."

Easily, she pulled him away and walked the length of the dance floor.

"*Merci beaucoup*," he whispered.

She looked up with a smile. "You're welcome. Come to safe harbor with the Barefoot Brides." She guided him to a back table where the other two wedding planners, one with a checklist, another gathering linens and centerpieces, stood talking.

"So how was your first wedding?" Willow asked as they arrived.

"Surprisingly nice. You ladies do excellent work."

The three of them shared smiles of pride.

"I wish Hailey had worn this off to her wedding night, though." He fluttered the veil's lace on Gussie's arm. "I would have liked to have shot it falling to the sand as she walked away."

"But it seemed like you got a lot of fantastic pictures," Ari said. "I can't believe you actually climbed on top of the gazebo. We've never had a photographer up there."

"You've never had me," he said simply.

Willow tapped the clipboard she'd had in her hand the entire day. "Rhonda's already bugging us for a proof sheet. Any idea when you'll have one?"

"I'll need to do some work to pull everything together," he said. "Gimme a day or two."

"We'll hold off the dogs," Ari assured him. "And thank you so much, Tom, for stepping in and saving us for this wedding."

"I was, uh, well persuaded." He couldn't help looking at Gussie, noticing that she looked a little tired and her makeup wasn't quite as sharp as it had been that morning, though her false eyelashes were secure, fanning bottle brushes up to her arched brows. They were another thing he wanted to rip off her, if only to get to the real woman beneath.

"Well, we owe you," Willow said.

"Then let your partner go, and we'll call it even," he replied.

"To France?" Ari asked with an expectant smile.

"To the dressing room, so she can unload the bride's belongings and review the initial shots. Unless the stylist isn't in charge of the wedding album?"

Even in the flickering torchlight, he could see some color rise in Gussie's face. She knew exactly what he had in mind in the dressing room.

"Go, Gus," Willow said. "We've got this covered."

"Seriously, you guys are done," Ari told them. "Call it a night. And thank you, Tom. The bridal party loved you."

"Understatement alert," Gussie teased, discreetly pointing to where they'd left Kayla. "I already saved him from the maid of honor."

"For which I am eternally grateful." He underscored that with one hand on her shoulder, the other hoisting his camera bag. "You need help carrying anything?"

"I got this." She lifted the veil, jacket, and shoes.

They said good-bye to the others and circled past the band, currently striking their set, when Gussie put her hand on his arm and said, "I don't want to run into anyone from the wedding, because the guys are drunk and the women will attack you. Let's go through the back entrance."

It meant crossing about fifty feet of sand, but he agreed. They stopped, and Tom kicked off his shoes and gave her an arm while she did the same with her sandals. She adjusted the items in her arms, and they made their way across the cool sand.

Neither of them spoke, letting the night noises from the wedding breakdown and the soft splash of the surf fill the thick, warm air.

"You did a great job," she finally said.

"You haven't seen the shots yet."

"I know your work. And thanks for not taking pictures of the stylist."

"The night is young." He slipped his arm around her, pulling her close. "And we're not finished yet."

He felt her stiffen, then give in, settling closer and letting their bodies touch. "All right, what do you have in mind?"

"Let's just say…you're not the only one who can pull off a transformation."

She gave him a look, questioning and curious, then he could see her relinquish the fight. At least for now.

"I do still need a closing shot for our album." He had a good storyboard in his head and knew he'd blow them all away with the power of these shots. Mr. and Mrs. Bernard would never have a traditional wedding album, not if his name was on it. "I need something symbolic and pretty. Can you help?"

"Of course." She lifted the lace veil and let the slight breeze pick it up. "I could let it float through the air."

He considered that, eyeing the moon and imagining the shot. "Maybe, but…no."

"Spread on the sand? Floating on the water?"

He smiled. "I love the way you think, Gussie. Every style idea you've had today has been right-on." When she beamed up at him, he couldn't resist pulling her a little closer, only the shoes and clothes she carried between them. "So, what did you decide?"

"About?"

"France."

She inhaled slowly and closed her eyes as she breathed out. "I knew that was coming sooner or later."

"Of course. Look what a great time we had today. You could come to the photo shoots, or even work with the stylists…"

"And he's sweetening the deal. If I drag this out any longer, you'll let me be a LaVie model."

God, he'd love that. "Would that put you over the edge?"

"The edge of sanity," she told him, slowing her step to get even closer. Surprising him, she leaned forward and kissed his chin. "I told you, I hate having my picture taken."

"Then you've never had it taken by me."

"The photographer doesn't change anything."

He slammed his fist against his heart, as if he could feel the dagger there.

"I mean, you can't make me enjoy the process, no matter how good you are."

"You willing to bet on that?"

She laughed. "I only bet candy. What do you have?"

He reached into his pocket and pulled out a pack of gum. "Will this do?"

"No."

"How about"—he turned her to face him—"a trip to France?"

She frowned, shaking her head.

"Come on, Gus. If I can prove to you that getting your picture taken—by *me*—can be a pleasurable experience, then you let go of all your reservations and go."

She snagged the gum. "We'll see."

Yes, they would. He nudged her toward the back of the resort, keeping an arm firmly around her. At the back door, he kissed her, sliding his hand down her back, low enough to appreciate the curve of her backside. She arched into him, nibbling his neck and burying her nose in his hair.

By the time they reached the Barefoot Brides dressing room, they were both a little breathless with anticipation. She dropped the tuxedo jacket and one shoe while trying to get the door unlocked, laughing as they bumped heads picking them up.

"I don't know about this…" she said.

"Yes, you do."

As she opened the door, he dumped everything he was holding onto the floor and pulled Gussie into him for another long, hot, deep kiss.

With a soft moan, she kissed back, letting him walk her one step backward so he could latch the door and lock them in. He lifted his head, and she gave him a look mixed with uncertainty and desire. Her lips were wet from his, naturally pink since her lipstick had long ago worn off.

He searched her face, trying to see it without anything except lust brightening the color of her cheeks.

"C'mere," he whispered, shaking all the things she held out of her hands until shoes and jacket hit the floor again. "But keep the veil."

"I can't tell if you're planning to kiss the holy hell out of me or trying to get your final shot with that veil."

"Neither," he said, his mind already whirring with

potential while his blood stirred with need. "I want you to do exactly as I say. Everything I say, okay?"

Her eyes were wide as she slowly shook her head. "I'm not into anything kinky," she said.

He laughed. "You can trust me."

But she stared at him. "I don't think—"

He captured her chin with his hand, holding her still, quieting her. "Don't think, Gussie. That's how we'll get the shot."

"What shot?"

"The one that will transform you."

"I'm the transformer in this room," she argued.

"Not tonight. You're trusting me. Okay?"

She started to argue, then let out something between a sigh of resignation and a slow gasp of anticipation. "Okay."

He took her across the room, tossed the veil onto the ottoman, but continued to the makeup table, where all the tools of her trade were still spread out over the marble counter top.

"Sit down."

"What?"

"What part of 'you can trust me' don't you understand?"

"Pretty much every word, but carry on." She slipped into the chair, and he looked around, spying a packet of makeup-removal cloths. He turned the chair a little and slid between the counter and chair, so her face was directly in front of his stomach.

"Let's make you even more beautiful." He snapped a cloth open, but she looked up with skepticism in her eyes. "You are, Gussie. How can you not realize that?"

"I am not beautiful," she said simply, but her gaze dropped back to his midsection. "But that is." She pushed her nose against his stomach. "So, if you're going to take off my barriers, then you have to do the same."

Without a word, he grabbed the bottom of his T-shirt and dragged it over his head, tossing it to the side. "There. Look all you want."

"Look? I want to lick."

"Knock yourself out."

She flicked her tongue against his skin and then lifted her face to him, eyes closed to let him wipe the cloth over her skin slowly, taking off some color from her cheek. When he stopped, she took another taste. Inches below that, the blood started to flow, making everything harder. Concentration, control, and his dick. *Everything* was getting hard.

But he took the rest of her foundation off, not at all surprised to find a pale, creamy complexion below.

When he put that cloth down, she leaned forward, put her hands on his hips and kissed his bare stomach again, making him hiss. Then she smiled up at him.

"I could get used to this game," she said.

"This game could get serious if you go any lower," he warned. Then he put two of his fingers on the outside edge of her false eyelashes. "Why did you wear these today?"

"Habit."

"A habit you should break." He stripped it off with one quick pull. "You have nice long lashes."

"And you have nice hard"—she nibbled on his stomach—"abs."

He removed the other lash and went to work taking her eye makeup off, eager to see her face with no paint, only ivory skin and spring-meadow eyes.

"Damn," he whispered. "Look at you."

She held his gaze, but it wasn't easy, he could tell.

"Why is it so hard for the girl who makes other people

beautiful to see how gorgeous she is?" He tipped her chin to get another, even more attractive angle.

"Another old habit," she said.

"Along with this one." He slipped his hands into her hair, feeling the netting of the wig.

She winced for a second, then stilled as he slowly removed the dark red wig to reveal her natural hair. She'd pinned it up in such a way that nearly covered her bald spot.

He took out one pin, then another, and the hair fell in waves of soft, golden honey over her shoulders.

"And if I never turn around, I'm perfectly fine."

"Even if you do, you're fine. So, so fine." He held her face in both of his hands, rubbing his thumbs over her cheeks, then her eyelids, then her mouth and jaw. Her face was small, heart-shaped, and precious in his hands.

"Has anyone ever seen you like this?"

"Few who have lived to tell the tale."

He smiled, but didn't reply as he appreciated her face.

"I thought you wanted a picture. Why am I letting you do this, again?"

"Why do you think?"

She narrowed her eyes, considering her response. "You know that this is more intimate than sex to me." It wasn't a question. And, yes, he knew.

Slowly, he bent forward so their mouths could meet. After the kiss, he pulled her up from the chair. "Let's get that shot. Come on, over here."

He led her to the white-satin hassock where the veil waited, the shot already forming in his mind. "Sit there and let me get my camera. All you're going to do is hold the veil."

He could feel her pulse kick up against his palm, her hands growing damp.

"Just tell me this isn't going to be on Rhonda's proof sheet."

"It isn't," he assured her. "So don't be uncomfortable."

"I'm already uncomfortable. I feel naked."

He smiled, then turned to get his camera. "I wish you were."

"You do?"

"More than anything, but I've pushed you far enough for the sake of a great shot."

He found the right lens, attached it, and checked the aperture before he turned.

Then he almost dropped thirty-grand worth of camera when he saw her shouldering out of her top. She gave him a sweet smile, almost as blindingly attractive as the cream lace bra that covered her beautiful breasts, sheer enough for him to see the outlines of her nipples. And there went his hard-on again.

He never got an erection while taking pictures. It was work. He was seeing a subject with an artist's eye, not a man's hungry gaze. But with Gussie, it was different. Damn it, with Gussie, *everything* was different.

Chapter Twelve

T om's reaction was instant, and real, and made Gussie fall a little deeper into the fantasy he'd created. He sucked in a slow breath, his gaze burning as walked slowly to her, taking the cap off the lens without taking his eyes off her.

"Take that veil and lay it over your chest." The order shot more fire through her and left no room for argument or questions. "Lie back."

"And you're *not* going to use this in their wedding album?"

He laughed softly. "I've got the shots I need for the album, but we'll both like the picture. Consider it a bonus for a job well done today."

His bonus or hers? Still, she did exactly as she was told, draping the lace over her bra, dropping her head back to the cushion, almost closing her eyes.

He snapped a picture. Then another. Then another.

With each click of the camera, her nerves tingled, little sparks of white-hot anticipation prickling her skin, tightening her muscles, stealing her breath.

This is what *gorgeous* felt like. Free and sexy and wanton and wonderful.

Holding the camera to the side, he reached under the lace veil, lifting her slightly, so close she could count his lashes and see his blue eyes darken with arousal. She bowed her back and let him easily unhook her bra.

"That's what I want," he murmured, like a confident photographer...and a needy lover.

Heat pooled between her legs as he dragged the bra off and let it fall, replacing it with the sheer lace of the veil. As he adjusted the fabric, he let his knuckles graze her budded nipples, staring at her, his jaw slack enough that she knew he wanted to put his mouth on her.

"One more shot," he whispered, angling her face and arranging her hair over her shoulder and the ivory satin.

She inhaled, sucking in the fragrance of him mixed with the scents of her favorite room, the heady, crazy whiff of sex that suddenly oozed from every pore.

And she wasn't scared. Or ashamed. Or...ugly.

He got down on one knee in front of her, so close his lens had to pick up every thread in the lace...and the bare breasts below.

She waited as he considered her pose, looked at her through his camera, scrutinized every inch. She waited for a wash of vulnerability and humiliation. She waited for the sense of lacking that had plagued her her whole life.

But all she felt was...*desirable.*

Finally, he put down the camera and looked at her.

"You don't want to take a picture?" she asked, hating that little note of inadequacy that sneaked in despite her sudden sense of security.

"I want to kiss you." He slid the veil to the side and lowered his head. "Everywhere."

And, God, he did. First, her breast, sucking and licking until he pulled a moan of pure delight from her, then planting more kisses up her throat to settle on her lips.

Burrowing her fingers into his long, silky hair, she clutched tightly, pulled him onto her, and fell harder into the bliss of his body against hers. Her hips moved with a rhythm of their own, rising and falling as the world slipped away and took all her hang-ups along with it.

All that mattered was the two of them, their connection, their kiss, their insane heat.

Tom lifted his head, the blue of his eyes already disappearing behind arousal-darkened pupils. "This is how I like you best."

She laughed a little, still holding his head. "Flat on my back, half naked, and helpless?"

"You're anything but helpless." He leaned over her, his hair falling around his face, nearly touching her cheeks. "I don't like all that crap you wear."

"Like tops and bras?"

"You know what I mean."

Of course she did. She pushed the thought away and pulled him back to her. "Keep kissing."

"With pleasure." His kisses were hot and wet and warm, while his hands sent electrical impulses to every needy place, touching her with confidence and ease, making her writhe with an inner battle of contentment and desire, wanting more of both.

He lifted his head and stared at her breasts as he caressed them, circling her nipple with one sure finger. Then he stroked her throat, her mouth, her cheeks, and her eyes. "Why don't you let go of all that and be yourself?"

"Easy for a man of physical perfection to say. Can we not talk now?" She punctuated the question by rocking her hips into his and getting the answer from a deliciously hard ridge of man.

Heartbeats passed. Slow, ragged breaths. Then he kissed her again, his tongue exploring with the same determination and power as his hand slid down her belly to—

"Gussie? You better still be in here!" The demand was accompanied by a hard rap that made Gussie gasp and an impatient rattle of the doorknob that made Tom stifle a groan. "Gussie! It's Kayla! I left my phone in there."

Seriously? This was happening now?

"Our maid of honor," Gussie rasped, frustration clawing through her.

"Gussie!" Kayla banged again. "God, please don't tell me you've left for the night."

Tom put his finger over his lips and shook his head. He underscored the demand with a little more weight, pinning her on the ottoman.

"Her phone," Gussie mouthed.

"Tough shit," he whispered back.

"What are you doing back here, Kayla?" Another female voice came from the other side of the door.

Great, now half the wedding party was out there, and Gussie was in the dressing room draped in the bride's veil.

"What are *you*?" The edge was clear in Kayla's voice, but then she and Courtney had sniped at each other quite a few times that day.

"I, um, left something in here. What about you?"

"My phone," Kayla said.

Gussie grunted. "Jeez, I told them to get everything when they left the last time." Still pinned, she reached to the side to find her shirt.

"You're lying," Courtney said. "I know exactly why you're back here."

Gussie froze at the tone, looking up at Tom. Again, he shook his head to keep her quiet.

"I left my phone in here," Kayla insisted. After a beat, they heard her say, "Oh, thanks. Where was it?"

"At the table. You came down to find the photographer, didn't you?"

Gussie choked a laugh, but Tom put his hand over her mouth.

"Screw you, Courtney."

"Or screw him, which would be better, but you're wasting your time, because I'm pretty sure he's boning the stylist. Didn't you see how they looked at each other?"

Gussie bit her lip, not sure if she wanted to laugh or cry. He was *not* boning the stylist...yet.

"Are you kidding?" Courtney asked. "Her?"

Tom shot up instantly, but Gussie grabbed him. "Don't. She's drunk."

Ignoring her, he marched to the door and unlocked it. "Get the hell out of here, both of you."

Gussie pushed up enough to see the two shocked faces on the other side of the door. And then she met Courtney's gaze as her eyes drifted past Tom and into the room.

Courtney grabbed the other woman's arm. "Let's go."

But Kayla stayed riveted at the sight of Gussie. "Dude, really? Her over me?"

The words fell like lead on the floor. Tom slammed the door in their faces, but Gussie rolled over and snagged her shirt.

"Gussie!" He strode back across the room, but she waved him off with one hand.

"Not now."

"Yes, now." He knelt beside her, one strong hand stopping her next move. "Surely you are not going to let some plastered and pathetic bridesmaid bother you."

She searched his face, digging for a quip, a comment, an

139

out. Nothing. If she opened her mouth, God only knew what she'd tell him. So she clamped it shut.

"I want you." He slid his hand into her hair, forcing her to face him. "And not just here and now. I *want* you…"

She shook her head, a hand on his chest to keep him back. "There's *only* a here and now with a guy like you, Tom. And here and now just got ruined."

He pulled her closer. "Don't give them that power. Don't give anyone that power over you."

Too late. "Let me get dressed."

"Gussie, you can't believe her. You do have eyes, don't you?"

She swallowed hard, arranging her thoughts like swatches of fabric that had to coordinate and make sense. "I don't see myself…like you do," she said. "I'm not saying that because I want pity or compliments or reassurances. I don't see beauty. I see plain." Worse than plain, but anytime she'd ever admitted that, she'd been told she was nuts, blind, or insecure.

She was definitely one of those three, and she didn't like that, but couldn't change it. Insecurities were cockroaches. They never died.

He pulled her up, shocking her with the force. "Come here." Ignoring her reluctance, he led her to the mirror, making her stand in front of it. Naked from the waist up, her hair tumbling over her shoulders, her face clean of any color or enhancement, she could barely look. "Gussie."

She looked down. "I can't do this," she admitted. Especially with him right behind her, facing her scar. But his eyes were on the mirror, and the woman in it.

"You *can* do this," he said. He kissed her shoulder. "With me. Just me. No one else."

The words were as tender as his kisses and had almost the same effect.

"Exercising your superpower, are you?" She tried for a tease, but it came out like the serious question it was. "Get your subject to reveal all?"

"No superpowers, Pink. I like you. I care about you. I'd like to hear the rest of your story."

The fact that he knew there *was* more to her story stunned her a little, but it warmed her, too. She wanted to tell it.

Still, she had to take a few slow, deep breaths before she jumped off this particular cliff. And she needed clothes.

She walked to the ottoman and picked up her blouse again, and this time, Tom helped her slide it on, sitting next to her and silently closing a few buttons while he waited and she gathered her words.

"Luke," she finally whispered.

He lifted his eyebrows in question.

"It all sort of begins and ends with my brother."

"How?"

She sighed. "Well, he got blamed for everything that happened the night of my accident. And he carried the guilt—no, I imagine he probably *still* carries the guilt to this day."

"But you were really in the wrong place at the wrong time."

She closed her eyes and dug her fingers into a fold of satin and velvet. "It was all my fault." The last word got trapped by the band wrapped around her chest.

"I thought there was a fireworks accident."

"There was, and it happened exactly as I told you. But the timing, the moment, the whole event wasn't because of something Luke did. It was me."

He didn't say a word or give a reaction, but waited for her to continue.

"I liked one of his friends." She shook her head, hating the simplicity and stupidity of it all over again. "I liked a lot of his friends, to be honest. I was a typical boy-crazy fifteen-year-old who craved attention from the opposite sex, but I was not the kind of fifteen-year-old who got it."

No, Gussie McBain had been at the height of her awkward, ugly stage. It may have evolved over the years, but somehow, time had frozen at that moment, and there she stayed, even now, fifteen years later.

"I had zits, and a narrow face, and an oversized nose, and a body that hadn't even begun to develop like my friends. I was not pretty. But I felt like if one guy—only one, any one—would notice me, then that would change, so I basically threw myself at one of his friends. Brian Grimsby. I can still see him right now." Not very tall, thin, but he'd had beautiful black hair and dark, dark eyes.

"What did Brian do with the honor of you throwing yourself at him?"

Act like an asshole. "I don't think he was honored. But he was an eighteen-year-old boy, so when we got far away from the crowd to make out, he took every advantage of me."

Tom's eyes widened in surprise, and she realized what he thought.

"No, not *every* advantage, but we rounded a few bases, and I freaked out when he whipped out his dipstick and started pushing me to my knees."

"What'd you do?"

"Said no and saw his interest fade in the blink of an eye. He zipped up and blew me off, so I downed the Solo cup of vodka he left behind." She wiped her lip absently, still tasting the burn and shame. "I kind of stumbled away and almost instantly felt sick. I went to go behind some bleachers that had been set up for real fireworks, and I heard him telling some of his friends that he'd just gotten a blow job, which, I swear to God, wasn't true."

"Gussie," he said, a little pity and sympathy in his voice. "Guys say stupid shit and no one believes them."

Of course she knew that. "His friends asked who, of course, and he told them, and they…they all started laughing and barking like dogs and joking about how"—her voice betrayed her with a hitch—"how Luke had it all, and I had nothing. He had looks, brains, sports, friends, but mostly looks. They were cracking jokes for what seemed like an hour but was probably two minutes. But I was mad and a little drunk and hurt beyond description."

She covered her mouth with her hands, shaking her head, hating this memory.

"Fact was, I despised my brother right then," she admitted. "He *did* have everything—he was great-looking, beloved, brilliant, bigger than life. Everything I didn't have, Luke had in spades. So I marched off to tell him, to rat on Brian, and take out my fury at how life had cheated me."

And that, right there, was the stupidest thing she'd ever done. "I saw him throwing the bottle rockets, and I recklessly ran right into the line of fire. The next thing I knew, my hair was on fire."

"Oh, God, Gussie." He reached for her hands. "I can't imagine what that must have been like."

No one could. The flash, the heat, the pain, the screaming, the ambulance, and the aftermath. Her mother losing her mind, her father bawling in the hospital, and Luke, stricken with guilt for something that hadn't been his fault.

"That stupid move cost us a family. Losing him was way worse than losing my hair."

"And you have no idea where he is?"

"Not a clue," she sighed. "After the accident, oh, it was horrible. I told you he was insane with guilt, certain it was entirely his fault for being drunk and dumb. My parents were..." She shook her head. "They refused to talk to him, which, I know now, they regret. When he turned eighteen, not long after I came home from the hospital, he left."

"He ran away?"

She shrugged. "At eighteen, it's not running away. It's breaking up a perfectly happy, healthy, wonderful life." She sighed on the last word. "I miss that family so much."

The lump in her throat grew so big it actually hurt to talk, so she didn't, waiting for the pain to subside.

"I know what it feels like to lose a family, Gussie."

The pain in his voice stabbed her, and when she looked at him, the agony in his eyes sliced right through her.

Of course he knew that. He'd lost his parents at seventeen and his sister just last month. And, clearly, that pain had not yet healed, not if the dampness in his eyes and the sorrow in his tone were any indication.

"I know you do," she said, rubbing her hand on his back in sympathy. "I don't mean to act like no one else ever had their family break apart. If it affected you like it did me, well, then, you know why family means so much to me."

He nodded, his jaw tight as if he didn't trust his own response.

"Have you tried to find him?" he asked after a moment.

She frowned. "You mean like use an investigator? No. I think my parents might have, but we never talked about it. Everything got broken and weird and ruined after the accident. Which"—she took a shuddering breath—"wasn't really an accident since I basically caused it by acting like an idiot. So, there you have it." She dabbed a tear carefully, forgetting for a minute that she didn't have a drop of makeup on. "My story of insecurity and heartache. Time kind of stood still for me that night."

He studied her, not answering right away. "It explains a lot."

"But doesn't change anything," she said quickly. "Telling the truth doesn't make it hurt any less or take away any impossible-to-understand repercussions."

"I would think," he said slowly, trailing a finger over her cheekbone, "that some dickhead who called you unattractive wouldn't have any power after that."

"You would think that." She closed her eyes and enjoyed the touch, but then moved away. "And, to some extent, you'd be right. Brian and his comments were forgotten for the most part in the trauma of what ensued. But I was the butt of jokes and then I let them…wreck everything. I don't know how or why that's affected me all these years, and maybe some high-priced therapist could tell me, but I haven't bothered to find out. My insecurities don't matter, though. What matters is that I lost my brother. And"—she touched her hair—"I got even less attractive in the process, which sometimes feels like…" She couldn't get the words out.

"Like retribution for what you did," he supplied.

Her heart slipped a little, with gratitude and relief to find someone who absolutely understood. "Yes. Payback for my mistake."

He shook his head. "You know it doesn't work that way."

Did she? She shrugged, trying to find some bright side to her sad tale. "I did discover wigs."

"In every color."

"It was right around the time that some companies were making them in colors, and it was my little form of rebellion.

Then I felt lost under the fake hair, my plain features seeming even...more so. My interest in fashion and makeup really took off then, and I started experimenting on myself. Next thing I knew, I always wore...a mask."

"Ever consider going without it?"

She shrugged. "Too many people know me this way, and it would take all kinds of explanation and...no," she finished. "I don't."

"Not even for a little while, as an experiment to see how you feel? Not even, say, for a couple of weeks in another country where no one knows you?"

It took a few seconds for the real meaning of the question to hit her. France. She smiled and jabbed him with an elbow. "You're a tricky one, Tommy."

"Come with me, Gus. Take off your mask and"—he slid an arm around her, pulling her closer—"just be you, with me."

"You want help with Alex."

His expression dropped in disappointment. "Do you *really* think that? If that were true, I'd take you up on your offer to keep her while I go. No." He gave his head a strong, vehement shake. "No. That's not why I'm asking."

"Then why are you asking?"

He puffed a surprised breath. "Are your insecurities that deep?"

"Have we not spent half an hour discussing them?"

He put both hands on her face and held her still, forcing their eyes to lock. "Augusta McBain, come with me and leave your mask behind. Consider it your therapy that you never got. You can walk the Promenade, eat the best food in the world, watch glorious sunrises, come to the set, and sleep"—he leaned closer and put his forehead against hers—"wherever you like, but preferably in my arms."

Seduction. This was what it felt like. Tempting and sweet and agonizingly *good*, no matter how bad it would be later. The very idea intoxicated her...weeks with him, in France, and Alex, who gave her a different kind of joy. No wigs, no makeup, no mask.

How could she say no to that?

Yes, when it was over, it would be, well, over. She knew that going in. He'd be "always alone," and she'd still be exactly the same. But if she said no, she'd spend the rest of her days regretting the decision. Hadn't she regretted enough in her life?

"Yes," she whispered into a light kiss. "I'll go."

Chapter Thirteen

*T*homas Jefferson DeMille, you are on dangerous
ground.

Although, to be fair, he was currently about thirty
thousand feet above the Atlantic Ocean in an elegantly
appointed Gulfstream G280.

Sipping a cold bottle of—what else?—LaVie, Tom
glanced across the wide aisle to see Gussie leaning her head
against her window, her eyes closed or focused on the
cushion of clouds below. The soft hum of the jet engines
lulled the cabin into a quiet cocoon, made even more private
now that Alex had dropped off to sleep on the sofa in the
back.

From his vantage point, Tom could see Gussie's chest
rise and fall with each breath, making him think she
might have fallen asleep, too. With her hair pulled back in a
ponytail that peaked at the crown of her head, she'd
easily covered most of the scar that troubled her so much,
and he could truly appreciate the slopes and angles of her
profile.

She had a slight overbite, and her chin was a little too
small. Without the bounty of fake hair around her face, he
could really see the angles of her delicate bone structure,

which might, before she'd developed into a woman, have been considered unexotic enough to be "plain."

Yet, she was beautiful to him. The way she made Alex laugh, or when she gave him her full attention and listened to what he was saying, or when she talked about a particularly crazy bride, he was enchanted. It attracted him on a level that had nothing to do with looks.

And the last time that happened…he'd suffered.

But here he was, barreling back toward a scary place at hundreds of miles an hour.

Of course, this was different. He wasn't attached. He wasn't even close to committed beyond the promise of what would be some romance and, he hoped, satisfying sex.

Surely he couldn't deny himself that just because he found her attractive, right? Spending his life "alone" meant no family, no ties, no chance of losing everything again. That didn't mean he couldn't be with someone, did it?

He shifted in his seat, making enough noise against the leather to get Gussie to open her eyes and look at him. For a moment, neither spoke or smiled or blinked or, hell, took a breath of air.

He really should tell her everything about his past. But he never told anyone. And, obviously, his sister hadn't even told Alex, or she'd surely have brought it up by now. Once he'd shared the pain, they'd be closer and then—

Gussie unlatched her seat belt and slipped across the wide aisle to sit next to him.

"I'm thirsty."

Why the hell was that so sexy? Was it the sultry tone of her voice? The almost sleepy look in her eyes? The subtle scent of something floral she always wore? It didn't matter. He gave her the bottle and watched her drink. She tilted her head and shuttered her eyes and looked at him from under her lashes. And inspiration struck.

"Don't move."

She froze, though her eyes got wider.

"Seriously, don't put that bottle down." He had his phone out in a second and tapped the camera.

She dipped the bottle. "You're—"

"Gussie, please." And took another shot. "Look at that," he said, showing her the screen. "*Look* at that."

The LaVie logo was perfectly visible, with the tip of one finger—bare of any polish, in keeping with their deal—brushing the stylized V. Her expression was pure satisfaction, and the bottle was partially reflected in her eyes. Best of all, those eyes matched the bright green in the iconic turquoise and chartreuse LaVie label.

"Perfection," he murmured, looking at the shot. "That could go right in the LaVie storyboard today."

"Well, it better not."

"No one will see the board shots but the crew and me," he promised. "Think of that picture as my taking a note so I don't forget the concept. Not that I could."

"A model would be better."

"A model wouldn't be real." He leaned back into the buttery leather again. "I'd love to use real women on this campaign, but they are so dead set on it being 'high fashion' and including the faces and bodies of supermodels."

"Why do they think that's going to get people to drink the water? Like, the more LaVie you drink, the more you'll look like a supermodel?"

"They want the bottle as an accessory." He reached to the floor and got his tablet, opening it to a campaign storyboard.

The shots were sketches, drawn to mirror a designer's pencil, with the emphasis as much on the clothes and accessories as the model or the lightly drawn scenery in the background.

"You think that's going to sell water?"

"They do. It's not my job to think about it."

"But it kind of is," she countered.

He looked skyward. "This is why I hate commercial photography. I'm all about creating the story and capturing the essence, not selling a bottle of water."

"Then why did you take this job?"

"My feet itch." At her confused expression, he added, "I don't just like to travel, Gussie. I hate staying in one place for too long. For me, it's like not being able to function."

He may have added too much emphasis on that last point, but that was the way it came out.

"I can't even imagine not having a home anywhere. Where do you keep your stuff?"

"My only stuff is photography related, and it comes with me or stays in storage."

"Your books?"

"On my tablet."

"Clothes?"

"In a suitcase."

"Favorite coffee cup?"

"Whatever holds my coffee when I want it is fine."

"Pictures, memories, and gifts from friends?"

He shrugged. "Pictures I have enough of, memories are in my brain, and my friends know better than to give me gifts."

"Do you even have friends?"

The question threw him, since the rhythm of the verbal volley suddenly evaporated. "Of course I do. I have friends all over the world, in all kinds of professions." He added a smile. "I stay at their homes when I'm traveling."

She shook her head. "I do not envy you that life. I like

my stuff. What happens when you get old?" she asked.

Again, a lob from left field he hadn't been expecting. "I'm only thirty-six. I have plenty of time to worry about the future."

She looked up at him. "No, you don't. The future is now." She pointed her thumb to the back. "The future is sleeping twenty feet away with a bruised heart and a notebook full of what I suspect is teen-girl poetry, but I don't want to intrude by asking."

Of course, Gussie knew exactly what *not* to ask with Alex. He'd prodded and gotten nowhere. "She can't possibly want to live with me."

"She's twelve. I don't think she has a lot of say in the matter."

He let go of her hand, stabbing his fingers into his hair to drag it back with a low sigh. "I'm going to figure something out." He had to. "As soon as we get back from France. Maybe she'll like life on the road, and I can, I don't know, get her homeschooled or something."

Her eyes tapered with a very clear message that he was dreaming.

"Look, these past few days are the first time I've gotten her to say ten consecutive words," he said. "And, let's be honest, *I* haven't gotten her to do that, *you* have."

"What are you saying?"

"Gussie, I just told you I don't even have a favorite coffee cup, let alone a…a…normal home life. And I don't want one," he added, a little too harshly. Had it, lost it, never want that again.

"Why not?" she asked.

Was this the time to tell her? He took her hand again to pull her closer, but a footfall behind them stopped him.

"Are we in France yet?" Alex wiped sleep from her eyes

and curled into the seat that faced theirs. "And what time will it be when we get there?"

Tom checked his watch, but Gussie leaned forward and put a hand on Alex's leg. "It'll be the middle of the night, and even on a private plane, we'll have to get through Customs and to the apartment, so you should keep sleeping."

She shook her head, eyeing one, then the other, and then her attention remaining on Gussie. "Can I ask you a question?"

"Of course," Gussie replied.

"Why'd you stop wearing wigs?"

"She's not wearing wigs or hats or makeup on this trip," Tom said quickly, hoping the question didn't make Gussie uncomfortable, but once again not having any clue if he should reprimand Alex or use the situation as some kind of an object lesson.

"Because we're taking a freecation," Gussie said.

"A what?" Tom and Alex asked in unison.

"A freecation. A vacation from the things that...weigh down our lives and keep us from being free."

And, no surprise, she had the perfect reply.

"And wigs and hats and false eyelashes weigh too much?"

"Essentially."

"I don't wear makeup," Alex announced. "My mom said it would make my skin break out more."

"She was right, especially the cheap stuff," Gussie replied. "I can probably find something that wouldn't hurt your skin."

"Then what should I be free of on the freecation?"

Gussie shrugged. "Whatever feels like too much to carry around for a while."

153

She considered that, nodding, then her mouth turned down. "I guess, you know, thinking about my mom."

"You shouldn't stop that," Gussie said, leaning closer to take both of Alex's hands. "But I'm certain she wouldn't want you to be sad in France. Is there anything else you want to be free of? Bad habits or things that make you feel not so great?"

How did she come up with these amazingly simple ways to talk to Alex? Who dreamed up a *freecation* and made it sound like so much fun that he wanted to take one?

"No, there's nothing else," Alex said, but she didn't sound too sure of that. Whatever she might want to unload, Tom was pretty sure Gussie would figure it out. "How about you, Uncle Tommy? What are you going to be free of on this trip?"

"Your uncle lives his life on a freecation," Gussie said when he didn't answer immediately. "So he's here to help keep us on track."

"But you have to give up something," Alex insisted. "There has to be something you want to be free of while we're here."

"I guess I'm giving up being alone all the time," he admitted.

Fact was, he'd have two people to worry about, a place he'd call "home" for a while, and the closest thing to a family he'd had since…a long time.

"You sure you can handle that, big boy?" Gussie asked with a nudge to his elbow.

No, he wasn't sure at all. "Guess I'm about to find out."

Jet lag wrecked Alex, but Gussie was too excited to sleep once they settled into the luxurious apartment in Nice. Although it wasn't light yet when their driver had picked them up at the airport and chauffeured them through the streets of Nice, Gussie had inhaled the incredible city nestled into the Côte d'Azur. The sedan's headlights flashed on glimpses of old European buildings with columns and arches mixed with wrought iron-laced balconies. The streets were wide, brick and, in spite of the predawn hour, already alive with vendors setting up food and flower stands.

Their apartment was in the middle of town, up three flights of stairs to one of two units on the top floor. Inside, they found a spacious living area, modern kitchen, and three bedrooms, beautifully decorated. French doors in the living room opened onto a balcony that spanned the length of the apartment, offering an unobstructed view of the lights out to the blackness of the Mediterranean.

Gussie nearly cried at the beauty and kicked herself for even thinking about turning down this experience.

After a hot shower, she eyed the fluffy comforter and bed, but despite the fact that her body thought it was midnight, it was six a.m. in the south of France. She was restless and ready for the day.

Assuming Tom and Alex were both in their rooms asleep, Gussie wandered into the living area of the darkened apartment, drawn by the tantalizing scent of…coffee?

Yes. Coffee. Tom must have brewed it, she decided, as she poured a generous cupful, not caring that there'd be no sleep this morning. She'd nap later. This was all too irresistible.

Taking the cup to the open balcony doors, she stood long enough to enjoy a warm breeze and the salty scent of the sea.

And soap, drawing her gaze from the breathtaking vista outside to the one lounging on the sofa.

His own mug in hand, Tom wore nothing but thin cotton sleep pants, his hair still wet from a shower and dribbling water over his bare shoulders and chest, his head back and eyes closed.

"Long way from Barefoot Bay," he said without opening his eyes.

"It is a bay, though." She gazed out to the first lavender rays of sunrise over the Mediterranean, taking in the wide curve of the shore.

"You're looking at Angels' Bay or Bay of the Angels, depending on where you're from."

"That has to be the prettiest piece of real estate on the planet."

"One of them," he said with the confidence of a well-traveled man. And something else tinged his voice. Sadness? Maybe exhaustion.

"I thought you'd be asleep, since our bodies think it's midnight."

"My body knows what time it is," he said. "And every artist who has ever been in this city knows about the light. I'm waiting for it."

"The light?"

He turned to her, his eyes flickering as he noticed she wore nearly as little as he did. A cotton tank and wispy shorts, which had seemed perfect for the warm summer night a few minutes ago, felt woefully thin when he looked at her that way.

"C'mere, Pink." He gestured toward the space next to him. "I'll tell you about the light in Nice. It's special."

The nickname reminded her that she wasn't pink...or black or purple or even blond anymore. Her natural hair was still damp and pulled back into the hasty braid that she always slept in, with no effort to hide her scar. But she could have been shaved bald and covered with charcoal, and that wouldn't have stopped her from taking that spot next to him on the couch. There, she had to fight the urge to cuddle closer and trace her fingers over the swirls and curls of dark ink on his arm and bare chest.

He tucked hair behind his ear and gave her a half smile, lifting his mug. "Glad you found the coffee."

"Called to me like a siren song."

"The coffee here is amazing. And the food. And the wine." His eyes shuttered as he took a deep inhale. "And the lemon soap you used."

"I almost took a bite of the bar," she admitted.

"Get used to it," he told her. "Everything in Nice is so achingly perfect that you want to eat it."

Like you, she thought as she devoured every inch of his face with her eyes. He looked serious this morning, his whiskers making his chiseled cheeks look dark, his wet hair screaming for her fingers to comb through it.

"Tell me about the light," she whispered.

"You're going to see it for yourself in a few minutes, and I suspect you have a good enough eye to know what you're looking at." He sighed, draping his arm behind her, looking out to the scenery beyond them. "It's the light that called to Cézanne and Chagall. Light that inspired Henri Matisse to make this his home. There is something wistful and tender about the sunlight on the Mediterranean and something magical about the orange and coral buildings and the sky. The light in Nice is unlike anywhere else on earth."

He grew silent, but she felt he wanted to say more, so she waited, almost feeling him tense.

"It's the original *portokali* sky," he finally said. "Do you know what that is?"

She thought about the words, familiar enough, but her connection couldn't be what he meant. "Portokali Sky's the name of a line of bags and accessories I love. Very beachy and bright."

"Probably named for the Greek expression. The Greeks used to roam this city in ancient days, and they know a good sunrise and sunset. *Portokali* sky means 'orange sky,' but it's a special kind of orange, heartbreaking and brief, that comes on with a sudden intensity and is gone before you've had time to…to truly appreciate what you had." It sounded like his voice was about to crack, but he covered that with a sip of coffee.

Light made him emotional, she thought, which was probably why he was a master at his art. *Something* had made him emotional.

"Anyway," he said, composure firmly back in place. "You're about to see one."

She turned toward the sky, aware of the very first hint of color floating over the horizon, the shadows on the hillsides, and the steeples and taller buildings stretched like fingers reaching up to God.

"I'm happy to be here," she whispered under her breath.

He curled his fingers over her shoulder, tickling her skin. "Good."

The words floated over her like the light on the city of Nice, soft and sweet and a little unexpected. "Are you glad I'm here?"

He cocked an eyebrow as if he had no time for that stupid question.

"It's a legit question," she said. "Wouldn't you rather be here alone, free, without the responsibility of Alex and me?"

He didn't answer, staring at the view, thinking. "I'm a little surprised by it, too," he finally said, turning to melt her with his intense blue gaze. "But I wouldn't want to be here alone. I can't say that I understand why, but it's true."

"Maybe you don't like that loner life as much as you think you do."

"Or maybe I just like you." He sounded wistful, and amazed.

She leaned in to kiss him, tasting coffee and mint and sunrise and his sincerity. Unable to resist the temptation any longer, she splayed her hand over his chest, surprised to feel the accelerated rate of his heartbeat.

He moaned into her mouth, pulling her closer. "Kissing you when the sun comes up is perfection."

In silent agreement, they paused in the kissing to put their coffee cups on the tables beside them, then settled deeper into the couch and each other.

His tongue slipped over hers, so sweet and quick it sent a thousand lightning flashes through her body, a soft whimper escaping as he caressed her arm and shoulder and slid his hand down to her breasts.

As she trailed kisses down his neck, he whispered, "Look, Gussie. Look."

She sighed into the next kiss, lifting her head to sneak a peek at the view, her body torn between the beauty and fire of the vision and the rising desire that made her want to close her eyes and let him touch her. Everything was bathed in a peachy tone right then. The world, this man, this incredible prelude to making love.

She clung to his head, his neck, his shoulders, taking a breath to inhale it all. He eased one tank top strap over her shoulder, finding new spots to burn with his kisses.

White heat arced through her, melting every cell, pooling

need low in her belly. Without a word, he pushed her down to the soft cushions and got on top of her, his erection pressing against her stomach.

"Tommy," she whispered, grabbing two handfuls of hair and lifting his face so she could look at him.

He moaned, and not with pleasure. "I hate that name."

"Why? I think it's kind of hot."

He closed his eyes and went back to kissing her neck, rolling against her as if his hard-on could shut her up if his *kisses* couldn't.

"Why do you hate it?" she asked as he dragged her tank top up to gain another form of access to her bare breasts.

"Why do you talk when we're making out?"

"Because I want to know you."

"Well, I want to know you, too. So hush." He had her top all the way up, her breasts fully exposed. "Oh." It was barely a breath, barely a whisper, but so full of awe and admiration that Gussie felt her throat close up with emotion.

"You've seen me before."

"Not in this light. Light from heaven, light like nothing else on earth."

The sunrise was even more powerfully orange now, spilling tones of ginger and persimmon over the rooftops of Nice. "So, so pretty."

"Yes, it is." He wasn't looking at the sky. Instead, he flicked his tongue over her nipple, sucking and licking, pulling pleasure and sweet grunts of need from her throat. His hair brushed her skin, exactly the way she'd imagined it would.

The feathery touch tickled and teased and made her crazier.

Finally, he lifted his head and met her gaze, the shadows of his face stark and stunning in the light.

The light! She could see it now—see what it did to everything it touched. Like a sprinkle of something divine, the light of Nice made everything more exquisite, including the man in her arms. Dear God, he was stunning.

"I've never kissed a more beautiful man," she confessed.

"It's the light," he said.

"No, it's the man."

"It's the light," he repeated, dragging his hand lower, over her belly, down to the ribbon drawstring, the ends of that grosgrain as frayed as her nerve endings. "Let me touch you," he whispered.

She barely breathed, "Yes."

He snaked his hand between them, sliding hot fingers lower and letting out a satisfied sigh when he realized she wore nothing but the sleep shorts.

With a kiss on her cheek and a groan of desire, he stroked her once, enough to make her hips rise in precious agony.

"Tommy."

He laughed, dry and mirthless. "You know what I'm going to do if you keep calling me that?"

"I hope so." Bowing her back, she gave his fingers entrance to her body, gripping his biceps for some kind of stability.

"You like that?"

She couldn't answer as the first torturous waves of an orgasm threatened.

"Pink," he repeated.

She shuddered. "Yeah?"

"No, not you." His fingers stilled as he kissed her cheek again, using his mouth to make her face turn toward the view. "Now the light is pink."

She managed to open her eyes and inhale in pure wonder. That color. That *color*. She almost sat up, but he had her securely under him, his hands starting their assault again.

Everything hurt in the best possible way. Her eyes ached from the beauty of the view. Her body twisted with the need to release itself against him. Her fingers throbbed from squeezing his muscles so hard. And her heart...oh, Lord, her heart was one big pain in her chest.

He stroked her again, forcing her to divide her appreciation between her body and the outside world. Gussie blinked at the sight, her senses assailed by the splendor, her body under siege by his touch and a wholly different splendor.

His hand worked its magic, like the sky, and Gussie watched the world explode in a rainbow of tropical pastels until she had to close her eyes and surrender to the colors in her head, and the pressure and pain and pleasure as her body rocked and came helplessly.

"That was beautiful," she managed to whisper.

He pressed his lips to her cheek. "So are you."

God help her, she was starting to believe him.

Chapter Fourteen

Citrus. Sweet lemon and tangy lime. The smell invaded Tom's nose and danced through his senses, waking him slowly. Warm skin and an unforgiving morning erection fought for attention against soft hair on his arm and the sweet curves of a woman pressed against him.

Tom blinked his eyes open, and even with his back to the railing and sky, he could tell that it was near-noonday sun that drenched the balcony, hot and relentless despite the breeze that floated from the Mediterranean.

Well, there were shittier ways to wake up than outside on the Côte d'Azur with a sexy woman in his arms. Gussie was pinned between him and the back of the sofa, still on her back, her eyes firmly shut and each breath steady and slow, in the depths of jet-lagged sleep.

They hadn't taken things any further, too relaxed to move into his bedroom and too out in the open to continue what they'd started. Anyway, they'd both fallen sound asleep.

He didn't move for a moment, then gave in to the urge to stroke some strands of hair off her face in the hopes that she'd wake slowly like he had. But she sighed and turned her head, her honey-gold hair sliding over her arm. And her scar was suddenly right in front of his face.

The scar from the night that had shaped her. He could see it, and it didn't bother him a bit. What would she think of the scars he hid from her?

He closed his eyes and waited for the inevitable—the memory of another woman, with black eyes and ebony hair, with a hearty laugh and a throaty voice.

But that woman didn't appear in his mind. When he inhaled the citrus scent, he wasn't transported to the hills of Karpathos, to a kitchen full of raucous voices and a family that lived and loved and laughed with such passion.

He smelled sweet Gussie, a woman who would appreciate all that, but didn't have it.

He studied the burn scar, the cause of her emptiness and insecurities. He wanted to touch it, but didn't, instead studying the shape—roughly the outline of the continent of Australia—and the size, about four and a half inches in diameter.

It had to have been a doozy of a burn. He'd done a little research after she told him about it, learning that the burn had to have been third or fourth degree if a hair transplant was impossible. It was high enough on the crown that it was difficult, even with the long, thick hair she had, to cover it completely. One good gust of wind, and it would be out there for the world to see.

Which was no doubt why she wore those pain-in-the-ass wigs. Well, now she was on freecation. No wigs or makeup, just morning make-out sessions and lazy naps in the sunshine.

He placed a light, gentle kiss on her shoulder, but that didn't get so much as a change in her breathing. Getting up very slowly, he inched off the sofa without making a sound, reaching over the back for a cotton afghan. He covered her to protect her from the sun and because the gesture felt natural and right.

After he did, he stroked her hair and carefully eased some locks over the back of her head, covering the scar to protect it from the direct sun. He took one more look at her and turned, smacking right into Alex.

"Whoa," he exclaimed quietly. How long had she been there? He didn't ask, and she didn't offer, staring up at him with a gaze that looked softer and more vulnerable than usual.

For some reason, it felt like progress, and he wanted to grab that with both hands.

"It's not so bad, is it?" she asked.

For a second, he couldn't imagine what she was talking about, then her gaze shifted, and he followed, landing on the hair that covered the scar.

"Not at all," he agreed. "Come on, let's let her sleep."

He ushered Alex back inside, closing the French doors behind him. "How are you feeling?" he asked.

"'Kay." He heard her stomach growl, and she tried to cover that by crossing her arms, making her skinny shoulders stick out of the sleeveless T-shirt that hung over cotton sleep pants covered with pictures of kittens.

"You sound hungry." He opened the fridge, which their hosts had stocked with LaVie, naturally, and a few other essentials, including eggs, but he had a better idea. "We're going to the best bakery on earth. Go get dressed."

But she stood frozen, staring at him, her expression unreadable.

"Look, Alex. I have an idea. Let's add something to the freecation."

She still simply looked at him, waiting. Swallowing hard, he forged on. "Let's both be free of the awkwardness and discomfort that seems to invade every conversation we have. Let's just get to know each other, and you meet me halfway without me feeling like I have somehow broken a cardinal rule of guardianship."

He watched her consider the suggestion, waiting for the fight or rationale why that was a bad idea and they should continue to walk on eggshells.

"You think they'll have croissants with chocolate chips?" she asked.

Thank *God*. "Like you have never tasted in your entire life."

She hinted at a smile and disappeared down the hall to her bedroom, which was across from the room that Gussie had taken. A small, but tangible, victory.

A few minutes later, he found Alex waiting for him in the living room, wearing shorts and a T-shirt and sneakers, looking adorably American and quite young. She gestured at his linen pants and understated collared shirt. "Why are you all dressed up?"

It wasn't quite as formal as Paris, but he suspected she'd figure out soon enough that the white sneakers and cutoffs branded her as an outsider in Nice. "Just dressed."

"Should I wake Gussie so she can come with us?" she asked, hope in her voice.

He peeked through the French doors to see she hadn't moved. "Let her sleep. We'll bring her a basket of baked goods and some fruit and coffee."

Alex looked a little horrified that she had to be alone with him, but he chose to ignore that.

"She'll be fine," he assured her, grabbing the house key they'd left on the counter. "Better if she catches up on sleep."

"But I like her."

"Then let her sleep. It's the most thoughtful thing you can do for someone you like."

"Or you can cover them up with a blanket and *kiss* them."
It was the closest thing to a tease she'd ever given him.

"Busted." He headed to the door, letting her out first, his
heart lighter than it had been since Ruthie died.

Crossing the street, he got his bearings of the southeast
section of Nice, the neighborhood tucked into a beautiful
section walking distance from the beach and Old Town. "If I
recall, the bakery is that way." He gestured them past a few
restaurants and boutiques, a salon and spa, and a small but
packed café.

"Can't we eat at one of these?"

"We could, but it isn't quite what I had in mind." A few
pedestrians brushed by, their gazes distant or down, like all
Frenchmen who refused direct eye contact. At the
intersection, a truck rumbled by at high speed, and
instinctively, Tom grabbed Alex's hand and tugged her back
a few feet to safety.

"Whoa, there. You okay, kid?"

Eyes wide, she nodded, still holding his hand. "Not a lot
of drivers like that in Florida." Staying close, they walked
past an iron gate around a lush garden, then by a stone
cathedral, and Alex practically stumbled on the cobblestones
trying to drink everything in.

As they walked, he told her tidbits about Nice, and she
soaked everything up, asking a few questions and even
making comments all the way to the red-and-white striped
awning of Le Pain.

Inside the little shop, she crooned over the chocolate,
cinnamon, and butter-rich aroma of a truly great French
bakery.

"Holy wow, that smells fantastic." Alex twirled a bit,
pulled to the glass cases full of petit fours and croissants,
cream puffs and macaroons. Behind the cases were stacks

upon stacks of baguettes and breads, glistening with golden crusts, every one uniformly made despite the fact that each was created by hand a few hours ago.

After some discussion in broken French with the baker, they settled on croissants, with coffee for Tom and milk for Alex, and then took their purchases outside to find a corner table to eat and people watch.

"Why does everyone dress so fancy?" she asked.

"Well, there are a lot of rich tourists, and this is France, where fashion reigns."

She lifted her sneakered feet and grinned around a big piece of chocolaty crust. "Whoops."

"No worries. Gussie can help you do a little shopping if you want to get some clothes that don't scream Mimosa Key, Florida."

She narrowed her eyes at him as she swallowed. "You know there's nothing wrong with Mimosa Key. We have tourists there, and some of them are even billionaires. Nobody cares if they wear sneakers and shorts. In fact, we encourage it."

"*Touché.* But you're in France."

She looked around again, clearly in awe of this new world. She loved traveling, he thought suddenly. She'd probably take to it like a pro. And maybe...

He sipped his coffee, considering exactly how to broach the subject. "You know, Alex, I travel a lot."

She nodded, brushing crumbs from her mouth. "I know."

"Traveling's the best education you'd ever get."

She shot him a look, setting down the remainder of croissant to drink milk. "I need to go to school," she said after she swallowed.

"Of course, but, you know, you can learn on the road."

She looked up at him, worry darkening her eyes, the tasty

food forgotten. "Is that what you think we're going to do? Travel all over the world while you take pictures and I get taught by people I don't know?"

"Does that really sound so bad to you?" He wasn't trying to argue, but he wanted to understand if his lifestyle could *ever* appeal to her.

"Yes, it sounds bad to me. It sounds weird. Like, who would be my friends?"

"I never see you with any friends."

"But I have them! I have school and a house I love, and it's home."

"Home is where you make it," he said. "And there's a great big world out there that—"

"No!" Her color rose as high as the note in her voice. "I don't want to leave Mimosa Key."

"Then what are we going to do?" he asked, actually hoping she'd have a solution, even though he knew better.

She pushed her seat back with a loud scrape against cobblestone, nearly toppling her chair. "That's not my problem!"

"Alex—"

"I'm not going to live like some homeless freak because you can't figure it out. You're not going to drag me around like an extra piece of luggage. I'm a person. I'm someone's *daughter*."

"Alex!"

But she was off like a bullet, using those white sneakers to fly down the Rue de la Something and disappear around a corner.

In the distance, Gussie heard a pounding, a persistent *tap tap smack* that hammered her out of her sleep. It was Ari, of course. She always came down way too early to have coffee.

"Gussie! Let me in!"

Gussie rolled over and fell right off the bed onto the floor with a painful thud. "Ouch! Holy sh..." She blinked into sunshine, shocked into consciousness. "What the hell?"

Oh, yeah. France. Nice. The Riviera. Crazy hot orgasms at sunrise. She swiped her hand through her hair, her braid long ago lost.

"That wasn't a dream," she murmured with a sleepy smile.

"Gussie! Please!"

And that wasn't Ari. She shot up, grabbing the railing for stability, stealing a look at the stunning view over rooftops and through trees, then hurried to the closed French doors. Why had they left her out here?

And why was Alex pounding on the front door of the apartment? And where was Tom? She reached the door just as Alex stopped knocking, the muffled sound of a woman's voice on the other side.

"Alex?" Gussie fumbled with the lock and latch, finally getting it to open. There, she came face-to-face with a teary Alex and a woman standing in the doorway of the next apartment, holding a large platter, her face smudged with two different colors of blue paint, big brown eyes wide under a halo of blond curls.

"Is everything all right?" the woman asked, her clipped tone decidedly English.

"Are you okay?" Gussie asked Alex, seeing a whirlwind of emotion on the young girl's face, but not at all able to read it. "Where were you? Where's Tom?"

"We went to some bakery down the street for breakfast."

"Oh, I hope it was Le Pain," the woman said, stepping farther into the hall. "I eat at least a baguette a day from that amazing baker." She gave them a huge smile and held out her hand, a long, thin-tipped paint brush balanced between fingers. "Oh." She seemed to realize she had it, then set it on the platter—no, palette—full of bright splotches of paint. Wiping her hand on a similarly splotched smock, she offered it again.

"I'm Anne Stone, and I presume I'm your neighbor."

Alex looked at her, so Gussie stepped forward to shake the woman's hand. "Hello. I'm Gussie McBain, and this is Alex. We arrived last night."

"For the rest of the season or are you a weekly?"

"We're here for a few weeks," Gussie said.

"Oh, lovely! I can't stand when there's a parade of newcomers every few days. And you with a youngster!" She turned her blinding smile on Alex. "You must be about the same age as my Lizzie or Eddie. Thirteen?"

"Almost," she said.

"Closer to Eddie, then. He's already thirteen. And Lizzie is eleven going on thirty-five." She gave a quick laugh at her joke. "On holiday, I suppose?" she asked.

"Um…sort of a working holiday," Gussie said. "Are you a painter?"

She hooted again, as though the question tickled her to death. "Let's say I put color on a canvas and try to make a picture. Georgia O'Keeffe I am not." She hoisted the paint palette as though she had a tray full of pastries. "However, I put my heart and soul into it, and that's all that matters."

"And you live here?" Gussie asked.

"Only for the summer. We go back to London in September." She let out the softest sigh. "So I'm trying to make the most of every—"

"Mum! Where are you?" a young boy's voice with the same lilting British accent called from inside the other apartment.

"In the hall, luv. Come and meet our new neighbors."

In a second, a boy stuck his head out, his hair as blond as his mother's, but not curly, his angular face twisted as he looked questioningly into the hall.

"And they have a child your age!" Anne said as if this was a great gift.

Gray-blue eyes shifted from Gussie to Alex, landing on her with a second of interest, then a flash of disappointment. "A girl."

Alex choked softly, spearing him with a look.

"Edward Stone!" Anne chided. "Get out here and be a proper gentleman."

With a puff of teen disgust, he stepped out and nodded. "Greetings, neighbors," he said stiffly, his freckled face stiff as a board as he carefully avoided eye contact with either of them. Then, to his mother, "Are the biscuits ready?"

"Where is everyone?" This time, a girl came into the hall, a smaller, younger but similar version of the boy. "Oh, goodness." She put her hand to her chest self-consciously. "Hello."

"And this is Elizabeth, but we call her Lizzie," Anne continued. "Meet our new neighbors, Gussie and Alex, who is right in between you and Eddie on the age scale. Isn't that convenient to have another mate your age around?"

"Oh, yes," Lizzie said, walking right up to Alex with wide eyes. "And you're American!"

Alex nodded. "Yeah."

"Have you met Justin Bieber?"

"Lizzie, are you daft?" Eddie scowled at his sister. "That's like her asking if you've met One Direction."

172

"Have you?" Alex asked.

Both girls burst out laughing, making Anne beam with joy. "And we have instant friends," she announced. "Are you alone or is your husb—"

"Alex!" Tom's sharp bark silenced all of them, echoing through the long stone hallway as he made his way up the stairs. "You shouldn't have run away like that."

Appearing at the corner, he marched toward them.

"Oh, dear," Anne whispered. "Someone's in a pickle with Dad."

"He's not my dad!" Alex shot back under her breath.

Anne lifted her brows and looked at Gussie, but Tom reached them before she could reply.

"Not cool," he ground out, his frustration and anger palpable. "You don't run away in a foreign city!"

"We best be going then," Anne said brightly. "Let's have a cuppa sometime, Gussie? And you young ones can play." She shooed her kids back into the apartment with a quick but silent hello to Tom, obviously recognizing that this was not the time for a neighborly introduction.

"What happened?" Gussie asked.

"Inside," Tom said, nudging both of them back into their apartment. His eyes blazed like blue flames, locked on Alex. She hustled into the apartment ahead of both of them, marching down the hall to her room, giving the door a dramatic slam. Gussie turned and put her hand on Tom's chest to stop him from following her.

"What is going on?" she demanded.

"She bolted in the middle of breakfast, and I wasn't even sure she knew how to get back here."

"Why?"

He huffed in resignation. "I brought up the subject of the future and the possibility of her traveling with me."

"And she hated that?"

"Hate would be a slight understatement." He raked his hands through his hair, frustration etched on every handsome feature. "It's like everything I do with her is wrong. How do you do it? How do you manage to get through to her so easily?"

"I mostly listen."

"You do more than that. But before we argued, it was great. We were checking out the scenery, talking about Nice, and having a fine time. Then I screwed it up and talked about the big, fat elephant in the room."

Which would be: what he was going to do with her.

Gussie's heart folded in half, feeling both their pain and aching to do something to fix it. "I'll go talk to her for you."

"Talk to her for *her*," he corrected, putting his lips on Gussie's forehead. "I need to leave anyway."

"Where are you going?"

"I got a text from the head of marketing at LaVie asking if I could come in for an emergency creative session before we finalize the location and shoot schedule. I said I would go. I'd love for you to come with me."

And she'd love to go, but… "I'll stay with Alex."

"They offered to send a sitter."

Gussie shook her head, listening to her head over her heart. "Bad idea right now."

He closed his eyes, pulling her closer. "I swear I didn't bring you to be her nanny."

"I know, but it would be wrong to leave her when she's feeling so tender."

"You know you're too good for me."

"I know," she teased.

"I'm serious." He gave her shoulders a squeeze. "And you can't solve my problems for me."

"Not long term. But I can help out while we're here. It's the least I can do for the vacation of my dreams."

He still looked torn, then he leaned closer and kissed her forehead again. "We're getting tangled up," he murmured, a note of something that hovered between fear and excitement in his deep voice.

"We'll get untangled." Eventually. There was no other way.

Chapter Fifteen

There was a metric buttload of money in water. That much was obvious to Tom as the driver steered the car up to one of the highest points in the rolling hills an hour north of Nice.

L'Eau LaVie S.A. was a village unto itself, with at least two dozen red-tile-topped buildings situated up and down the hillside with a grand castle-like headquarters at the peak.

The internationally recognized lime-green and Tiffany-blue LaVie logo was everywhere, including on the flag that fluttered atop a rounded tower where, Tom's driver informed him, the CEO had his offices.

But the marketing department was no less impressive, taking up a whole wing of the stone building, with a commanding view of the countryside even from the stone driveway where they finally stopped.

In an instant, a dark-haired woman in her fifties, sharply dressed in a black and white suit and sky-high heels, snapped her way across the stone, barely waiting for the driver to open Tom's door before she extended a hand demanding to be shaken.

"*Monsieur* DeMille! You have arrived!"

He greeted Suzette Voudreaux with a standard two-cheek air kiss, then followed her on a brief tour that included the history of LaVie bottled water. They finished in a massive conference room that had a glass wall that showed a breathtaking view of southern France as far as the eye could see.

But Tom was more interested in the opposite wall, which held a series of poster-size sketches that would be his working storyboard for the next few weeks of shooting. The room was nearly filled with a dozen or more advertising types, a mix of loose creative experts and uptight marketing machines.

For the next hour or so, he listened to all of them, appreciating how they made every effort to speak English for him, getting their ideas across until someone inevitably argued and a heated discussion broke out. After they finalized the shots and locations, a number of executives left, and a few more from casting came in with the head shots of models. Suzette led this session, showing him the selected faces, many of whom were familiar to him.

"So you're definitely using high-fashion editorial models," he mused, turning one of the eight-by-tens around and recognizing the woman as one he'd shot in Italy for *Marie Claire* last year, someone cold and self-absorbed who went by one name.

She had exaggerated features and cheekbones that could slice butter, so he could certainly see the appeal for the ad. All of the models were *Vogue* quality, in keeping with the fashion flair of the campaign. He could shoot the hell out of this, and they'd get every penny they were paying for.

But would the results push one drop of bottled water?

He looked at the next eight-by-ten, barely aware that he was shaking his head.

"*Monsieur* DeMille," Suzette said, "you do not like Johanna?"

"No, I like her fine, it's just that..."

"We can pick a different model. We wanted to use her in the Monaco campaign, but you'll recall we have six specific locations—beach, city, mountains, home, country, and village. All French settings, of course, and perhaps she would fit somewhere better."

She belonged in Monaco, actually. But not in an ad for water.

Thinking, he walked to the wall of images and eyed the sketch, imagining the actual photo. Suddenly, he pulled his phone out of his pocket and thumbed through the last shots on his camera, stopping at the picture of Gussie drinking LaVie on the plane.

Now *that* would sell water. He felt that shot right down to his bones.

"*Monsieur*?"

"Hear me out," he said slowly, turning to them. "How hard is it for a woman like that"—he pointed to the eight-by-ten glossy on the table—"to make a bottle of water look fashionable? Not difficult. That woman could make a Hefty bag look like a designer accessory."

He got enough frowns to know that most of them didn't know what a Hefty bag was. But not Suzette. Her eyes were narrowed and intent as she listened.

"I can give you the shots you want and make this campaign look like it got pulled out of the editorial pages of *Vogue*. I get that you're trying to do that, and it makes sense, and I'm the right photographer for you. But..."

For a long second, no one breathed.

"I might have a better idea," he finished. Slowly, he

walked back to Suzette and handed her his phone. "Maybe something more like this."

She stared at it for a second. "Excellent composition," she said. He didn't bother to say thank you. Composition was like breathing to him.

A man whose name Tom had forgotten looked over Suzette's shoulder. "Yes, nice. But she's not *extraordinaire*."

Oh, but she is. "She looks like a real woman," Tom replied. "Like a woman who buys water who thinks the water—not the photographer—can make her look extraordinary." He pointed to the poster. "Women need to feel like they have a chance to look like that, you know."

"Who is this model?" Suzette asked.

"She's not a model, she's my"—*soon-to-be lover*—"friend." God, that wasn't good enough for Gussie, but he let it go. "I brought her with me."

"Oh?" Suzette looked interested. Then, suddenly, she spun around and looked at the others seated at the long table, spewing a string of French that was mostly unintelligible to him. He did get a few words, like "*C'est incredible!*" and "*Une bonne idée!*"

And it *was* an incredibly good idea. Ordinary women turned extraordinary by the water, and the shot.

Suzette passed his phone to another woman so she could look.

"*Ecoutez.*" She snapped her fingers to demand they listen, and then nodded to Tom, silently apologizing for all the French. "I adore this idea of *Monsieur* DeMille's. We do not use famed supermodels. We use *la femme ordinaire* and make her look like a famed supermodel. There is no photographer more capable than this one to do that."

The rumble of both dissension and agreement traveled

around the table, along with his cell phone. Half of them loved the idea, half of them hated it. Arguments broke out in French, most of which he got the gist of because they were nothing if not vocal and emotional.

Suzette made an impassioned argument, mostly in French, so much of it wasn't clear. What was clear was the fact that her opinion carried quite a bit of weight at the company, and a few of the fence-sitters joined her side. Enough that she won a majority.

"It is decided then. We will shoot tomorrow with your friend."

"What?" How had he missed that? "No, no. She's not a model—"

"*Exactement*! No models. Not a single one. The entire campaign will be regular women who are made into supermodels with the right accessories, including, of course, a bottle of LaVie!"

"I think that's brilliant," Tom admitted. "But—"

"Of course you do, *monsieur*! It was your idea!"

That cracked the whole room up, and while they laughed, Tom imagined how this would go over with Gussie. Not well.

"But we will find models or even off-the-street French women who can model for us," he insisted. "Not my...Gussie."

"Gussie?" Suzette asked, lifting her voice and her lips in a smile. "Perfection!"

No, she's not. At least she didn't think she was. "She's actually a professional stylist," he said, speaking slowly to make sure he got that across. "Maybe she could help in that department, but she doesn't want to model."

"Merely to test the concept, of course," Suzette said, ignoring every word, as she did when she wanted to get her way. "If we agree it works, we will find women for the campaign who are not models."

One of the men spouted off something in French, too fast for Tom to follow, but Suzette agreed excitedly. "Christophe brings up a very good point, *monsieur*. This will be a fantastic campaign for…what do you call it? Public relations. We will address the media with the opportunity and test real women for the job."

"I like that," Tom agreed. "But how much time will it take?"

"Not long, a week or so. It may stretch your time in France, but we will accommodate you until, *non*?"

How would Gussie—and Alex—feel about an extra week in France?

"But for tomorrow, you will bring your friend," Suzette said. "And we will use her to test against the professional and make our final decision, weighing time and cost."

"What if she doesn't want to do it?"

"It's a test!" She waved her hand as if anyone would love the opportunity. "You convince her. I'm sure you can."

But he wasn't sure of that at all.

"Why are you putting a hat on?" Alex stood outside Gussie's room, stuffing a towel into a beach bag.

"'Cause we're going to the beach with the neighbors." Gussie had been relieved and happy when Anne Stone and her daughter, Lizzie, knocked on the door a few minutes earlier and invited them to join them for an afternoon on the Promenade. Gussie hadn't slept enough to have the energy for sightseeing and really didn't want to explore

Nice without Tom, who seemed to know the city so well.

A day at the shore was exactly what she needed—along with a hat.

"I thought you weren't going to, you know, cover up? I thought the whole idea of you coming to France without your wigs and stuff was to be free."

"Alex, ninety percent of the women you'll see at the beach will be wearing hats, I'm certain of that. Tops? I'm not so certain."

Alex clutched her bright blue bikini top that covered very small preteen breasts. "I'm keeping mine on."

"Good call, since your uncle would probably kill me if you decided to join the French in their toplessness."

"What about you?"

"I'm going to scream American and stay dressed. My guess is Anne will do the same." She adjusted the brim of her baseball cap, her ponytail pulled through the opening in the back. She tapped the hat where it covered her scar. "And 'dressed' includes protecting my delicate skin."

Alex eyed her suspiciously. "That's not why you're wearing that hat," she said.

"Well, why I'm wearing it is irrelevant. I'm wearing it." Because she sure as hell didn't want Anne staring at her scar or have one of her kids say, "Eww," and point at it. Not that she hadn't endured that before, but—

"What happened to the freecation?" Alex asked.

Gussie propped her hands on her hips and angled her head, hat and all. "Not to put too fine a point on it or anything, but exactly whose side are you on?"

"Are there sides?"

Good question. "Well, I have agreed, at your uncle's urging, to try to see what life is like if I don't cover my head with wigs and wear a lot of makeup and give in to"—

insecurities—"my need to cover up. But I thought you and I were, you know, like…friends."

"Aren't you friends with him, too?"

Friends with benefits. Oh, would she have to explain that to Alex, too? "Let's go. Anne's waiting, and I'm sure her kids are anxious to get to the beach."

Alex headed down the hall, with Gussie behind her doing a mental inventory of what she thought they might need. Sunscreen, towels, water, money—

She walked right into Alex, who'd stopped dead in her tracks. "I just figured something out," Alex said. "It makes perfect sense."

"What?"

She turned around, her brown eyes wide, as though she'd made a huge discovery. "He's kind of, what's the word, *obsessed* with the idea of freedom. Have you ever noticed?"

"I have noticed." She managed to keep the sarcasm out of her voice, because how could you not be around Tom for any amount of time and not figure that out?

"And he wants you to feel that way," Alex said.

Gussie nodded. "Yes, and I do feel free when my head's not stuffed into a wig, but I don't think they are the same kind of freedoms. He likes the ability to move around the world unencumbered, and I just want the wind in my hair."

"So, Gussie." She struggled for a minute with her thoughts, and Gussie had to rein in the desire to reach out to help her. "How can I possibly fit into his life?"

And she had no answer for that. "You might not fit, not the way you expect to."

"Then what am I going to do?"

Of course she was terrified. Writhing with her own worry of what her life would look like without her mother.

Gussie touched Alex's cheek. "You have to get used to being outside your comfort zone."

Alex gave her a questioning look, which Gussie answered by reaching up to the brim of her hat. "And if you can do it, so can I." She dragged her ponytail back through the opening in the back and stuffed the cap in her bag.

Alex's smile was a little shaky. "Sometimes you really remind me of my mom," she said quietly.

Gussie inhaled lightly, the compliment stealing her breath. "Because you win the arguments?"

"Because you totally get me."

Something folded over Gussie's heart, making it hurt a little. "That's really sweet, Alex. I'm touched."

"She was the most incredibly hopeful person," Alex continued. "The glass wasn't half full, it was half full of the best-tasting drink ever and nobody had ever had anything so delicious."

Gussie laughed, getting a great image of Ruthie. "I'm not that optimistic."

"But you're, you know, positive. And he's..." She rolled her eyes. "He couldn't hate me any more if he tried."

"Alex!" Gussie reached out. "He doesn't hate you. He cares very much for you."

"He doesn't act like it."

"He doesn't *know* how to act," Gussie said, the defense making her voice rise. "He's totally in over his head with a twelve-year-old girl."

"Well, good thing you're here."

She pulled Alex closer. "It sure is."

"Are you ready?" A loud rap accompanied the young girl's voice outside.

Gussie gave Alex a soft push toward the door. "Let's go play with our new friends." She leaned a little closer.

"And don't you dare tell me you don't think Eddie is cute."

Alex threw a look over her shoulder, her face deepening in color.

"Ha! Knew it." Gussie tapped her back. "Your secret's safe with me. But if I decide to put this hat on and you make a fuss, I might spill the beans."

"You can wear the hat if you need to." Alex opened the door to greet Anne, Eddie, and Lizzie, all decked out for the beach. The kids went ahead—well, the girls went ahead, as Alex was dragged off by a very enthusiastic Lizzie. Eddie followed a few steps behind, too cool to dart along with the girls, while Anne and Gussie brought up the rear, chatting as they made their way down the stairs into the vibrant streets of Nice.

There was noise and color, vendors and cars, cafés and boutiques, and so much sunshine that Gussie couldn't help smiling as they trekked along side streets and worked their way to the massive crescent-shaped walkway that followed the beach from one end of the bay to the other.

Nearly three lanes of pedestrian traffic hummed along the Promenade des Anglais, a French-flavored boardwalk that Lizzie happily informed them had been named for the many English people who took their holiday in Nice for centuries.

They found empty chairs along the railing overlooking the beach, perfect for relaxing, sunning, and people watching. But that lasted about five minutes with the kids, who wanted to get on the sand—which was far rockier than any in Florida—and into the water.

Gussie and Anne settled in their high-back chairs with cold bottles of LaVie to keep an eye on the kids who headed to the shore. The companionship was instant and smooth, easing the sting of not seeing Ari or Willow after their many hours of working and hanging out together.

"Okay, so forgive me if I'm butting in where I shouldn't," Anne said a few minutes after they were alone. "But I'm not sure I quite understand this bit of a triangle. Alex is not your daughter, she's that gentleman's niece, but you are not his wife or girlfriend. Yet the three of you are on holiday together." She tipped her sunglasses down and peered over the rim. "It's quite confusing in a typical American way."

Gussie laughed. "It's an unconventional little gathering, I'll give you that. I recently met Tom, and he had to come here on business. About a month ago, he was named Alex's guardian when her mother passed away."

Anne's face fell in sorrow. "Oh, I'm so sorry. What a tragedy for her. Where's her father?"

"It *is* a tragedy. I didn't know her mother, but it seems they were very close. I have no idea about the father, but he appears to be entirely out of the picture since a long-ago divorce. Alex is wrecked, of course, so when the opportunity came up for her uncle to take this assignment, it seemed like a good way to give her a change of scenery and possibly lift her spirits." She peered at the threesome, the dynamic of growing friendship between the two girls obvious even from a distance. Then the blond boy said something, and Alex laughed, picking up a shell or stone to throw it into the water. "I think it's working," she added. "It's really nice to see her have fun with other kids."

"I may have to kidnap her, then, because my two are about to kill each other, and they need a distraction and another person to be a referee. Lizzie, especially, is aching for her school chums this summer, so I'm happy to have you next door, but terribly sorry for little Alex."

"The whole trip is all due to these people." Gussie held up her bottle of LaVie, the green and blue label matching the sun and sky around them. "They are paying for everything."

"Really? Jolly good of them." Anne used her bottle to

toast. "And what shall you be doing while you're in Nice?"

"Maybe a little shopping for my wedding clients. I work as a stylist for my destination-wedding company back in Florida."

"Oh, really?" Anne made a face. "Lots of bridezillas and way too much saccharine for my taste."

Gussie acknowledged both with a nod. "The brides can be, you know, emotional. But for the most part, it's fun. And I don't mind the saccharine. Nothing like a supersweet wedding to renew your faith in romance."

Anne curled her lip. "Nothing can renew my faith in romance after my divorce."

"Oh, a bad one?"

"Bloody brutal would be more like it. Also, acrimonious, hateful, nasty, and expensive would be perfect descriptions. At least the expensive part is his problem, and I get to spend the summer in France."

"Oh, I'm sorry about that. The kids seem to be handling it well."

Anne sipped her water, studying the children in the distance. "Lizzie is strong and flexible, but Eddie has retreated so much. He's moody and fluctuates between tears and swearing."

"He is a thirteen-year-old boy, and I suppose the raging hormones are difficult enough."

"Speaking of hormones, look." She tipped her bottle toward the kids, and Gussie caught a moment of intense conversation between Eddie and Alex. "Sweet."

"Says the woman who moments ago decried romance in any way, shape, or form."

Anne hooted. "Touché, luv." She pushed her sunglasses back over her curls, letting her eyes sparkle. "I like you, you know that?"

"And here I've been told the English are so reserved." Gussie winked.

"Oh, I can keep my upper lip stiff when I have to, if that's what you mean. But here in France? I like to pretend I'm a different person."

"Funny, that's kind of why I'm here, too."

"Really? Well, let's do this. Let's keep our old selves at home, and you and I can be friends with the new selves. You can call me Annie and pretend I really know how to paint and that my husband leaving me for a twentysomthing woman he met on Twitter hasn't turned me into a bitter, hissing crone. No, I'm carefree and happy."

Gussie gave her a knuckle tap. "Carefree Annie you are."

"And you?"

"I'm Gussie on any continent, but here, I'm going to be...natural. No pretenses, no hiding, no wishing I were"— Different. Better. Unscarred—"more comfortable in my own skin."

"Your skin looks comfortable to me," she shot back.

"You're very sweet," Gussie said. "And happy. And unjaded. And what else did you say you wanted to be?"

"An amazing painter."

"Michel*annie*gelo, they call you."

Anne—*Annie*—giggled. "Right you are." She put her head back and closed her eyes. "I want to remember this lovely moment next winter when I'm freezing in London and the kids are spending the weekend with Twatter."

Gussie snorted at the name. "That reminds me." She reached into her bag. "I need pictures."

When she took out her phone, she saw a text from Tom that she'd missed. Tapping it, she angled the screen to read the words.

Any chance we can get some alone time tonight?

"Oh…"

Annie looked sharply at her. "Everything okay?"

Gussie stared at the words, but with the reflection of the light on the screen, she really only saw her own face and couldn't help noticing the smile working on her lips. "Yes, I got a text from Tom."

Annie looked hard at her. "Just a friend, is he?"

"A friend with some unexpected benefits."

Her eyebrow launched north. "He's not married?" she demanded.

"Oh, God, no. He can't commit to life with a houseplant let alone a wife. Look up Single Until He Dies in the dictionary, and you'll see a nice picture of him."

She grinned and inched closer, pretending to look at the phone. "So what benefits is he asking for?"

"Time alone tonight."

Annie nodded and pointed toward the kids racing around as if they were playing tag. They were too far away for their laughter to carry, but it was clear they were having fun.

"Then text him back and tell him Alex is having dinner with us tonight."

"Really?"

"Unless you'd rather not have a romantic dinner in Nice with a handsome man offering, uh, what did you call it? Benefits?" Annie grinned. "And who knows? It might turn into a sleepover."

"For Alex or me?" Gussie asked with a laugh.

"Well, you were the one who came here to get comfortable in your own skin. You might start by showing him some."

She might.

Chapter Sixteen

"You want to know the truth?" Gussie asked, sliding her fork tines through the delicate whipped cream and chocolate sauce of a profiterole.

Across from her, Tom sat with his elbows on the table, his chin resting on his knuckles, his gaze where it had been the whole meal—firmly on her. He'd chosen a secluded restaurant in Old Town on the second floor of a house, only four tables in the whole place, and theirs was on the open balcony, the sights and sounds of Vieux Nice surrounding them as they enjoyed an insanely delicious meal. And company that equaled it.

"Always and only the truth," he said, the answer making her eyes glint like emeralds in the reflection of a full moon and flickering candlelight.

"This has been one of the best days of my life."

He lifted his brows, surprised. "But I didn't spend that much of it with you."

She laughed. "What an ego. We've been together for hours."

"Seems like minutes."

She pointed her fork at him. "Dude, the flirting is heavy. But don't stop. I like it."

He crossed his arms and leaned even closer. The table was small enough that a few more inches and he could kiss her. "Tell me why this day was so wonderful." Because, if he went ahead and even suggested what he'd been discussing in the meeting this afternoon, he had a feeling her wonderful day would head south in a hurry.

"It started at sunrise." She gave him a slow, sexy smile that reached right down to his gut and twisted everything into a knot.

"That was a nice sunrise," he agreed.

"The colors and all."

"And all."

She lifted a bite of profiterole to her lips, flicking whipped cream with her tongue while staring at him.

"Speaking of heavy flirting," he teased.

She looked down, her lashes spreading against her cheekbones. "Hey," he said, tapping her arm. "You cheated. You have mascara on."

"That's all. Look." She crinkled her nose. "You can even see my freckles."

"And they are so, so pretty." In fact, freckles would be gorgeous in the shot he had in mind. Somehow, in between "this is the dumbest idea ever" and "I'll talk to her tonight," Tom had come around to Suzette's way of thinking. But would Gussie? Even for a test shot?

For the first time since he'd met her, Gussie didn't roll her eyes or tsk or wave off his compliment. Instead, she smiled her thanks. "You want to know why else it was a great day?"

"You went to the beach?"

"Yes, and I made a new friend, Annie."

"Love that she has kids Alex's age," he said. "Alex didn't even seem the least bit bothered that we were going out."

"Because she likes that boy."

"What?" He practically shot forward. "He's a child. *She's* a child."

"Thirteen—or almost thirteen—is not a child. And you, my friend, are starting to sound like a...*guardian*."

"Which I happen to be. Do I have to get LaVie to hire bodyguards?"

Gussie laughed. "They'll be under the supervision of Annie or me, so keep the bullet catchers away. She's having a little summer adventure, Tom. What better way to help her to heal from the hurt of a lifetime than to make new friends? Even of the opposite gender."

Of course she was right. And he sounded like some kind of ogre, not wanting the girl to make a new friend just because that friend was a boy.

"You know what I think?" Gussie asked gently. "I think you are much more protective, caring, and family-oriented than you let on."

Every word stung, because...well, because she didn't know the truth. Without answering, he looked down at the words on his arm, the constant reminder.

Πάντα μόνος.

He would never again be protective, caring, or family-oriented.

She slid her hand over his arm, trailing her finger over the tattoo as if she'd followed his gaze or his thoughts.

"Where did you get this?" she asked.

"The Blood Brothers tattoo parlor in Cyprus," he replied without hesitation, remembering the night all too well.

"What happened?"

He swallowed, and she added some pressure on his arm.

"What was her name, Tom?"

God, was he that transparent? When he tried so hard not

to be? "Her name was Sophia, which is surprisingly simple, I guess."

"What's simple? The name or the fact that the declaration of independence on your arm was caused by a woman?"

"Both, I guess, but I meant the name. Nothing exotic or unusual."

"So, let me guess. She tried to rope and tie you down and get a binding contract from the justice of the peace?"

Each word twisted the knife in his heart a little bit more. "Something like that." Let her think Sophia had wanted to rope and tie him down, and it had been his inability to commit that ended…everything.

"And the tattoo? A reminder never to get that close to disaster again?"

"Precisely," he confirmed. The truth bubbled up, but he didn't want to let it out. She'd be sympathetic and understanding. She'd share his pain and ask poignant questions. She'd tell him it wasn't his fault and life was tough and maybe he'd find someone again.

She'd try to heal a wound that he didn't want to heal.

"It's like I'm an open book or something," he said, going for as light as he could make the dark topic.

"Well, your story *is* written all over you."

Not the full story. Not by a long shot. "Are you done?" he asked, glancing at the remains of profiterole.

"Done talking about Sophia or done with dessert?"

He pushed back, the check paid long ago. "I'm done with both," he said, getting a slightly surprised look for his gruffness and regretting it immediately. "Let's go walk through Old Town."

She hesitated for a moment as he stood, so he held his hand out to her. "I want to show you my favorite alley."

"Your favorite alley?" Holding his hand, she stood

slowly. "Who even has one of those? Is it perfect for taking pictures?"

"It's perfect for kissing." And forgetting old aches. "Come on." He slid his arm around her and ushered her out, stopping to thank the owner and chef again, then stepping out into the dim and narrow cobblestone street.

"This way." He guided her down the next side street, past a café and dimly lit art gallery. "Off Rue Droite."

Like all the streets in Vieux Nice, the main drag had no vehicles but plenty of pedestrians, all vying for space in the narrow maze that made up the small section in the southeast corner of the city. They were forced to walk arm in arm, and he tucked Gussie close into his side and stayed with the foot traffic.

They stopped to listen to a violinist on the corner, then wandered among the street vendors selling scarves and flowers and hand-painted porcelain.

"Souvenir?" he offered, picking up a heart-shaped box with the words *Vieux Nice* painted on the top.

She took it, opening the tiny latch to reveal a mother-of-pearl inlay. "Pretty," she said. "I bet Alex would like this."

A little guilt pinged, since he hadn't thought of that. "Then I'll get two, one for each of you."

He paid the vendor, who wrapped each box in tissue and slipped them into a tiny bag.

"Thank you," Gussie said, smiling up at him. "Not necessary to butter me up, since I'm already on my way to the kissing alley." She leaned into him, purposely coy. "Aren't we?"

"We are." He turned her around one corner, past another café, then along the side of a very ornate but small church, and into the alley.

He slowed their step and leaned her against a cool stone

wall, the narrow alley barely big enough for both of them.

Looking up at him, she let her lips relax, ready for a kiss. But he looked at her, studying her face in the moonlight and shadows. "Damn, I want to take a picture of you as much as I want to kiss you."

"Don't," she ordered. "Kiss."

"I do have my phone."

She curled her hand around his neck and pulled his head to her. "Keep it in your pocket, big boy."

He captured her lips under his, holding her face in his hands, angling her to get the maximum amount of her mouth against his.

She leaned into him, opening her lips to let their tongues tangle, threading his hair in her fingers. With an easy arch of her back, her breasts pressed against his shirt, sending the first hot rush of blood south in his body, starting a war with his head and his hard-on.

Did he need to tell her everything about his past before they slept together?

Son of a *bitch*. He knew the answer to that, and hated it.

"Hey." She dragged her hands over his shoulders, squeezing gently. "You're thinking about something." She squinted, playful but still determined. "Sophia?"

The name—just the name—sliced through him.

"It's tough to explain." A miserable story with a sad ending and a broken man. Who'd want to fall into bed with that?

She drew her brows in a frown. "That sounds serious."

And he wasn't going there now. So he'd tell her about the LaVie deal and let her think that's what troubled him: her fury over decisions made without her input this afternoon.

So much easier than talking about his past and his pain.

195

"It is serious." He stroked her hair, sliding it behind her ear. "Can you handle serious?"

"Maybe. Probably. Did the kissing alley just become the confession alley?"

He didn't answer, but pulled her into him, dropping his forehead against hers. "I need to tell you something, but I'm not sure."

"Not sure of what?"

"Of whether I want everything to change. It might guarantee that you won't come to my bed at midnight, like I'd hoped."

She fought a smile. "Is that what you hoped?"

"Yes."

The single syllable elicited a tiny intake of breath from her. "Oh, well. What are you going to tell me then that could change that?"

"I want you to let me take your picture—"

"What?" She laughed. "In bed at midnight? Is that what you're into?"

"No, tomorrow in broad daylight. As one of the models in the LaVie campaign."

Total shock, mild confusion, and something that might have been amusement flickered in her eyes. "Excuse me?"

"It's not the real shoot," he said quickly. "It's a test. They want to test using non-models and regular women, like you. I showed them that picture on my phone—"

"You *did*?"

"—and the client went crazy, and they all decided we needed to try it, and since we have the shoot and equipment set up for tomorrow, we're going to test a model and a non-model, who would be you."

She opened her mouth, then shut it again, a move he was

used to by now. Then she closed her eyes, dropped her head against his chest, and started laughing.

"Gussie?"

She chuckled harder, finally lifting her face to show tears of mirth in her eyes.

"Did you hear me?" he asked. "Do you understand what I'm asking?"

"Yes, I heard you. No, I don't understand."

"Then why are you laughing?"

He braced for the inevitable response. *No way! Are you out of your mind? I told you I don't like my picture taken!*

She angled her head with a great big smile. "Okay."

"*Okay?*"

"Yes," she laughed. "I'll do it. Freecation means free of everything, including my stupid hang-ups about having my picture taken. It might be fun."

Oh, God, why had he doubted her? "It will be fun," he assured her. "Because everything with you is fun."

Her eyes sparkled at the compliment, then that light faded. "Now that sounded serious again. Like it's killing you that you have fun with me. Why?"

Because he wasn't going to fall for her. He couldn't. He wouldn't. He *wasn't.*

"Nothing's killing me except the fact that we have to walk all the way home and figure out a way to sneak into my room without Alex knowing so that I can..." He lifted her face and looked at her.

"So that you can what?" she urged.

Not fall for her.

But it might be too late.

"Take a guess, Pink."

Alex stared into the bathroom mirror, a little shocked at how pale her face was even after a day in the sun, how big her eyes looked, how really *young* she looked at that moment. Too young? No, not too young for this. But way, way too alone.

Momma always said it would happen when you least expect it, when you're not even thinking about it, the whole thing would catch you by surprise. Well, this certainly had *not* been something she'd been expecting when she came to France.

Still, it happened, and now she had to figure out what the heck to do about it. Tell Miss Annie? No, Alex would die of embarrassment. Lizzie? She might be too young to understand. Maybe her mom hadn't told her all about it yet.

She gripped the sink and looked at her reflection, seeing her mother's eyes and not her own. God, she'd give anything, anything in the world, to walk out of this bathroom and into Momma's arms and say, "Guess what happened?"

She'd probably want to eat ice cream, because Ruthie Whitman had celebrated all things with ice cream. She closed her eyes, tears threatening at the thought.

"Alex?" Miss Annie tapped on the bathroom door. "Gussie texted that they're almost back from dinner. Do you want to call her and tell her you're spending the night with us?"

No way she was spending the night now. Gussie wasn't Momma, but she was the next best thing. She opened the door slowly and gave Miss Annie a smile, wondering if anything was obvious.

"Are you okay, honey?" Guess it was obvious.

"I'm just, you know…" *Missing my mother.*

"Homesick?"

"A little, so I don't think I'll stay tonight."

"What?" Lizzie came shooting out from around the corner, her freckles bright with the day's sunburn. "Eddie set up that Monopoly game Mum found in the closet. You have to stay." Her voice grew whiny, and instantly Miss Annie had her arm around her daughter. "You're tired, darling, and so is Alex. She has real jet lag from America."

"Are you leaving?" Eddie came into the hallway then, a lock of his blond hair falling over his brow, making him so cute Alex had to squeeze her hands into fists.

She nodded and nearly melted when he smiled.

"So, we'll see you tomorrow then, right?" He seemed eager and confident at the same time, like he had all day.

"Prob'ly," she said.

"Oh, I think I hear them now," Annie said, turning away to head to the front door. "Come along, Alex."

Lizzie threw her arms around Alex's head, her constant enthusiasm wearing a little thin right then.

"Until tomorrow, bestie!"

Alex laughed and looked past Lizzie's head to meet Eddie's gaze. His lip curled in a half smile, like they were sharing an inside joke about Lizzie's over-the-topness. "Tomorrow," he mouthed, making Alex's stomach flip like it did at the top loop on the Hulk at Universal Studios.

"I have to go," Alex said, disconnecting from Lizzie's tight squeeze. She hustled out to the living room, where Miss Annie stood at the door talking to Gussie and Uncle Tommy. As soon as Alex walked up, Annie stopped talking. Could she *know*? Could she be telling them? Oh, God, she'd die if her uncle knew.

"Oh, here she is now," Miss Annie said, stepping aside to make room for Alex.

Gussie and Uncle Tommy stood in the hallway, waiting for her. For one flash of a second, Alex felt like they were her parents, who'd come to pick her up at a friend's house. A longing so real and powerful nearly strangled her. *If only.*

"Hey, Alex." Her uncle's smile was easy and, at least now, seemed real. "Did you have fun?"

Like a dad would ask. But he wasn't her dad, and he never would be.

"Yeah." She glanced at Gussie, trying to silently communicate her desperation with her eyes. "Let's just...go."

While they said a quick round of good nights and thanks, Alex slipped out and got next to Gussie, quietly tugging her arm toward the apartment, just as she would have if her mother had been there.

Thank God, Gussie immediately got the message, speeding things along and heading toward their apartment, giving Alex a closer examination while they waited for Uncle Tommy to get the key and unlock the door.

"I need to talk to you," Alex mouthed behind him, darting her eyes toward the hall to their rooms, hoping that communicated that the talk had to be *alone.*

Gussie nodded and patted Alex's arm, which only made the lump in Alex's throat grow about six inches bigger. Why couldn't this be Momma? *Why?*

"I'm going to help Alex get ready for bed," Gussie said quickly, earning a surprised look from Alex's uncle. Who could blame him? She was long past the age of needing to be tucked in. In fact...

Remembering what she had to tell Gussie, Alex hoped that he bought it.

"I'm going to have a nightcap on the balcony," he said. "If you want to find me later." They shared a flash of a smile, and everything became instantly clear to Alex.

Maybe she *should* have stayed overnight with Lizzie. But no, she couldn't. Not now.

With Uncle Tommy gone, Gussie led them both into Alex's room, quietly closing the door, then giving her an expectant look.

"What happened?" she asked.

Alex's knees almost buckled. She so *got it*. She got it, and that was like being handed a pile of gold. Emotion welled up and choked her again, but this time, Alex didn't fight the sob that threatened. She was so grateful to have Gussie. What would she have done if this had happened and she'd had no one to tell?

Gussie launched forward to hold her. "Alex, what's the matter? Why are you crying?"

Because I miss my mother! She tamped down the obvious answer and hoped Gussie understood. "I'm b-b-bleeding."

Gussie gasped, inching back to search her face and body. "Where? What happened? Are you..." Her words trailed off as she finally read Alex's look.

Just to make sure it was clear, Alex pointed a finger...down there.

"Ohhh." Gussie dragged out the word, then her eyes widened. "First time?"

Alex nodded, still working not to cry.

"You know about this, right?" Gussie asked.

"Oh, yeah, my mom told me everything. I know what it is, but..."

"But it's still a shocker the first time."

Alex exhaled with relief. "It's just so...*red*."

Gussie smiled, taking Alex's hands. "Do you have anything?"

She shook her head. "I rolled up some toilet paper, but…" A little panic rose. "What do I do? You're not going to tell my uncle, are you?"

"God, no." She started to step away with a look of determination, then stopped, putting her hands on Alex's shoulders and slowly guiding her to the bed. "This must be hard for you. First time, and you're a million miles from home and your…your mom's not here."

There went the waterworks again. "Yeah," she admitted. "I really…"

"I know you miss her," Gussie finished, and her own voice hitched. And her eyes misted up, which only made Alex want to cry more. "Oh, you poor thing." Gussie pulled her all the way into a hug, which was nothing like Lizzie's but everything like Momma's. Warm and tight and utterly secure.

"I thought I wet my pants laughing," she admitted. "But then I went to the bathroom and…"

"Well, at least you were having a good time."

Alex felt a smile pull. "I was flirting with Eddie Stone."

"Ah." Gussie's eyes twinkled. "The cute boy."

"Yeah, but I had to get out of there."

"Of course you did. Now let me see what I have for you in my room." Gussie got up, but before she left, she leaned over and kissed Alex on the head. "I think I'm supposed to say something about how you're a woman now and maybe some drivel about the fact that you can have babies, but if you even think about that, I'll have to kill you."

Which meant she cared. Alex almost collapsed in half at the thought. While Gussie disappeared across the hall, Alex pulled up her knees and gave herself a little hug. This was going to be fine, even without Momma. This life was going to happen, without Momma, and there was nothing she could do to change that.

For the first time, that thought didn't make her want to tear her hair out and scream in misery. For the first time since Momma died, a spark of...of something...flickered in her heart. Hope? Maybe that was it. Gussie gave her hope that life could be near normal someday.

Gussie breezed back into the room, carrying two different pink and blue boxes. "I have options," she announced. "We can start with one and work our way up to the other. Tomorrow, I'll sneak out and get you something different if this isn't comfortable or working. Oh, that reminds me. Your uncle signed me up to be a model in his campaign."

Alex took the boxes, but her physical predicament was suddenly forgotten. "*Huh?*"

Gussie laughed. "I know, right? Listen, you go do what you need to do. And I'm going to tell him—"

"No!"

She grinned. "That I'm not going to stay up any longer."

"It's okay."

Gussie reached to stroke Alex's hair. "Would you feel more comfortable if I hung out in here until you fall asleep? Would that make you feel better?"

For a second, Alex couldn't breathe. She closed her eyes and put her head down and simply couldn't breathe. It was stupid that she wanted to say yes. Immature and babyish. It was her period, for crying out loud. Everyone knew it was coming sooner or later.

"Alex?"

"Yeah, I would." The words were rough on her throat and pride, but she said them anyway.

"Oh, honey." Gussie folded right down on her knees and

wrapped both arms around Alex's waist. "Don't worry. You're not alone in this."

Alex nodded and put her cheek on Gussie's head, giving back the embrace. Without thinking, Alex hugged hard, like she would have if it were her own mother. As she stroked Gussie's head, her fingers suddenly hit the smooth skin where most people had hair.

"Did you say you're going to model for the water ad?" The question popped out so fast, Alex couldn't stop it. And immediately regretted that. They both knew why she sounded surprised.

But Gussie laughed. "I'm praying for a hat, a wig, or really good Photoshop. And I'm not actually going to model, just be a test subject for them."

"It's so cool that you would do that."

"Cool or crazy. Will you come along or do you want to stay and flirt with British Boy?"

She giggled. "I want to come."

"All right, I'll go tell your uncle and then I'll be back. You go take care of things and don't be afraid. Of anything."

For the first time in a long time, she wasn't. "'Kay."

When she left, Alex stayed on the bed, staring at the boxes that seemed so foreign in her hand, but familiar, too. Her mom had used this brand.

"Momma," she whispered, digging her nail into the cardboard box. "Thank you for sending her."

Chapter Seventeen

They ended up in Cannes after a forty-five-minute limo ride through the Riviera, which would have been enough of a thrill, but the final destination was a high-end studio where movies and commercials were made, including promotions for the famous film festival. So Tom told them to expect a top-of-the-line crew and stylists, all connected to a huge set that took up two picturesque city blocks.

Tom disappeared minutes after they arrived, and Gussie and Alex were swept into a waiting room that looked down over the wide boulevard where they'd be shooting.

While they waited, Alex munched on the over-the-top buffet, chatting with Gussie and pressing her face against the window to see the goings-on below. Gussie tried not to chew her lip while she tried to figure out how she'd gotten herself into this particular predicament. It was supposed to be liberating and exhilarating and once-in-a-lifetimey.

Instead, she felt raw and terrified, every flaw exposed.

"Holy crap, she must be the professional model."

Gussie joined Alex to get a look. Oh, yes. The model. Of course she was a tall, stunning, jaw-dropper of a blonde with the longest legs Gussie had ever seen climbing out of a limo.

A glamazon of pure perfection with a mane of whiskey-gold hair, wicked-sharp cheekbones, and a body that made couture designers weep with joy.

"Her name's Johanna Holt," Alex said. "I heard one of those guys with the headsets who brought us up here call her your competition."

Gussie rolled her eyes. "Like that's a fair match."

Alex scowled. "You're not going to back out, are you, Gussie? I'd hate that."

She could hear the honesty in the girl's voice and knew if she changed her mind, then she'd somehow let Alex down. Not to mention Tom.

"I'm not," she promised. "But I still don't know why one of the other three billion women in the world who aren't models couldn't do this."

"But you represent *la femme ordinaire*!" She grinned at Alex's perfect imitation of Madame Suzette.

"*Viva l'ordinaire!*" Gussie joked, giving her knuckles.

"Look at all those people she brought." Alex pointed back to the model, who glided across the street trailed by three men, one carting garment bags, one rolling an oversize makeup case, and the other a beefy bruiser who was no doubt carrying a Glock.

"Bodyguard," Gussie murmured.

Alex turned, her eyes wide and jaw loose. "No way. She gets a bodyguard to come to her shoot?"

"Well, I get you."

That made Alex laugh while they watched more people scamper around Johanna like she was royalty. The last group to arrive on the scene included Tom, who was on the phone, camera around his neck, a few hangers-on following him.

He greeted Johanna with a warm smile and a two-sided Euro air kiss.

"Don't be jealous," Alex said.

Gussie snorted. "Why would I be jealous?"

"Because you like him."

"One of us has to."

"*Mademoiselle* McBain?" The door popped open, and their escort, a young man wearing a headset, came into the room. "*Je regret* the delay. *Mademoiselle* Holt was slightly delayed. Can you come to hair and makeup now, *s'il vous plait*?" He stepped away from the door and started speaking in French into a microphone.

"Hair and makeup are my favorite words," Gussie quipped. But this time? Not so much.

"C'mon," Alex whispered, nudging her a little, probably sensing Gussie's hesitation. "You can do this."

Gussie shot her a look of gratitude.

"It's your birthday and your freecation," Alex added.

"How do you know it's my birthday?" Gussie asked, shocked by the revelation.

"You told me the day I met you that you were born on August first. And I know you're not forty."

Gussie laughed, shaking her head, oddly touched.

"I told my uncle. Didn't he say happy birthday yet?"

"No, but he's a little preoccupied."

"He will." Alex sounded so certain, it was kind of endearing.

The French escort made his impatience known with a dramatic clearing of his throat. "Jean Claude is waiting."

Gussie made a quick face at Alex, who giggled some more.

"Then by all means," Gussie said, nudging Alex ahead, "let's get to my personal idea of…" *Hell.*

But she didn't want to reveal that to Alex. Being camera shy and insecure were such unattractive traits and not something she'd like to model for this impressionable young girl. On the contrary, she longed to show Alex the importance of strength, confidence, and fearlessness. Conquering her own fears was a great way to do that. Agonizing, but great.

"Your personal idea of what?" Alex prompted.

"Challenge," she said, reaching for Alex's hand. "Come on, I need moral support."

She squeezed her fingers around Gussie's. "You got it."

They followed their escort to another floor into a styling salon, where he directed Gussie to a makeup chair. Alex took the empty one next to her.

Another man came in seconds later, clapping his hands like a schoolteacher. "The world's greatest beauty specialist has arrived," he announced in a heavy French accent. "I am Jean Claude. And you must be my test *du jour*."

Might as well get right out there and be the ugly American. Literally. "Brace yourself, *monsieur*. I'm opinionated and"—she lifted her ponytail—"I'm partially bald."

"I am more bald, *mademoiselle*." He rubbed his own hairless head and adjusted hipster-style black-rimmed glasses to get a better look at her scar, then gently pulled her hair out of the silky tieback. Gussie watched his expression in the mirror, waiting for the usual sympathy or even disgust.

He frowned, gnawing on his lip, angling his head from one side to the other, studying her scar like it was a work of art he couldn't quite understand.

"Mmm." He looked into the mirror to meet her eyes. "May I?" He fluttered his fingers.

"You may."

He started to lift and finger-comb her hair, which was

208

thick enough in the front and sides that from this angle, she looked perfectly normal.

"I know several styles that can almost completely cover it," she said. "If you just—"

"*Non!*" He barked the word, startling her. Then he broke into a grin. "We can use it."

Use it? "Um, don't you want a wig? I can't wear extensions because—"

"Marie!" He clapped his hands as he called the name, and instantly an assistant appeared. Then he spewed a string of incomprehensible French.

Marie nodded. "*Et* Suzette?" she asked.

"*Oui, oui, oui!*" He clapped again, dismissing her. "We do makeup first."

"And then…"

He glared at her like she was a disobedient child. "Makeup first." More clapping. More assistants appeared, one carrying a load of color palettes, the other rolling out a satin bag of makeup brushes with the same flair as a chef presenting his cutlery.

"What is all this stuff?" Alex whispered as the others chattered in French.

"Other than heavenly?" Gussie asked. "Oh, Alex, those are Kevyn Aucoin brushes that retail for about a hundred apiece."

No less than three artists went to work with those pricey brushes on Gussie's face, speaking rapid French with no regard for the fact that she didn't understand them.

"You have perfect skin," Jean Claude said, brushing Gussie's cheek. "Marie says it is like a baby's ass."

Alex snorted.

"And your bow!" He tapped her upper lip. "Deep and delicious. Made for kissing."

This time, Alex cleared her throat in her own distinct *ahem*.

"But it is your lovely symmetry that makes you a true beauty, *cherie*." He stroked her face from cheekbone to cheekbone. "You have been kissed by the beauty gods."

And here she thought she'd been *dissed* by them.

When they finished, Gussie opened her eyes and blinked, stunned at the results. For her, makeup was extreme or nothing, but this was subtle, warm, and beautiful. Before she could comment, the door opened, and six more people crammed into the room, led by the stately LaVie executive Suzette, who was obviously calling the shots today.

French volleyed back and forth, the conversation loud and bubbling with constant interruptions, with all attention riveted to her scar.

Due to the perfectly applied foundation, Gussie couldn't see her face flush, but she could feel her entire body burn with embarrassment. They looked at her like she was some kind of museum exhibit.

During the discussion, Alex slipped off her chair and took Gussie's hand. The simple moved cracked Gussie's heart, opening it like she had to make room for the girl. They exchanged a smile, and then, suddenly, all of the French people went silent.

Every eye in the room fell on Suzette, who stared at the scar with her arms crossed.

Gussie couldn't take it anymore. "I wear wigs," she said. "I wear them very well, as a matter of fact. Would you like to see how well?"

Suzette finally took her gaze from the back of Gussie's head to meet her eyes. "A wig? *La femme ordinaire* does not wear wigs."

Well, la bald femme did. "I'm sure we can find one that's

very natural." Gussie swallowed hard, but refused to let her voice waver. "Or another model."

Suzette shook her head. "No. I like it. I like it very much." She gave a gesture of permission to Jean Claude. "He will finish up," she said, the English clearly for Gussie's benefit. "Johanna's set is nearly complete, and they will be ready in fifteen minutes." She smiled coolly at Gussie. "You are perfect."

Gussie gave a sardonic grunt. "Since you just had a twenty-minute discussion about how imperfect I am, that's really not true."

"*Au contraire, mademoiselle*. Our campaign celebrates the beauty on the inside. Beauty that is more enhanced by LaVie than any of this." She swept her hand over the makeup brushes strewn on the counter. "I believe your imperfection, as you see it, is something women can relate to."

"Not exactly," Gussie said. "A few extra pounds, less-than-creamy skin, a weak chin. These are flaws women can relate to. A scar that leaves a bald spot on the back of your head? That's not relatable."

"We shall see," she countered. "We all have the scars, inside and out. And in the hands of TJ DeMille, you will be indescribably beautiful."

She'd like to be in the hands of TJ DeMille right now. And not for sunrise sexy times. She'd really rather strangle him for putting her in this situation.

As quickly as they'd arrived, the French contingent of marketing geniuses disappeared, and without a word, Jean Claude went to work styling Gussie's hair.

She'd lost the fight, so she closed her eyes and endured combing, clipping, and more hands-on attention than her hair had gotten in the fifteen years and...twenty-eight days since the accident.

211

Not that she was counting or anything.

She didn't open her eyes until she heard his comb hit the counter and Alex gasped audibly. And then she had to blink to make sure she wasn't dreaming.

"Wow," Gussie whispered. "You're good."

Jean Claude threw up his hands as if to say, "It's about time you realized that." Then he gave a sly French half grin, clearly pleased with his work. As he should be. Her hair had been cut into layers—something she'd never dared attempt—and now had a bounciness she'd never even tried to achieve. Why bother? She hated her hair because it wasn't all there.

No, she hated her hair because it was a constant, endless reminder of the worst day of her life.

"Would you like to see the back?" he asked, holding a hand mirror.

She generally avoided that angle, but she had to look. Taking the mirror, she gasped at how beautifully he'd styled the back. The scar was visible, but somehow he'd cut and layered the hair around it so it wasn't quite so ugly. Why couldn't she have done that?

Because she'd never really tried. Instead, she hid her hair and scar, as if she could hide away her pain of that night.

She lowered the hand mirror and looked at the bald Frenchman beaming in front of her. "Thank you," she mouthed, worried that if she spoke, her voice would crack, then the tears would pour and she'd wreck her makeup, and Jean Claude would kill her.

Instead, she was going to kill this photo shoot.

Chapter Eighteen

On one knee, Tom angled his lens away from the sun, checking the last set of shots after they'd dismissed Johanna.

"No one's going to buy water from her," he murmured to Monique, the only assistant who spoke decent English.

"Three-thousand-dollar shoes, yes," Monique agreed. "But not water. This woman, though"—she tapped him on the shoulder to get his attention—"could sell me anything."

Tom looked up, blinking into the sun and shadows that fell on the backstreet of Cannes.

"Whoa." For a second, he froze the frame in his mental lens, letting the background fade away to a blur, but Gussie burned in stark clarity, taking his breath away.

"And she's *not* a professional," Monique said, unaware, like most of the freelancers in Cannes, that he and Gussie knew each other. "This is the *femme ordinaire* test shot."

But, damn, there was nothing *ordinary* about that woman.

It wasn't just the way her hair was styled, although it was natural and pretty, utterly pleasing to the eye. Nor was it the lacy white sundress that floated above her knees, giving her an unexpected innocence, or the subtle makeup that enhanced a face he already admired.

No, it was something inside Gussie McBain that had her striding with confidently squared shoulders and an air of authority. She tossed a comment to Alex, who laughed with a spirit he'd yet to see much of, and then the two gave each other a friendly knuckle tap and a quick hug as Alex stepped away from the set.

Tom tried to take it all in—the woman, the moment, the ease of her relationships—but instead of a single coherent thought, he stood there with his heart racing unnaturally.

Only when she gave him a nod of acknowledgment did he walk across the cobblestone street to meet her.

"You know what I'm going to say, don't you?" she teased.

"Let me guess... 'I'm ready for my close-up, Mr. DeMille'?"

She laughed guiltily. "I guess you've heard that about a hundred times."

"A thousand." Suddenly, he was aware of the crew closing in, Monique close enough to overhear, and Suzette watching hawklike from twenty feet away.

"Come with me." He took Gussie by the arm and whisked her past all the others, under an awning to talk privately.

"Okay. Tell me what you want me to do."

"What I want you to do can't be done here." He lifted a lock of her hair and eased back to check her out head to toe. "But I will warn you that if I ever hear you even imply that you aren't beautiful, I'm going to force you to look at the pictures I'm about to take."

She smiled, her confidence unwavering. "I know, right? And look what he did." Spinning, she showed him how the stylist had fixed her hair to almost cover the scar, cleverly cutting and combing it in a way that looked completely natural. He could still see that hair didn't grow there, but it wasn't unattractive, it was...Gussie. Flawed, but then, who wasn't?

"How will I capture that in a picture?" he mused.

She turned back, frowning. "Aren't you going to, you know, play it down?"

"Gussie, they're trying to appeal to every woman. Every slightly imperfect, real, unvarnished woman. Our job is to convince them you are happy, healthy, glowing, and gorgeous from the inside out, thanks to the water."

"That's a tall order, considering I'm all those things thanks to a spunky little Frenchman named Jean Claude." She glanced at the set behind him. "So, what do I do?"

"First and foremost"—he put both hands on her shoulders and inched her closer—"trust me. You have to completely let go and allow me to take the pictures I want from whatever angle I decide, close, far, up, or down." Her shoulders tensed under his touch. "Trust me," he repeated, lowering his head to place his lips right over her ear. "You are in the best possible hands."

She shivered. And sighed. "Okay. But only because this is a test shot and a favor and a personal challenge and you promised that no one will ever see it."

"No one will, except some marketing yahoos whose opinions will be outvoted by Suzette. So all you need to do is relax and have fun."

"Aren't you supposed to tell me to, you know, make love to the camera or something?"

"How about this?" he asked, pressing a kiss on the top of her head, inhaling the scents of the salon and sunshine. "Make love to the guy who holds the camera."

She looked up at him, tenderness and desire making her eyes so gorgeous he wanted to take that picture right then and there. "That's what you want me to think about?"

"That's what I'm thinking about," he admitted.

A few seconds passed as they stared at each other, electricity arcing and drawing them closer.

Until someone coughed loudly. And someone else dragged a spotlight into position. Tom didn't move, but Gussie slipped out of his touch and gestured to the people watching from the set. "Um, Tom. They're waiting."

He shot the crew a look that got them to scatter to their various stations, then walked Gussie through the storyboard, emphasizing the breakpoints and the need for a natural look.

"Basically, you're walking down the street," he concluded. "You're window shopping, talking on the phone, waiting to meet a friend, living life. But mostly, you're enjoying your water. *Really* enjoying the hell out of your water."

"Got it. So no actual posing?"

"Not for a second. What I want you to do, Gussie, is forget I'm here, forget this is a set, forget you're being watched. Think in, not out."

She frowned. "I have no idea what that means."

"Just…go in there." He tapped her heart. "Find out what makes that beat." Because, God knew, he wanted to do exactly that.

Suzette clattered up next to him, bearing an armload of handbags. "People are already talking," she said brightly.

"Let 'em. We don't care. Right, Pink?"

Suzette waved off his comment. "Not about you. *Me*. The word on the street, as you Americans say, is that I'm a genius."

"No surprise, since this street is our set and everyone spreading the word is being paid by you."

She gave a classic French shrug and held out her bags.

"Final accessories, and we're leaving it up to you. Which of these bags would *la femme ordinaire* choose to carry?" she asked.

Gussie glanced at the offerings. "Not Chanel or Kate Spade, lovely as they are." Suzette removed those two bags from her collection.

"Oh, is that Portokali Sky?" Gussie reached for a bright orange baguette-style purse. "That's my favorite"—she winked at Tom—"designer." Slipping the bag on her shoulder, she earned a nod of approval from the client.

"Okay," Tom said, trying to shoo Suzette without actually telling her to get the hell out of his way. "Lighting's good. Accessory's chosen. We've talked. She has this."

"But she does not have the water, *monsieur*." She snapped her fingers at a production assistant behind her.

Damn it. He'd forgotten the product. *That's* what Gussie did to him.

Once Gussie had a freshly open bottle of LaVie, they started.

"Walk by the café," Tom instructed. "Let your dress flutter in the breeze, and I'll be right behind you."

That got him a sharp look. "*Behind* me?"

"Yeah." He reached out and arranged her hair, caressing the exposed skin of her shoulder. "Behind you, next to you, in front of you..." He purposely didn't finish all the places he'd like to be. Like on top and underneath.

But her eyes registered the unspoken comments, darkening slightly, a Mona Lisa smile threatening.

"Walk," he instructed, following her as he lifted the camera.

She started slowly, visibly shaking him off, taking a minute to get her head in the game. As she sauntered up the street, Tom stayed a few feet away, lining up a shot.

"You're alone in France," he coaxed, helping her get into the part. "You're thinking about someone special. Who is it, Pink?" Him, he hoped.

She slid him a sideways look, and he snapped it, getting the flirt and fun, and the vaguest shadow on the back of her head.

"Now you're shopping. Look at the shoes. Imagine wearing them." She paused in front of a boutique, lightly placing the fingertips of one hand on the glass, using the other to take a sip of water. All the while, she peered at a pair of Louboutins with a look of longing that reminded him of Alex and croissants. He captured raw desire and a hint of regret, which he loved because, of course, *la femme ordinaire* couldn't afford those shoes. But LaVie could quench her thirst for luxury.

And, to please Suzette, he also captured the perfect angle of her fingers wrapped around the bottle.

"Keep going, Gussie. To the flower stand."

In the distance, he could hear Suzette natter on in French, her excitement for the shoot building.

A few feet ahead, a flower vendor—actually an actor with props—waited with baskets overloaded with lilacs, daisies, and bright purple jacaranda flowers. They didn't exchange a word, but Gussie rounded the stand, fingered the flowers, and accepted a bouquet with a toast of her bottle of LaVie.

In his lens, Tom managed three different angles, each one a study of joy and inner serenity as she examined the flowers.

"You're killing it, Gus," he said, but she was so into the moment, she didn't break character at all. Instead, she reached a hand to the old flower vendor, and they shared a casual touch, and Tom caught the millisecond of connection between the two.

"Now I need pensive, not so happy," he said. "You've been waiting for someone, and he's late. Maybe not showing. You've been waiting a long time."

She played the game with him, her expression perfectly depicting expectation, longing, and a little disappointment as she peered down the street.

"Perfect," he assured her. "Now, wait here at the planter."

She reached a brick and stone street decoration filled with more flowering plants. She leaned against it, sipping her water, letting her dress spread out enough to make a flowing, pretty picture.

"This is going to be our money shot, honey." He switched to his secondary camera, wanting the optimized high-res lens. "You ready?"

She threw him a look that was out of her newly assumed character, but insanely *Gussie* in attitude, and he snagged it, loving the mix of uncertainty and confidence, a cocktail of sexy.

Each shot was magic. *Gussie was magic.*

God, he hadn't felt like that about a woman since...a long time.

The realization hit him hard, making him stand up straight and lower the camera, looking at her with his naked eye.

"What?" she asked. "Am I doing something wrong?"

No, *no*. She wasn't doing *anything* wrong. His gaze shifted to the words on his arm, a constant reminder, then back to the woman who'd captivated him on the most fundamental level.

He'd rather look at Gussie. He'd rather be with Gussie...than alone.

And that scared the shit out of him.

"Tom?"

What the hell was wrong with him? "Lean against the stone, Gus. And, for God's sake, take a drink of water before Suzette births a goat."

She laughed at the joke, and he caught that, too. So real and natural, like the stupid water.

Damn, she was good.

"Okay, I'm moving in now," he warned. "No more body shots. I'm getting close enough to get emotion."

She nodded, as if to say, *I can do this*. And she could. As well as Johanna, if not better. Without the affectation. Without the training. Just pure, raw, genuine woman.

Suzette *was* fricking brilliant, he had to admit it. The real-woman campaign might have been his idea, but she was smart enough to execute it, and he couldn't say that for most marketing stiffs.

"Look at me," he whispered, going a few steps closer. "Lift the bottle, tilt your head this way, hold it lightly, now look right at me, Gussie."

She followed every instruction as he got closer, snapping every shot, using the light, working with the angle, adjusting everything but the one thing he couldn't adjust. Her eyes. Her story. Her *truth*.

This was the moment he found the soft spot, the vulnerability that would translate into honesty and beauty, the glimmer of gold that connected with every woman who looked at this shot. The deepest, darkest, sweetest, truest Gussie.

"Honey," he whispered, knowing no one could hear her but him.

She looked at him, waiting for his next word.

"Who are you waiting for?"

Her eyes flickered, confused at first—and he got that shot—and then she relaxed. But still, she was able to communicate a sense of waiting, of anticipation, of longing.

"Someone special, right?" he prodded.

A true professional, she turned to give him her profile, looking down the street in expectation, a hint of lift in her heels, the LaVie bottle poised a few inches from her mouth as if she couldn't take a sip until she saw whoever she imagined she was waiting for.

But the shot was flat. He needed more emotion. Less hope and more heartache. He knew how to get that by playing a story game with her. He did it all the time, and the best models caught on. And she was clearly one of the best.

"He's not coming, is he, Gussie?"

Her eyes nearly shuttered closed, as if he'd hit the mark, and he got the shot.

"You're waiting and waiting, but you know he's not on his way."

She closed her eyes and took a tiny sip, as if the water named for life itself could ease her pain. Perfect shot. He had her now. Had her.

"Do you see him, Gussie? That person who'll make you feel finished? Complete? Whole? Do you see him?"

Because, damn it, he is right here taking pictures of you.

A wistful look crossed her face as she tucked her lower lip under her teeth. She wasn't acting, he realized. He'd taken her to a real place.

"Do you?" he prodded.

She shook her head infinitesimally, enough that he knew she was trying to shake off the question and yet acknowledge that her pretend man wasn't there.

She pushed her hair over her shoulder, and he snapped the shot.

"You want to see him, though, don't you?"

She turned and looked directly at the camera, a stunning

world of hurt shadowing her eyes. The beauty was there, along with so, so much pain. He didn't take that shot, but slowly inched his camera down.

"Gussie?"

Still holding the bottle close to her mouth, the label perfectly readable, as it would be in the hands of a pro, she shifted her gaze down the street, an aura of anticipation, as if she were on hold for his next question.

He angled the camera, changed the aperture, checked the focus. This was it. He wanted this shot. "Who are you waiting for?" he whispered.

In partial profile, she lifted the bottle to her mouth, pressing glossy lips to the opening. All the heartbreak he wanted tinged her expression. The last rays of sun glistened over her as a sea breeze lifted her hair and fluttered a few strands, revealing her scar. He had it all, every angle and color and shadow of her.

"Who are you waiting for, Pink?"

"Luke," she whispered. "I'm waiting for my brother."

All the anguish, all the vulnerability, all the longing, and all the exposure he wanted filled the lens and broke his heart.

For a long time, they stared at each other, ignoring the hoots and hollers of Suzette and the crew. He lowered the camera. "That's a wrap," he whispered, then walked to Gussie and folded her into his arms.

Chapter Nineteen

B y her second glass of champagne and a few bits of escargot so luscious it could have made a grown woman weep, Gussie had nearly forgotten her inexplicable meltdown at the end of the photo shoot.

Though maybe it wasn't so inexplicable. Her ache for Luke, for her family, for the very essence of her childhood, was always right there beneath the surface. Maybe that whole act of facing down her insecurities—so tied up with what happened that night—had brought her pain bubbling to the surface.

Maybe the fact that for the first time in fifteen years, she forgot her scar and realized how utterly different her life would have been if she hadn't made that stupid mistake.

Or maybe it was Tom, exercising his superpower, making her vulnerable.

Whatever caused her distress, the wounds seemed less severe tonight, and everyone seemed happy, including Gussie. She sipped the Dom Perignon that Ari and Willow had arranged to have sent to the table during the surprise birthday party that Tom had confessed he'd planned before they'd even arrived in France.

Not only had he managed to get a table for six at

Chantecler, one of the best and most exclusive restaurants in Nice at a gorgeous hotel, there'd been a single white rose at her place setting.

She glanced at Tom, who was next to her, his arm securely across the back of her chair, the position protective, proprietary, and public.

"Thanks for doing this," she whispered. "It would have been easy to stay in tonight after the long day of work."

He added a little pressure on her shoulder. "Thirty only comes once, Pink."

"And you gave me what I value the most." She looked around the table, half Americans, half Brits, all animated and all dear to her.

"A party?"

"A group of people I care about." She gave a soft, self-deprecating laugh. "I mean, I know I've been here two days, but…"

"But that's what you do. You have a gift for it, you know."

"For what, exactly?"

He thought for a moment, glancing around. "For making something out of nothing. For making…" He swallowed, as if the realization of whatever he was going to say had an unexpected impact on him.

"Fun?" she supplied.

"I was going to say family."

She sighed. "I guess I do."

Leaning closer, he whispered. "You're okay now, right?"

"More than okay," she assured him. If there hadn't been a table full of friends gathered to celebrate, she'd probably have given in to the lure of his blue, blue eyes and spent the next two hours talking about her brother. But not tonight. Not now.

"So how does it feel to be thirty?" Annie asked, leaning away from the children back to the adult side of the table.

"It feels"—she lifted her champagne flute in a playful toast—"not as old as it sounds."

"Pfft!" Annie flicked off the comment. "Wait until you hit thirty-five." She leaned closer. "And your husband decides he prefers twenty-three."

"All the more chance for you to find love again," Gussie quipped.

"Spoken like a true wedding planner. Do you firmly believe in the elusive happily ever after?" Annie asked.

Tom's arm tensed ever so slightly, barely enough to notice. But Gussie did, and her stomach flipped, because she knew he was listening intently.

"I do," Gussie said.

Annie narrowed her eyes, and Gussie braced for the vitriol of a newly divorced woman. "And those are exactly the words you'll say when you find it."

Gussie smiled at the unexpected response. "And here I thought you were going to bury me in bitter."

"Not tonight," she said. "You inspire me, Gussie. Young, optimistic." She shifted her gaze to Tom. "What about you, handsome photographer to the stars? Are you a believer in fairy tales?"

Gussie gave an exaggerated cough, not only to tease him, but because hearing the truth from this loner might put a damper on a perfectly wonderful evening. "This is a man without a permanent address," she told Annie. "So he's obviously not planning on any fairy tales."

Annie's eyebrows lifted. "You're homeless?"

"I have a loft in New York," Tom said, picking up the bottle to refill Gussie's glass.

She gave him a sharp look. "Really? I thought you said you didn't actually have a home."

"Define *home*. Mine happens to be a six-hundred-square-foot apartment I use to store equipment, but it does qualify as a permanent address for my passport."

"And your expired driver's license," she reminded him.

"Passport's all I need."

It would be to a man like Tom.

"Pity," Annie said on a sad sigh.

"Why is that a pity?" he asked.

She angled her head as if to communicate what a stupid question that was.

"Because of Alex," Gussie whispered, though she was certain Alex, Lizzie, and Eddie were deep into their own conversation, their three heads together as they looked at something on one of their phones.

"No," Annie said. "Because of you."

"Me?"

"Her?"

Gussie and Tom asked their questions in total harmony, only it didn't sound harmonious at all. More like a couple of bats that accidentally flew into sunlight.

Annie laughed. "Denial is not a pretty thing, my friends."

Tom picked up his drink rather than respond. Gussie opened her mouth, and for a change, nothing came out. Annie found this even more amusing.

"Oh, would you two stop bloody acting like it's not real?" She threw a glance at the kids and added in a stage whisper, "The only two who have more chemistry at this table are Alex and Eddie."

"They do?" Tom practically spewed his drink. And suddenly, the kids stopped talking, their radar for a more interesting conversation in perfect working order. "You have got to be kidding," he said.

"Kidding about what?" Alex asked.

"About this—"

"Nothing." Gussie smashed her foot into his. "Nothing, Alex. We're talking about"—what was the most boring thing in the world to a kid?—"the value of the euro versus the dollar."

Alex rolled her eyes, and instantly, all three of them went back to something far more riveting on the phone.

Tom shifted in his seat and narrowed his eyes at Gussie. "Why are you protecting her?"

"Because you were about to ruin her night, if not her life."

He grunted and looked at the ceiling at the hyperbole. "Are you concerned?" he asked Annie.

Smiling, she shook her head slowly. "Well, I am for poor Alex if you're going to react like that to a harmless summer friendship between two kids."

"You made it sound like more than friendship."

"I doubt he'll be proposing tonight," Annie said dryly.

"Especially with Lizzie in the middle of it," Gussie added.

Tom sat forward. "I need to talk to her and—"

Gussie put her hand firmly on his thigh. "Do you actually want her to die of embarrassment?" She heard the edge in her voice, but couldn't help it. "She's tender and uncertain, on top of being in mourning for her mother. She doesn't need a bodyguard. She needs a strong and empathetic male figure in her life."

That got another eye roll, but his disgust was directed inwardly. "Can we change the subject?"

"Please," Gussie said, turning more in her seat so Alex

couldn't see her face. "If she hears us, she'll never forgive me."

Tom looked hard at her. "Forgive *you*? You're not responsible for her, Gussie."

For a long moment, neither spoke, and Annie took a drink to cover the awkwardness. Gussie bit her lip, but that didn't work. The words were not going to be held back. "I'm not responsible for her, Tom, but she has my heart."

His eyes flashed, but he didn't say a word.

"Maybe you don't understand that," she said on a harsh whisper. "Maybe when you don't have a heart to give, you don't understand when someone takes yours."

He stared at her. "And maybe you'd be wrong about that."

"Um, excuse me," Annie said, putting a hand on Gussie's arm, obviously uncomfortable. "But, Gussie, your phone is about to explode."

Gussie took the excuse to look away, seeing text after text popping up on her home screen.

"Birthday messages," she guessed, picking it up, welcoming the distraction. What did he mean she'd be wrong about that?

She focused on the messages, but none of them mentioned her birthday. In fact, none of them even made sense.

Instagram...photos...LaVie
campaign...congratulations!!!

Her arms suddenly felt heavy. Her chest vibrated with a sudden shot of adrenaline. Around her, the restaurant noise and heated discussion faded away, taken over by the pulse in her head.

"What are they talking about?" She tapped the first message. Then the second. Then the third. And, oh, no, there were more.

"What's going on?" Tom asked.

Blame and fury welled up. "You released the photos?"

"Of course not."

"They're on Instagram."

"*What?*"

"And Twitter. And Facebook. They're all...over...the..."

"Hey, Gussie!" Alex shouted, holding up her phone. "Did you see this?"

Oh, God. Oh, *God*.

"Give that to me," Tom demanded.

Gussie didn't want to look. Instead, she stared straight ahead. "No one will see the pictures except a few marketing yahoos," she whispered, throwing his empty promise back at him.

"Son of a bitch," he murmured, staring at the screen. "LaVie took the test to social media, asking for people's opinions."

Gussie grabbed her glass and downed the entire thing like a frat boy playing beer pong.

When she slammed the flute on the table, she turned to him, praying for the brain-numbing buzz to hit. "How did this happen?"

"I don't know, but you're winning," he said. "In a landslide. Everyone loves you, Gussie."

Tom didn't get to talk to Suzette until late the next afternoon, while he, Gussie, and Alex perused Cours Saleya, the expansive food and flower market that spilled from one end of the street to the other in Old Town.

Alex and Gussie were under a brightly striped awning,

tasting grapes and olives from a bucket, laughing with the street vendor, when Tom's phone finally rang with the call he'd been waiting to get since the night before.

"It's Suzette," he said to Gussie, holding up his phone. "I'll be right over on that bench, so don't go far."

She popped an olive into his mouth. "Tell her she's a dead woman."

He munched the olive and nodded, heading toward some privacy before he took the call, answering it the minute he swallowed the briny bite. "You're a dead woman."

A soft laugh was the only response.

"I'm serious, Suzette. What the hell were you thinking putting out those shots? Turning it into some kind of social media contest? Gussie is furious and, frankly, so am I. As far as I'm concerned, you posted unauthorized, copyrighted photos, that I let you preview, in a total breach of confidence and contract, and I demand you take them down or I'm off the job and you better have a slew of attorneys, because this is going to cost LaVie a fortune."

Another laugh, which irritated the shit out of him. "Are you finished, *monsieur*?"

"I haven't even started."

"But will you listen to me, *s'il vous plait*?"

He answered with a low, unhappy sigh as he sat on the bench, his gaze settling on Gussie and Alex. Side by side, they paid for a small container of olives and moved to the next stand, spilling over with fuchsia begonias, deep-red roses, and playfully angled sunflowers. Even through the crowd and with a phone to his ear, he could hear Gussie's laughter float across the marketplace and touch something deep in his heart.

She gave Alex a fistful of violets, getting a look of sheer joy from the girl who gazed up at her. If he hadn't been on

230

his phone, he'd have taken the shot, profile to profile, smile to smile, woman to girl.

"…So we hardly had anything to do with that leak and simply don't know who on the crew put the photos out." Suzette's lame-ass excuse finally got through to his addled brain. "But, Tom, the results are astounding, and we've been in nonstop marketing meetings to figure out the very best way to…to *exploit*…is that the word?"

"I'm afraid that's exactly the word."

"No, no, *utilize*—that's it. The best way to utilize this fascinating information."

He moved the phone to the other ear since the first one already hurt, bracing his elbows on his knees to observe Alex and Gussie move on to the next stall, then suddenly change their minds and scamper over to another flower stall. A man a few feet behind them made the same sudden change, making Tom wonder what was so interesting about that stall.

"We must work fast." Suzette's lilting, French-accented enthusiasm brought him back to the conversation. "Instantly, in fact, to launch this campaign before another company takes this unexpected gold mine of market information and beats us to the slap."

"The punch," he corrected, leaning to the side to try to keep an eye on Gussie and Alex, who'd disappeared around a mountain of strawberries and apples.

"And it would hurt like one."

He closed his eyes to focus. "What gold mine of market information?"

"*Monsieur*, have you not looked at the statistics on these social sites? Eight hundred thousand views! Ninety percent women, who are our target audience. And over half of them have voted, and the results are *extraordinaire*! Consumers prefer Gussie nine times to one, and the comments! They're relating to her bit of scarring. Really, how have you done anything but read them?"

"For one reason, I've spent much of the last day and a half assuring her that I had nothing to do with this and that you would pull these posts from every site immediately." Which had cost him any intimacy he had hoped for and had made him even more frustrated than Gussie.

"*Non, non.* That cannot be done, *je regret.*"

She did not sound like she *regretted* anything. "Oh, we could pull anything that is on LaVie's Facebook, Instagram, Pinterest, and the like pages," she continued. "But the photos, especially the one that contrasts Gussie and Johanna, have gone viral. You know the picture I mean?"

"I know it." Someone—possibly the someone he was talking to right now—had used a shot he'd taken of Johanna standing in front of the stone planter on the Cannes street. It was a lousy shot, a throwaway, as far as he was concerned, because she looked cold, haughty, and flawless. But the real problem was that the water bottle was utterly lost in her human perfection.

But edited next to that shot was Gussie in the same location, a breeze lifting her skirt and hair in the same way, a profile shot that caught her scar. The angle of her face showed an expression of someone who'd survived and thrived, a woman who had her priorities in order, a woman who knew her true beauty came from the inside. And in that shot, he'd gotten the bottle perfect, the label like a flashing neon sign that said her inner beauty was fired and fueled by what she put in her body...LaVie.

Damn it, why had he made the shot so perfect? For a *test.* Across the market, he tracked Gussie and Alex. They'd moved about a block away, to a vegetable stand, and Gussie stood back, taking a picture of Alex, who playfully dangled a bright red pepper before dropping it into a basket.

He was about to answer Suzette when he noticed that same man, the one who'd made the sudden turn that they had, and he, too, had his phone out and was taking a picture...of them. Instantly, Tom stood, scowling.

"Tom, you must see that we have hit the ballpark!"

He choked at the idiom, as screwed up as this situation. But his focus was really on the stranger.

"Our brand is highlighted. Our message is clear. And our audience has responded exactly as we'd hoped," she continued excitedly. "In fact, in one of the comments, we found the theme for the whole campaign. Are you ready?"

Gussie and Alex disappeared again, rounding a flower cart out of sight. And the man—a bit taller and huskier than Tom, with a short, military-style haircut—followed. Gussie and Alex were a good city block away from him, so Tom got up and moved fast.

"We're changing the entire campaign."

He lost the guy at the flower cart.

"Don't you want to know our new theme, Tom?"

Was this because Gussie had gotten famous overnight? Now she had stalkers? Or was he some pedophile after Alex? Tom dodged a few tourists without an apology.

"We're working on 'Beauty isn't perfect, but LaVie is.'" She made a soft shriek. "We love it! Don't you? Our whole campaign will feature not just real women, as you suggested, but *flawed* women. Women who celebrate their imperfections and find—"

They were all out of view now, and Tom's pulse pumped along with his legs as he practically ran through the market now. "I have to go."

"Don't you love it?"

"It's fine. I have to go, Suzette."

"Be sure to tell Gussie she has inspired the whole campaign!"

"I will." *If she's still alive.* The thought spurred him on, elbowing through a pack of shoppers who scowled at him. He ended the call with a jab of his thumb, pocketing the phone as he reached the flower cart and whipped around to the other side.

And there they were, picking flowers one stem at a time, laughing and talking and totally safe.

Breathless, he scanned the area, searching for the man in the black T-shirt and jeans, but he was gone.

"What's the matter?" Gussie asked him.

"Are you okay? No one talked to you? No man?"

She drew back, fighting a smile. "No, but are you worried one might?"

"He's jealous," Alex teased.

"No, no, I'm…" He looked again, peering at a guy standing next to a display of hanging Persian rugs, but that dude was about fifty. The one following them hadn't been a day over thirty-five, if that. "I saw someone taking a picture of you."

"Really?" Gussie's eyes widened, and then she puffed out a breath that sank her shoulders on the exhale. "Well, I guess if a person wants to get over a weird phobia about having her picture taken, getting her face splattered all over the Internet for a million people to see is the way to go."

"Only eight hundred thousand," he corrected, giving up his search.

Gussie grunted and closed her eyes. "Are they taking it down? Did you fight her? Did you tell her you didn't give permission to—"

"What did he look like?" Alex's question stopped Gussie short.

"Who, honey?" Gussie asked.

"The man. The one taking our picture. The one you saw." Alex was trying to stay calm, he could tell, but the low-grade desperation in her voice came through loud and clear.

"Oh, Alex, there's nothing to worry about," Gussie assured her. "It was a tourist—"

"Are you sure? Uncle Tommy seems to be concerned." She looked from side to side, spinning again, searching the crowds. "Did you see his face?"

"Gussie's right," Tom said, although he didn't agree completely. No reason for the girl to be worried. "A tourist or, more likely, one of those eight hundred thousand views."

Gussie handed the bouquet she'd been making to Alex. "You can finish picking the flowers, honey. What did Suzette say, Tom?"

They took a few steps away, but Alex was still peering hard at every man in the flower market.

"Damn, I hope I didn't scare her," he whispered to Gussie.

"I don't think she's scared, more like hopeful."

He frowned, then suddenly understood. "Her father?"

Gussie lifted a shoulder. "She harbors the hope."

Hope that would never be fulfilled, he knew. "I'll fill you in later," he said quickly, something instinctive making him walk back to his niece. "Come on, Alex." He put a protective hand on her narrow shoulder, guiding her away and kicking himself for overreacting. "Let's pay for those and finish shopping. I promised you I'd cook a true Niçoise dinner, and we can't make that out of daisies and violets."

She took one more look over her shoulder, then fell into step with him. Gussie joined him on the other side, and without thinking too much about it, he held her hand and led the three of them through the market.

He tried really hard not to think about how good and right and, damn it, *permanent* it felt to be flanked by two people who suddenly mattered a whole hell of a lot more than he'd ever expected them to.

"I can't have dinner with you guys tonight," Alex said.

"Don't tell me, you have a date," Tom said dryly.

She giggled and turned as red as the roses she clutched to her chest. "Miss Annie invited me to go to the French cinema with Lizzie."

"And Eddie?" he asked.

More blood rushed to her face, and Gussie squeezed his hand in warning. "Well, yeah, he'll be there. Is that okay?"

"Over my dead body."

"Uncle Tommy!"

Another squeeze tempered his reply, so he patted Alex's shoulder. "Of course it's okay. I was playing with you, Alex," he said.

She looked up at him, her eyes a little uncertain before she broke into a smile. "Well, that's a first."

It sure was. Inside, he could almost feel something click in his chest. An adrenaline dump from the chase or something else? Something like...an adjustment of his heart.

Chapter Twenty

Gussie settled more comfortably on the barstool at the island counter, mesmerized by Tom's ease and competence in the kitchen. Okay, his ass in jeans and his biceps in a loose-fitting T-shirt were kind of compelling, also.

The tangy aroma of sautéed onions and shallots wafted through the air, the glow of the day hung over every inch of the cozy apartment, and the man who cooked for her had Gussie's every nerve ending tingling with anticipation and interest.

This was good. This was all so flipping *good.*

So, of course, the familiar sensation of dread crawled up her spine and spread all over those tingling nerve endings, promising to numb every sensation like a bucket of ice water.

"I hate when this happens to me," she whispered, mostly to herself, but he turned from the stove, always tuned in to those kinds of comments.

"You hate what?"

She tipped the glass with what she hoped was a flippancy that wouldn't give away her real worries. "Oh, you know, when someone exceedingly hot cooks dinner for me after a dreamy day in the south of France and I have to watch while sipping perfectly chilled chardonnay." She went for a light smile. "I hate that."

He shook the sauté pan, spreading the garlic and oil with an expert touch. "You had me at exceedingly hot."

She rolled her eyes. "As if this is a big shock to you."

"But you're lying," he said.

"Lying? I may have my own personal issues, big guy, but if you try to pretend you don't know that you are…what do we say back in the old USofA? A stone-cold fox, then you're pretty blind for a man who uses his eyes to make a living."

He left the stove to pick up the cutting board covered with sliced vegetables. "I meant you're lying about why you whispered that you hate this. You hate something, and it's not me, the day, or the food. I call bullshit. What do you hate?"

If he hadn't been so dang adept at getting inside her head like that, she'd have laughed. Or lied. But why bother? "I get nervous around anything that's too good to be true," she admitted.

He snorted as he dumped mushrooms and onions into the pan. "I hope you don't mean me, 'cause we both know I'm not."

"I didn't mean you." Yes, she did. "I meant"—she made a quick, sweeping gesture that encompassed everything around her—"this. This day, this trip, this place, this"—*go ahead, admit it*—"this man."

He splashed some wine from his glass into the pan, causing a sudden flare and sizzle. "I thought you were still stewing over the LaVie situation."

"Not stewing, exactly. Trying to get used to it. I certainly have never sought fame or fortune, but Ari and Willow seem to think the whole thing is cool and might even help the

Brides business. Alex thinks it's a riot, of course, and you..." He hadn't really tipped his hand yet. "I'm not sure how you feel about anything."

She glanced at her glass, still nearly full, but maybe the wine was too potent for her if she was going to start confessing things better kept inside.

"My opinion doesn't matter."

Like hell it didn't.

Leaving the stove, he came around the counter behind her, setting his glass next to hers. "So what are you hating?" he asked, genuine confusion in eyes the same blue as the flames flickering under the burner.

"I just told you...all of this is too...good." Wonderful, really. Impossibly, perfectly wonderful.

He slid his hands over her bare shoulders, his thumbs slipping right under the straps of her tank top. "But why is that a problem, Gussie?"

She tipped her head to the side to rub her cheek against his knuckles, a hungry puppy taking all the affection he gave her. "Because it's too good to be true." *Too good to last.*

"But it is true." He rubbed his thumbs in circles, causing a cascade of chill bumps on her arms.

"And it is too good," she cooed into his touch. "When things are really nice and easy and swell and sweet, then I'm in suspended animation, waiting for it all to blow up in my face."

He was quiet for a moment, then she felt his lips press against the back of her head, over the hair that partially covered her scar. "Understandable, I guess," he whispered. "Since your good life did once blow up more or less in your face."

More chills exploded, but not because of his warm lips or gentle hands. It was the softness of his words and sympathy that gave her a slight shiver. This man *understood* her like no one she'd ever met.

And that slayed her heart.

"You know, Tom, I'd really appreciate it if you wouldn't be quite so ideal." She turned the stool to face him. "That way, when it blows up—or over, as the case may be—it won't hurt so much."

He searched her face, his eyes piercing, his mouth unsmiling. "What do you want me to say to that?" he asked.

How about…*It's not going to blow up, Pink.*

Except that would have been a lie. And Tom didn't lie.

"I want you to say exactly what you feel," she said. "Because that's what you get me to do. So do the same for me. Tell me exactly what you feel."

She could take it. She could take his explanation of how he liked her, but he was a loner, drifter, desperado type, and the end was inevitable, and this couldn't la—

"Let's skip dinner and go right to bed."

She choked on her unfinished thought. "Why didn't I see that coming?"

"You did." He leaned in and whispered the words over her mouth. "I want you."

And every single cell that carried a double-X chromosome started marching in order, preparing for the onslaught. Yes, yes, *yes.*

"Skip dinner? I'm hungry," she lied. Well, she *was* hungry. But not for chicken *chasseur*.

"You're scared."

"No shit."

He opened his mouth and scared her some more, this time with plenty of tongue. She put both hands on his shoulders, ready to ease him back, but that didn't work at all. The moment she touched his arms, all she could do was dig in and pull him closer to kiss some more.

"Don't be scared," he murmured.

She laughed into the kiss. "Easy for you to say."

He drew back, opening his eyes slowly. "No, Gussie, it's not easy at all." All the sexual playfulness evaporated at his tone. "I'm scared, too."

"Forgive me if I find that a little hard to believe."

"Why?" He took his hands off her, and immediately, she felt cold, but she followed suit and let go of his arms. "Why is that so hard to believe?" he asked. "You think I'm fearless?"

"I think you're the leaver. You're the mover. You're the guy who lives for his independence and tattoos proclamations of solitude on his arm."

"Proving my point," he fired back. "A man who embraces his solitude has a lot more to lose when faced with…"

She froze, not even breathing as she waited for him to finish. But he shut down, shaking his head.

"With what?" she demanded.

"This." The word was barely audible.

This. This? "What exactly is this?" she asked.

"This is"—he swiped his hand through his hair—"getting complicated."

"And falling into bed together is really going to simplify things."

He started to turn away, then froze, taking in a quick breath. In a flash, he wrapped her in his arms and pulled her off the chair, practically lifting her to nearly the same height, crushing her chest against his.

"No, it isn't," he ground out the words. "But when I'm with you, I keep thinking I can…clean up the mess later." He punctuated that with a swift kiss, squeezing her so tight breathing wasn't an option.

She wanted to push away, knew she should slow this pain train before it flattened her on the tracks, but then he eased her feet back to the floor so his hands traveled up her sides, over her breasts, under her throat, into her hair. His mouth burned kisses along her jaw, and he kept pushing her back until she hit the counter and he could really press himself into her.

Her skin sizzled like the onions in hot oil, his hands making every tender spot crackle with the fire of his touch.

She couldn't stop, couldn't fight the urgency that made her touch all the same places on his body, over his shoulders, down his abs, lower to get her hands on the rock-hard—

The door latch echoed through the whole apartment, jerking them apart.

"Oh, hi." Alex walked in as they somehow let go of each other, all three of them blinking in surprise. "I...I..."

"Hi, Alex," Tom managed. "You're back early."

"Yeah, I know. I'm...sorry."

"Nothing to be sorry about," Gussie said quickly. "We're just making"—*out*—"dinner." She gave a tug to her T-shirt.

Great, just *great*. Some role model she was.

"Well, I'm not staying, if that's okay. I'm going to spend the night with Lizzie and—"

"Spend the night?" Tom asked. "There's a boy over there."

Alex battled a little smile. "I don't think he's going to be in our room," she said. "And Miss Annie is there, and she said it was fine. Isn't it fine, Gussie?"

"Of course it's..." Not her place to give permission, she remembered. She turned to Tom. "I think it's fine," she said. Better, even, since it left them alone in the apartment.

But that side benefit hadn't even registered with Tom, who was still frowning with a parental-like concern. "You sure Anne is there?"

"Uh, yeah." Alex shifted from one foot to the other. "Do you need to talk to her or anything?"

He hesitated for a moment, then shook his head. "No, it's okay."

Alex looked from one to the other, no doubt taking in exactly what she saw. "You want me to call or text before I come home?"

Oh, Lord. "Absolutely not," Gussie said quickly, not caring if it was her place to say or not. "You have a key, and you can come and go as you please, as long as we know where you are."

We. Why did she say that?

"Cool." Alex headed back to her room, leaving them a few feet apart and a million miles away from where they had just been.

"Shit." He picked up his wineglass and lifted it for a mock toast. "Here's to 'do as I say and not as I do,' right?"

Gussie smiled and returned the toast with her own glass. "Told you all good things must come to an end."

Over his glass, tapered blue eyes warned her loud and clear. The end wasn't in sight…yet.

Maybe it was because Alex had unexpectedly popped in on them, but Tom managed to focus his attention on getting dinner on the table and quit trying to drag Gussie to bed. They were both a little gun-shy after the interruption, so they enjoyed the food, the view, the company and, in the back of his mind, the fact that they'd be alone overnight.

"I have to say something." Gussie toyed with her last few bites, finally setting down the fork without taking one.

"Not sure I like the sound of that."

"No, it's a good thing. I mean, it's an observation I've made about you. An incongruity in your character, if you will."

"Nope, definitely not going to like this." He stabbed a piece of chicken the way he'd like to stab any conversation about *incongruity in his character*, whatever the hell that could mean.

She ignored his comment, sipping ice water before making any pronouncements. "For a guy who is, you know, hell-bent for leather to stay completely free of any responsibilities, you sure take yours seriously."

"What am I going to let her do? She's my..." He shook his head and gave up on the last bit of chicken. "Look, I had to take care of my sister when she was a teenager. The first thing she did when she turned eighteen was hook up with an idiot and get pregnant. Can you blame me if I get a little nervous about history repeating itself?"

"But in the flower market today, when you thought someone was on our tail? You were as protective as a paid bodyguard."

Hardly. "A good one would have taken that asshole down for getting pictures of you."

"But we know why he was doing it. He's probably on Instagram or Facebook."

Tom thought about that, the echo of Suzette's marketing stats still in his head. Ninety percent of the people who'd seen the shots were women. That guy had been kind of a bruiser, with muscles and a look of intensity on his face that still made Tom uneasy.

"You can admit it," she urged. "You have a protective streak. I think, deep inside, there's a man who wants to care for his loved ones and, you know, guard the cave."

He looked skyward at the phrase. "Excuse me if I don't grunt and drag you by the hair." Then he winked at her. "Although, the idea has merit."

"Scoff if you want," she said. "But I think there's hope for you, *panta monos*. You'll have to find the right…situation. Then maybe you won't have to stamp an expiration date on your other arm."

She went for a teasing tone, but the words hit him hard anyway. "I don't expire, Gussie… Other people do." He felt the sensations well up, familiar and dark. He looked away, trying to manage them, but the view of a sun-streaked sky melting into twilight took him back to…

"What do you mean?" she asked.

"I mean that, for me, in my life, I've lost the people that I…" Damn it, his voice would crack if he said the word *love*.

"I'm sorry." She shifted in her seat and started to reach out to him, but stopped as if the look on his face warned her not to touch him right then.

But he didn't want to push her away. Not now. Not…ever. "Don't apologize, Gussie. You've only been real and open with me." He took her hand, threading their fingers together, already wanting her support for what he knew was about to come out.

"And you?" she asked, tracing her thumb over his knuckle, the touch sexy and intimate and better than any conversation. "Have you been completely open?"

Swallowing, he studied their joined hands, her long, tanned fingers and his blunt-tipped, stronger ones. Intertwined like lovers. But, of course, they couldn't be lovers. Not yet. Not until he told her everything.

"I haven't lied," he finally said. "But there's more."

Her thumb stilled on his knuckle. "Really?"

"Really."

They sat in silence for at least thirty seconds. Gussie didn't move, patiently waiting for him to continue, but Tom couldn't move, paralyzed by his thoughts and the memories that he liked to bury.

"I guess I am protective," he finally said. "I don't want to lose anyone else in my life."

She nodded sympathetically. "You've lost both your parents and your sister. That's more than a lot of people have to endure at such a young age, Tom."

"But they aren't all I've lost."

He felt her fingers tense as she waited.

He tried to swallow, but his throat was dry and his stomach was tight and, son of a bitch, something hot was burning his eyelids.

"Who else have you lost?" She whispered the question, as if she really didn't want to know the answer.

"My wife and son."

Chapter Twenty-One

Gussie stared at him, all the blood draining from her head to land in a pool in her stomach. "You were married." She barely breathed the words. "With a son?"

Taking a deep inhale, he held it in his lungs for a long time before letting it out in a long, tattered puff of sorrow.

"My wife, Sophia, had been six months pregnant when she hemorrhaged. Both she and our son died before she could get medical help." He slipped his hand out of her grasp, pushing his chair back from the table slightly. "So, no, I haven't always been alone."

A rush of blood and sympathy and, whoa, understanding rolled through her. No wonder…no damn wonder he wanted to be alone.

"Tom, I'm so sorry." Lame, hollow words. "Can you talk about it?"

"No," he said with a mirthless laugh. "But I guess I'm about to."

"Why have you never mentioned it?"

"Because it's easier to pretend it never happened."

Who would want to do that? Why? "Why has Alex never mentioned it?" Surely she knew her uncle had been married and had a baby on the way and then…oh, God, it was sad.

"Alex doesn't know."

"Did Ruthie?"

He nodded slowly. "Alex was only seven when Sophia…when it happened. I suspect Ruthie hadn't told her, then never mentioned it after Sophia died. I'd been around to see my sister only sporadically before that, and she never met my wife."

His *wife*. The very word sounded foreign on his lips.

If Alex had been seven, then this must have happened about five years ago.

"So that's why I don't do well with connections," he explained. "When Ruthie died, it was like…" He made a guttural sound. "How many people does a person have to lose before they know it's better not to have any…any…"

"Any family," she supplied. "And yet Ruthie made sure that didn't happen by leaving Alex with you."

Another grunt of unexplained emotion. "Which was why when I found out and got to Florida, I was just a shithead from the word go."

"No, you weren't. You tried. You are still trying to reach her."

"I didn't want another family," he ground out. "I was actually so angry at Ruthie, I didn't mourn her properly. I still haven't."

But he was, in his own way.

"Anyway, that's my story, and better you know before you get in any deeper."

Too late. She was deep. "Can you tell me more? Tell me about her?"

He shrugged. "She was amazing. Awesome. One of a kind."

Gussie was ashamed at the twinge of jealousy, tamping it

down quickly. Of course he would marry someone like that…like himself. "I'm glad you found her, then."

He shot her a look that said he wasn't so glad at all. That it really wasn't better to have loved and lost.

"We really wanted the baby," he said, giving her a mental image of a young couple, blissfully expecting, which came with yet another twist of envy. He pushed away from the table completely. "He wasn't planned, but…we were…"

He shook his head and walked out to the balcony, leaving his thought unfinished. But Gussie could already imagine what he and Sophia were—happy. Excited. Anticipating great things.

For a moment, Gussie stayed right where she was because running after him to demand to know more wasn't going to help him at all. She could see his silhouette, leaning against the railing, head down as he worked to shovel his emotions back into wherever he stored them under lock and key.

She wondered how a person survived that kind of heartache. No, the question she was asking was, how would *she* survive that kind of heartache? It was clear how Tom had coped.

Always alone.

Well, not now, buddy. Not this time.

Taking a steadying breath, Gussie got up and joined him in the balmy evening air. Wordlessly, she put her hand on his back and turned him toward her, and then she wrapped her arms around his waist and rested her head on his chest.

He kissed the top of her head and fell a little closer into her, still silent.

She had so many questions, but the logistics of his sorrowful story didn't seem as important as holding him right then and just letting him hurt against her.

They stood like that until darkness fell, and only then did Tom ease back and look at Gussie with gratitude in his blue eyes.

"She was a real estate agent in Athens," he said. "I met her trying to buy a place to live, of all things."

She almost smiled. "So you're not really a man with no home or country."

"I loved Greece and decided to get a place there when I got financially secure and stable. Then I met Sophia and started staying at her apartment, and before we knew it, she was pregnant."

"Before you were married?"

He gave a dry laugh. "Now you sound like her dad, who did threaten to kill me. Or drown me in ouzo and whiskey." His smile grew wider and his gaze distant with a memory. "Her family lived—*lives*—on an island in the middle of the southeast Aegean Sea, Karpathos. They're farmers up north, in a village so old school that women run around in traditional dress. They live close to the earth, close to each other, close to God. But with so much life and love and wine and food and family, it was…unbelievable."

Jealousy got its grip on Gussie's heart. *Now* she ached with wanting something she didn't have.

"We got married right there in the front of her farm, in a really small ceremony because she was already showing, so it was just her family." His smile faded as quickly as it came. "But they couldn't help her when she needed it the most."

Even though part of her almost didn't want to know, she asked anyway. "What happened?"

He turned toward the view, so she couldn't see the pain etched on his features. "She was staying with them because the pregnancy hadn't been easy. She had problems from the beginning and, as much as I wanted her to stay in Athens, near her doctor, when I was out of town, she insisted on going home. It was where she felt safer, being pregnant I guess, because her mother and sisters were there."

Quiet for a minute, he stared straight ahead, and Gussie waited, bracing for a tough story.

"I had to go to London for a week-long shoot when she was pretty far along." He closed his eyes as though a surge of guilt hit. "Apparently, it was all very fast, and they tried, but the village is notoriously remote, with one treacherous road an hour from the only real town on the island. And even there, all they have is a medical center, no hospital. She didn't make it, and neither did the baby."

She closed her eyes, feeling the impact of his words. "God, I'm sorry."

"We were going to name him Uly, short for Ulysses." He could barely say the name. "It's Greek, and we thought I shouldn't be the only one in the family with a historical and hysterical name. Plus, it beat Homer."

She heard the attempt at humor, an echo of what she imagined were inside jokes shared with a woman he loved while they planned for their life as a family.

"Anyway," he said, stiffening as any hope of humor faded. "I made a decision to stay completely alone after that."

"*Panta monos*," she whispered.

"I never want to lose like that again. I never want to feel that kind of pain, like someone ripped a limb from my body, and while they were at it, they tore out my heart." He cleared his throat as if the jagged words actually hurt to speak them, then stepped away, looking hard at her, as if this were the first time since the conversation started that he actually saw her.

"Gussie." He dragged his hands to her shoulders, gripping her there. "I don't tell people this story."

"Then I feel special."

"That's the problem," he said gruffly. "You are."

Her heart flipped at how his dead-flat tone didn't match his promising words. "Why, exactly, is that a problem?" Except, really, she already knew the answer to that question.

"Nothing can change this." He raised his arm so the Greek letters were visible. "In fact, someone like you—no, *you in particular*—will only make me even more certain of my decision never to..." His voice trailed off.

"Never to live? Never to love?" She jerked back a little, the force of her emotions jolting her. "Really? No one has a chance with you, ever?"

He gave his head a nearly imperceptible shake, the minuscule move firing her even more.

"That's awful damn selfish of you, Tom."

He flinched a little, then acknowledged it. "Self-protective."

"Self*ish*," she fired back. "Because people are going to love you, whether you want them to or not. People like Alex and"—*me*—"people you meet. Friends. Associates. It's not fair to hold everyone off."

"It's fair to me."

Fury punched her. "And that's all that matters to you?"

"Gussie, please, I just bared my soul to you—"

"And that soul is scarred, like the back of my head. I get it, Tom. I get it, and my heart hurts for what you've been through and what you've lost. It's unthinkable. But—"

"There is no but," he interjected.

"But," she continued through grinding teeth, "you can't stop living because someone else died."

"Too late. I already did."

252

"You *can't*," she insisted, refusing to hear him. "You have Alex, you have a job, you have..." She frowned as something else hit her. "You have a family in Greece, living in a remote village, surrounded by food and wine and friends."

"They're not my family."

"Do you still see them?"

"I haven't seen them since the funeral. I barely said good-bye, just went to Cyprus to mourn and drink and..." He gestured toward the tattoo on his arm. "Set a course for the rest of my life."

"Is she buried on that island?"

"Yes. On a hillside under her favorite willow tree."

"And you've never been to there to visit her grave?"

He shook his head, too ashamed to make the admission out loud.

"Well, you need to."

He closed his eyes and huffed out a breath strong enough to quiver his nostrils. "Stop this."

"Stop what? Telling you what you don't want to hear? The truth?"

"The only truth I know is that it hurts more than a human can bear to lose a person you love, so it's better not to love." He pivoted to the French door, heading right back into the living room.

"Tom!"

He kept on going through the room, disappearing into the shadows. Gussie's throat closed up as she stared into the dimly lit rooms, hearing his bedroom door close. She felt her whole body want to follow him, pound on the door, demand he talk and think and *change*.

But he wasn't going to change any more than that tattoo would disappear from his arm. And that was bad, bad news for a woman who might be falling for him, or a girl who might have already fallen...into his care.

Gripping the railing, she stared out at the night lights of Nice, the reality of what she now knew about him settling over her like the warm night air. He'd been so busy getting her to reveal her old heartaches that she'd completely missed what he was hiding. His pain was so deeply embedded that it was impossible to see, even in close conversation.

Behind her in the apartment, she heard footsteps, and she tightened her fingers, waiting for him to join her. What would he say? Would he argue more or throw his arms around her and tell her she was right and maybe she could be the one to heal—

The front door clicked closed, and the apartment went silent.

Gussie didn't move, the impact of that noise and the fact that he'd left rolling over her like ice-cold water. Ten seconds later, she saw him walking down the shadowy streets a few stories below, his head down, his hands in his pockets, his shoulders slumped as he disappeared into the city.

Alone, like always.

"Allez! Allez! On se lève!" The words, barked with indignant French fury, slapped Tom awake. *"Pas d'sans-abri ici, c'est interdit!"*

Blinking into the rising sun, Tom grabbed the arms of the Promenade sun chair, attempting a sleepy mental translation. All he could get was "homeless" and "forbidden," which was enough to tell him what the gruff

French policeman meant. *Get the hell off the beach. Nobody sleeps here.*

"*Maintenant!*" the man ordered. *Now.*

"All right, I'll go." Tom waved him off, pushing up from the chair to stumble away, not bothering to even try to explain that he wasn't homeless.

Because, shit, he kind of was.

He had no home, no family, no wife, no...what had Gussie once called her friends? No foundation.

He stood still for a moment, pressing his feet into the concrete as though it were a material reminder of what it would feel like to have that kind of foundation in his life. Other than terrifying, of course.

He closed his eyes, burning from the lack of real sleep and overactive tear ducts.

Damn, he hadn't cried over Sophia and the baby for a long, long time. He'd hardened that part of him, let the scar tissue form. Walking again, he let another metaphor create a mental image—this one similar to the rutted tissue that covered a spot on Gussie's head, only his was over his heart. And like Gussie and her wigs and hats, he'd tried desperately to cover that scar with work and travel and solitude.

But she'd exposed his scar, like he'd gotten her to reveal hers.

He threaded his fingers through his hair and lifted his head from a study of the pavement to catch a glimmer of the morning sky.

Which only made him think about Gussie and how he should be waking up with her right now, holding her naked body against his, making love as the sun painted Nice a *portokali* sky. Maybe he should have told her that Sophia had taught him that word—or maybe she'd figured it out by now.

He shook off the sky, the poignancy of it too much for him right then, instead turning a corner to head back to the apartment where he would...what?

Apologize for being a dick?

And then what? As much as he wanted her in his arms, and his bed, Gussie was right about how it would only make things worse when this inevitably ended.

He swore under his breath and caught a whiff of rich coffee aroma floating over the morning air. Without thinking, he followed his nose to a small café that hadn't quite opened its doors for the earliest of risers. He had to negotiate in broken French and slip a few euro, but a few minutes later, he sat at an outdoor table and sipped creamy *café au lait*.

From there, he watched the few passersby hustling to daybreak jobs and vendors carrying baskets of fruit and flowers toward Old Town for today's market.

One passed him rolling a barrow of spices, a whiff of coriander, vanilla, and clove drop-kicking him into memories of the Karras kitchen. The sounds of Sophia's mother and sisters chattering and cooking, music playing, sun pouring in through windows that looked out over the Aegean Sea.

His eyes shuttered with the echo of Gussie's words.

You have a family in Greece.

And he missed them. Missed the colors and scents of Karpathos, the jagged terrain, the whitewashed buildings in the gleaming sunshine. He missed Papa Nico's laugh, and Mama Christa's nurturing. The music, the food, the whiskey on the patio...the wholeness of a family who'd taken him in and loved him like a son.

And yet, if she hadn't insisted on being there when Tom was out of town, Sophia might still be alive and Uly...

No. It was easier to let them all go.

He looked up from his coffee to take one more memory-infused sniff of the spice cart, and as it moved, he caught a glimpse of a man across the street, scant seconds before he disappeared around a corner. As he rubbed sleep-deprived eyes, the image of another man flashed in Tom's head. The same muscular build, the same dark hair cut short, a green T-shirt this time, but the same faded jeans.

What the hell? He shot up from the table so fast coffee splashed onto the saucer. Without hesitation, he darted into the street and around the corner. No sign of him. He paused for a second, peering up and down the road, then realized where he stood right now. Blocks from the apartment, if someone knew to take that next alleyway.

He jogged toward it, his heart rate already increased, his sixth sense on high alert. Nice was not a huge city, so what were the chances it *wasn't* the same guy?

As he turned the corner to the street where their apartment was, his view was blocked by a vegetable truck rumbling down the street. Impatient, he darted behind it, half-hoping he'd see the man, half-hoping he was imagining this.

But there he was, walking briskly...*right toward their building.*

Tom stayed back, far enough away not to be seen, but close enough to get a good look at him. His features were strong and distinctive, his body language both ready and centered—military trained, he'd guess.

The man slowed as he reached the yellow stucco apartment building, crossing the street to lean against another building and look right up at the very balcony where Tom last stood with Gussie.

What the hell?

Tom waited, ready to run or pounce. But the man stayed perfectly still, his gaze locked on the balcony like some kind of stalker creep. Tom's hands itched and his legs ached to have at the guy, but he had to wait to see what he was—

The sound of female voices floated down the street as Gussie and Alex stepped out of the front entrance of the building, arm in arm. Tom wanted to call to them, but as soon as the man saw them, he dropped into the closest alcove doorway and hid. Gussie and Alex walked up the street in the opposite direction, their heads close as they chatted.

Tom had no idea where they'd be going this early, but his entire being was focused on the man, who stepped back out into the street, took out his phone, and started taking pictures.

Bastard! Tom ran toward the guy from behind, careful not to make a sound on approach. Gussie and Alex disappeared around the next corner, just as Tom jumped. He whipped the guy around, slammed an elbow into his gut, sent the phone flying, and smacked him against the wall with a loud grunt.

"What the fuck do you think you're doing?" Tom demanded.

Horrified hazel eyes popped wide open, and he fought for breath.

Tom pressed a little harder, ready to knee the prick in the balls if he had to. "Why are you taking pictures of them?"

He shook his head frantically, and for a second, Tom assumed he didn't speak English.

"I don't want to hurt her," he murmured, killing that theory. He not only spoke English, he was as American as Tom.

But that didn't make him let up any pressure. "Then why are you following them?"

"I just...I wanted..." He closed his eyes. "I wanted to see how she turned out."

Her? Who did he mean? Tom searched every inch of the guy's face, digging for anything that would be a clue as to who the hell he was and what he was talking about.

"I had to...see her." He wasn't even trying to push Tom away anymore. "I had to."

And then Tom knew exactly who he had pinned against the wall.

Chapter Twenty-Two

Alex and Gussie wandered through the backstreets, taking the scenic route to what Alex liked to think of as The Best Bakery in the World.

"Stop for a second," Gussie said, putting her hand on Alex's arm. "Look, right there, down that incline to the corner. What does it look like to you?"

Alex frowned into the view, taking in the yellow buildings and low gray stone wall along the side of one road. It did look like something…

"Delfino Square!" She almost jumped up and down, thinking of the race route in Mario Kart. "This is totally like the first intersection right after the roundabout."

"Exactly," Gussie agreed, throwing an arm around her. "And up there is like that main road where it gets busy and I always, always get creamed."

Just then, a bus rolled by, so close that Gussie and Alex had to step closer to the buildings. It turned the corner and headed for a large building surrounded by twenty other giant buses exactly like it.

"Jeez," Gussie said. "It's about as dangerous as Mario Kart, too. Next thing, they'll be flinging banana peels at us from the…*gare routière*. Which I believe means *bus station*."

"You're getting good at French," Alex said, fighting the urge to hold Gussie's hand when the light changed and they could cross. "Do you think Mario Kart based that course here? I thought it was supposed to be Italy."

"It's Europe," Gussie said. "Who cares? Still feels like we're living in our video game."

Our video game. When did that happen? Alex waited for a surge of disloyalty—after all, Mario Kart *was* Momma's game—but that guilty feeling never came. Just something she hadn't felt in a long time, something like peace or contentment.

Then Gussie yawned so loud and long, it drowned out all sounds and peace and made Alex giggle. "Whoa. That was pretty," she teased. "Pretty ugly."

Gussie elbowed her. "Shut up. I didn't sleep all night."

Alex looked down at her feet, not really able to meet Gussie's gaze because she knew why she had been awake.

Even though Gussie had been in her own room and Uncle Tommy's door had been closed when Alex had come home this morning, she *knew*. They *had* to be doing it. She and Lizzie had talked about it for hours, laughing so hard they cried. And Miss Annie made enough comments about what a cute couple they made and how they looked at each other that Alex had it all figured out.

The question was…did that mean they would be, like, boyfriend and girlfriend? Or *more*? Because living with Uncle Tommy as her guardian, just the two of them—that was not an option and it felt like time to tell Gussie.

Because the dream that her father would show up out of the blue and want to take her away to raise her—that wasn't happening. Although, she'd hoped when Uncle Tommy had said some guy had followed them in the market. Of course, she'd prayed it was her father.

But that was crazy. When she woke up this morning, next to her new friend Lizzie, Alex had a certainty about her father that she hadn't felt since Momma died. He wasn't going to swoop in and save her, so she had to tell Gussie…what she wanted. She'd even gone back to the apartment early to tell her, finding her up. When Gussie suggested they go for croissants, Alex was sure this was her perfect opportunity.

Except she was scared Gussie would say no.

"Can I have coffee, too?" she asked.

"I think in France kids can have coffee *and* wine, but let's start with a little *café au lait*." Gussie put a hand on Alex's shoulder. "And one of those incredibly sinful chocolate croissants while you tell me all about your evening with the Stone family. I want every gory detail." She fake-coughed and muffled the word, "Eddie."

A little shiver shot through Alex, because that was so something Momma would have done. And she'd said so many times how she couldn't wait for Alex to like boys so they could talk about each one of them for hours and decide whether they were boyfriend material.

A sudden wave of sadness so powerful and strong she could taste it washed over Alex. Momma would never, ever get to know about any one of her boyfriends. Ever.

"Um, Alex?" Gussie nudged her. "Someone just went off to la-la land. And I can only imagine why."

Let her think it was Eddie who took over Alex's thoughts. She wished it was. She wished she could think about Momma a few less times every minute.

"Do you like our next-door-neighbor boy?" Gussie asked in a singsong voice.

Just like Momma, no beating around the bush. "He's cute."

"Very."

"And nice."

"Seems so."

"But he cheated at Monopoly."

"Ugh!" Gussie made a face as she yanked the bakery door open. "Cheaters are not boyfriend material."

Alex froze. "Boyfriend material?" Only Momma said that!

"Oh, don't pretend you haven't thought about it," Gussie said, holding the door so Alex could walk right into the smell of heaven. "But you are too young for a boyfriend, you know."

"I know, but who says that?" *Besides my mother?*

"Everyone."

Alex's heart dropped a little. "Oh, I thought..." *That it was a sign.* "Never mind."

Gussie took a noisy sniff. "I could crawl into that mountain of baguettes and live there."

Alex smiled, still thinking how Gussie sounded like Momma when she said things like that. After they got their goodies, they went outside, and Gussie picked a table by the street.

"This is the same table where I sat with Uncle Tommy the other day," Alex said. "Hopefully, this will be more fun."

"Oh, Alex, come on." Gussie handed her the bag. "You have to give the guy a chance."

She didn't have to. Without answering, she spread out the wax paper, taking a second to admire the perfection of the croissant.

Gussie sipped coffee, her gaze off in some distant place, brows pulled in a slight frown. With red eyes and the shadows under her lids, she definitely looked like she'd been awake all night.

"Why are you staring at me?" Gussie asked.

"Still getting used to you with no makeup," Alex lied, looking away.

Gussie sighed. "Me, too." She closed those shadowed eyes and exhaled noisily. "Alex, I might go back to Mimosa Key soon."

"What?" Alex sat straight up, punched by the announcement. "Why? What would you do that for? You can't leave now."

"I might need to…" She looked away again, and Alex could have sworn she was about to cry. What happened last night? Alex was almost afraid to ask. Instead, she tried guilt.

"But you promised to stay, to have a freecation, to be with us like…like a family." She was whining, but she didn't care.

Gussie's expression softened as she reached over the crumbs and bag to take Alex's hand. "Oh, honey, I'm not really your family."

Alex stared at her, willing her eyes not to fill as the words hit her heart. She failed. Gussie never talked like that. She was never negative.

"Alex." She squeezed her hand. "Please, don't cry. I'll start, too, and then we'll be two blubbery messes."

How could she not cry? "Don't you want to stay?"

She didn't answer, but shifted around in her seat as if the iron bottom hurt her. Or the conversation did. "I may have to go home," she finally said.

"There's no wedding for you to work on, you said so. And your friend isn't getting married until the end of the month." Nothing was working. "How can you leave Uncle Tommy?"

Gussie gave her a *get real* look. "Um, easily?"

Really? "But he really likes you. He loves you!"

Gussie blinked at her, color draining from her face. "No, he doesn't, honey." The hitch in her voice told Alex a whole heck of a lot. Like Gussie really liked him, but he didn't like her back. Did that happen to grown-ups, too? Grown-ups as pretty and cool as Gussie?

"Miss Annie thinks he loves you."

Gussie smiled. "For a woman in the throes of divorce, that says a lot about her optimism." She shook her head. "Enough about me. Tell me about this Monopoly cheater you like."

No, she wouldn't let her change the subject. "You'll never get him to fall in love with you if you leave, Gussie."

"I'll never get him to fall in love with me, period." Her voice was tight, like she was trying to make a joke, but it wasn't funny. "He's determined to be alone." As soon as she said that, she must have realized what it sounded like, because she squeezed Alex's hand even harder. "Not *alone* alone," she corrected. "I mean alone without, you know, a woman in his life."

Alex pulled her hand free so she could make a fist under the table. "So, if you don't marry him—"

Gussie snorted hard. "I'm not going to marry him, Alex."

"Then..." She took a deep breath and spilled her idea. "Could you take me and be my guardian and take care of me?" She rushed through the question so fast she wasn't sure if Gussie understood.

Maybe she didn't, based on the look of complete confusion on her face.

"Would you? Could you?" God, she sounded like a Dr. Seuss book.

"Alex, I—"

"Think about it before you say no, okay? Think really

hard. You are such a natural at being a mom, and I'm an orphan, so—"

"Alex, you're not—"

"I think we could have so much fun, and I don't eat much, and I promise I would be so neat, my room is never messy, and I won't spend a lot of money. In fact, I could get a—"

"Stop."

She swallowed her promises, letting the big lump in her throat the size of the whole croissant she'd eaten choke her with the truth. "You don't want me."

"Alex, that's not true, not for one second, and you know it."

But Gussie was the only person who seemed to understand her, who made her feel safe, who could possibly replace the giant hole left by her mother.

"A person can't just take someone's child to raise," Gussie said softly.

But she wasn't *anyone's* child now. Except her father's. And he—

"There are courts and legalities and what your mother wanted—"

"She didn't want me to end up with her stupid brother!" Oh, great, now she was bawling like a two-year-old.

"Shh." Gussie instantly moved her chair to the side of the table, getting closer to Alex. "Calm down and listen to me."

Alex bit her lip, trying to do exactly that, but her head was buzzing.

"If she really and truly didn't want you with your uncle, then she'd have changed her will. She wants you with family, Alex."

"What is family? It's the people you like to be around, right?"

Gussie opened her mouth and shut it. "You know, I was going to tell you that family is blood, but I know that's not true. When you're older, you'll make friends who will seem like sisters to you. But, until then, you can't choose your family."

Alex shot her a look, hating the tears that blurred her vision. "Why don't you choose me?" she sobbed.

"Oh, Alex." Gussie's voice cracked as she hugged Alex. "I would if I could. You're sweet and good, and I love you already."

She clung to every word, every syllable. There was hope.

"But I told you, it isn't that easy to take someone from their legal guardian."

She jerked back. "He'd let you have me! He doesn't even have a heart."

Gussie's green eyes were completely wet, and when she blinked, a tear rolled down her face. "He does have a heart, honey, but something happened to break it."

She inched back, taking in this new information. "How do you know that?"

"He told me, and it made me understand him a little better."

But what did it mean? "Can you...fix him?"

She smiled sadly. "I don't think I'm the person to do that, but maybe you are."

"Me? He hates me."

"No, he doesn't, Alex." She stroked a soothing hand over Alex's face. "He doesn't understand you."

Alex leaned into Gussie's soft fingers, aching everywhere for how much she wanted Gussie to take her. "Gussie, will you make me a promise?"

"If I can."

"Talk to him."

"And try to make things better between you two? Yes, I promise you, Alex. I'll talk to him—"

"No, ask him." She reached out to hold Gussie's hand. "Ask him about you adopting me. Please, talk to him about the possibility. I need to know there's a chance."

Gussie's eyes shuttered half closed.

Please, Gussie, please. Alex silently squeezed her plea into her grip on Gussie's hand.

"Okay, I'll tell him we talked about it."

That's all she needed to hear. "Then I won't go and try to find my dad."

Gussie gasped. "You would never!"

"I was thinking about it."

"Well, don't think about it. Ever again. Come on, let's go."

"And you'll talk to him?"

"I will."

Holding on to that hope—he might say yes!—Alex stood and let Gussie put her arm around her as they started walking home.

"I'm not going into that apartment until you tell me whether you like Eddie," Gussie said as they headed down the sidewalk.

She was trying to get things back to normal, so Alex went along with it. "Not that much. A little, maybe. He definitely likes me."

"Really?" Gussie gave her a squeeze. "How can you tell?"

"Every time I look at him, he's looking at me."

"Oh, dead giveaway."

Which was funny, since Alex had seen Uncle Tommy staring at Gussie for what seemed like hours on end. "And when he cheated at Monopoly, it was to help me win."

"Ohh." She turned them into the apartment building, that lightness in her step again. "He's not a cheater, he's a helper. We can forgive that."

"Lizzie couldn't." They trotted up the stairs. "They fought so hard about it."

"Well, brothers and sisters fight, you know. At that age, Luke and I wanted to kill each other." She opened the front door, and they both stopped at the sound of men's voices coming from the balcony.

"Who's here?" Alex asked.

"I have no idea." Gussie ventured farther into the room, peering out toward the balcony doors. Behind her, Alex looked in the same direction, seeing a man talking to Uncle Tommy, a complete stranger. As tall as Uncle Tommy, with short hair, he turned when they got closer, a huge smile breaking over his face.

"I found you," he whispered.

The words floated over Alex's ears, grabbing her heart and squeezing every drop of blood out if it. Her knees nearly buckled, and every cell in her body went completely numb.

He was here! Her father had come for her! She covered her mouth to hold back a scream, tears she thought had completely dried up sprang to her eyes.

Nothing came out of her mouth. Nothing. Not *Daddy* or *Mr. Whitman* or—

Next to her, Gussie made a weird whimpering sound. Her hands were over her mouth, too, and her face was bone white.

Gussie shook her head like she couldn't speak, like she couldn't even breathe. All she did was open her arms and fall against the man, murmuring the same thing over and over again.

"Luke! Luke! Luke!"

Chapter Twenty-Three

He was here! In her arms! It wasn't a dream or fantasy or trick of the light.

Gussie embraced her brother until her arms hurt, fighting a sob of joy and relief and more joy.

Shaking, crying, still trying to get her breath, she drew back to look at him, and that made her let out another sob and hug him again.

"Oh my God, oh my God. I can't believe it." She was blubbering, but didn't care, finally hugged out enough to pull away and look at this grown-up version of Luke. He was so different than the boy who'd left, but still so distinctly…Luke. His slash of dark brow, his wide cheekbones and strong jaw. But all if it was so magnified and masculine. This was no boy, that was for sure.

Luke was bigger, better, and…a little scary-looking. A faded scar on his temple and the shadow of his whiskers added to that, but it was something else. He was all muscles, his hair was nearly shorn, but it was his eyes that had changed the most.

Still a muddy mix of green and brown, still fringed with unfairly long lashes, but the light behind them had dimmed and darkened to more of a glint. A serious, cynical, harsh glint.

Even when he smiled, which he was doing as he examined her with the very same scrutiny, no doubt balancing his memories of a girl with the woman in front of him.

"Auggie, you got hot."

She tried to laugh, but it came out as another half sob. "Well, that takes away any of my doubt that it's you." The nickname usually earned a death threat from her. This time, she hugged him again, her heart finally slowing down to something close to normal.

"How is this possible?" She pressed her cheek against a shoulder that was close to twice the size of the one she'd last seen on him. Her gaze landed on Tom, who stood silent a few feet away. His expression was unreadable, maybe a little dark, as he searched her face as if he needed to know how she felt.

"Did you do this?" she mouthed.

He almost shrugged then shook his head.

"He *did* do this," Luke said. "Honest, I was only trying to see you from a distance."

"Why?"

For a second, he didn't answer, then looked down. "I can't stand it if you hate me."

"Hate you? Lucas John McBain, have you even met me?"

"Not for a long time, and…" He took a slow breath. "I wouldn't blame you if you did, Gus."

"Well, I don't!" she exclaimed. "I don't blame you now, and I didn't blame you then."

She saw his eyes flash for a millisecond, then he was Luke again and shook his head. "You don't have to say that, I know—"

"You don't know anything," she fired back. "Because you've been gone for fifteen years. So the only thing I blame

271

you for is leaving and making us all worried and miserable. That was a dumb move, Luke."

"That was my only move, Gus."

"Then why didn't you come back?"

"Couldn't. Sorry."

Couldn't? *Sorry*? Under any other circumstances, she'd have lashed at him for that lame-ass answer, but nothing could make her mad at him now. Nothing was worth the risk of losing him again. But first, Tom.

Tom. The other man she wanted to wrap her arms around. He looked as wretched as she felt after a sleepless night, the last conversation they'd had still shadowing his eyes, but he had an air of satisfaction, too. The look of a man who knew he'd given the perfect gift.

"How did you find him?" she asked, no small note of hero worship slipping into the question.

"He was the guy in the flower market."

She gasped, unable to fathom that she'd been that close to Luke and hadn't even known it.

"I'm usually better at stealth," Luke said. "But I took a risk and tried to get your picture."

Why? Why not approach her? Why not call her? Why not *come home*? She swallowed all the demanding questions, still terrified he'd disappear as magically as he'd arrived.

Instead, she drank him in some more, marveling at the man he'd become. Gone was a college-bound superstar who roamed the halls of Framingham High like he was king of the world. All signs of youth, innocence, and his anticipation of life had morphed into a rough, rugged man with an air of...danger.

He was built like a tank, with a solid chest and...what was around his neck? A dog tag? She lifted the metal pendant, the shape different from anything she'd seen. This was decidedly French with a stylized fleur-de-lis with the words *Legio Patria Nostra*. On the back, the name Luc McBain.

She looked up at him and met a hazel gaze darkened with a warning that she wasn't going to love what she was about to hear.

"French Foreign Legion," he said simply.

She took a slow step backward, unable to comprehend this. "You joined the French Foreign Legion?"

"Fourteen years ago."

The French Foreign Legion? "Is there still such a thing? I...I thought that was some romantic, fictional group of mercenaries from the movies."

"The only thing accurate in that statement is mercenaries, but very few stay in it for the money."

"So, you're like a paid soldier for other countries?" Her brother, the ultimate pacifist? The diplomat that everyone said would either be president or the chief justice of the Supreme Court? The best debater in the state of Massachusetts had become a professional soldier?

"I am a French citizen now, and to be clear, I'm no longer in the Legion."

Words failed as incredulity took over. Her brother, born and raised on the outskirts of Boston, as American as Paul Revere. "Then where do you live? What do you do?"

"France. I have a construction business in Lyon. When you said on your blog you would be so close—"

"You read my blog?"

"Every post. So I came down here to snoop around, then that picture of you went viral, and you were easy to find."

She pressed her hands against her chest, taking another step backward. Almost instantly, Tom was next to her, his arm around her. "I'm sure he'll answer all your questions, Gus—"

"Maybe not all of them," Luke said.

"Well, how about just the big ones," Gussie replied, curling her arm into Tom's for the support. "Like why you left and never called or came home."

"I called Dad a few times."

She'd known that. Brief, uninformative "I'm alive, don't look for me" calls that ripped open the wound every time Dad told her about one. All Luke had ever done was assure them he wasn't dead. Beyond that…nothing.

She resented it, but not enough to let it derail this reunion. The past didn't matter, because he was right in front of her. Finally.

"Gussie." Luke reached for her, his tone and eyes telling her their thoughts aligned. "I want to explain some things to you. I couldn't go back to the States for a lot of reasons, but I'm here now, and I can talk to you." He searched her face, a whole lifetime of pain she didn't understand on his. "Please?"

She felt her shoulders soften and fall as she turned to Tom. "I want to talk to him." As much as she loved Tom's support, she needed to be alone with Luke.

"Of course." He nodded. "I'll go see what's going on with Alex."

Alex! Gussie had promised her she'd talk to Tom. But now—

As if he could read her mind, Tom squeezed her hand and shook his head. "One family crisis at a time, Pink. Talk to Luke."

Gratitude rolled over her, and she impulsively hugged him, holding him long and close and hard. "Thank you," she whispered, which seemed incredibly inadequate.

He kissed her on the forehead before he left, the simple, single gesture like being handed a diamond.

When he left, Luke pulled her onto the sofa next to him. "Gussie, let me get this right out there. I did what I had to do to survive."

She nodded, still not entirely getting it. "You know, you could have survived at home."

"I couldn't stand it."

"But the whole incident ended." She turned, as if to prove that one scar was all that remained. "Once all the hospital and doctor stuff was over, we would have made it as a family, Luke. We were the McBains, remember?"

"I never forget that," he said. "And we still are the McBains."

She gave him a wary look. "Mom and Dad split up."

He closed his eyes like a bullet hit his heart. "I know. Because of me."

"Because the family broke apart," she said. "But it can be put back together." Hope gripped her heart. "I know it can. I believe it can."

"I damn near killed you. I know it was an accident, but I—"

"No, it wasn't." She held up her hand. "I mean, it was, but it wasn't your fault, and you need to stop thinking that right now."

"Don't try to change history. I was there."

"So was I, Luke. I ran right into the line of fire, or whatever you call the direction a firework is going."

"But you didn't know—"

"Yes, I did. And I didn't care. I'd downed a glass of vodka 'cause your stupid friend Brian Grimsby hurt me, and I thought I'd get attention and maybe make you look bad and…" Her voice faded as the blood drained from his tanned face. It was like she could see him replaying the moment in his mind, from a different angle, with a different possibility, and a different outcome for his whole life.

A band squeezed around her chest, aching and tight and impossible.

"I still shouldn't have thrown a bottle rocket. It was stupid."

"Luke, kids do stupid things. Adults forgive and forget."

He looked down, his jaw clenched. "After I left, I got into trouble. Big trouble. Bad trouble. So I ended up in Europe, and there was more trouble."

She shook her head on an exhale. "The golden boy of Framingham who never got a freaking detention in school."

"I changed."

"I see that." She reached to touch his face, tracing her finger along the scar at his temple. "And, obviously, I'm as much to blame for your scars as you are for mine."

"No, I've made my own." He kept looking down, his gaze on his clasped hands, his elbows on his knees.

"I fought wars for money," he said simply. "I survived in jungles and deserts and caves and…worse. I've been all over the world. I've fought in Bosnia, Iraq, Somalia, Rwanda, and the Ivory Coast. My family are brothers from Austria, Serbia, Nepal, and New Zealand. I've seen shit that can't ever be unseen but still haunts me at night. I've almost died so many times I stopped counting. But not one day have I forgotten you, Mom or Dad, or what I left."

Her stomach tightened and turned at what he'd been through. "Is it…over now?"

"More or less."

What the hell did that mean?

He looked up, managing a smile. "I can stay in Nice for a few days. Can we hang out or am I intruding on your family time?"

Her family time? That would be…and then an idea hit her so hard she almost shrieked.

"What?" he asked, obviously reading her expression.

Would he agree to it? Only one way to find out. "Luke, of course you can stay. I want you here. I want you to never leave my life. But…"

He swallowed, as if waiting for his sentencing.

"But that's not good enough," she whispered.

"What else do you want?" He looked down again, as if he couldn't face whatever request was coming.

"I want to be the McBain family again, Luke. I want Mom and Dad here, too. Will you do that? If we can get them here, will you stay for a family reunion? Please?" She reached over and put her hands over his, squeezing. "Would you stay if they come here, too?"

When he looked up, his eyes were wet with unshed tears. For a long moment, he said nothing, but then he blinked, sending a tear rolling over his rough-skinned cheek. "Yes. I will."

Chapter Twenty-Four

"Wag your tail!" Lizzie cried out.

"Fish ... water ... eyelashes!" Annie screamed.

"I know, I know!" Alex bounced on the living room sofa, laughing so hard at Luke's inane charade that she could barely speak. "*The Little Mermaid*!"

Luke dramatically pointed right at Alex, then touched his nose, making her break out into applause, the happiest she'd been in hours. Tom gave Gussie's hand a quick squeeze, and they exchanged a look—again. They still hadn't had a chance to talk alone today. Somehow, the hours had unfolded into a day at the beach, a dinner with neighbors, a silent truce thanks to Gussie's obvious joy at having her brother back in her life.

But Tom wanted to talk now, so when Gussie pushed up from the sofa and begged off the next round of charades to straighten up the kitchen, he followed.

When he came up behind her at the sink and slipped his arms around her waist, she stiffened. Undaunted, he pressed her into the counter and buried his face in her hair and neck.

"What's a guy gotta do to be alone with his girl around here?"

He felt her shudder—either from the kiss or the endearment. "Dishes." She held a dessert plate over her shoulder. "You can dry."

He took the plate with one hand, but squeezed her waist with the other. "Are we okay?"

Slowly, still in his arm, she turned. "I didn't know we were a *we* or that I was *your girl.*"

A hundred responses played in his head. *Maybe we could be. Let's give it a try. Just for France. Just for now.*

All were wrong.

"I don't know what we are," he admitted. "Other than crazy about each other and inches apart and dying to kiss."

"We are all that."

"It's good to see you so happy, Pink."

The smile reached her eyes, making them bright green and blissful. "Happy? My brother is here, my parents are packing to join us, and there's a living room full of people laughing. I don't get happier than this."

"Really?" Because where did he fit in that scenario of happiness? Nowhere. Which was what he wanted, right?

She reached up and cupped his cheek. "This has to be hard for you," she said. "All this family. Constant reminders. I'm sorry. I'm sorry you lost so much, and if I'm putting salt in the wound."

His heart dipped a little, as if her words and feelings were pressing right down on his chest. "Sometimes," he admitted in a soft voice, "when I'm holding you and I want you so much, I feel more lonely than alone."

He saw her work to swallow, then she bit her lip.

"Whatever it is, Gussie, let it out. Say what you're thinking, no matter how hard you're trying not to."

She fought a smile, busted. But then she shook her head.

"Then tell me later, when everyone's asleep and you sneak into my room tonight."

"Your room?"

"Yes." He added pressure with his hips. "It's the most secluded, and the bed is big and I want you there." It was a simple truth, and she didn't have to know how monumental it was for him to feel that way. "What do you want, Gussie?"

She looked a little surprised by the directness of the question. "I have what I want right now."

He stared at her, but she backed away at the sound of footsteps. Luke stepped into the kitchen, his face relaxed, his wineglass raised in a toast. "You're a nice couple," he said. "I think Mom will approve. I'm going back to my apartment, Gus. Will you walk me down to the street?"

"You promise you'll be back tomorrow?" she asked.

"If tomorrow comes."

Gussie laughed. "What kind of defeatist attitude is that, Luke?"

"Realist, not defeatist." He reached out to shake Tom's hand. "Thanks for the sneak attack this morning, my man. You proved you really love my sister, and for that reason, I won't kill you for kissing her."

Tom blinked at him, a denial on his lips that simply wouldn't come out. But Gussie was smiling when she left. Of course she was. She had everything she wanted.

Gussie walked with Luke to the door and down to the street to say good-bye.

"You could stay here, Luke, and crash on the couch."

"Or I could sleep in your room since you'll be shacked up with your boyfriend."

"He's not. And he doesn't love me."

Luke snorted. "I thought you were smarter than that, Gus."

"I am and you're wrong. We, you know, like each other."

"No, I don't know."

"No one in your life, Luke? Never been in love?"

He gave a dry laugh. "You definitely don't know about life in the Legion. I'm alone, and that's all that matters."

She grunted. "Oh, you men and your need to be alone. How does this world even procreate with a generation of isolation junkies?"

"Look, sis, forget me. Your issue's upstairs waiting for you in bed."

"We've never slept together," she fired back.

He made an *I'm impressed* face. "Mom will like that."

"Yet."

Laughing, he put an arm around her. "Brotherly advice?"

"I guess."

"Seize the day, or the night, as it might be. You never know what's going to happen. So live for this day, this moment, this feeling. 'Cause you could be numb or dead when the sun comes up."

"Wow, that's a pretty miserable way to look at the world."

"The world is miserable," he shot back. "My advice is have some fun, and stop trying to fight whatever you're trying to fight. What's the worst that could happen?"

"My heart could get stomped on."

"Oh, it will. But that's how you know you're alive."

She scowled up at him, reaching to touch his face. "What

happened to you, Luke? What made you so bitter and fatalistic?"

"I'm not bitter or fatalistic. I told you, I'm a realist. And that guy up there? He's a pretty real dude, too. And he likes you. In fact, I'm sure he's more afraid of you than you are of him." He gave her a quick kiss on the cheek, fluffing her hair, but letting his fingers brush lightly over the scar she'd been beginning to forget was there. "You turned out real good, Gus. I'm glad to see that."

With that, he was gone, leaving Gussie unexpectedly torn in two.

Back upstairs, Annie and her kids were letting themselves into their own apartment, and they all shared a quick hug.

When the kids said good night, Annie lingered in the doorway, leaning close to Gussie to whisper, "Check on Alex when you have a sec, luv."

"Is she okay?"

"She's been a bit off today. Haven't you noticed?"

"I noticed she was quiet, but not during charades. She had a blast."

"Who wouldn't with your dazzling brother?"

He was dazzling, even now, after fifteen years, Luke still captivated everyone around him. "I guess I've been so focused on him, I didn't give Alex my usual attention. Is she with Tom now?"

"She went to bed as soon as you walked out."

And Gussie knew why; she hadn't mentioned their conversation to Tom yet. How could she with a day like today? Still, she gave Annie an impulsive kiss. "You're a good friend already. How does that happen?"

"It's you, dear." She laughed. "You fold people into your arms and heart, and they never want to leave."

The compliment warmed her right down to her toes. "Gosh, Annie, thanks." She laughed. "Except Tom, who might want to be in my arms, but he surely will want to leave."

Annie drew back and gave her a serious look. "He's struggling as much as you and Alex," she said. "All that dreamy bachelorhood about to go down the loo."

But he hadn't always been a bachelor. She shook her head, not ready, willing, or even free to share his story. "If only it were that easy," she said instead. Adding an impulsive hug, she slipped back into the apartment to check on Alex.

Tom was quietly cleaning up the rest of the kitchen, waiting expectantly when she entered. "You done for the night, Pink?"

"Actually, I'm going to check on Alex."

"What's wrong with her?" he asked, frowning.

She hesitated a moment, not at all prepared to tell him that his niece not only didn't want his guardianship, she wanted Gussie's. The conversation would be hurtful and horrible and, honestly, the idea was unrealistic. After the emotional rollercoaster she'd been on today, she simply couldn't bear to dive into something that heavy.

"She's been a little weird all day," she said, purposefully vague.

"Damn it, I didn't even notice." He put up his hands in frustration. "How can I miss something like that?"

"It's okay," she assured him. "But really sweet that you care."

"I do care," he insisted.

"I didn't notice, either," Gussie admitted. "I was all focused on my brother."

"Which is understandable," he said. "He's your long-lost brother, but I should be more in tune with her." He set down his dishtowel. "I'm going to talk to her."

And Alex might bring up the whole topic of guardianship. At the very least, Gussie should be there. "I'll come with you."

"That's a good idea. I can learn from an expert."

She slipped her hand into his, and they walked down the hall together, a weird, buzzy feeling between them. It wasn't just attraction—that was always there. It wasn't that they had a joint mission—they both cared about Alex, so it made sense. It was more like...

This is what family did. What parents did. What two people who loved a third and made a unit—

"Gussie." He stopped her before the door. "What's the matter with you?"

She didn't dare blink, because her eyes had filled. Along with her heart. God, she wanted this so much. She wanted this to be real, not a freecation.

"I'm worried about her, that's all."

He slipped his arm around her and tapped on the door with his free hand. "We got this," he whispered.

Which only made it worse.

"I'm asleep."

"Funny, you sound awake," Gussie said.

"I'm tired, Gussie." But the slight hiccup gave away the truth. She was crying.

Sharing a quick look, Gussie nodded and Tom turned the knob, and the light instantly clicked off. The bedclothes rustled as she feigned sleep.

"What do you want?" Alex asked. "Why are you both here?"

"Because we both are worried about you," Tom said, his voice as gentle as Gussie had ever heard it.

"I'm fine."

"You don't sound fine," Gussie said, going to sit on the edge of the twin bed. She reached for Alex's cheek, but the girl whipped to the side and Gussie barely grazed her. It was enough to feel the tears.

"Why are you crying?" Gussie asked.

"Why do you think?"

"You miss your mom," Tom said, coming up behind Gussie and putting strong hands on her shoulders, the support so real and welcome.

"Actually, not this very minute."

"In other words, you're crying about something else," Tom said.

She didn't answer, which meant yes.

"Too dark for charades. Should we do twenty questions?" Gussie suggested. When there was more silence, she took a stab. "Did one of us do something to upset you?"

In the bit of moonlight in the room, Gussie could see Alex turn to face them, looking from one to the other, her eyes wide. As if she thought it was weird that they came in together, too. Weird and a little wonderful.

Alex and Gussie were on the same page there.

"How about that boy?" Tom said, making Gussie smile at the Dad-like tone in his voice.

"Eddie's fine," she said with a sniff. "And so's Lizzie."

Gussie thought for a minute, stumped. "Then what is it? Are you homesick? Physically sick? Reading a sad book?"

Alex sighed. "It was Luke."

"Luke?" Gussie startled at the unexpected answer. "My brother made you cry?"

Alex shot up and reached for the light, the sudden brightness making them all blink but instantly revealing how hard Alex had been weeping.

"Why couldn't he have been my dad?" she burst out. "I mean, first, he shows up, and I was sure...I was so sure that when we walked in he was going to, like, throw his arms around me and say, 'Alex! My daughter!'" She swiped at snot and tears, her eyes fierce with sadness and shame.

"Oh, Alex." Gussie sat on the bed to hug her, totally and completely understanding why she would have thought that. "I'm sorry you thought that's who he was."

She pushed back, shuddering on a sob and clearly ready to let it all out now. "And then he has to be so nice. And funny. And everyone loves him."

Gussie gave a dry laugh. "He was born that way."

"Well, why can't I have a father like that? Or..." She looked up. "An uncle?"

Ouch.

Tom's grip on Gussie's shoulders tightened a little. "Don't think I'll ever play charades that well."

The poor attempt at humor in the face of harsh criticism nearly folded Gussie in half. Alex was wrong, and the comment wasn't fair. She reached up to put her hand over Tom's in solidarity.

"Listen, Alex, I know that a strange man arriving here and the way he looked—I totally get that you might have had that moment of joy, only to have it fall apart into disappointment. That's a real pain, and you're entitled to feel it. But you're not entitled to insult and compare and hurt your uncle." She leaned forward, getting close to Alex's teary face, trying to capture her thoughts so they had the most impact and effect on Alex.

"Let me tell you as a woman who has had and lost a family in a lifetime, a person who comes into your life and is willing and able and ready to love you to the best of his or her ability—whether they are related by blood or not—is a gift from God. Accept it graciously, honey. No matter if it's exactly what you wanted or not. It's what you have."

Alex stared at her, and after a long moment, she lifted her gaze to meet Tom's. "Sorry," she said.

"S'okay, kid. Luke's a great guy, and think of it this way, now you have two uncles."

Gussie's heart flipped. What did he mean by that?

Alex didn't quite get the full unspoken message, but she seemed appeased—and maybe that's why he said that—and tired. She nodded and reached out to hug Gussie. She even let Tom kiss her on the cheek.

Gussie tucked the blanket under Alex's chin, turned the light out, and walked to the door where Tom waited.

She took each breath slowly, stepping into the hall as he closed the door.

"What did you—"

Silently, he leaned her into the wall and kissed away the question. And any comments, teasing, or discussion about what just happened.

"I don't want to be alone," he whispered gruffly. "Not for one more minute." He lifted her a little off the floor, scooped his arm under her knees, and started carrying her to the opposite end of the apartment.

Chapter Twenty-Five

He might have kicked the door too hard and snapped the lock with too much force. Didn't care. He might have hit the bed with too much pressure. Whatever. He might have had a little more finesse, but all that would come sometime, next time, later, when he wasn't crazed with the need to explore and examine and excite every inch of Gussie.

And no "might" about it, Tom definitely heard a seam tear as he furiously worked to get them both undressed, but he didn't give a crap. If he paused to so much as whisper a word to Gussie, then he'd start to think. Right now, he did not want to think.

He wanted to feel. Close. Warm. Naked. Gussie. He wanted dear, sweet, funny, sexy Gussie to be all his in the most intimate way, and from the way she was kissing, touching, and stripping, the feeling was utterly mutual.

By the time they were naked on the sheets, both were breathing too hard and kissing too much and moaning too often to talk or think or second-guess their actions.

He flicked his tongue along her jaw and throat, his hands already at home on her breasts and stomach. Under his lips, he heard her groan and whimper, nails lightly scraping his back as they rolled over and found their fit. Which was perfect.

Everything was perfect.

And then she dragged her fingers down his abdomen and closed her hands over him with a feminine sound of pure, raw satisfaction and appreciation. Like she'd been yearning to touch him.

Fire shot from one end of his hard-on to the other, agonizing and fierce, forcing him to rock into her fist and damn near howl with the intensity of the feeling.

He eased out of her touch and pinned her arms so she couldn't have him shooting off like a desperate teenager in a minute. Instead, he concentrated on kissing her, tasting every curve and dip and slope he could find.

But he needed his hands to touch, and when he released her, she instantly clutched his head, digging into his hair, guiding his mouth from pleasure point to pleasure point.

Her sighs, her scent, her every move shot more blood and need into him, making him harder and hungrier.

"Too good," she murmured, lifting her hips so he could suckle her belly button. "Too good."

"Don't worry," he laughed into a kiss. "Nothing's too good, Pink." He proved that by feathering more kisses, lower and lower, until his tongue touched that one single point of perfection, and she gasped.

"That is." She began to move against his mouth, her fingers stabbing his scalp. "Too good. Too...good." She tasted exactly as he'd imagined—too many times—tangy and salty. "It can't last. Can't."

He lifted his head and looked at her face in the dark shadows. "Don't think about that now, okay? We have tonight. All night."

They held each other's gazes for a long moment, then she

closed her eyes on a long, jagged exhale. "Okay. Then do that some more."

He found his way south again. "I could"—he kissed her inner thigh—"do this"—and the other one—"for hours." He licked her quickly, teasing another moan out of her. Looking up, he caught her head lolling from side to side.

Skin flushed, eyes closed, hair tousled, she was the sexiest woman he'd ever seen. Her nipples protruded, wet from his mouth, pink and juicy and inviting. Her abdomen squeezed tight, her arms extended to him.

"You're lucky I don't have a camera, 'cause this angle? Insane."

Her eyes popped open. "You wouldn't dare. I'd kill you."

"But I'd die happy." He crawled back up to her, planting kisses on all those beautiful places he'd just admired and ending up at her mouth. "I'm content to take that picture with my mind. It's one I won't forget."

He nestled close to her, lining up their warm bodies and sliding a leg over her thighs. He grazed the rise of her breasts, appreciating the feminine undulation and round shapes. Chill bumps blossomed on her skin, and her nipples budded like cherries.

He kissed one, then leaned back to caress her some more.

Blood thrummed and sweat tingled and something deep and low inside him threatened to splinter from the sheer goodness of Gussie. Maybe not so low...since that fractured feeling was more in his chest.

In the vicinity of his heart, damn it.

She wet her lips and gave a single nod, the order all he needed to get where he wanted. He grabbed the condom he'd left on the nightstand and opened it to sheath himself, resenting even that moment of letting her go.

Finally, he dropped down to the bed, held her gaze for a

long moment, and eased himself into her. Both of them hissed at first contact, but then they moved in concert, each breath in syncopation as he moved inside her, slow and easy, before sliding into fast and hard.

His brain flatlined when he fit all the way, her wet, warm womanhood stretched around him, too intoxicating for him to think.

"This is good, Gussie. So good."

"Shh." She quieted him with a kiss.

"No talking?"

"No talking about how good it is."

He tried to scowl at her, but that took too much effort away from the achy pleasure of each thrust into her.

"'Cause good always ends," she whispered.

He slowed, then stopped, throbbing in her but determined not to plunge into her one more time until she was completely quiet on the subject of *ending*. "Stop talking about the end," he ground out. "In fact, stop talking, period."

She looked up at him, and for the first time, he saw sadness in her eyes. Moonlight made them glimmer, but a deep, deep darkness stole the smile from her eyes.

No, Gussie. Don't feel. Don't think. Don't take that chance.

He squeezed his eyes closed and wiped his brain of every word, strictly *feeling*. Feeling pressure grow into a scorching need for release, feeling his pulse pounding in his veins, feeling the heavy, savage punch when he lost the battle to last one second longer.

But she lost it first, biting her lip to hold back a scream, digging her nails into his skin, and bucking hard into his hips.

He came watching Gussie lose all control, a hazy, hot spill that made him tremble and groan and, finally, fall onto her to smash his mouth against her mouth and helplessly kiss her. And kiss her. And kiss her some more.

And that cracking feeling in his chest started again, and this time, he knew why. Oh, man, he knew exactly why he felt that way, and it wasn't good.

"Shit."

She snorted softly. "Is that postcoital poetry?"

He hadn't even realized he'd spoken aloud. "Sorry."

She pushed him away enough to look in his eyes. "You are not apologizing for that."

"Not for what we just did."

She pushed harder. "Then what are you sorry for?"

For a long time, as long as it took both of their heartbeats to get to anything that resembled normal and their breathing to turn smooth and steady, he looked into Gussie's eyes and thought of all the different ways he could answer that question, settling on light and easy instead of the truth.

"I'm sorry I dragged you caveman-style and threw you on the bed."

"Are you kidding? Best move ever. I may tell all my friends. Hell, I might blog about it."

He laughed, hoping he'd deflected questions.

"Now tell me what you're really sorry for, Tom."

He hadn't deflected anything. He looked away. "I could have, you know, asked first."

"I'd have said yes. I was fully prepared to say yes." She turned his face, forcing him to look at her. "*Yes.*" She smiled. "But you do have some explaining to do."

"Really? I don't want to talk now. I want to sleep." He took a moment to clean them up, then settled under the covers, curling his whole body around her.

"You think I'm going to fall asleep and not ask for an explanation?"

"What's to explain, Gus? I'm crazy about you. I've had a hard-on since I met you. You're adorable, amazing, loving, funny, and...and..."

"Don't stop now."

But he had to before he said too much. Way too much. Because now that the urgency had faded and his body was sated, now that they were done, shouldn't he suggest she go to her own bed? He had a perfect excuse—Alex could wake up at any moment.

Yet, he didn't say a word. He held her and let every inch of their bodies touch, their heartbeats right next to each other, their mouths a kiss apart. Seconds drifted into minutes and minutes into a half hour of nothing but matching breaths.

He stroked her hair and repositioned them to a classic spoon, wrapping his arm around her stomach and a sliding a leg over hers, locking her down.

He kissed the back of her head, purposely letting his lips touch her scar, adding pressure, trying to communicate how he felt about her, no matter what scars and flaws she had.

"Okay, Pink, what kind of explanation were you looking for?"

She didn't answer, just breathed her next, even breath, sound asleep in his arms.

For the first time in five years, four months, and nine days, Tom didn't sleep alone. Maybe he should start keeping track of time differently now, no matter how scary that was.

Maybe this should be night number one...of many.

In the recesses of her mind, Gussie heard a noise, a footfall, a door creak. But sleep so totally owned her right then, she didn't move. Sleep and the weight of a masculine leg wrapped around her, not to mention a strong man's hand on her stomach and the delicious pressure of an urgent erection nestled against her rear end. Add to that the heaviness that comes with a contented heart, the feeling that all is right—or will be—with the world.

She wrapped her hand around Tom's, entwining their fingers before she brought his knuckles to her lips to kiss, trailing her mouth over his forearm to his tattoo.

Panta monos.

Why was she doing this to herself? Why was she falling so hard and completely into this man who did not want the kind of forever connection she craved? And why did it have to feel so good, even though she knew that when it was over, it would hurt like a bitch on wheels.

Warm, soft lips pressed against the back of her head, directly on the mottled skin that used to make her cry in her bed every night. She could cry in this bed, too. Of joy.

Instead, she reached behind her and got her hand around Tom's morning erection, sighing as he pulsed and grew in her hand.

He let out a low, slow groan of pleasure, immediately fondling her breasts as he rocked against her.

"I think Alex might be awake," she whispered. "Was my bedroom door closed?"

"You expect me to remember that?" He tweaked her nipple and slowly turned her onto her back.

"I have to brush my teeth before I kiss you," she said.

"We won't kiss on the mouth." He proved that by taking his morning kiss of her already protruding nipple, his fingers walking south to search and destroy whatever he could find there.

"I'm not quite awake yet."

"You will be in about one minute." He slipped one finger inside of her, making her eyes pop with surprise. "Good morning, gorgeous."

Why should she fight this? How? Instead, she held on to his head, guided him all over her body, took another fifteen minutes doing the same to him, and finally, she gave up on the no-kissing rule while he made love to her again, this time much slower and sweeter than last night, but every bit as satisfying.

When they lay still, breath caught, hearts slowed, skin chilled, slivers of orange stabbed through the blinds, lighting the room.

"It's a *portokali* sky," she whispered.

He closed his eyes and nodded.

"Want to look at it?"

He didn't answer, except some muscles tensed and his pulse jumped a little.

"It reminds you of Sophia," she guessed.

"It reminds me of Greece in general," he replied.

"You should go back."

He didn't answer, but swallowed loud enough for her to hear.

"Why don't you?" she asked.

"I can't face some memories. That sky, that place..."

The answer didn't tweak any sense of jealousy in her, but plenty of sympathy.

She slid out of bed.

"Hey." He grabbed for her arm. "Where are you going?"

"To make a new memory. Come on." She managed to get him out of bed, dragging the sheet with her. His French doors opened to another, smaller balcony, private, but with the same view they had from the living room.

She spread the doors wide open to let the golden-orange

light of sunrise pour over both of them. Wrapping the sheet around herself, she stepped outside.

But Tom stayed in the doorway, magnificently naked, his around-the-world tattoos—including a blackbird's head and jaguar paw below the waist—stark against his skin, his manly form like a sculpture in perfect artist's light. His hair was tousled, his cheeks shadowed by morning stubble, his lips a little swollen from all the kissing.

She stared at him, bathed in orange, the singularly most beautiful man she'd ever seen.

"Wait a second," she whispered. "Don't move."

"What are you doing?"

She grinned. "I want to take a picture."

The irony of that made him laugh. She swept by in her sheet, grabbing his phone off the dresser. Back on the balcony, she faced him and clicked.

"I can't believe you're taking nudes."

"And you're going to send them to me."

He rolled his eyes and reached for her hand. "C'mere. Let's get one together." He turned them around so the sunrise was behind them, wrapping them both in her sheet before tapping the camera to take a selfie together.

They put their heads close, smiled, and he took the picture.

"One more," he whispered. "Look at me."

When she did, he kissed her, and snapped the camera again and again and again.

Laughing, he set it down, and Gussie wrapped them both in the sheet cocoon. They stayed like that, naked bodies pressed together, facing the *portokali* sky, silent until footsteps, loud and determined now, pounded down the hall, followed by a hard tap on the door.

"Gussie? Are you in there?"

Alex. They both looked at each other, too stunned to laugh or gasp at how totally busted they were.

"Gussie!" Alex's voice rose to a slight level of panic. "Your parents are almost here!"

"What?" She spun the sheet off Tom and flew to the door, opening it a crack so Alex couldn't see in. "They're not supposed to be here until this afternoon."

Alex inched back, looking up and down at Gussie in her sheet.

Shit. "I…uh…I…um…" *Shit shit shit!*

"You slept in here," Alex supplied. "Which is why I'm telling you that your brother called my phone because he couldn't get an answer on yours and wanted to be sure you were ready for your parents since they got on a much-earlier connecting flight out of Paris and will be here soon."

Bless that boy. And Alex for not judging, at least not openly. And, oh, God! The reunion of her dreams was minutes away.

"Yikes!" She opened the door and slipped out, leaving Tom behind. "I gotta get dressed!"

As she ran down the hall, all she could hear was Alex laughing.

For a moment, one silly, crazy moment, Gussie couldn't imagine being any happier.

And that was never a good sign.

Chapter Twenty-Six

At some point in the afternoon, Tom realized he was sitting in the same Promenade deck chair where he'd spent the other night. Only, he wasn't sleeping as a refugee now. He was reclining in the sun, surrounded by tourists and locals, watching the beach scene unfold from under his lashes.

"You asleep, Uncle Tommy?"

Next to him, Alex curled into her chair with a giant plastic cup of gelato and berries, her gaze fixed on the same scene.

"Mmm. Awake."

"So what do you think?"

He turned to her, the vast open-endedness of the question a little overwhelming. What did he think of Gussie's parents and the tearful reunion he'd witnessed? What did he think of how tangled up he'd gotten with a woman who wanted everything he wanted to run away from? What did he think of how the McBain family of four somehow walked the beach as one unit, despite the years and heartache that had broken them all up? 'Cause he thought that was nothing less than a miracle.

"What do I think of what?"

"Didn't Gussie tell you?"

He frowned, thinking of all Gussie had told him, much of it unrepeatable to a twelve-year-old who was already a tad smug since she knew what they were doing behind closed doors.

He played along. "Didn't Gussie tell me what?"

She looked hard at him, a spoonful of bright pink gelato poised between the cup and her mouth, which hung open. "She didn't tell you."

At the hurt and hint of anger in her voice, Tom sat up, shifting his full attention to Alex. "I can't be sure until you tell me what it is."

"Oh, you'd know if she told you." She dropped the uneaten spoonful back in the cup and turned her body in the chair so she was no longer facing him.

"Alex, tell me."

She shook her head. "Never mind. It isn't important."

"Of course it is, Alex, come on."

Another firm shake.

"Well, don't be too mad at her," he said. "Her brother showed up, and her whole life changed in a day. She hasn't had time for much else."

She speared him with a look. "She had all night in your room."

He felt the blood drain from his face. "We didn't talk about"—much—"you."

Looking down, she dug for another bite of gelato, the circles on her cheeks nearly the same color as her treat. "Of course not."

"Alex." He reached over. "Whatever you wanted her to tell me, you can tell me yourself. I'll listen, I promise. We don't have to talk to each other through Gussie."

She still wouldn't meet his gaze. "It's easier that way, don't you think?"

"No, I don't. I'm here and I'm listening. You can share anything. You can tell me about a boy you like or a problem in school or some dress you want to buy or how much you miss your mother. You can talk to me." He might not have a clue how to answer, but they had to start somewhere.

She finally looked at him. "I want to live with Gussie, not you."

For a second, he couldn't speak. He opened his mouth, tried to make a sound, but nothing came out.

"I would be so happy to be part of"—she pointed her spoon at the McBain family, huddled in a circle on the rocks near the shore—"that."

Tom still stared at her.

"That's what I want," she said. "I want to be"—her voice nearly snapped in two—"whole again. I can't be that way with you. I can't go on photo shoots or have a nanny or live in hotels. I can't and I don't want to, and I don't think that's what Momma wanted, either. She just forgot about hings. About signing papers and making arrangements. She didn't think she'd ever die."

Oh, God. What could he possibly say to that? "I can't..." *Give you up.*

When did that happen? He didn't know, but Alex was his, whole and completely, and that might suck logistically, but she was the only...

He turned and looked at Gussie and her family again, jealousy shocking him as it made a slow stomp up his chest.

Alex was the only family he had. And he *wasn't about to give her up.*

He turned to her, but she was standing, hoisting a canvas bag onto her shoulder. "I told you it wasn't important."

Not important? "Where are you going?"

"Back to the apartment."

"No, no." He stood, too, wanting to reach for her, wanting to find the words. But he had no words. He never had words. He spoke with a camera and...and...

He glanced at his arm.

And permanent ink. Why was he so surprised when people listened?

Alex was already ten feet away. "Alex!" He rushed toward her, reaching for her arm. "Please stay and talk to me."

She shook out of his grasp. "Really, Uncle Tommy, it's not that big a deal. I'm tired and want to go home. Or, you know, back to the apartment. It's not really home."

She took off at a good clip, but he could have easily caught her. Instead, he stood frozen, watching her hair swing as she darted away, feeling incredibly helpless and hopeless.

"Tom! Tom, guess what?" Gussie practically pranced toward him, breaking a few feet away from her family, the smile she'd worn all day firmly in place. "Where's Alex?" she asked when she reached him.

He had to tell her. He had to tell her the entire conversation, but her parents and brother were twenty feet away, and throwing his own situation with Alex into the mix would put a damper on Gussie's perfect day.

"She went back to the apartment," he said.

"Alone? Is she with the Stone kids?"

"No, she said she was tired."

"And you let her go alone?" A note of concern lifted her voice, of course. She cared. Deeply and truly.

"She was..." He shook his head as the others arrived, hoping she understood the conversation should be private.

"I better go check on her then," Gussie said. "But I have to tell you something so exciting. We've made a huge decision."

"Really?" He glanced at the others, all of them wearing expressions of joy. Whatever they'd talked about out there on the beach, this family was solid.

"We're going back to the States," Gussie's father said in his strong New England accent as he put a hand on Luke's shoulder.

Tom drew back. "You just got here."

"I know," Gussie agreed. "But we were talking, and we all feel like, as a family, we need to be home. And Luke's coming with us!"

"To heal." Wendy McBain's green eyes, sixty-year-old versions of Gussie's, danced. "I still live in the same house these two grew up in, you know, and this is what I want."

"Oh, that's…great." But Tom didn't think it was great at all. "I…" *Hate the idea*. But he had no right to say that. He had his own family problems to deal with. And this was Gussie's greatest dream. "That's really awesome for you."

"I have an idea," Gussie's mother said. "Why don't you two figure out the logistics while we go back to Luke's hotel? And we'll call you with the final travel plans in a bit."

"Okay," Gussie agreed, giving them all reluctant kisses and hugs. "Don't be long."

After they said good-bye, Tom slipped his arm around her, swallowing all the arguments against her going. She had to do this, and he needed to understand. "You really do have everything you wanted," he said, giving her a hug. "I'm happy for you."

"Except you don't want me to go," she whispered.

"Of course I don't, but that doesn't mean I can't be happy for you."

She looked up at him, the smile faltering for the first time since she'd awakened in his arms. "You know it's inevitable that we're going our ways."

He managed a nod, even though that inevitability felt less and less, well, inevitable every minute they were together.

"Come on." She tugged at him. "Let's tell Alex. I doubt she'll be any happier than you are."

"She's definitely not thrilled with me now," he said as they walked in the direction of the apartment, wending through the flow of tourists on the wide beach walkway.

"What happened, Tom?"

He puffed out a breath. "I guess she thought you were going to tell me that—"

She slammed a hand over her mouth. "Oh my God, I never told you about that conversation. We got home and Luke was there and the day was crazy and then, last night was so...good. And this morning my parents came. Damn. She told you what she asked me?"

"Yes."

"What did you say?"

He just looked at her, hardly remembering his words because he'd been so sucker-punched by the request, he hadn't really responded. "Not much, I'm afraid."

"Are you sure she's gone to the apartment?" She yanked him into a trot.

"Yes." He thought she had. "Why wouldn't she?"

"Tom, she told me if she couldn't live with me, then she's going to try to find her father."

He froze midstep. "Like, now? From France?"

"I don't know, but let's find her."

Holding hands so the crowds didn't separate them, they snaked their way back to the apartment, silent in their determination. To find her father? She wouldn't do anything that foolish, would she?

Of course she would. The child desperately wanted a parent, and all Tom had done was worry about his stupid job

303

and travel and lifestyle. What the hell was wrong with him?

At the bottom of the stairway, they nearly smacked into Annie and her two kids.

"Oh! Thank God," Gussie exclaimed. "Did you see Alex up there?"

Annie shook her head, frowning. "She's not home."

"Are you sure?" Tom barked the question.

"Well, no one answered when we knocked, so we figured—"

Tom didn't wait for her to finish, but took off up the steps, snippets of the conversation behind him fading as he barged into the apartment.

"Alex?"

Nothing. He charged down the hall.

"Alex!"

Her door was wide open, her bed made, her room neat, her suitcase under the bed...gone.

"Alex." He dropped to his knees, spying the notebook she was always writing in, tucked against the wall as if it had accidentally slipped behind the bed.

He reached for it, grabbing the edge with his fingertips and dragging it out. Should he read it? Should he invade her privacy?

"What does it say?" Gussie dropped to her knees next to him. "Open it, Tom. Maybe she left us a note."

He flipped the cover and read the girlish scrawling.

Dear Daddy...I wait every day for you to call.

He turned to a few more pages.

Dear Daddy...I would love to send you pictures from France.

And to the last page.

Dear Daddy...I found your name on Facebook and I think I can find your house.

All this time, he'd thought it was her diary, or bad poetry, or whatever preteen girls wrote about. He never dreamed she'd been writing *to her father*.

He had to be that for her, whether he wanted to or not. The thing was, he *wanted* to. "Tom." Gussie reached up and touched his cheek, her fingers sliding over a tear he hadn't even realized he'd shed.

"How do we find her?" he asked. "Where would she go? The airport? A—"

"*Gare routière!*"

"The bus station?"

"She knows exactly where it is," Gussie said. "Let's go!"

He froze for a second, a punch of pain slamming his gut. "Would she really do that?"

Gussie yanked at him. "Do not underestimate the willpower of a girl who wants a family. A real family."

He closed his eyes. "Let's find her and give her one."

Chapter Twenty-Seven

Gare routière. *Gare routière.* She had to get there, fast, because they might come after her.

But who knew? Uncle Tommy certainly made it clear he didn't want her, and Gussie was so wrapped up with her family, she probably hadn't even noticed Alex was missing. Fighting a sting of tears, she paused on a street corner, turning around with one hand on the roller bag she'd packed. Where was the *gare routière*? Hadn't they been right here when Gussie had read the name and translated it to *bus station*?

But the streets were so much more crowded this afternoon than they'd been early in the morning with Gussie. And Alex was turned around, confused, and scared to death.

But fear was not going to stop her. She had one chance, and she was taking it. She knew Steve Whitman lived in someplace called Bend, Oregon, and that place was small enough that she could find him. First, she had to get out of Nice, and then France, and then…take it one step at a time. She had an emergency credit card that her mother had given her a long time ago, about fifty dollars, and a passport.

She could do this.

It just wouldn't be easy.

Well, nothing worth having is easy, Momma used to say. Oh, she used to say so many things, like how a woman can never be overeducated or overdressed. And how you can tell how good a man is by the way he treats animals. And how no one can hurt you if you don't give them power.

So she would not give them the power. She'd give it to her father, and if he didn't want her after she turned up at his front door, then...then...then she'd kill herself and be with Momma.

She turned one more time, this time glancing at passersby, trying to find someone who would help her. But the French never looked right at anyone, and the tourists ignored her, so like always, she felt completely alone.

Not always. Not with Momma. And not with Gussie, but...

She hadn't even talked to him about it! Biting back Gussie's betrayal, Alex made a decision and charged across the street with the crowd, her bag clunking on cobblestones until it tipped over, off its wheels.

"Oh, shoot! Come *on!*" she cried, trying to right the bag in the middle of the street.

"You need help?" a man asked.

She looked up and met the gaze of an older man, maybe a little older than her uncle.

Nearly thirteen years of stranger-danger lessons bubbled up. "No," she said quickly, shaking her head.

"Looking for the bus station?" he asked in French-accented English.

Maybe she shouldn't ignore a stranger. After all, her very own father would be one when she knocked on his door. "Um, yeah, actually, I am."

He gave a slight nod in the other direction. "Right over there and around the next corner."

"Oh, thank you!" She gushed gratitude because she was headed in exactly the wrong direction. She pivoted, bungled the bag, then gave up and scooped it up by the regular handle, hauling it across the next street.

Her sneakers pounded on the pavement—her white sneakers that screamed American tourist—but she didn't care. She had to get to the *gare routière.*

She finally reached the corner, turned it, and—

A park? "Come on!" she moaned. Instinctively, she turned back the way she'd come and saw the same man not fifty feet behind her, walking slowly in her direction.

Fear clutched at her, freezing her for a minute before she turned again, the fear quickly icing into panic. Now what? Cross the street! She had to cross the street.

She looked again, and he was on a phone.

Oh my God, what if he was calling in more men? They would surround her and kidnap her. Things like that happened in foreign countries.

She darted toward the street, barely slowing to look one way then the other, trying to find a break in the traffic.

It looked like she could make it, so she started to cross the street, getting a loud honk from a car that had to swerve around her, the surprise making her almost drop her bag.

She glanced again, and the man was still coming! Hoisting the suitcase, she darted to the next corner, hoping for a better chance to cross the street.

At the curb, she tried to get next to some other people for safety, but they gave her dirty looks. Should she tell them? *A man is after me!* Who would believe her? Who spoke English?

Another horn honked, and a bus rumbled by and—

"Alex!"

Did someone call her name? Did the man know her?

Refusing to look, she stepped to the very edge of the high curb. She sneaked one more peek, through the crowd, getting a direct shot of the man who walked calmly in her direction. What if he wanted to get her into that park alone and do...bad things?

Oh, God, Momma had told her about stuff like this.

He was so close.

She looked up and down the street, and there were cars, but far away. She could make it without a light. And he'd be stuck on the corner. Yes, this was perfect.

"Alex!"

Taking a deep breath, she grabbed the suitcase and stepped off the curb, just as a bus the size of a country came barreling around the corner and someone screamed—

"Alexandra Whitman!"

She turned at the sound of her name, so fast her foot slipped on the curb, her ankle popping as she fell, her whole body tumbling toward the street. She dropped in slow motion, the suitcase rolling out of her hand. Only thing she could see was the bright green grille of the bus as it rolled right over her suitcase, making it explode clothes everywhere.

Her shoulder hit the concrete with a thud, and then suddenly, she was yanked up with lightning speed. The bus's deafening horn was drowned out by the screams of people everywhere and a man—no, not a man, Uncle Tommy— saying her name over and over again as he dragged her back to the sidewalk.

She'd almost died. Right in front of him, inches from his fingertips, so close.

He'd almost lost someone...*again*.

The realization slammed Tom with the same force as the bus that nearly took Alex's life.

"Alex, oh my God, Alex!" Gussie swooped in on them, wrapping Alex in an embrace, the two of them pulling away from the melee on the sidewalk.

But Tom stood, utterly frozen in shock.

It was him. He was a curse, or he was cursed. Didn't matter if that was real or not, it happened again and again and again to people he loved.

And he did love Alex. He didn't know how it happened, or when, or why, but she was family and blood and the child of his little sister. Who was probably up in heaven, watching this in total disgust.

What kind of guardian was he? The worst of all kinds. The kind that loses people.

But he loved her and—

"Over here." Gussie was guiding a thoroughly shaken Alex away from the crowd, thanking people as they gathered the busted-up suitcase and bits of clothes, soothing Gussie to a bistro table.

"Tom, come here," Gussie called. "Don't worry about the clothes."

His legs like lead, he walked to the table, the waterfall of adrenaline through his system like a shot of whiskey.

"Please don't yell at me," Alex cried. "Don't be mad. It was dumb. A dumb idea."

"Shh." Gussie stroked her cheek and hair. "No one is yelling."

Alex looked up at him, no doubt expecting a reprimand. But he was so damn relieved she was alive because...he loved her.

And that was why there was only one thing he could do, without a moment to waste.

He gripped the backrest of a wrought iron chair, more for support than anything. "I'm not going to yell at you, Alex," he said. "I'm simply going to do the right thing."

Both of them stared up at him.

"You belong with Gussie. With her family, in her life."

"But she won't—"

"Oh, yes, I will!" Gussie instantly put both arms around Alex, looking up at Tom with a mix of confusion and relief, and some hurt, too. "I will take care of her. I will raise her. I will love her. I already do."

"Oh my God," Alex whispered, her fingers covering her mouth. "Could you, Gussie? Would you?"

No hesitation, not so much as a shadow of doubt flickered in Gussie's eyes. "You always have a home with me."

Alex dropped her hands into her face and cried silently, a bittersweet sound of rejoicing mixed with anguish. Gussie held her and lifted her eyes to meet Tom's gaze. Did she see the anguish in his eyes? Or did she just think that he was doing what he wanted to do all along?

It didn't matter. They were both happy, and they belonged together.

And him?

All he knew was if he had to feel this empty for the rest of his life, he might throw himself under the next bus. But he had to do the right thing for these two whom he loved. He had to step aside and let them have each other.

And he could go back to always alone.

The Air France terminal at the Nice Côte d'Azur Airport was empty before the late-evening flight to Paris, so they lingered before heading through security, making a strange group.

Mom and Dad huddled close to Luke—and each other—talking in hushed tones. Lizzie and Eddie flanked Alex, neither one happy their new friend was leaving for the States. Annie stayed a few steps away, taking pictures.

And Gussie stood near Tom, trying to still the steady pounding of her pulse as their good-bye grew closer.

"We're going to get something to read," Luke said, indicating that he was taking Mom and Dad with him.

"And I'll take the kids to get snacks," Annie offered.

In other words, they were all leaving so Tom and Gussie could have a private moment.

A moment Gussie really didn't want to have, but clearly, he did. They'd barely talked all day after getting Alex home. Everyone was consumed with packing and preparations, and Tom had gone out and gotten dinner for the entire gang. The one thing about having family around, Gussie remembered, there's little time for one-on-one conversations.

But they had time now.

"C'mere," Tom said, his voice low as he reached for her hand. They walked in silence to a quiet corner of the airport. Standing close, Tom took her hand, and her heart nearly stopped.

"I guess it would be stupid to ask if you're certain about taking this trip." The statement surprised her, but not as much as the pain in his voice.

"Not stupid. It's a reasonable question," she replied. "And I'm only okay if you're okay. I mean, with me taking Alex back to the US." *And we have no idea when we'll see you again.*

"I meant"—he closed his eyes and sighed—"leaving me."

"It had to happen eventually," she said, fighting to keep it light and to resist touching him.

But she lost both fights. She heard the sadness in her own voice and reached for his hand, grazing his forearm. "After all, you warned me." She lifted his hand to see the Greek tattoo. "I've always said there should be an expiration date stamped on you."

He twisted out of her touch, wrapping both arms around her. "Stop joking."

"It's all I can do, Tom."

He kissed her, hard on the lips, trapping his name in her mouth.

When he ended the kiss, his eyes were as fierce and intense. And Gussie was confused. "You want this, don't you?" she asked.

Because, if she hadn't known better, she'd have sworn he was as torn up about this as she was.

"I don't know what I want," he admitted. "Except for you and Alex to be happy."

Then stay with us. "I know what I want."

He closed his eyes, as if he didn't want to hear it. But that wasn't going to stop her.

"I want to be the one who finds the space in your heart that you are so determined to fill with...nothing," she whispered. "I want to be the one who makes you hate being alone. I want to be the person who is so important that you are willing to take a chance to lose again because that bet is worth making."

He was silent, except for the pain in his eyes. She could read that loud and clear.

"I feel like this is best," he said.

"Of course you do," Gussie fired back. "Best for you. But

you know what, Mr. TJ DeMille? Until you take off your own mask, the only thing true about your life is the phrase you stamped on your arm. Always alone." She shook her head. "Fact is, you're hiding worse scars than I was."

"I'm not hiding scars, Gussie. I'm trying to avoid…inflicting any more."

She narrowed her eyes at him. "I hate to break it to you, but life is scars. Life is one long series of little cuts and bruises and burns that leave marks on your heart, but when you are surrounded by the people who matter, those wounds heal. Those scars make you who you are, Tom. Hiding them is like trying to hide from the world."

The realization was so wonderful and liberating, she almost laughed. "Thanks for helping me figure that out," she added.

It was his turn to look away, the impact of her words making him clench his jaw and fight for composure.

"Gussie, I have lost two parents, a sister, a wife, and a child."

She let out a shuddering sigh, the full impact of those five deaths hitting her hard.

"And I almost lost one more this morning."

She couldn't deny that, the moment that they'd almost lost Alex still fresh in her brain.

"This 'family' you want so bad? It scares the crap out of me," he admitted. "I don't think I'm cut out for it."

"Gussie! Augusta!" Her mother came hustling toward them. "They're boarding our plane soon. We better go." She smiled up at Tom. "Thanks for being the one to bring our whole family back together, Tom." She leaned up and gave him an impulsive kiss. "You keep in touch, now."

Mom grabbed Gussie's arm and pulled her. "Come on, honey. Let's go."

She let herself be led, turning to Tom as she walked away. "Bye," she mouthed.

"Gussie. I…I…"

"Come on." Mom tugged, taking her back to the cocoon of her family. But Tom's eyes locked on her and held her and finished the sentence he was having so much trouble saying.

"You know where to find me," she called. "To find us!"

She kept walking with her mom, crossing the aisle, looking for Luke and Alex because they were her family now. With each step, she half-expected Tom's hand to land on her shoulder, to spin her around…and…tell her…

No. No, that was crazy. She had her family now, so all her dreams had come true. She had to remember that every time her heart ached for him. Which was now and possibly…always.

Chapter Twenty-Eight

On a good day, when the impetuous *meltemi* winds cooperated and no goats decided to linger in the middle of the pine-lined road that led to the rugged northern tip of Karpathos, it took an hour for a Jeep to reach the sugar-cube, white-washed home of the Karras family. It had taken Tom much longer, though, because he'd done everything to delay his arrival.

He'd lingered on the stone streets full of carts and olive oil and women wearing insanely bright scarves and vests. He'd taken time to drink in the baskets of fruit and spices, and listen to the odd mix of Greek and English that filled the air.

But he was delaying the inevitable—he'd done it successfully for several weeks now. Oh, who was he kidding? He'd delayed for five *years*, but it wasn't until a few weeks ago in the Nice airport when he'd actually decided he'd make the trip when the LaVie shoot was over.

As always, he finished a job and headed to the airport. But this time, he wasn't jetting off to the next assignment. This time, he was going to see the Karras family.

Eventually, he made his way around the hamlet, taking the Jeep to the old farm where each crop was stacked in the terraced fields, inhaling the briny smell olives and the sea on his way.

He shouldn't have waited, he realized within minutes of arriving and greeting some of Sophia's sisters and then her mother, Christa. There were tears, of course, and hugs, and long sighs of missed years, but Nico was out in the fields, and somehow, talking to the women was easy. Their English was broken, but far better than Tom's Greek, and they were too classy to demand to know where he'd been all these years.

But the rumbling of cart wheels on the drive outside told him that explanation was about to end.

He glanced at Christa, who cast her dark eyes down and nodded as her husband arrived. "Go to him," she whispered.

Tom walked outside into the late-afternoon sun and knew immediately that Nico had been told they had a visitor. The older man didn't look surprised as he climbed out of his farm cart, his broad shoulders stooped as though the weight of the world pressed on him. And despite his picturesque island home, large and loving family, and his simple life, that weight never left his heart.

For a moment, the two of them stared at each other, sizing up what time and mourning had done, and before Tom had a chance to say a word, he was folded into Papa Nico's massive arms.

"I've missed you, son."

That was it. No other words were necessary. Tom closed his eyes and hugged the bear of a man, wondering why on earth he thought Nico would be any different today than he'd been at the noisy Greek wedding that took place right on this spot all those years ago.

Nico gestured for Tom to follow him out to the back terrace, up a dirt path to an olive orchard, mostly silent until

317

Nico slowed and looked at him. "It was very, very fast."

Sophia's death. It was like Nico not to hem and haw, or try to pretend they didn't all know the reason Tom had stayed away for so long. The funeral had been brief and sad, with almost no words exchanged at the time.

"We tried, we moved so quick, but..."

Tom swallowed, waiting for a wave of blame that blessedly didn't rise up. This was where Sophia had wanted to be, more than their apartment in Athens, more than on the road with Tom. She had known the risks of being in her home village. She had not been the first to die here for lack of modern health care.

Nico waited, his eyes as dark as the olives hanging from a branch behind him, lines of worry and grief engraved on his sun-weathered face. "I need you to forgive me," Nico said gruffly. "I need that."

"So do I," Tom admitted. "I've been gone too long."

The older man reached out, and Tom did the same, both of them patting each other's backs for a long embrace. He could feel Nico's full-body sigh, as if one of the many weights he carried had been taken away.

They continued to walk, higher into the hills, leaving Tom no doubt where they were going. But the walk was slow, and the air warm and redolent with the smells of earth and sky.

"*Yiati?*" Nico asked after they'd walked for a few minutes.

Why? Tom didn't answer the question because Nico could have been referring to so many things. "*Yiati?*" Tom said, making his confusion known.

Nico reached up and grabbed a handful of Tom's hair. "Why all this hair?"

He almost laughed. "I haven't cut it since..." He flicked

318

the hair, which, to be fair, he'd trimmed himself to keep it from going past his shoulders, and sometimes, he'd had someone on a photo set clip off an inch or two, but the short cut he had worn when he was with Sophia? Gone.

"And why?" Nico lifted his arm and pointed to some new tattoos. "Because of Sophia?"

Some of them. Tom shrugged and fought a smile. "Anything else?"

Nico's gaze dropped to Tom's left hand, which he took in his own dinner-plate-size paw and lifted to his face, pointing at the empty ring finger. "Why *not*?"

He understood the question, and all its implications. He couldn't shrug it off. That would have been disrespectful.

"I haven't..." But he had. He'd met a wonderful woman with light in her eyes and good in her heart.

His heart stuttered as they reached the western slope, with its direct view out to the Aegean Sea, nothing breaking the endless blue but the mountains of Crete on the horizon. There was an ancient willow where he and Sophia once had a picnic, and she'd told him it was her secret childhood hideaway.

And now it was the gravesite she shared with their unborn child.

As they neared the gnarled tree, Nico stopped and put his hand on Tom's shoulder. "Alone or with me?"

He started to answer the way he'd answered for the past five years...but then swallowed the word he'd had tattooed on his arm. "With you," he replied.

Together, they walked to the willow that wept over Sophia's grave. It was marked with two Greek Orthodox crosses, and someone had put fresh flowers there within the last day or two.

Tom dropped to the grass, staring at the cluster of purple

bougainvillea until it all blurred before his eyes. Tears came swift and hard, choking him. He remembered his wife, her laugh, her heart, her many plans to be the best mother in the world. He closed his eyes and whispered, "I miss you, Soph."

A breeze rustled the willow tree, but Sophia's father stood stone silent.

Tom took a deep breath and pushed up to stand, studying the light on the violet blossoms and the shadow made by the cross. Suddenly, he reached for his phone, tapping it so he could take a picture.

"Ahh." Nico leaned in, looking at the screen with interest. "Now I understand."

The phone screen was filled with the last picture he'd taken—Gussie and Tom wrapped in a sheet on a balcony in Nice. Her eyes danced, her skin glowed, and her smile nearly blinded him.

Nico launched a bushy brow. "This is why." The older man nodded several times, slowly and with such great knowledge. "You need..." He searched for the English word, but it clearly eluded him. "Permission," he finally said.

Did he? Is that why he'd traveled to Greece and driven across treacherous terrain to this ancient village? To get Nico Karras's permission to love again?

Maybe it was.

Nico put his hands on Tom's shoulders and flattened him with a hard look. "Here is what you do."

Tom nodded and waited for the sage counsel that could only come from a man whose ancestors went back to Alexander the Great, who worked the land, raised five children, and pressed oil from olives. A man who knew what was what. Whatever he said, Tom would do.

"Cut your hair."

He fought a laugh. It was so Nico, and Sophia would have loved that.

"Do not sleep alone."

Okay, but would she have loved that? Tom stayed perfectly still. This wasn't about who he slept with—it was about forever family.

Then Nico lifted his arm and pointed to the Greek letters on his arm. "God did not intend for you to be alone, Thomas. And neither did Sophia. Of this, I am certain."

"But what if...what if..." What if *he* was the reason for all this loss?

"Life is a series of 'what ifs,' young man. If you let that kind of fear rule you, you aren't living. Sophia wanted you to live—and love—again."

"You don't know that."

Nico's eyes grew fierce. "She died in my arms," Nico said. "I know that. And if you'd have come to me, I would have told you." He pulled Tom into his chest again. "Now, please go make children, make money, make laughter, and make your Greek family happy."

Peace and contentment washed over him. And happiness. So much happiness. This had been what he'd needed to do all along. Of course, Gussie knew that.

After the embrace, Tom lifted his phone to take a picture of the grave, but Nico stopped him, pushing the phone away to prevent the shot.

"That." He pointed over Tom's shoulder. "That is your picture. The *portokali* sky."

He turned, stunned by the richness of the orange sunset, an aching, brilliant, heart-stopping palette. Yes, he needed to get this picture...for Gussie.

He snapped it and put his arm around Nico, and the two men walked side by side back to the house.

On the stone porch, Christa waited. "Thomas?" They always called him that here. He was used to it. "I have some...things. Sophia's. For you. Yes?"

She was asking if he was ready to see them, of course. "Yes," he agreed.

He drank a toast with Nico, and they sat in silence for a few minutes, until Christa returned with a small ceramic box painted with classic Greek cobalt blue. He wasn't sure what she had, but he accepted the box with a smile.

Immediately, Nico stood, poured Tom another shot, and left with no more than a touch on his shoulder.

Alone, he opened the lid and saw Sophia's engagement and wedding rings, tied together with a white satin ribbon that he suspected had been on her bouquet. He lifted the rings, swallowed hard, and studied the diamonds that had made her so happy.

These were his to give away, of course. He set the rings aside, knowing already that he would give them to Christa to keep in her family. There were some pictures of Tom and Sophia together, and several of her progressing pregnancy. He glanced at them quickly, unable to linger.

Underneath all that, some mail, unopened. A doctor's bill, insurance papers, a credit card statement. All pretty...old. Those bills were long paid, that credit card closed.

He set them to the side, but a letter in between slipped out and fell to the ground. Reaching over to retrieve it, his gaze fell on the return address and his heart quite literally stopped for a moment.

Ruth Whitman.

A letter from his sister? To Sophia? He turned it over,

realizing that it had never been opened. He peered at the date and realized it must have arrived within days of Sophia's death. Written, no doubt, before that.

Why would Ruthie write to a sister-in-law she'd never met?

He tore open the envelope and pulled out the single page covered in flowing handwriting, his eyes falling on the greeting "Dear Sister." He took a deep breath, sipped the shot of whiskey, and smoothed the page on the table to read.

I can call you that, I hope! I am writing to you because I've decided to come and visit with my daughter and we want to surprise Tommy! If it would be easier to email or talk by phone, my number and email are at the bottom of this letter.

Sophia, I know my brother and I haven't been all that close, but I really want that to change now that he has you. I've always believed that if he could find someone special and he understood what love is, he might forgive me for thinking I was in it all those years ago when I got pregnant. And once you two have this baby, I am certain he will understand why I kept her, and how I love her.

In fact, I recently met with an attorney who recommended I update my Last Will & Testament. (What a thought, huh?) I still have Tommy listed as the person to take Alex if anything ever happens to me. I didn't change it, though, and I hope that's okay with you.

I almost did. I thought about it, but, you know, I think Tommy was the best brother in the world and he will make an unbelievable father. And if anything ever happens to me, God forbid, there is no one I'd want raising my daughter except my wonderful brother.

Anyway, that's not going to happen! Long lives ahead and lots more babies for both of us, right? Please call me or email me after you get this and we can start the arrangements for my SURPRISE trip! Can't wait!

Love xxxxooooxxx (kisses and hugs in America)

Ruthie

He sat staring at her words, her name, her kisses and hugs, for a long time. Mostly, though, he reread the same sentence over and over again, unable to ignore the irony that while he'd come to say his good-byes to Sophia, the message that he got in return came from his sister.

There is no one I'd want raising my daughter except my wonderful brother.

And then, he knew exactly what his next flight and destination had to be. Home. Family. Forever.

No, no, not yet. He had to make one more stop in Cyprus first.

Chapter Twenty-Nine

"**F**ritos? For lunch, Alex?"

Alex made a face at Gussie, but put the bag back on the shelf, sliding down to the protein bar section of the Super Min.

"You can eat a regular lunch at the camp," Gussie said. "You're a junior counselor, not a camper."

"I know, but I get so busy with the little ones, especially that adorable one, Dylan. He has to spell everything he E-A-T-S."

Gussie laughed, remembering Alex's stories of the little boy at the Casa Blanca Kids Club who loved to spell. Having Alex work at the resort children's camp had been a huge blessing, giving her a way to make friends and get acclimated after they'd returned from Boston a few weeks ago.

"I can't believe I only have one more week, then school starts." She chose a few different protein bars. "It's going to be so different this year."

"Middle school is different," Gussie agreed as they walked to the counter. "It's a slightly lower-level hell."

They headed to the cash register, but instead of her usual open examination followed by judgment, the Super Min's owner didn't lift her head from the magazine she was reading.

"Hello, Charity," Gussie said as they laid their purchases on the counter.

She held up her finger. "Wait, wait. I'm busy reading all about you right now, Miss *Au Naturel*." Finally, she peered over her readers, a mix of amusement and amazement in her gray eyes. "Color me stunned that you singlehandedly made a major corporation change its entire advertising campaign."

"What?"

Charity twirled the magazine around as Alex sidled up to the counter to see it, too.

"Oh my gosh, Gussie. Look!"

The two-story spread had a bold headline: *LaVie Launches 'Beauty Isn't Perfect' Campaign.*

The first thing Gussie saw was the bright green and blue logo of LaVie water, but then her eyes moved to the woman in the picture, striding along a city street. The brunette wore a sunny summer dress, snazzy heels, and the most gorgeous smile. She held a bottle of LaVie in one hand, but her other arm, resting over a sleek blue clutch, ended at the elbow, the result of an accident or birth defect. Under her, the words: *Beauty Isn't Perfect...But Your Water Can Be.*

"Would you get a load of that crap?" Charity choked. "I guess it means I can charge more for that stuff now."

Alex and Gussie pressed together to read while Charity's red nail pointed to a sidebar in the corner. It featured the now-familiar shot of Gussie on a Cannes street, the wind gust showing her bald spot as clearly as the label on the water bottle in her hand.

"You're a regular Heidi Klum," Charity said. "Only, you know, not."

Gussie read the sidebar, which explained that she'd only

been doing a test shot, but "the bald girl" had gone viral, and the positive public reaction had prompted LaVie's revised campaign strategy.

"Does it say anything about the photographer?" Gussie asked, unable to hide how much she wanted to know something—*anything*—about Tom. He'd texted a few times since Nice, to check on Alex and the trip to Boston, but nothing personal, nothing real, nothing that reflected the feelings they'd had. Still had, in Gussie's case.

"The long-haired hippie?" Charity asked.

Alex pointed to a few paragraphs about the world-famous photographer chosen for the campaign to capture the beauty of "every" woman, even those society dismisses as flawed.

"I suppose you want me to give you that magazine for free now," Charity said.

"Nope." Gussie threw it on the counter, getting a flashback of another time and another person who'd tossed a magazine right there. "It's not in our family budget."

"You're not a family."

This time, they both glared at her. "News flash, Happy Face." Gussie snapped her fingers with a sassy wave. "Families come in all shapes and sizes." She wrapped an arm around Alex. "Including this one."

Charity's eyes tapered and then, unexpectedly, softened. Wordlessly, she grabbed the magazine and stuffed it in their bag. "Don't expect it ever again," she said gruffly. "That one's for all the ugly gals you give hope to."

As always, Gussie wasn't sure whether to laugh or sigh, but Alex beamed at her. "Thank you, Charity. And you give hope to all the bullies in the world."

Cracking up, Gussie and Alex left for the parking lot.

"Speaking of families," Alex said. "Any word from Luke?"

327

"He called last night." Gussie climbed into the driver's seat, thinking of the blissful, tearful, awesome days they'd all shared up in Boston. "He's nailed down that construction job and he'll be here this weekend to start. Isn't that awesome? He's really coming to Mimosa Key."

"How long will he be here?"

"I don't know," Gussie said. But since they'd never been closer, she hoped a good, long time.

"Will he be here in time for Willow's wedding?" Alex asked.

"Maybe."

"That'd be nice. I wish..." Alex suddenly reached over and turned on the car radio.

Gussie snapped it off. "You wish your uncle was going to be here."

"Of course not."

"Alex, I know what you were going to say. You miss him."

"*Miss* isn't exactly the word," she admitted. "But he did kind of grow on me."

"Welcome to the club."

Alex grew silent, as she often did when the subject of Tom came up. It was easier for both of them to pretend he'd never existed, but, of course, that wasn't feasible. He'd come back, eventually. But neither of them knew what that would mean, if anything.

Tamping down a cocktail of uncertainty and disappointment, Gussie pulled through the gates of Casa Blanca and drove to the far end of the parking lot to the outdoor camp check-in.

"Oh, look, there's the speller," Alex said as she gathered her stuff. "Dylan Ivory."

"Did you know his dad is Nate Ivory of the Ivory Glass billions?" Gussie asked.

"He's one of those billionaires?" Alex's eyes grew wide. "Wonder if he has any friends for you."

Gussie smiled, a burst of affection for Alex exploding in her heart. "He has plenty of friends, all rich. They're building a baseball stadium over on the east side of Barefoot Bay. But..." She had to be honest, since that had been her M.O. with Alex from the start. "I'm not interested."

"You miss him, too, don't you?"

And got direct questions in response. "Lesson number one, little grasshopper. Don't fall in love with a guy who has 'I want to be alone for the rest of my life so stay far away from me' tattooed on his arm."

Alex patted her hand. "I knew you were in love with him."

Dang it! Had she said that? She barely admitted that to herself, except on lonely nights when she cried herself to sleep. Before she could answer, Alex was out of the car, saying hello to campers while Dylan Ivory danced around her singing, "H-E-L-L-O!"

Gussie took one second to enjoy the scene, then drove to park in the employee area. Willow was taking the week off to spend time with her parents, who were in town for the wedding, and Ari had a meeting on the mainland with a vendor, so Gussie skipped the office stop and headed straight to the bridal dressing room to get some things in order for this weekend.

Inside, the room was dim and cool, normally a sanctuary from the hustle and bustle of the resort. She stood perfectly still for a moment, closing her eyes to picture what would take place here in a few days, but found herself thinking about what *had* taken place in this room about a month ago.

TJ DeMille had gotten under her wig and under her shirt and under her skin.

"Ugh! Get over him already. Think about Willow."

Following that self-imposed order, she went to the gown closet to retrieve the dress and hang it for some last-minute tweaks by Willow's mother, Ona, who'd designed it exclusively for her daughter.

After draping the wedding gown on the dress form, she went back into the closet and lifted the veil off the mold and carried it out, holding the lace-trimmed tulle like precious cargo. She paused at the mirror, stopping at the very spot where Tom had removed her makeup and wig. After that, she'd never put a wig on again. And she'd toned down the makeup, too.

No more masks for Gussie McBain.

Why bother hiding behind wigs and makeup now that the whole world had seen her and, apparently, judged her acceptable? The world...but not the one man she wanted.

She pulled her hair forward over her shoulders in a way she rarely wore it because the style left her scar out in the open. But if she were getting married, this was how she'd wear it.

And she'd cover the spot with a veil.

Lifting the gossamer netting, she slipped it on, taking a moment to admire the vision, but suddenly she felt unstable. Knocked over by the sensation of longing, of desire, of envy even, for every woman who'd ever had this moment for real.

What would it feel like to be loved that much?

She spread the veil over her shoulders, lifted her chin to a better angle, and then—

Click.

She spun around at the sound.

Click.

There was no one there, but the distinct sound of a camera. A chill tiptoed up her spine, lodging at the base of her neck, sending a spray of goose bumps over her arm.

Click. Click. Click. A man with a camera stepped out from behind the oversize cheval mirror. "What are you—"

He lowered the camera to show his face. Not a man...*the* man.

"—doing here?" The question ended with a hitch of disbelief and joy and love.

"Heard there was a wedding this weekend and thought you might need a photographer."

Tom. She stared for a minute, not quite able to accept reality.

"We, uh, have one. Maggie's back in town." She dug for composure, finding nothing but happiness. Raw, real, full-body happiness. "What happened to your hair?"

He ruffled one hand through what was left of his locks, a quarter inch of black spikes that somehow managed to look exactly right on him. "Someone told me to cut it."

Suddenly, she was aware that she stood like a little girl playing dress-up, in a veil that didn't belong to her. She reached up to yank it off, but he held out his hand.

"Don't. Please, don't. I want that shot."

No, no, he wasn't doing this to her. Ignoring his request, she managed to get the veil off, carefully laying it over the counter. "What are you doing here?"

"I told you, I heard—"

"For real," she interjected, maybe a little more sharply than she'd meant to.

He held up the camera. "I am offering my services for Willow's wedding. Free of charge." At her narrowed eyes, he added, "Although I may ask to dance with one of the bridesmaids."

331

She let out the breath she'd probably been holding since he appeared. She wanted to reach for him and hold him and kiss him, but she shook her head to squash the urge. "So, how are you?"

"Lonely."

"Just the way you like it."

He didn't answer, but looked hard at her, then lifted his camera. "Don't move."

"Tom, don't—"

"Please." He took a step closer. "I want to get that look on your face."

"My 'I can't believe you showed up out of the blue' look?" Is that how it would be from now on? He'd pop in when he was *lonely*?

"The 'you're trying to hide how happy you are to see me' look." He put the camera on a chair and slid his hands into the pockets of khaki pants, staring at her. "I went to Greece."

Her jaw opened a little in shock.

"You were right," he said, taking another step closer. "You were right about everything, it turns out."

Not exactly sure why that sounded like it was loaded with extra meaning, she waited for the rest.

"I spent time with my in-laws, and I got a letter from Ruthie."

"What?"

He pulled out an envelope and handed it to her. "It was addressed to Sophia, but she never got to read it."

Gussie took a few slow breaths, steadying herself for what she was about to read.

The words ran together, until close to the end.

There is no one I'd want raising my daughter except my wonderful brother.

That sentence jumped out in painful clarity, stabbing her. "You're taking her back?"

"I'm coming home."

"This isn't your home."

"What do they say? Home is where the family is."

"Heart," she corrected. Like the one shattering in her chest.

"Same difference." He closed the rest of the space, only the letter she held between them. "I'm supposed to raise Alex."

Oh, Lord, it was one thing to lose him—or have him pop in to torture her periodically. But Alex, too? She already loved Alex.

And she already loved him. "Tom, I thought we'd agreed *I'm* supposed to raise Alex."

"You are. You will." He slid the letter out of her hands and let it flutter on top of Willow's veil. "With me. Together. I sure as hell can't do it alone." Taking both her hands in his, he pulled her knuckles to his lips.

"But you do everything alone."

"Not anymore."

She wanted to believe that. Wanted to believe the insane pounding of her heart and the look of love in his eyes. "But, you know, that tattoo?"

"Oh, yeah, that." He reached to the cuff of his long-sleeved shirt. "I got another one." He unbuttoned and started rolling the material back on his other arm. "I got to thinking about how you always said I should come with an expiration date. So I went to my pal the tattoo artist in Cyprus and got one."

She swallowed hard, finally looking at his exposed forearm. When would her time be up with him? Right then, it didn't matter. She'd take anything. A day, a week, a month, a year.

Forever.

He ran his fingertip over the word, small but legible, purple and rimmed in the pinkness of a fresh tattoo. "I put this one in English so you can read it. Every day and every night, I hope."

Forever.

"You think you can keep me on the shelf that long, Pink?"

"Forever." She almost sobbed on the word, the world blurry with tears and happiness and hope. "Tom, what changed?"

"Everything. Gussie, we both changed." He reached for her head, threading her hair, letting his fingertips graze the scar he'd made her forget. He pulled her into him, whispering before his lips touched hers, "We changed each other."

Yes, they did. They certainly did.

"Give me a chance to show you how much," he whispered. "Give me a chance."

Like there was ever a possibility she wouldn't.

Chapter Thirty

"Where have you been?" Gussie barked the question when Ari came flying into the Barefoot Brides office, her long hair tumbling out of a ponytail, her shorts, T-shirt, and sneakers even more of a shock than the fact that she'd *finally* decided to show up for Willow's wedding—an hour before they walked down the aisle.

Ari froze, her dark eyes wide. "What are you doing in here?"

"Better question, why aren't *you* in the dressing room with the rest of the bridal party? Clean, showered, made up, and ready to put our dresses on for Willow's wedding?" Her voice rose with the frustration she'd been feeling since not being able to reach Ari for the past few hours. "Why didn't you answer your phone?"

"I was...out."

Gussie glowered at her. "Do you mind telling me what is more important than the fact that one of your best friends is getting married and you are a co-maid of honor?"

Ari blinked guiltily. "I had to go somewhere."

"Where?"

She bit her lip, giving her head a shake.

335

"Tell me," Gussie ordered.

"Not important."

Gussie's blood pressure spiked. "I've been keeping Willow calm, assuring her you'd be here, lying for you when I couldn't reach you so she didn't become the freaked-out bride we all swore we'd never be, so yes, Arielle Chandler, you *are* telling me."

"You'll think I'm nuts."

"Too late." Gussie narrowed her eyes and gripped the paperwork for the florist that she'd come to retrieve. "What's going on? Where were you?"

"I had to do something."

"Now? Today?"

Ari held up her hands as if she had to stop Gussie's onslaught. "I had to..." She closed her eyes. "I think I met him."

"What?" Gussie's screwed her face up, completely unable to follow the conversation. "You met who?"

"Him. I met...*him*. You know, him. My one, my only, my destiny."

Gussie stared at her, delicately balanced between howling in laughter and screeching in frustration. "Ari, you know I think your new-age superstitions are precious and you believe in love at first—"

"No, I don't. It's not love at first sight. It might not be, anyway. It's fate. It's destiny. It's—"

"Hogwash." Gussie came around the desk, a rush of sympathy at the look of torment on Ari's striking features. "You know what's happening, don't you? Willow is getting married. Tom and I are together. That leaves you as the only one of the three of us..." *Alone.* She didn't want to use the harsh word, especially because Ari's state of singlehood was ridiculously self-imposed. Men flocked to her, but her whacked-out beliefs in "a one and only" kept every potential guy at arm's length.

Ari shook off the touch of sympathy. "I'm not mooning over the fact that my two best friends and business partners have found their mates, Gussie."

"Mates. You make it sound like we're dolphins, for crying out loud."

Ari pressed her fists against her mouth. "But there's a problem."

"There always is. What? He's the wrong sign? His aura is bad? What's his fatal flaw?"

She shook her head again, not laughing like she usually would. "I think he's going to hate me."

"Sounds like the start of a fabulous relationship." Gussie nudged her to the door. "You can tell me all about him on the way to the...what?"

All the color had drained from Ari's face as she looked over Gussie's shoulder. "Who...is...that?"

Gussie whipped around to look out the window, a smile pulling the minute she recognized the man who crossed the parking log. "Luke made it! He was supposed to get in this afternoon, but he didn't show up at the apartment." She turned back to Ari. "He's here to..." Then she started laughing, giving Ari a gentle push. "I know, he's hot. But, please, can we go before Willow hits Bridal Defcon 1?"

But Ari just stared, her jaw slack, the color still gone from her creamy, olive complexion. "That's...Luke?"

"So much for Mr. Soul Mate you just met, huh? I thought you were—"

"You guys!" Willow practically squawked as she barged into the room, her color high, her hair in the fat curlers Gussie had rolled, her dressing gown nearly falling off. "Where in the hell are you two? I am officially having a breakdown. I'm getting married in less than an hour." Her voice rose and hitched. "I'm getting married in less than an hour!" she repeated, putting her hand over her mouth as tears sprang to her eyes. "I'm so happy and scared and excited and happy!"

Gussie and Ari shared a knowing look, but Willow held her arms out for a group hug.

"Now I understand!" Willow exclaimed.

"Why brides freak out?" Gussie asked.

"Yes! It's so amazing. Isn't it amazing? I'm marrying the man of my dreams, and I am going to spend my whole life with him, and I can't believe this is happening for real! It's amazing!"

Gussie laughed and tried to get them all to the door, catching Ari looking once more out the window. "Let's go," she insisted. "It'd be pretty sad if the wedding planners were late to one of their own weddings."

Gussie led them all down the back hall to the bridal dressing room, Willow floating like she was a foot off the ground, where she stayed while they dressed in silk and lace, drank some bubbly, and shed a few happy tears with Willow's colorful mom and dad.

They all followed the stone path together, stopping at the tiny bridge that crossed the sea oats and led to the wedding set, where about sixty excited people and one beaming groom waited.

Gussie was first, but before she started her walk, the three of them took a deep breath and had one last "we're all still single" best friend hug. Already Gussie could feel the sting behind her lids, tears of pure joy and anticipation for her own moment like this.

Something told her it wasn't far off—something like the look on Tom's face every day since he'd been back.

"Listen," Willow whispered. "I know we always said no weddings for us."

"That was the wine talking," Gussie joked.

"The voices of jaded wedding planners," Ari agreed.

Willow shook her head. "It was fear, plain and simple." She gave both women a squeeze. "I was scared of losing control, and when I did, it was awesome. And you." She looked at Gussie. "You're terrified of not being good enough, but I think that Tom has proven you wrong."

"He sure has."

"And you'll find your one true love, Ari."

Ari was peering into the crowd a few hundred feet away, but turned back to the small circle, her eyes bright. "I know," she said quietly. "But right now, Willow? There's a man standing up there who's been waiting for you for ten years. Go marry him and live happily ever after."

Willow smiled. "Sure would like you girls to join me."

"We're right here," Ari said.

"That's not what I mean." With one last hug, Willow gave Gussie a slight nudge toward the bridge covered with white rose petals that lined the sandy aisle.

As she reached the guests, Gussie felt Tom's presence, stealing one sideways glance and getting a wink that fried her right down to her bare toes. Holding on to that sensation, she finished the walk, and turned to watch Willow, escorted by her parents, walk the aisle to exchange vows with Nick.

The tears didn't quite dry during the ceremony, or when the bride and groom kissed, and certainly not when they walked back down the aisle as husband and wife.

Gussie just stared as one teardrop rolled down her cheek.

"Tears of joy, Pink?"

Tom's voice came from right behind her, followed by his strong hands on her shoulders, pulling her into his chest. She looked up, unashamed of those tears or the smile he brought to her face every time she looked at him.

"Utter joy," she confirmed. "I predict a long and happy marriage for Mr. and Mrs. Hershey."

"How do you know?"

"Oh, I can always tell," she said. "After you've seen enough weddings, the forever couples stand out."

He turned her in his arms to face him. Gussie still wasn't used to his short hair, but she loved how it made his handsome features even more striking.

"How can you tell?" he asked.

"There's...peace...in each other's arms." Which was exactly how she felt right this very minute.

His smile was slow. "How else can you be sure if a marriage is going to last?"

She glanced at Willow and Nick, holding hands, laughing, hugging friends and family. "There's no friction. There's no push or pull. They just *work* together."

She closed her eyes and settled closer to him, feeling that last barrier taken down, the last remnants of her lonely facade melting into a...partnership. "There are no walls between them."

"What about space? Is there space between them?"

Almost none, now. She and Tom were like one. For now, anyway.

"No." And she hated to admit that to a man who traveled so extensively. There'd always be space between them—possibly half a world. "They're together, like a unit."

He brushed a hair off her face, cupping her chin. "Do they usually know each other for a long time?"

"Nick and Willow met in college, ten years ago."

A frown pulled. "No one ever has a whirlwind romance that lasts a lifetime?"

"I won't discount a whirlwind romance to last a lifetime if the foundation is strong."

He nodded. "Okay, so that's it? Peace, comfort, no barriers, no space, and newcomers can apply? No other criteria?"

"And love." She laughed softly. "But that goes without saying."

"Actually, it doesn't." He threaded his hands in her hair again, sliding his warm palms over her neck, blanketing her with an affectionate gaze. "Love should never go without saying."

For a long moment, neither one of them spoke, but, then, sometimes they didn't have to and they still heard each other loud and clear.

"Then let's start with that and work backward," he said.

"Start with what?"

"Love." He pulled her closer. "You know, that feeling when you can't breathe if you think you're going to go a minute without seeing each other? When you wake and sleep and eat and work with one person on your brain and in your heart? When you only care about how they feel, what they think, and if they are happy? You know that feeling?"

She sure did. Her throat grew a little tight, so she nodded.

"That's love," he repeated.

Then she was in it.

"And next, you have time. There's no law that says these successful marriages have to be grounded in a multiyear or multimonth relationship, so one that started, oh, a month ago? It could work."

It definitely could.

"As for peace and comfort, I don't know about you, Gussie, but I've never been more at peace or more comfortable than I am right this minute, with my arms around you."

A shudder danced through her as she agreed with a nod.

"We kicked that barrier thing in the ass, too."

"Walls are gone," she confirmed. "Along with wigs."

"Then that leaves space." He inhaled deeply and sighed, taking Gussie's heart on a little ride it almost couldn't stand.

"I approved a new contract today, I'm happy to say."

And that ride stopped...along with her heart. This would be life with him. Contracts. Assignments. Constant travel. Could she take it? "Where are you going?"

"Nowhere. That's the new contract. Anyone hiring me will either have to bring the job to me, accommodate my family by flying us to the job site, or wait until I'm good and ready to travel."

She blinked at him, processing all that, stuck on one word. *Family*. Well, two words. *My family*.

"I'll work my travel schedule around Alex's school and your weddings and our life. But, spacewise, we need a bigger house. I've seen a few in south Mimosa Key I think we would love. Still home to Alex, but a fresh start for all of us."

Her knees felt weak, but she managed not to buckle with the happiness that pressed all over her. "So, do we meet the criteria for a happy marriage that lasts"—he lifted his arm, showing the new tattoo he was so damn proud of—"forever?"

"I think we do," she whispered, not trusting her voice completely.

"Then let's go tell Alex the good news."

But she didn't move. "The good news?"

"That we're getting married."

She laughed. "You haven't asked yet."

"Can't do that without the rest of our family." He turned

and waved to Alex who, Gussie realized, had been standing about twenty feet away, watching the whole exchange.

"Now?" Alex asked.

"Now."

They'd *talked* about it? Gussie didn't know quite what to make of that, but she didn't have time to think because Alex came bounding over, kicking sand under her bare feet. She held out a small box to Tom, grinning like a fool.

"Here you go." As she held it out, Gussie recognized the container as the porcelain box Tom had bought on the streets of Nice. Gussie pressed both hands to her chest.

"Come here," Tom said to Alex, gesturing to his side. "Like we planned."

They'd *planned* this?

"But, Uncle Tommy, you have to—"

He quieted her with one raised hand. "I got this, kid." Turning to Gussie, Tom slowly got down on one knee. Gussie pressed so hard on her chest, she was sure she'd crack her breastbone if her heart didn't do it from the inside first.

"I love you, Gussie McBain." He was so matter-of-fact that Gussie had to smile. "I love your spirit and your heart and your soul and your mind. I love your body, your beauty, and your flaws. I love who I am when I'm with you and who I'm going to be after we spend our lives together."

Alex made a sweet little whimper that echoed the one Gussie was fighting not to let out.

"And whatever lies ahead in that great unknown," he continued, "I know that I will never stop loving you."

She nodded in agreement, her eyes filled to the point that he blurred.

"So will you marry me, Gussie, and make me the

happiest man on earth?" He opened the box and nearly blinded her with the glint of an oval diamond.

Aiex cleared her throat.

"And make Alex the happiest girl along with me?" he added.

She didn't answer right away, because the moment was just too precious and poignant to end. Instead, she stood perfectly still, letting the setting sun warm her and the gulf breeze lift her hair and tickle her skin. She wanted to remember the salty smell in the air, the soft sand under her toes, and the joy that ricocheted through her body.

She'd never forget this.

"Um, Gussie?" Alex said, a note of worry in her voice. "Yes?"

Gussie laughed. "Yes! I would be honored to marry you, Thomas Jefferson DeMille."

Tom stood instantly, but before he put the ring on her finger, Gussie opened her arms and pulled him and Alex close to her and made a different kind of ring, every bit as beautiful. Her family.

THE END

There's more love on the horizon of Barefoot Bay! Be sure to look for these other stories set on this island.

The Barefoot Billionaires
Secrets on the Sand
Seduction on the Sand
Scandal on the Sand

The Barefoot Bay Quartet
Barefoot in the Sand
Barefoot in the Rain
Barefoot in the Sun
Barefoot by the Sea

Sneak Peek

Barefoot in Pearls

The Barefoot Bay Brides #3

If you wonder where Ari was when she was so late for Willow's wedding, read on for a sneak peek at Ari's story, Barefoot in Pearls, coming soon!

Arielle Chandler never prayed, not in the classic head-bowed, hands-folded, beg-for-help kind of way. Raised by a Bible-thumping Oklahoma man of God and a new age healer with Native American blood coursing through her veins, Ari never really chose sides on the subject of The Powers That Be. When she wanted answers, though, she took things up with a nebulous force she thought of as "the universe" and hoped it covered all the bases.

Which was why she wasn't in the bridal dressing room right now. She checked the sky to gauge the time, certain she had at least fifteen more minutes until she had to tear across the island and get back to Barefoot Bay for Willow's wedding. Until then, she kept walking up the one and only hill she'd ever found on this island, making her supreme displeasure known to the universe.

"I'm happy for them," she said out loud. "I mean, who wouldn't be happy when best friend number one is about to say 'I do' and best friend number two just fell hard for the man of her dreams? Of course I say, 'Way to go, girls.'"

The words rang hollow, and not just because this little stretch of land on the northern tip of Mimosa Key was always abandoned. Someone must have lived here once, though, because there was a dilapidated old bungalow at the bottom of the hill, missing most of its roof and all of its windows.

Nearly at the top of the hill, Ari stopped and looked out to the distant horizon. "I just want my turn," she whispered. "I just want…"

She closed her mouth, purposely silent. The universe would laugh at her. Like her friends tried not to do when she told them that she'd been raised to believe there is *one and only one person* meant for everyone on earth.

As the years had gone by and Ari failed to meet The One, she couldn't help wondering if the idea was merely something her God-fearing father and crystal-loving mother had cooked up to explain their bizarre, yet wildly successful, union.

But she'd heard the promise since childhood and stubbornly clung to the hope that it was true. Mom had assured her she'd recognize her one true love by the way her heart would feel like it was literally expanding in her chest, because it was "making room for love that will last a lifetime."

Dad said her spine would tingle, sending sparks out to her fingertips that couldn't be stopped until she touched the man who was destined for her. Just to make things worse, her sister had found The One and told Ari it hurt to look at her beloved because white lights went off in her head when they met, and her brother, just as fortunate, said he'd gone numb when he laid eyes on a woman he married six months later. None of them, reportedly, could breathe.

Frankly, they all sounded like they needed a drink, or had one too many. But Ari, the youngest and most impressionable, believed they must be on to *something* since they were all happily married, lovingly connected, and wonderfully in love.

But she was not, and had never been. How did the universe explain that?

The flutter of bird's wings pulled her attention, as though the answer were right over her head. She looked up, expecting an ibis or even a seagull, but big, black wings beat the air, the long gray tips spread wide and menacing over her.

A vulture. She ducked instinctively as the bird swooped low, dropped a massive dollop of poop on the ground, then soared back into the air like a poor man's eagle.

"Eww!" She backed away, disgust and disbelief rocking through her. Is *that* what the universe thought of her dreams and longings? A vulture who pooped all over...

What *was* that? The bird dropping had landed on something white, shiny, and long that looked like an ivory-colored snake curled into the grass. Ari stepped closer and leaned over to examine a string of tiny misshapen stones curled along a section of dirt.

Were those...*pearls*?

Leaning over, she squinted at the row of at least a dozen stones, the droplets of bird doo still wet on the ridged surface. Reaching into the pocket of her shorts, she fished for a tissue or receipt or, much more likely, a candy wrapper, but came up with nothing that could wipe the stones clean.

So she'd have to man up and touch them, because they were absolutely stunning. Kneeling closer, she squinted at the bluish-purple color of the largest stone. Wiping her hand on her shorts, she extended two fingers gingerly toward the end of the strand.

These were not your basic jewelry-store freshwater pearls. These had an ancient, handmade look, the string between each pearl clumsily knotted and frayed with age. A memory came drifting through her mind, barely more than a wisp of smoke, but Ari closed her eyes and went back to a Native American festival she'd once attended with her mother.

There were pearl necklaces among the artifacts, found in...*Indian burial mounds*.

She gasped, blinking at the punch of realization. What if this hill—on an island that had no other hills—wasn't a *hill* at all?

What if—

A rhythmic pounding broke the silence, but not a bird's wings this time. The sound was steady, strong, a drumbeat of...feet.

Ari whipped around to see a man jogging—no, seriously *running*—full speed toward her, bare-chested and bronzed.

She blinked as if the sun were playing tricks on her, highlighting the glistening muscles of his torso and abs, the powerful thighs as he took each stride, the tanned, sweaty shoulders held straight and strong as he powered up the hill, directly at her.

He had earbuds in, short, dark hair, and a mouth set in a grim line. He wore sunglasses so she couldn't see his eyes, but he made no effort to change his path as he barreled forward.

It happened so fast. With no time to stand, she threw herself back with a shriek to get out of his way, but he stumbled over her foot and barked a word that sounded like a black curse in a foreign language. He danced a little to get his balance, and the sunglasses went flying.

"Whoa!" He fought to stop his own momentum "Where the hell did you come from?"

Her? What about him? "What do you think you're doing?"

"Running up a hill." He practically spit the words at her, wiping sweat off his forehead, his chest heaving with a shallow breath. "What are you doing here?"

Really? It was *her* fault he rammed into her? "How did you not see me?"

"My eyes were closed."

What?

"In the zone," he added, as if that explained why anyone would run with eyes closed and ears plugged. He reached for her hand to help her up. "You okay?"

She started to wave off the help, but he clasped her wrist, wrapping huge, masculine fingers around her, giving her an effortless tug that brought her right to her feet. She still had to look up at him and still needed to squint, but not because of the sunlight. Because he was as menacing as the vulture who just bombed her.

He wasn't handsome, not in any conventional way. Just rough and dark with heavy whiskers over a jaw that looked like it might have met a few fists in its day. And big. His chest and shoulders dwarfed her, with cuts to define every single muscle.

"Really sorry," he said again. But he didn't sound sorry, or look it, either. He scanned her face and made no effort to unlock his grip on her wrist.

She should yank free. She should step away. She should stop staring. She should...breathe.

But right that minute, bathed in sunlight and pinned by a green-gold gaze the color of hammered bronze, Ari Chandler couldn't do any of those things. Because her whole body was kind of tingling and buzzing and sparking, like she'd just stuck her entire arm in an electrical socket.

"You sure you're okay?" he asked. "'Cause you look like I rung your bell."

He rang...something. There was no other explanation for how lightheaded she suddenly felt.

"I...I'm...I think..." Words failed her. No chance of a coherent sentence.

His brows pulled into a frown as he gently turned her arm and placed a thumb over her pulse, which just hit warp speed.

"Whoa. Your heart's going faster than mine." He started to tug her back to the ground. "I have some water in my truck. Should I get it?"

Ari let him guide her to the ground, staring up as he crouched in front of her. "Who runs with their eyes closed?"

"I was trained that way."

"For what? Suicide missions?"

"Something like that." The words, low and charged with mystery, sent another cascade of chills down her spine, a shocking feeling that had no place dancing over her in this heat and humidity.

"Really, what are you doing here?" she asked. "I've never seen another person in all the times I've been here."

He glanced around. "I'm checking the place out."

"With your eyes closed?"

He almost smiled, just enough to show a hint of dimples and straight white teeth. Just enough to take the edge off his face and turn it into something...arresting. She needed to look away, but all she could do was blink at the white lights flashing behind her eyes.

Had she hit her head or...or...oh, no. *No.*

"No," she murmured. "No, this isn't...you can't be...no." This wasn't possible.

"No...what?" he asked, concern darkening his eyes. "I can't check the place out? I have the owner's permission. Do you?"

But it *was* possible. He could be... No, that was her imagination, not the universe answering her plea. Right? "No."

For one long, suspended second, everything around her became crystal clear, making her hyperaware of every color, scent, and sound. The slow roll of a bead of sweat, trickling over a scar on his temple. The flecks of amber and jade that somehow mixed to make his eyes a haunting shade she'd never seen before. The timbre of his voice, low and sweet, even the rhythmic breathing as the run caught up with him, was musical. He smelled like sunshine, and his hand, still wrapped around her, was like a hot brand of man against her skin.

"Miss?" She blinked at him, letting the very real possibility of what was happening sink in.

He was The One.

"Hey." He snapped his fingers in front of her face, making her jump. "Do you know your name?" he asked sharply.

"Arielle Chandler."

"Place of birth?"

"Sacramento, California."

"Husband's name?"

"I don't have one."

His eyes flickered. "Phone number?"

The paused, but not because she couldn't remember it. Because his smile went from *almost* to *full force*, and the impact kind of…hurt.

She could practically hear her sister's voice describing the same thing.

"No way!" She shook her head, still not believing it.

"Hey, it was worth a try." Still smiling, he leaned back on his haunches. "Since you're coherent enough to turn me down, I guess you're okay, Arielle Chandler. In fact, you're…" He let his gaze drop over her. "Fine."

And every cell in her body just went numb.

After a few seconds, he scooped up his sunglasses and stood. "So, by the way, if you don't have the owner's permission, you won't be able to come here when construction starts."

She looked up at him, digging deep for some semblance of sanity and cool, when all she wanted to do was jump up and down and tell him exactly who he was. Her future…

Wait a second. "Did you say construction?"

"That old shack that got messed up in Hurricane Damien? It's history, along with this hill, which the owner said will block his water view when he builds his new house."

Another, different kind of buzz hummed through her head. "It's history?" Yes, it *was*. Her gaze shifted to the right, to the string of pearls not an inch away. "How can you get rid of a hill?" Especially when it might not be a "hill" at all?

He lifted one mighty shoulder, as if she'd asked how to remove an ant hill...and not something that might be sacred ground. "Easily with a front loader and a bulldozer." He wiped some more sweat and lifted his eyes to the water. "I personally think he ought to put the house up here for the best view, but hey, I'm just the builder, not the guy with the money."

She pushed up, sputtering a little. "You can't build on this."

"Oh, he can and will. Well, I will. He'll just pay for it." He angled his head and looked closely at her, his stare so intent her heart ached like it was...expanding.

For the man who wanted to bulldoze sacred ground? Oh, this was not good. Not good at all.

"You positive you're okay?" he asked, sliding on his sunglasses.

"Yes, I'm fine."

"All right, then. Maybe I'll, uh, run into you again." He gave a quick laugh at the joke.

"Oh, I'm sure you will." She closed her fingers around the pearls. She'd have to find out the truth about these and this land. And if it turned out she was sitting on a Native American burial ground, this man would *not* bulldoze it away.

She'd do anything to stop him...even if that cost her The One.

355

Other Books by Roxanne St. Claire

The Guardian Angelinos (Romantic Suspense)
Edge of Sight
Shiver of Fear
Face of Danger

The Bullet Catchers (Romantic Suspense)
Kill Me Twice
Thrill Me to Death
Take Me Tonight
First You Run
Then You Hide
Now You Die
Hunt Her Down
Make Her Pay
Pick Your Poison (a novella)

Stand-alone Novels (Romance and Suspense)
Space in His Heart
Hit Reply
Tropical Getaway
French Twist
Killer Curves
Don't You Wish (Young Adult)

About the Author

Roxanne St. Claire is a *New York Times* and *USA Today* bestselling author of nearly forty novels of suspense and romance, including several popular series (*The Bullet Catchers*, *The Guardian Angelinos*, and *Barefoot Bay*) and multiple stand-alone books. Her entire backlist, including excerpts and buy links, can be found at www.roxannestclaire.com.

In addition to being a six-time nominee and one-time winner of the prestigious Romance Writers of America RITA Award, Roxanne's novels have won the National Reader's Choice Award for best romantic suspense three times, and the Borders Top Pick in Romance, as well as the Daphne du Maurier Award, the HOLT Medallion, the Maggie, Booksellers Best, Book Buyers Best, the Award of Excellence, and many others. Her books have been translated into dozens of languages and are routinely included as a Doubleday/Rhapsody Book Club Selection of the Month.

Roxanne lives in Florida with her family (and dogs!), and can be reached via her website, www.roxannestclaire.com or on her Facebook Reader page, www.facebook.com/roxannestclaire and on Twitter at www.twitter.com/roxannestclaire.

CPSIA information can be obtained at www.ICGtesting.com
Printed in the USA
LVOW09s1942071114

412567LV00003B/145/P